Neil Rose is 33. He ⬛⬛⬛⬛⬛⬛⬛⬛⬛⬛⬛⬛⬛⬛⬛⬛ ng
a lifelong desire to w⬛⬛⬛⬛⬛⬛⬛⬛⬛⬛⬛⬛⬛⬛ ys
and features editor of⬛⬛⬛⬛⬛⬛⬛⬛⬛⬛⬛⬛⬛ e
lives in north-west L⬛⬛⬛⬛⬛⬛⬛⬛⬛⬛⬛⬛⬛ d
seemingly immortal g⬛⬛⬛⬛⬛⬛⬛⬛⬛⬛⬛⬛⬛ d
novel.

Also by Neil Rose
Bagels For Breakfast

Brief Encounters

Neil Rose

PIATKUS

Copyright © 2003 by Neil Rose

First published in Great Britain in 2003 by
Judy Piatkus (Publishers) Ltd of
5 Windmill Street, London W1T 2JA
email: info@piatkus.co.uk

The moral right of the author has been asserted

A catalogue record for this book is available from the British Library

ISBN 0 7499 3386 0

Set in Times by
Action Publishing Technology, Gloucester

Printed & bound in Great Britain by
Bookmarque, Croydon

Once again, I owe great thanks to Heather Eyles and the various people in her Wednesday night writing group in Tufnell Park for motivating me to write, and providing wise guidance both when I knew I needed it and thought I didn't.

On this occasion, equal thanks for the same reasons must also go to the Cornflake Club, and especially Juliette Adair, Shona McIntosh and David Ogunmuyiwa, all hugely talented writers themselves in whose own acknowledgements I fully expect to feature in time. That they are sometimes rude enough to seal the Malteser sweets from the box of Celebrations, when they know they're my favourites, is the only bad thing I can think to say about them.

Gillian at Piatkus has made this book a far less stressful experience than I had a right to expect, for which I am truly grateful. And everyone in the book is, of course, entirely a product of my own fevered imagination.

Fiona Rose provided valuable reading services, and did so in the honest way I expected.

Whenever my fabulous nieces, Sarah and Emma, go into a bookstore, they search out *Bagels for Breakfast* and place any copies prominently on shelves and tables, an attitude I heartily applaud and recommend to all. I hope that Fiona and Neville ensure they redouble their efforts now there is a second book.

My parents, Maureen and Harvey, and Aunty Hazel, have all taken great pride in me and my writing – I'm still trying to make up for not being a lawyer and hopefully this will continue to make up the deficit.

The final word, of course, must go to my wife, Rebecca, for being, well, herself. For picking me up when I need it and knocking me down when I deserve it. For showing a reasonable amount of patience when I come to bed very late after a night writing. For being my sounding board, and not sounding bored while I pace the living room. For at least pretending to listen when I witter on about the law. For making me laugh every day and for making me happy.

For my parents

Chapter One

'Why did you become a lawyer, Charles?'

'Erm ...' I goggled quietly at Graham Bentley, my supervising partner. It was the last question I expected at the end of my appraisal. I mean, I was here, wasn't I? Had been for eight brain-grinding, morale-sucking, sleep-depriving years. Wasn't it a little late to ask?

'For the money' was the obvious answer, but nobody was allowed to say that. The unspoken but unbreakable code for young solicitors at top London law firms like mine is that we never, ever admit to this. So what that we originally had £10,000 of debt from university and law school which we wanted to transform magically overnight into a trendy flat in Hampstead and wine bar lifestyle?

'It's Michael Cusack's fault. And Arnie Becker's fault and Victor Sifuentes's fault' was far closer to the mark but not quite what he was looking for. I mean, why didn't *LA Law* come with some kind of parental advisory? 'The practice of law in reality bears absolutely no resemblance to this programme.' That might have put me off. Perhaps I should sue. Win an award for most ironic legal action of the year.

But who wouldn't want to become a lawyer when you could live like them? The lawyers of McKenzie Brackman had it all: glamorous lives, piles of cash, fast cars, women on demand, and yet they still retained their consciences and only did what was right. It was in so many ways, I now know, too good to be true.

'For the good of society' was out. Nobody at Babbington Botts would believe it for a nanosecond. In our firm, pro bono didn't mean free legal advice for the underprivileged; it was assumed to be some fancy make of dog food that the partners' wives bought. When I began helping out at a legal advice bureau once a month to keep in contact with real people, Graham looked at me as if I'd told him I was popping home to Jupiter every four weeks.

'Because the work is really challenging' was a possibility, but not for someone fighting their way up the ranks. The only challenge I've faced over the years, as I wade through frightening piles of photocopying and ceiling-high stacks of paper which need numbering individually, is fighting off the desire to jump out of the window.

'Because I find the law a stimulating discipline' worked with the more bookish lawyers, of which there are many – hence my collective term, 'a bore of lawyers' – but Graham was more stimulated by talking about shagging trainee solicitors.

'Because I absolutely love suing people and making them sweat' showed I was into my work, but in all was a touch too aggressive.

'Because my mum and dad wanted me to do it' enjoyed an admirable ring of truth, but struck me as somewhat lame. Get a profession behind you, they'd advised with middle-class urgency. Put your life behind you too, they'd failed to add.

'Because it is giving me a very sound grounding in business, and is a good qualification to have whatever I go on to do' was OK, but hinted that I might not want to expel my last breath behind my desk at Babbington Botts – for a firm where loyalty is all, this is not a career-enhancing reply.

'Well, Graham,' I eventually said, 'it's what I always wanted to do.'

2

This was a lie only insofar as it wasn't the truth. There may be those who sit in their cots and consider that a late feeding constitutes an actionable claim for negligence, but I wasn't one of them.

But having gone through my footballer phase (too unco-ordinated), fireman phase (too afraid of getting stuck on the pole and not sliding down), secret agent phase (too indiscreet), zookeeper phase (overwhelming fear of ante-lope), bohemian artist phase (too talentless even to pull that off) and finally teacher phase (way, way too poorly paid), I settled on law. Frankly, like many solicitors I know, I couldn't think of anything better to do, but plenty of other vocations which didn't pay as well. And Arnie Becker seemed to have a new woman in his bed every week, so there was that to look forward to as well.

I flush with shame when I recall how idealism also played its part in the fatal decision. With a naivety that would nowadays see me booted out in the time it takes to say 'legal aid', I envisaged myself championing the under-dog against the bully state, confounding the establishment at every turn. The fantasy sadly had not extended to being the tiniest cog in the mammoth machine that is Babbington Botts, a faceless City monolith where the validity of the cause is in direct proportion to the speed with which the client coughs up our fees.

This, after all, is a firm where a bill is known among junior staff as an HM – 'How much?' Or, at the top end, an OMGHM – 'Oh my God, how much?' The firm's central philosophy is that we don't get paid lots if we don't have clients who can pay lots.

Unsure exactly what I wanted to do as I reached the end of my law degree, I'd applied to a range of different law firms. Before my first interview with Babbingtons, my parents wisely drafted in a friend of a friend who was a partner at another big corporate law firm.

'So, Charlie,' he said over tea in our front lounge, 'why do you want to become a lawyer?'

That was an easy one. 'I want to help people.'

3

He nodded encouragingly while eyeing the Jammy Dodgers with dismay. 'Good. Excellent. Help them in what way?'

'Well, the law's a pretty scary thing—' I began.

'If you use it right, it certainly can be,' he agreed.

'No, I mean, from the other side, it's pretty scary. People need help to fight against it.'

'Sounds like anarchy to me,' he chuckled.

My dad looked alarmed. 'You're not an anarchist, are you, Charlie?'

'Please God, no,' my mum went on. Whatever would the neighbours think? 'Or worse, a nihilist?' She'd just finished a night class in political theory – she'd wanted to get on a cookery course, but it was full by the time she signed up. 'The washing doesn't get done in a nihilist household, mark my words, Charlie.'

'And don't think the anarchists are any better,' Dad cautioned. 'They leave their gardens in a right old mess.'

The lawyer looked gravely at me. 'You see, Charlie, the law is a wonderful thing. It helps many people in many different ways. Sure, you can go and do legal aid work, but I've got to be honest: it doesn't pay well and you get no thanks afterwards.'

That didn't appeal at all. I wanted to save the world and be properly rewarded for doing so, financially and morally.

'But what a firm like Babbington Botts offers is a chance to help those people who make the world go round. Who make the food that the ordinary people eat, for example. Do you understand? It's a higher calling, in a way.'

I and a few fellow law students at university had formed Student Lawyers Against Greed (which became Student Lawyers Against Corporate Greed following an emergency council meeting over the acronym issue), so I knew my stuff. I wasn't going to be taken in so easily. 'What you mean is help the rich get richer.'

The lawyer laughed, and my parents joined in syco- phantically. 'Let me put it another way. Change the system

4

if you want, but you've got to be inside to do it.' And I was callow enough to believe him.

Faced with a series of very tempting job offers from big law firms, the members of SLACG agreed that an inside job was our best option. We, and the world, are still waiting. Our group song, ironic at the time, less so ten years on, was The Clash's 'I Fought the Law and the Law Won'.

Where had the time gone? And was I much closer to achieving anything of note? I was thirty-one. I still had my life ahead of me. Sure, there was the odd shoot of grey to be found in my dark hair, and my face wasn't as unlined as it had been when I bounded through the door eight years before like a puppy on acid. But I had yet to develop a lawyer's stoop from hunching for hours over my desk, was dimly aware of the world beyond my ivory tower and had against staggering odds maintained a sunny (or at least sunny-ish) outlook on life.

When I tell people I'm a lawyer, some of them look at me kind of funny, like I've quietly acquired cloven hooves and a pointy tail. I'm a nice guy, I want to explain. I don't eat babies, I only have one face, I actually give blood and have never been remotely tempted to suck it instead – while the last time I appealed to the devil was years ago during my law school exams (though I guess that did work). I don't get hardened criminals off murder charges, I have never slept with a client and I wouldn't dream of overcharging. No more than a meagre 10 per cent anyway. My clients would be insulted if I didn't.

And if they'd see the pleasure in my parents' faces when I decided my career path – ignoring for a moment the little pound signs that rang up in their eyes – they could not deny that the law is a force for good and social harmony.

I had unfinished business at Babbington Botts, however. I hadn't slaved my way through the last eight years only to be denied the chance to reach the pinnacle of partnership that was shortly to be in sight. Oh, the satisfaction. Oh, the kudos. Oh, the status. Oh, the money. I had a name to aspire to, after all.

Graham looked pained at having to impart bad news. 'A couple of partners have mentioned to me how they're not sure you're fully committed at times.'

As those times tended to be midnight and later, most people would not complain. But I existed in a culture where pulling all-nighters is the professional equivalent of notches on your bed-post – mine was whittled down to a sharp stump, but there were more than a few fanatics who didn't even have a bed left.

In any case, these unnamed partners were not far off; I was committed in much the same way that the fox is committed to the hounds. But how could I ever become a partner – and I really, really, really wanted to reach that sweet summit – without playing the game?

So I did my best to look upset. 'I can't imagine why they think that, Graham. I love it here.' Well, I love the money and for many, that's the same thing. The work has its moments too, if intermittently. In any case, I was always careful to show Graham my most joyful isn't-this-thrilling-working-on-a-file-at-three-in-the-morning-who-needs-a-life-anyway-when-you've-got-a-dictaphone-and-coffee-machine-for-company persona, so he was able to dismiss the criticisms.

'Where do you see yourself in five years, Charles?'

'Here.' The answer had to be as quick as it was decisive. I smiled playfully. 'And giving you a lift to partnership retreats.'

Graham smiled back. Ambition was good because it meant I would work as hard as it took. 'I think that just about wraps up the appraisal. I'm happy with your work, Charles, and that's what really matters. Any questions?'

It was time to take the bull by the horns. I had a habit of grabbing it by the testicles, but still. 'So ... should I be thinking about partnership yet?'

Graham smiled tolerantly. 'You can always think, Charles ... Just not on firm time.' He laughed loudly and I joined in with due enthusiasm.

I was dependent on his patronage and it made me feel

6

dirty. 'I feel I've learned so much from you. I want to take it to the next stage.'

Graham could just about see that I was bootlicking in a manner which even my fellow associates – a more competitive bunch you couldn't hope to find in an old Soviet bread queue – would find distasteful, but he was also just too vain to care.

He smiled again, putting away his gold pen. 'Let's see what we can do in the next few months. Maybe bring the old chargeable hours up a bit. We'll review and then decide whether to put you up for partnership. There's a good chance – let's leave it at that for now.'

Getting up to leave, I knew that until I finally mastered the chargeable hour, my rise would be thwarted. A key stage, I knew, was getting my charge-out rate up just £10 to hit the £250 an hour mark. It may be the bane of every solicitor's life, having to record any moment spent working on a file in ten-minute units, but it was also the road to partnership bliss.

The firm's most successful partners have famously liberal attitudes as to what constitutes 'working' on a file. Walking time to another partner's room to discuss it, casual telephone chats with the client about cricket, talking to the wife about what happened at work that day, and of course thinking time on the loo all find their way on to the best timesheets. To the extent that law is a creative profession – not a suggestion ever made in the vicinity of the tax department, naturally – then the timesheet is where legal stars are born.

Nowhere is time more flexible than on a lawyer's timesheet. There's an old joke about the lawyer who dies and finds himself at the Pearly Gates. 'It was your time,' St Peter intones.

'How come?' says the lawyer. 'I'm only forty-eight.'

'That's strange,' replies St Peter. 'According to your timesheets, you're 120.'

Graham looked at me meaningfully. 'Don't worry, Charles. We always look after each other around here, whatever happens.'

7

'Thank you, Graham,' I replied, resisting the temptation to bellow, 'And now would be a bloody good time to prove it, you sadist.' Instead I wondered what he was being meaningful about.

Back in my room, I swivelled my chair away from the door and looked out of the window; being an associate's window, all I could see was the neighbouring building, but it was status enough that I had a window at all. You might as well wave goodbye to partnership if you were surrounded by blank walls.

I silently apologised to Michael Cusack. If I was being absolutely honest, it actually wasn't his fault. 'You really want to know why I became a lawyer, Graham?' I muttered. 'Elly Bloody Gray, that's why.'

Chapter Two

'The guy's a Nazi,' Hannah said loudly, slamming down her Budweiser and making it froth out of the top.

'Rubbish. Nothing more than your average sadist, if you ask me,' Ash threw in.

Lucy pushed herself drunkenly forward in her chair. 'No, no, no, no. I think he just has a problem with intimacy.'

'So, we're agreed.' I brought the discussion about a particular property partner to an end. 'He's a fascist bully with a sensitive side. And that makes him our—' Ash gave us a drum-roll on the table with his hands and we all chorused loudly: 'Bastard Partner of the Week.'

Hannah giggled and leaned her head heavily on my shoulder. 'Oh Charlie, who would've thought that we would end up last ones standing. Of all people.'

This was what was left of The Partnership, as our group christened itself eight long years ago. The only four still with the firm from the original intake of forty-four bright-eyed law students. Ownership of a partner's telephone, with digital displays and all sorts of other status-enhancing features, was tantalisingly close. The rest had fallen by the wayside, mostly because they couldn't keep up, the

9

occasional one thanks to a desire for a better life – or any life, come to that – while a handful went in periodic culls the management carried out to keep everyone on their toes.

Nowhere was the traditional City law firm promotion policy of 'up or out' more ruthlessly practised than at Babbington Botts. There was more than an echo of the old Politburo about it; but instead of arriving at a meeting to find there was no chair for you and that you were on the fast track to the Gulag, lawyers would come in on a Monday morning to find their luxuriously padded swivel-chair replaced by an older, inferior model which didn't recline. That meant you were on the fast track to your leaving party.

A 'redeployment of reclinable resources' was the official explanation offered by an accompanying memo, ahead of the redeployment of your legal resources out of the front door. A Triple-R, as it was known, was seen as much less messy than giving the news direct.

The four of us held Partnership meetings in a wine bar every Friday night, where we would pick over the past seven days and nominate our Bastard Partner of the Week. Over the years, as the numbers had dwindled, so our bond had grown. While we were a hugely competitive and ambitious bunch – we were no use to the firm otherwise – there was a strong sense of Us against Them. Of course, at the same time we all ached to join Them.

All trainee solicitors have to undergo two years of training across the work of a law firm before qualifying, and at Babbingtons this involved spending six months in four different departments. Hannah and I were sent to the same departments each time. We soon found that we had similar backgrounds and attitudes to our chosen profession, becoming firm friends, both expecting the chop at any time. Nonetheless, we rose above others who had enthusiasm about the latest volume of case reports that Hannah and I spent many hours in the pub trying to figure out, but never emulate.

An appealing, curvey brunette with an open, welcoming

face, and shiny, long hair, Hannah was around a head shorter than my six foot-plus. We had toyed with the idea of getting together near the beginning – and even got so far as snogging in a cab on the way back to her flat – but that same evening rightly decided that we didn't want to complicate an uncomplicated friendship. She came from a loud family of north-west London Jews and she said that while I fitted her mother's criteria for a future husband by being a professional who would be able to support his wife properly once the grandchildren started flowing out of her, I fell down badly on the possession of a foreskin front. Since then I had happily spent many a night on her sofa.

'I had my appraisal today,' I told them. I was the first among us to have gone through the ordeal this year.

'And?' Hannah asked.

'And . . . I'm starting to wonder if I won't be Triple-R'd soon.' Ash snorted sceptically. 'I'm serious. Some sod's been complaining that I'm not committed enough. And then Graham suggested I bring my chargeables up a bit.' We all knew it was like saying I wasn't breathing enough – do more or die.

'Oh bugger,' said Ash, concerned. 'I mean, how much more do they want to screw out of us? Seventy-minute hours, that'll be the next thing, mark my words.' But he knew the rules well enough. The powers-that-be would only overlook the complaints if I was bringing in the cash. Could it be that the wear and tear of a constantly crushing workload was finally starting to show on me? It was lousy timing if so.

'But then Graham said he was happy with me and that we always look after each other around here, nudge nudge wink wink. So I don't know what to make of it.'

'Graham'll never stab you in the back,' Hannah predicted. 'You're like the son he never had.'

'Or the son he's never taken to lap-dancing clubs, at least,' Ash said.

'Well, his kids are only eight and six,' I pointed out. 'Their time will come, I promise you.'

Ash laughed. He was my mucker, always game for a laugh and a bit of mischief where we could get away with it. That he went by the full name of Ashok Chaudhry said all you needed to know about him. Coloured faces are rare at firms like Babbingtons outside of the typing pool and the partners just returned from long holidays in Antigua, so for Ash to have made it this far meant he was the real thing. He had a languid manner, thick and wavy hair, and long legs – Ash was something of an Asian Hugh Grant, a younger solicitor once sighed to me while I tried to chat her up – but behind it all lay a very sharp mind.

Yes, Babbingtons was a traditional City institution when it came to the old school tie and layers of prejudice, but in other ways it was also terrifically meritocratic. Such was the pace of change in the City that even firms of Babbingtons calibre were now letting – albeit with a quiet sigh of reluctance – the likes of Ash, Hannah and suburban middle-class oiks such as me through the door. When we joined, there were a couple of Asian guys who tried hard to be more English than muffins, but no more, although there were a handful of Jewish partners who managed to blend in. And anyone dare to be openly gay? Shut that door behind you as you pick up your P45.

But at least I came from the Home Counties, and kind of grew on people, but in a pleasant, non-fungal manner. I looked the part too: tall, athletic without actually being athletic, and not un-good-looking. My features were in reasonable proportion, my eyes a slate grey I've been told is very striking, while my happy smile had got me out of more than a few tight corners.

But all the time there was an even-stronger financial imperative. If you proved yourself to be an accomplished lawyer with excellent timesheet control and a good way with clients, there were now many – though by no means all – who didn't care if you were black, brown, yellow or even non-Oxbridge.

From our point of view, it was only because the firm attracted some of the best work in the City, with pay and benefits to match, and offered kudos and rewards beyond avarice for those lucky enough to become partners, that we tolerated the rubbish that came with it much of the time.

Lucy had been slumped on the table, staring intently at her gin and tonic as if it was the only thing making sense to her at that moment. 'Male partners are, let's face it, bastards,' she declared, rising carefully into an upright position holding her glass above her head for some reason. 'They should all be Bastard Partner of the Week, every week. Do you know why they employ women? Do you?'

'Yes, we do, Lucy,' I said wearily. 'You tell us every bloody week.'

'I'll tell you why,' she ploughed on. 'They only employ women because they like to fantasise about chasing us round a boardroom table in our underwear like it's an episode of the Benny Hill show. Whadd'ya think of that then?'

Lucy was something of an expert in that particular legal sport because a partner had once suggested it to her. She still can't get over it. She told him, famously, that he was welcome to try but she would be forced to break his penis into pieces, send part of it to his wife, another to the president of the Law Society and use the rest in an employment tribunal claim that would ruin his career quicker even than depenisisation (she swears that this was the very word she used) would curtail his sex life.

She was promoted from assistant solicitor to associate less than a month later – the first among us to reach the hallowed jump-off point to partner – with a recommendation from the same man that she had more balls than the rest of the department put together. 'More than he almost had, anyway,' she shouted in the pub that night.

Lucy was the real star of our group. What made her stand out was boundless energy, which could prove very annoying both at work – where she was one of those who was always offensively bright at four in the morning – and at play, where she would be the one urging everybody on to a club after last orders while the rest of us were finding just sitting down enough of a task.

Nobody was more charming, funny, thoughtful and self-effacing than Lucy; and she was admirably determined to succeed on her own account, not because she went by the full name of Lady Lucy Sommersdale. This gave her the confidence to expect a long future at Babbingtons and probably knocked at least a year off her wait for partnership, but we didn't hold it against her. That she was a tall, willowy blonde with an infectious laugh was yet another tick in her favour, of course. Like she needed it. She had a long face that was striking rather than beautiful, but cheekbones that any supermodel would go under the knife for.

'Depenisisation,' she declared far too loudly to surrounding tables. 'Too good for the lot of 'em.' Lucy lifted her glass and indicated to me that it was time for another. 'Oh, present company excluded, of course.'

'Thanks. And there I was thinking you couldn't wait to get your hands on my willy.'

'Funny guy, Fortune. Come on, get the drinks in. And who's up for a club after?'

'Oh please, Luce, not tonight. How can you after all you've drunk?'

She shook her glass at me more vigorously. 'That's why they call it tonic, my friend.'

'I don't believe you sometimes. I just can't keep up.'

She looked at me mockingly with big eyes. 'That's enough about your professional problems, Charles Fortune. Let's drink then dance.'

While I easily laughed off her jibe, underneath I sometimes found it genuinely hard being surrounded by such achievers. I considered myself something of a fraud. I had the academic record – largely the result of a compliant memory in the couple of days before exams – the quick answers and was good company in the pub. But there was always the fear that I was hanging on by my fingertips to this lot. How I had survived this long was a mystery.

University was where I realised. I arrived cocksure, top of my year at school, ready to take on anything and anyone.

14

But then I found that everyone on my course had been top of their year, some top of the year ahead of them too. I never quite recovered from the shock to my self-esteem. These were frighteningly clever people who seemed ready to become judges before I knew my way to the law library.

'Something's up,' said Lucy, suddenly far more alert as the first of many winds swept through her, when I'd returned with fresh drinks. 'I've been hearing stuff. This may be what Graham was talking about.'

'Such as?' I knew Lucy was plugged into the secretary network, always the most reliable source of information at the firm.

She looked darkly at us all. 'New face. Fresh brains. An associate but a . . . you're not going to like this.' Identical looks of concern flashed from Ash's face to Hannah's to mine. 'Yes, my friends and colleagues. The word on the street is that we are shortly to be joined by yet another six-year qualified. Like they haven't got enough in the gene pool already.' She gestured round the table.

It was as if a ghost had walked across our careers. This was a genuine threat. Babbingtons doesn't introduce new blood at a level as relatively senior as ours unless they are good. Really good. Really shoo-in-for-partner good. It almost certainly meant one less slot for us. All four of us were in the corporate department which, while huge, could only support a small number of new partners every year. 'Quality over quantity' many a partner would sniff.

'Do we know who this bastard is?' I asked.

'No, but word is we'll find out sooner rather than later.'

'You know, at most normal law firms,' Hannah grumbled, 'they'd have consulted us first. At least warned us.'

'That'll teach us not to work at a normal firm,' I said gloomily, but we all knew the upsides every time we checked our bank balances. The best way to save money, a partner had once explained to me in all seriousness, was to work so hard that you never have the time to spend it. He thought Babbingtons was doing me a service by giving me just that opportunity.

15

We stared at our drinks for a bit, before Ash said, 'But there's no point worrying about it right now, I guess.'

Lucy knew where he was going. 'So let's dance, yes? Who's up for it?'

Ash raised his hand and, with an amused sigh, so did Hannah. They turned to me. 'Come on, Charlie,' Hannah pleaded. 'It's August.' She was right. Thanks to most of our clients jetting off on their summer holidays in exclusive resorts around the world, this was the only time of the year we could really take the foot off the pedal. Rolling my eyes, I put up my hand too.

Lucy clapped in joy. 'They may doubt our legal ability,' she announced with pride, 'but let them not doubt our ability to get pissed and make fools of ourselves at discos.'

Rather than search out a club in the West End, we compromised on a nearby wine bar called The Witness Box, which ran a disco fronting a renowned pick-up joint. The place was heaving with young City professionals seeking respite from their week, although more than a few were simply slumped in corners drinking until they finally couldn't remember what they were drinking so much to forget.

Over the years, alcohol had played an increasingly important role in my life. Not to the level where I kept a bottle of whisky and revolver in my desk, but as a way to help release the tension that wracked my every fibre. I barely knew of a successful City solicitor – at least one without the sometimes calming influence of having a wife and family or of having a reliable dealer – who dealt with the stress in any other way.

The moment we arrived, Lucy and Hannah headed straight for the dance floor to throw themselves around enthusiastically, while Ash made for an attractive girl sitting forlornly by the bar. I began to trail after him but turned back when I saw the girl's body language perk up when he offered her a drink.

Instead, I leaned on a post by the dance floor, watching Lucy circle Hannah extravagantly and playfully push away some guy in a suit who was trying to follow her round.

16

Hannah beckoned me to join them, but with a grin, I declined. I always enjoyed watching her like this. When Abba came on, they launched into their patented disco routine, which involved a lot of bum-wiggling at the nearest men and proved to me just how drunk they were. I counted at least eight guys with their tongues hanging further down their shirts than their ties.

As I turned to see how Ash was faring – indeed, if he hadn't already whisked the girl off – I bumped into an arrestingly pretty blonde in one of those short floaty dresses that makes summer so worthwhile. She was dancing listlessly by herself and the impact spilled her wine.

'Sorry,' I said.

She shrugged, seemingly bored. 'Don't be. That's about the most exciting thing that's happened to me tonight.'

'Let me at least buy you another drink.'

Deciding whether more solo dancing or talking to me was the better option took slightly longer than it should have done, but then she said: 'Yeah, why not?'

We barged our way to the bar, although away from Ash, who already had his arm around his conquest to give her support.

My girl told me she was called Helena, and was a para-legal at a much smaller law firm known for being very posh and specialising in extremely rich individuals and thereby putting its partners in the same bracket. I guessed she was about twenty-five, with very pale and lightly freck-led skin, and the deepest dimples. I just wanted to grab her cheeks between my fingers and coo, 'You're so sweet, aren't you?' She had such a fresh look to her that I thought she should be advertising the joyful benefits of a breakfast cereal.

'The problem,' she was saying in a well-educated accent, 'is that I don't like City lawyers very much. So hypnotised by how wonderful they think they are that they don't realise there's a world beyond their own egos, the silly arses.'

I couldn't disagree with that as a general proposition. 'So I take it you don't enjoy your job.'

'It's OK, I suppose. There's a few who're all right, but by and large, they're a bunch of arses.' I just loved the way she said that. 'But it gets me through the week, to be fair. I'm only doing this until I can do what I really want.'

'What's that?'

'Marry a filthy rich guy from Chelsea and never do a second's work again in my life. I have a lot of lunching to catch up on.'

'You might want to start liking lawyers, then,' I suggested.

She smiled. 'Actually, I'm kind of an actress. I'm between roles, as they say. Have been for nine months. Only working here to save up as much money as I can so I can give it a real go. I'm really focused on that right now. Not interested in any other stuff, like relationships and so on.' She looked at me, and I got the point.

We chatted enjoyably about her ambitions and experiences so far – it turns out that the casting couch is less of a myth than I'd assumed – until she asked me what life was like at Babbingtons. 'Someone told me that it was where the word "sweatshop" originated.'

'There is a bit of that,' I conceded. 'But there's a real thrill working for such a top firm. Best clients, best work, best back-up, you know. It's great.'

Helena sipped away at her white wine, looking unimpressed. I wondered how I could've ever imagined that she would have thought 'cor, this guy's got all the stationery supplies he could need, I must go to bed with him.'

I moved on quickly. 'Given your opinion of my profession, I have to wonder why you're here at all.'

'The girls from the office come here every Friday. "Down the Box to get out of our box", that's their motto. Bit arsey, but there you go. You know what it's like – you have to join in with these things.'

'Indeed. So where are they?'

'Bunch of lightweights. Already gone.'

18

We chorused 'arses' and laughed. Helena shifted to stand closer just as Hannah and Lucy joined us, panting with the exertion and towing a couple of guys along.

There were rapid introductions and I could sense Helena shifting uncomfortably at my side.

'Actually, I'm at the same firm as Helena,' Hannah's guy said stiffly. 'I'm a trusts lawyer. I mean, a real lawyer, not a paralegal.' Hannah frowned unhappily at that and I knew the guy was toast.

I was unimpressed, anyway. Trusts lawyers are pretty low on the legal food chain, while it was almost a condition of working in the field that you have your personality surgically removed beforehand.

'Are you an arse then?' I asked him in my poshest voice.

'I'm sorry, I don't quite get your drift?'

'You know, an arse.' Helena began to shake with suppressed giggles. 'Don't worry about it, old chap. Fancy a dance, Helena?' She pulled me off to the dance floor before I could finish asking.

'You shouldn't have done that,' she admonished, smiling at me prettily.

'Well, he looks most arse-like.'

'He's the biggest arse in the department, more like. I really don't like him.'

We basked in our mutual dislike of trusts boy and I bent over unsteadily to kiss her. Helena regarded me for a moment once more. 'Yeah, why not?' she said again, and repeated it for the final time when I got her back to my flat an hour later.

Chapter Three

I woke the following morning to find Helena sitting on the side of the bed, her bra half on, poking me hard. The phone was ringing.

'I think it's better if you answer it. It might be your mother or something,' she said in a tone that implied that if I left it to her, she might take Mum to task for some inadequacies in her son. It was a conversation both mother and son could live without.

I rolled over and picked up the receiver.

'Morning, lover boy.' It was Lucy at full volume; another feature of Little Miss Hyperdrive was that she never suffered from hangovers. I didn't feel in a position to make a similar claim as I watched Helena stand up naked except for her bra and search for her panties. I silently congratulated myself on my achievement the night before. Helena was by far the prettiest girl to fall for the Fortune charm in some time.

'Whadda ya want?' I growled. Helena shot me a sideways look full of the morning-after regret that sobriety brings. I hardly looked my best in a threadbare T-shirt and emergency grey Y-fronts for when I hadn't got round to sending my normal trunks – selected solely on the grounds of the sex appeal promised by a major advertising campaign – through the washing machine.

'That's not the way to talk to one of your best buddies, is it?'

'It is at ... what time is it?'

'Eleven,' Lucy and Helena chimed, as Helena climbed into knickers so horrifying in their frillyness that she could only have borrowed them from her great-great-grand-mother. My Y-fronts suddenly seemed the height of fashion.

'Exactly. Go and be cheerful with someone else.'

Helena saw my look and cheerfully shuffled over back-wards to wave her bottom in my face. 'Cool, aren't they? Really cheap too. Picked them up in this great second-hand shop in Chelsea that sells absolutely everything. All part of my great economy drive. My mother would be horrified if she knew.'

'Now, now, stud, don't be coy with me,' Lucy said.

'Stop calling me that, would you?' I replied, and then said to Helena, 'You buy second-hand knickers? Isn't there a law against that kind of thing?'

Lucy laughed throatily. 'Ah, she's still there then.'

'Look, Y-front boy, you should be glad anyone agreed to sleep with you wearing those. They don't exactly spark a girl's passion, I can tell you.'

'Very much so,' I told Lucy. Helena was now busy squeezing herself back into her dress. I watched the oper-ation with regret; clearly I'd had my lot. 'How did you get on then?'

'When the guy I was dancing with whispered ever so sensuously that he wanted to show me his Thunderbirds duvet, I knew I was on to a loser.' I laughed. 'But before he realised it wouldn't be "Thunderbirds are go" last night, I did happen across some rather good information.'

Helena leaned over the dressing table to peer in the mirror, though whether it was with a 'look at the state of you' or a 'how on earth did you end up here?', I couldn't tell.

21

'What information is that then?'

'You know our soon-to-be sworn enemy, this high-flying new recruit?'

'May he get hit by a low-flying jumbo.'

'Not a he; a she. This guy works at her current firm.'

'And?'

'Her name's Eleanor Gray, apparently. Qualified same time we did. Real hot shot. Joins very soon with this partner who I'm told bills absolutely squillions.'

It took a moment to sink in. I felt panic rising and I squeezed my eyes shut in pain. I opened them to find Helena looking at me quizzically in the dressing-table mirror. 'Elly Gray?'

Helena turned around. 'No, you idiot. It's Helena. Helena Shalet. Don't you remember? That is so bloody typical.' She shovelled various girly things back in her bag with clear determination to be done with me soon.

'Not you,' I mouthed, pointing to the phone, finding it hard to focus on anything except those horrid two words, Eleanor Gray.

Helena harrumphed. 'Look, I've got to go,' she said. Yeah right. 'But I'm absolutely starving, so do you mind if I just go and grab some breakfast?' I waved her off, sad that she couldn't wait to get out. Noticing the outline of those knickers through her dress as she left – I must have been very far gone with passion or booze to have missed them last night, I was groping hard enough – I felt this was shaping up to be an extremely bad day.

'How do you know she's called Elly?' asked Lucy.

'If it's who I think it is, then I grew up with her. She's sharp, very sharp. As sharp as the pain you'll feel when she stabs you in the back.'

'Sounds like she'll fit right in.'

From the kitchen, I could hear doors slamming and Helena threatening the tea if it didn't stop hiding. 'Look, I think we need an emergency Partnership meeting over this.'

'Why?'

'This is extremely bad news for all of us, that's why. This woman is like the Duracell bunny only with a car battery shoved up its arse. She won't stop until she's trampled all over us, take my word for it.'

'Are you still pissed, or is overreacting the emotion of the day?'

'I'm serious. That smell you'll be detecting soon? That's your partnership going up in smoke.'

Lucy sounded unconvinced but said she was free at teatime, and I made her promise that she'd get the others to come along.

Elly Bloody Gray. There was a crash of china, and I reluctantly got up, threw on a dressing gown and went to save my kitchen from Helena. Not again. How many times did a vengeful God need to visit this plague upon me? Was I that awful a person? Were there not evil solicitors who padded their bills far more than me who deserved Elly Sodding Gray?

I am not, by nature, a vindictive person, I thought as I ushered Helena to the sofa and set about making breakfast. But if Elly Effing Gray were to die a horrible death that saw her head explode and body diced in wafer-thin slices, then nobody would hang out the bunting quicker than me.

The single emotion this woman inspires in me is spite. 'You ever done anything spiteful?' I asked Helena.

She mulled it over. 'I once put a tampon in a boyfriend's teapot when he dumped me. A used tampon, that is.'

'The personal touch – that was good of you.' Helena had the imagination that you'd expect from someone with a creative bent. 'I think that just about counts as spiteful.'

'I should say so. It was a fresh pot of tea.'

Very creative. 'Nice.'

She grinned nastily. 'Not what his mother said five minutes later.'

Note to self – part on good terms.

I started buttering toast. 'But I think spite is the single worst reason for making any decision in life. That I've made

23

most of my crucial ones from that standpoint probably explains much.' She stared at me blankly. And it's all because of Elly Hell-On-Earth Gray, I didn't add. If only she hadn't wanted to become a lawyer. And if only my mother hadn't sighed with such desperation at what a wonderful profession it was, just what any parent wants for their child.

I delivered up tea, toast and muffins, and Helena and I munched away in post-coital, pre-goodbye-forever silence. Any other day and I'd be trying my hardest to get her to stay, to arrange a date, to do anything but let her out of my grasp. But it was hard to think about anything other than Elly; for once, a woman's desire to clear the hell out of my flat was in both of our interests.

Breakfast over, Helena and I finally reached that stage of supreme morning-after-the-one-night-stand-before awkwardness where you part and both falls back with relief against opposite sides of the door thinking, 'Thank goodness that's over.'

'You haven't left any little gifts in my teapot, I hope?'

'Don't worry, you weren't that bad.' She grinned.

It was nice to know she cared enough, and the fact was that though I wanted her out right then, Helena was definitely worth another go. 'So, erm, see you some time, perhaps?' I heard myself and it sounded like I was fourteen and at the end of my very first date. I'd got pretty good with women over the years, but just hearing the name Eleanor Gray had unsettled me. So in the presence of someone as striking as Helena, the little boy in me who is going 'Wow, I just slept with her' occasionally seeps out.

Helena nodded with little enthusiasm. 'Maybe down The Witness Box sometime.'

'That'd be great,' I said. 'I'll look out for you. Perhaps next week?'

'Sure, see you then,' she said, and an expression washed over her face that said she'd be hanging out at a different bar for the next few weeks. She turned sharply and left, which was disappointing, but it allowed me to potter around for the next few hours, cleaning, watching TV, having lunch, cursing Elly Gray at every opportunity.

Next-door neighbours in commuter-belt Buckinghamshire, Elly and I were best friends throughout our childhood. We went to a local nursery and then primary school together, where we were the brightest kids, and continued to excel at secondary school even though Elly was always one step ahead of me. I used to insist this was a temporary state of affairs until my rate of maturity caught up with hers.

I was too young to realise it at first, but I have always found Elly gorgeous. She's had jet-black hair to her shoulders for as long as I can remember, with sparkling spinach-coloured eyes set against a not-too-pale face that enhances the colours. She was unduly disappointed that she didn't finish up at five foot seven, but however many times she made me measure her – and after I'd almost had to nail her feet flat to the floor – she always came out half an inch short. I always enjoyed our measuring sessions. She was, in the best sense of the word, a minx – mischievous, expressive, funny, impatient and generally joyful.

It was the summer of 1988, and everything was going exceptionally well. Elly and I had been dancing around each other for some years now, but the dancing was getting closer and I could envisage a time when we finally stepped over the line marked 'friends' to the side marked 'wahey, would you look at that'.

What made it a near racing certainty were our plans to go to university in Bristol together. We were going to live together, we were going to study together and surely, within a short period of time, our bodies would join together in a suitably sweaty manner.

I hadn't slept well the night before the A-level results, and I'd been up since early in the morning carefully adding rips to a new pair of jeans.

'What are you doing?' my mum demanded when she came in. 'I only just bought them for you. If you don't like them, I could've just taken them back.'

I rolled my eyes with the impatience of a teenager who

25

knows better than his parents. 'You are so untrendy, Mum,' I said. 'Everyone's got rips nowadays.'

She looked doubtful, but never liked to be thought of as behind the times. The following day, when my dad put on some suit trousers, he found them virtually shredded. 'Charlie says this is how people are dressing,' Mum said.

At last the envelope slipped through the letter-box and, confident though I was, I suffered a momentary shiver of fear that I had gone and buggered up my entire future. My parents watched on breathless as I opened it.

'Oh God, I failed,' I said, putting a distressed hand to my head.

My parents shared a look like that of a James Bond villain whose plans for world domination have just been thwarted. 'Oh well, Charlie,' my mum said almost instantly. 'There are plenty of careers you can do without going to university and still make a really good living.'

'I was talking about you to a friend of mine who works at a bank just the other day,' my dad offered. 'He said there may be a junior job going there, but you can get promoted really quickly.'

I gazed at them, more than a bit put out that they'd been busy making contingency plans. Great to know they had such faith in their only child. 'I only got a B in general studies,' I said, grinning. 'It's meaningless. Otherwise, three As.'

They fell on each other with relief, before remembering to give me a hug too. 'We always knew you'd do it,' my dad said, lying through his teeth in a manner that was to come in useful during my professional career.

Leaving my parents to telephone round the good news, I rushed over to Elly's. She was already at the door, looking sensational in the glow of happiness, and bounded out into my arms. Without thinking, we kissed with gusto, before she pushed me away gently. 'Well?' she said.

'Three As and a B.' The Fortune swagger, boosted by the taste of her lips, was in full flow. 'You?'

'Four As. So near and yet so far, Charlie.'

26

I could live with it this once and we hugged again with joy. 'We are going to have such a great time at Bristol, Elly. I can't wait.'

She pushed me away again. 'Erm, what do you mean, Bristol?' Her demeanour had suddenly turned very shifty.

Eloquence deserted me. 'What do you mean, "What do you mean, Bristol?"?'

There was a long pause. 'Charlie, I'm going to Cambridge.'

Oh God, my life was over. 'No, you're not. You're coming with me to Bristol.'

'I thought I told you, Charlie.' It was said with the same conviction as 'the dog ate the letter I wrote to you about this'.

All my romantic dreams of us becoming adults together – and my more sordid dreams of an awful lot of sex – were splintering. 'You didn't tell me anything. I thought we agreed we'd both apply for Bristol and not Cambridge because we knew we would both get in even if we didn't get three As.'

'You know I really wanted to go to Cambridge,' she said. Maybe, but I thought she really wanted to be at university with me more.

'You know I would have applied if you had,' I snapped. 'And I'd've got in, just like you.'

We argued some more before she shrugged, seemingly losing interest in the discussion. 'I dunno what happened, Charlie. I thought I told you. I'm sorry.'

And so it began. Our rivalry turned from friendly to hostile to Geneva convention. I was as sure as I could be that she hadn't done it as a way to get me out of her hair. I refused to believe that. My main suspicion was the ruthless sense of competition that occasionally overwhelmed her. She couldn't control it, even when I was the victim. Or maybe it was random nastiness. Or some kind of psychosis. Perhaps it was just her nature to turn on the people close to her. I packed sadly for Bristol and preferred to put it down to PMT. At least I could understand that.

But our lives remained entwined in a silent but deadly race for superiority, filtered through our mothers and fuelled by bitter encounters at regular joint family get-togethers neither of us could escape, even at this age. The need to achieve more than Elly drove me to Babbington Botts – a name which put even the pukka firm she joined in the shade – and, for all I knew, still drove me now, thirteen years down the line. But if the subject of Elly ever came up, I dealt with it in the only way I knew how: by becoming incredibly immature and vindictive. It had worked for thirteen years and I saw no reason to change now.

The emergency Partnership meeting came around quickly enough and we were soon convened around a table in the corner of a pub in Hampstead. It was a quiet afternoon; a few of the locals were watching football on the TV at the far end of the long bar, leaving us undisturbed.

Ash had sauntered in with a cat-that's-got-the-cream smile, but I wasn't in the mood for a game of one-upmanship, even though I was confident that for once I would beat him. Lucy and Hannah groaned and refused to discuss the night before, except to verify the source of the key information.

'So we trust the word of a man who owns a Thunderbirds duvet, do we?' Hannah was less than impressed.

'No reason not to,' Ash said. 'You've seen Charlie's Darstedly and Muttley duvet, I presume.'

'That's hardly the same,' I protested. 'Their determination and deviousness provide a daily inspiration for life at the firm.'

An argument ensued over which Wacky Races character would do best at Babbingtons – the gorgeous Penelope Pitstop, we decided, so long as she could bring herself to sleep with the right partners – until I called for quiet and explained about my history with Elly Gray. 'She's merciless, I promise you.'

'That was all a long time ago, Charlie,' said Hannah. 'You're probably overreacting.'

'What she's trying to say is that you're a raging para-noid,' Ash threw in.

'No, I'm not,' Hannah said. 'Not raging, anyway.'

'She's still like that. I see it in her eyes every time. Deadly, she is. Poison. Ultra-competitive.'

'Sounds like she has very expressive eyes,' said Ash.

'You could probably say that about any of us when the chips are down,' Hannah said. I stopped myself from disagreeing. Of all of us, Hannah was the one person I wouldn't say that about.

'Anyway,' said Lucy, 'we're bound to be in pole posi-tion. We've worked our way up at Babbingtons and you know what they think about loyalty.'

'And you also know that they wouldn't recruit someone as senior as Elly if she wasn't partnership material,' I countered. I could tell that had hit home. 'And if she's coming with this bit-hitting partner, he's probably cut a deal for her too.'

'There's nothing much we can do about it,' said Hannah. 'For some reason, they don't consult us over their recruit-ment policy. And let's face it, we could do with an extra pair of experienced hands around the place.'

'No, no, no, no, no,' I said, imploring. 'You're falling into her trap.'

'OK,' Hannah said, in an I'll keep him calm, you grab the straitjacket tone. 'I'm reassessing the raging paranoid thing now.'

I took a breath. 'I'm not paranoid. I know the world isn't out to get me.'

'Good,' said Hannah. 'You had us worried for a moment.'

'But without a shadow of a scintilla of doubt, Elly Gray is out to get me. So just promise me one thing.'

'What?' said Lucy.

'That you won't be friendly with her. You won't welcome her. You won't do anything that'll upset me by making her feel comfortable. We've got to keep her wrong-footed.'

29

'Of course,' said Ash.

'Wouldn't think of it,' said Hannah.

'Trust us, Charlie,' said Lucy. 'We're your friends.'

So what that none of us could have risen to where we are without knowing when to say the right thing at the right time? These were my friends, my future partners. I knew I could trust them.

About as far as I could throw the Babbingtons building, that is.

Chapter Four

My tension levels grew over the next few weeks as I waited for the fateful day when Elly hit town. Every morning while shaving I tried out a variety of super-cool expressions to greet her with, but instead I just felt my stomach acids fizz. It wasn't enough that the day-to-day stresses of work were burning a hole in my stomach lining; Elly had come along to finish the job.

But when the Monday dawned, I found myself imprisoned in meetings at a new client's office, explaining patiently to one wide-boy director after another now what they were proposing to do to their shareholders was at best totally immoral and at worst utterly illegal.

'But you're a lawyer,' one of them said, mystified. 'We're paying you to make the illegal things legal and ignore the immoral things.'

'To be honest,' said another, not getting the irony, 'we're surprised you recognise immorality. At least as something that's wrong.'

'I do have a higher duty, you know,' I said, a touch too piously. This bunch was very much out of the lawyer/liar school of thinking.

'Yeah, to billing us,' guffawed Robert, the chairman,

looking round to make sure his colleagues were laughing along. I'd privately nicknamed him Atlantic, for he truly seemed to be that wide.

How is it that a group of highly educated, highly trained professionals like lawyers, who in many cases do an awful lot of good for people unable to take on the might of the law themselves, have attained such an awful reputation? But Robert didn't seem quite the right person for a philosophical discussion.

I staggered back to the office about seven in the evening, having finally made it as clear as polite client relations would allow that I wasn't their 'legal bitch', as Robert had so charmingly shouted at me during one particularly tense exchange.

Normally this wasn't the kind of client the firm associated with – the typical Babbingtons client was rather more blue chip than blue collar – but Robert was the brother of a partner's wife. I'd not been back long when the partner, a litigation bulldog, called me to his office.

'Good day?' he asked.

'What is it they say in diplomatic communiqués? We had a frank exchange of views.'

'Robert can be a little difficult,' he agreed placidly. 'You should see him at Christmas – goes nuclear if he's not allowed to cut the turkey.'

I was surprised they let him near a knife. 'What's the best way to deal with him?'

'Swear back at him even harder. It's the only way to gain his respect. My aunt won't come to us for Christmas any more.'

'I'm not sure my vocabulary's up to it.'

He smiled at me teasingly. 'Telling you that this one's a freebie will probably help.'

He was right, but I bit my tongue and looked deeply pained instead. Not only had I lost the pleasure of constructive timesheet re-evaluation – that is, over-billing – but it would eat into my chargeables too. How could I ever exceed my targets if I was busy doing freebies for partners' in-laws?

'Don't worry,' he said, understanding fully. 'I'll clear it with Graham.' The upside was that helping out an influential partner like this couldn't do any harm.

Rather than return to my desk, I went looking for the others, only to find all their offices empty. Like most law firms, the open-plan fad hadn't made it to Babbingtons. Lawyers argue that the nature of their work requires privacy; the reality is that having separate offices means they don't have to put their – let's be polite and call them rusty – social skills to the test.

The main exception to this is the trainee solicitors, who have to be supervised through sharing a room with a senior solicitor and, more importantly, made to realise that the pecking order is everything. They are the modern equivalent of the public school fag, only swapping physical abuse for the most menial tasks the law can throw up – so we're talking breathtakingly tedious.

'They've gone down the pub,' the trainee who shared Ash's room told me. He had clearly been left there to salve Ash's conscience because the kid's desk was piled high with textbooks.

'Pulling a late one?' I asked.

He gestured at the books, moaning about some research. 'Ash said it has to be done by first thing tomorrow.'

He wore an expression I recognised all too well. 'And you had plans for this evening, yes?'

'Too right. This is about the fifth time running that I've had to blow my girlfriend out.'

I shrugged, finding it hard to care. It was a process we all went through. 'It'll get easier.'

'Will it?' he asked hopefully.

'Of course. She's bound to dump you soon.'

Narked that nobody had left me a message – even though there was only one place I'd find them on a Monday night if not in their offices – I packed up for the night and headed down to our local, an upmarket place with lots of brass and what appeared to be a policy of linking beer prices to Babbingtons charge-out rates. That made it possibly the most expensive pub in the world, but we liked the way it had lots of little booths for private bitching sessions.

My paranoia had got the better of me most of Sunday and I'd called in the evening to remind them all about what I'd insisted was the Elly Clause: No making friends, no offering encouragement, lots of hostility and bucket-loads of pro-Charlie support.

My mind went back continually to an occasion about five years back when we had both been at an old school friend's birthday party. I'd recently split up with a girl-friend I'd been keen on and, feeling insecure, wanted to build bridges with Elly. I needed a close friend and nobody had ever fitted the role as well as her. She ignored me most of the evening until I cornered her near the toilets.

'Elly, we need to talk,' I said.

'Why?' Her tone was less than welcoming.

'Because I don't want us to go on like this.'

'Blimey,' Harry Dobbs said as he passed us on the way to the toilet, 'you two are talking. Has the world gone mad?'

'I don't know what you mean,' said Elly to both of us.

'What's your problem?' I asked plaintively. 'Just tell me.'

'It's easy,' said Mandy Lowe, who neither of us had ever much liked, as she went into the ladies. 'It's that bloody great stick up her backside.'

Elly took a breath. 'Have you put on a bit of weight, Charlie? I noticed last time I saw you that you were letting yourself go a bit.'

Two could play at that game. 'Well, you know what it's like when you're working at the top law firm in the City. Oh, no, actually you don't, do you?' She was at a superb law firm, but one that wasn't quite at Babbingtons level.

She smiled thinly. 'I hear you just got dumped again. Sorry about that. Hope it wasn't too painful.'

'Still, it was nice to have been seeing someone in the last few months.' The line coming out of the Gray household, according to my mum, was that Elly was taking a break from dating so she could concentrate more on her work.

There was an unpleasant pause. 'Look, Charlie, we've grown up. We're not seventeen any more. Do we have to be friends?'

'Not if you don't want to be.' I was starting to get angry. 'You're acting like a child.'

'Am not.' Elly had turned sullen.

'Are too.'

'I don't know what you mean.' She bunched her fists, like she always did when she was tense. By the standards of our confrontations over the years, that was us being mature.

Harry came out of the toilet. 'Sounds like a really deep discussion,' he grinned. 'And to think we always reckoned you two would get married.'

I was fast losing my cool. 'You know something, Elly? Mandy's wrong. You couldn't shove a stick up your arse. There's not enough room what with your head already there.'

She shook her head wearily. 'Oh, Charlie. Just fuck off.' And she walked off, the casualness of the dismissal wounding me deeply.

So the Elly Clause it was. To ensure they stuck to it, I made them swear on all that was dear to them – Ash's condom drawer, Hannah's signed photo of the Bay City Rollers and Lucy's homemade Babbingtons underwear (for the ultimate in silent subversion, sit on your senior partner's face all day, she'd said when she first revealed them one exceptionally merry Friday night).

I really should have known better. I tracked them down to our favourite booth at the far end and counted four heads. Even before I reached them I recognised the black shoulder-length hair of the woman with her back to me. My heart galloped and I could feel my face flush. The last time I'd seen Elly was at our mothers' joint Easter party in our house, about seven months before. We'd carefully kept our distance until the mothers contrived to put us together in the kitchen. They looked on from the door, still desperate for us to get on, go out, get married, have children and link them together for ever. Uneasy for no other reason than it had been so long since we had spoken civilly to each other, we managed to talk about the law for a minute before the mothers were called away on a cake slice emergency. We held a silent gaze for a few seconds, and then Elly walked out.

But suddenly it was like we were best pals again. 'Hello, Charlie,' said Elly brightly. The others had the decency to look ashamed. 'I was just telling Lucy here how you liked to run down the street naked when you were younger.' I'd been about five at the time.

'Hello, Elly. That was a very long time ago, Lucy.' My teeth were already on edge.

'Of course,' said Elly. 'At least five years.'

Everyone laughed and I forced out a tight smile, while trying to suppress a surge of immature resentment.

'It used to be really funny at school,' I said. 'The boys called her Elly the Elephant.'

This time nobody laughed and the others looked uncomfortable. Serve them right, the traitors.

'I had a bit of a weight problem when I was about seven,' Elly said, unconcerned.

'Doesn't seem to be a problem any more.' Ash proffered a professional opinion.

Then Lucy suggested I get in a round. I agreed on condition that Hannah come and help. Reluctantly, she agreed.

At the bar I turned on her, upset and angry. 'Was it that hard? Was it asking too much?'

'Oh come on, Charlie. It's her first day. It was the least we could do.'

I felt genuinely betrayed. 'No, by definition the least you could do was nothing. Which is what you all promised me you'd do.'

'I'm sorry, really I am. But we had to. You know that. And she's not as bad as you made out, honest. Not until you turned up, at least.'

'No, no, no, no. That's what she does,' I said desperately. 'She's just spinning her web.'

'She's been very nice about you. Said you were always a star destined for big things.'

I stopped short. The last time I could remember Elly saying something so nice was when I helped her with her geography homework about fifteen years before.

'And then she said how her mother was desperate for her to marry you because you were so clearly the best man she'd ever met.'

Despite myself, I was curious. 'What did she say then?'

'Ash said that she obviously didn't get out much and she just smiled.'

'And?'

'Oooh, Charlie's interested all of a sudden.'

'No, I'm not.' My debating techniques hadn't improved greatly over the years.

'Are too.'

'Am not.'

'Are too.'

I dangled her wine in front of her. 'Just tell me what I want to know or the vino gets it.'

Hannah pouted. 'She was just telling us how close you two had been and that she regretted the way you two had drifted apart.'

I was interested but still annoyed. It took more than a bit of second-hand praise to undo the last thirteen years. I took a big gulp of her wine and Hannah looked alarmed. 'Hey, that's mine.'

'Not very nice when your friends take something from you, is it?'

'What have we taken from you?'

'My dignity.'

'Oh, please. You lost that when you ran naked down the street.'

'I was five, for pity's sake. The least you could have done is what I asked.'

Hannah slowly took the wine glass from me like a policeman disarming a criminal. 'Just come and talk to her.

Maybe she's changed. Just give it a go and if you really want us to ignore her, we will.'

It was my turn to pout. 'Promise?'

'As best we can, given that we have to work with her, yes I promise.' Always the proviso – a typical lawyer's answer.

We returned to the booth and I squeezed in next to Lucy and opposite Elly. We eyed each other, undercurrents running strong. It was such a shame, I realised. She was so very attractive and so very smart, and had once been almost everything to me. I'd imagined us being pals for life, and maybe more. But that was ancient history.

As the others started talking about a partner who had the pointiest head any of us had ever seen, Elly said quietly, 'I think we should talk.' I noticed her fists were clenched.

It was the way she said it that surprised me. Soft, almost friendly. I nodded instinctively. 'Later,' I mouthed, and she nodded back.

Strangely shaken, I tuned back into the conversation. 'In my learned opinion,' I said, 'he's had an accident with a giant pencil sharpener.'

Chapter Five

About an hour later, Lucy, Hannah and Ash drifted over to play a video quiz game which they were determined to crack. Normally I tried to dissuade them – their embarrassing performance only showed how little they knew about the world outside the office and caused a weekly 'we have no life' lament – but on this occasion I welcomed them leaving Elly and me alone.

We watched Ash shout excitedly 'Gloria Estefan' at the machine before it burbled with disappointment. 'Who's Ricky Martin then?' he asked plaintively.

'So?' I said eventually.

Elly gazed back steadily. 'So?'

'Here we are.'

'Indeed.'

'Just the two of us.'

'So it would seem. Observation's one of your strong points, isn't it?'

The conversation ground to an immediate halt, and I looked more closely at Elly, the first time I'd had a really good, unabashed, head-on stare for years. The ideal proportions of her features, an alluring half-smile and the startling green of her eyes made it a face which drew you in. She was one of those women who was sufficiently attractive that people forgave her things. And she knew it. I had been close to doing it myself countless times but resisted, however strong the temptation.

I could also tell she meant business; not with me necessarily, but just business in general. There was something about her eyes.

Women lawyers need that extra spark. Some men can rise up the ranks simply by knowing the name of the head waiter at the Savoy Grill and not dribbling too much. Whereas women eventually face the standard children dilemma: have them and you're considered to have wasted everybody's time from university lecturers on; don't and have the partners whisper that you're just a little too unladylike for their refined tastes.

Either way, they're not good chaps and the upper echelons of Babbingtons still resound to the good chap's code of conduct. Good chaps can rely on other good chaps, even if they are women, to be wholesome family chaps able to pull their weight at the office and present an acceptable public face for the firm. Acceptable meaning that the firm is full of good chaps, of course.

But there is a new breed of younger women lawyers like Elly and Lucy determined to have their cake – or children or whatever – and eat their slice of partnership too. I was less sure about Hannah; I could sometimes sense her ambivalence to the whole stellar career option, as if there was genuinely nothing she would rather do than trot off and plan a pine kitchen for a country cottage.

Flexible working was the new buzzword – and it no longer meant chaps sneaking off for an afternoon's golf with other chaps. Even Babbingtons, where some of the older partners have blue and white pinstripes flowing through their veins and no concept of working women beyond the waitresses at their clubs, was slowly coming to terms with this.

I tried again. 'So ... you knew I worked here.'

'Yes.'

'Then why did you come here?'

'Because it's the best firm for what I want to do.'

'And you knew I worked here.'

'Charles, let me know when you might say something beyond the blindingly obvious.'

She knew I didn't like being called Charles. 'Oh, come off it, Eleanor. You know exactly what I mean.'

It didn't have the same effect. She liked Eleanor because it sounded more lawyer-like than Elly. 'Ok, I confess that you being here did give me pause for thought.'

Perhaps I should have become a litigator; my interrogation almost had her at my mercy. 'But you still came. Why?'

She bared her teeth. 'I decided it would be unfair to judge Babbingtons just because they had a bozo like you working there'

Was it so hard to have a civilised conversation? 'You know, Elly, you're living proof that it is better to remain silent and be thought a fool, than to open your mouth and remove all doubt.'

'If only you would take your own advice, Charles, and just shut the hell up.'

We paused for breath, hostility crackling. Just like the good old days, I thought grimly.

Elly sighed deeply. 'Charlie, we need to talk properly because we can't go on like this. Just grow up. You expect me not to want to come to the best law firm in the City simply because you're working here? Why shouldn't I? Do you think I hate the idea of sharing the same space as you so much that I would alter my career plans?'

'You haven't shown much enthusiasm for sharing the same space with me for the past fifteen years.'

'So what? It's all a long time ago. You were immature, even I may have been immature.' Was that a dig or a confession? 'I'm not going to alter my career plans just because of some childish spat with you. My supervising partner was moving here and he asked me to come with him. It's a fantastic compliment and a fantastic opportunity.'

I'd already heard about Ian McPherson, who was supposedly so posh he made Prince Charles sound common. He came with a big reputation as both a lawyer and a womaniser. I couldn't help but wonder about him and Elly.

She read my mind, a trick she'd mastered when we were about six. 'I know what you're thinking, Charlie Fortune, and you can wash your head out with soap. There are a lot of rumours about Ian but in the office he's totally focused on his work. He tried it on with me once years ago but I think it's because I stood up to him that I won his respect.'

I tried to conceal my scepticism and that just made her more irritated. 'I want to be a partner, simple as that. If you don't like me being here, tough. Just deal with it.'

I could ignore her desire to snatch a beloved partnership away from me, but dismissing my carefully nursed hatred as a childish spat was too much. 'You're the one who started it, if you're going to be like that.'

We heard Lucy bang her fist on the bleeping quiz machine and insist that Tom Cruise couldn't have been in *Mission: Impossible* because it was made in the 60s. Elly sighed once more. 'It was a long time ago, Charlie. Time to let go, don't you think?'

Not seeing any great need to be mature, I just grunted my dissent.

'Would it help if I apologised?'

Now there was a welcome concession. 'It might do,' I said carefully. 'Would you mean it?'

She grinned. 'Of course not, but I'll do it if it'll shut you up.' She was taking this far too flippantly.

Genuine anger welled up in my chest, perhaps because of the way she'd been all these years, perhaps because she hadn't taken it as seriously as I had. 'I just do not believe you. For years you've ignored me, made me feel like there's a real grudge going on, and suddenly nothing's wrong? What's happening?'

Elly looked round to make sure the other three were occupied. 'At first there was, yes,' she said harshly. 'God,

42

it seems so long ago, but I still remember the way you kept on going out with all these girls and all the time you kept running back to me and saying how I was your best friend and everything. It wasn't easy, you know. I mean, if I'd known that sex was all it took to retain your attention—'

'Was that it? I find that hard to believe.'

'I was planning for us to get together the day our A-level results came out. I was so excited. But then you started getting so hostile—'

'Only because you were going to bloody Cambridge—'

'And I thought, sod him, if he wants to be like that, I can do it better. So I did.'

She'd been prepared to have sex with me? It may have been an age ago, but I felt sick. I'd spent several years leading up to the non-event and even more years after thinking about it, wondering about it. It sounded stupid but this was my first love, the girl – maybe idealised but still – against whom I'd measured all others and found them wanting in one way or another. It was a relief to learn that she'd have been perfectly happy to have sex with me, but then I recalled how much time I'd wasted thinking about it at the time. Shit, shit, shit, shit, shit.

And was that all there was to our animosity, I wondered fearfully? The competitiveness that made us such good lawyers getting totally out of hand? It was pretty bloody sad if that was true. But how was I to know she would have had sex with me?

I couldn't let her off lightly. 'Why didn't you tell me you were going to Cambridge? How could you have done that to me? I could've got in there.'

'It's hardly held you up, has it? You are a senior associate at Babbington Botts, after all. That's not bad for someone who didn't go to Cambridge.'

Could it be that she admired me still? Like she had when she would have had sex with me? 'That's not the point. Why did you do it?'

She shrugged violently. 'I don't know. It was a long time ago. Maybe I needed to make a fresh start. Maybe I

43

wanted to put one over on you. Maybe that's just how I am. I dunno.'

I sat back in silent amazement as Lucy yelled, 'Yes, yes, I know this, I know this. I was doing a deal with the Tokyo office last week. They're nine hours in front.'

'Of course, you became a complete idiot once you went to university, so you deserved it anyway,' Elly went on.

'How so?' asked Hannah, returning to the table.

I tried to signal that she should leave but Elly was happy to explain. 'Prepare yourself. We're talking pullovers lovingly wrapped around shoulders everywhere he went, and shiny slip-on shoes with little tassels. And he always looked so proud of himself too.'

Hannah stared at me in mock horror that she was associated with someone who could even entertain the thought that such an ensemble looked cool. Those shameful days when I thought I had the perfect attire of the aspiring lawyer down pat were fortunately long gone. Ted Baker was now my constant companion as I left squaredom far behind me.

'And there's more,' Elly smirked.

'No, surely not,' exclaimed Hannah.

'Ironed jeans with creases so sharp you could cut your finger on them.' Hannah giggled.

'It was cool at the time,' I insisted with little conviction.

'If that time was the 1950s, sure,' Elly said, but if I didn't know better, I'd say the recollection was almost fond. And all this from the woman who had been prepared to have sex with me. I still couldn't quite believe it. 'And then someone told me about this time he was wearing bermuda shorts with long black socks and—'

Who'd told her about that? 'I was in the middle of a washing crisis,' I protested.

'Please let it be the slip-on shoes with tassels, please,' begged Hannah.

Elly nodded gleefully and Hannah looked at me with warm pity. 'That's so sweet, Charlie. I've always thought that inside you there was a fully rounded geek just waiting to get out.'

44

I was feeling spiteful. 'Hannah, don't make me bring up your tattoo.'

Elly looked at her with interest as Hannah blushed; she'd sworn me to secrecy one Saturday night when the two of us had gone out, but the gloves were off now. Hannah was the easier target and I wanted her to shoo anyway. 'Will you show me?' asked Elly.

'Unlikely,' I said.

'Oh go on.'

Over the years, as the pressures of work had meant we had both lost contact with friends, we had increasingly relied on each other for entertainment, especially on Saturday nights. But this had been the only time I saw more of Hannah than a good friend normally does. We were at a club together and staggered giggling into the empty male toilets where she pulled down her trousers to display the word 'Simon's' on her bottom. It was small, but legible if you got close enough, which I did.

'One question,' I'd said, having admired her peach-like behind for longer than was strictly necessary to read a single word. 'Why?'

Hannah had flushed. 'We were going steady and becoming really serious, he had this thing about my bum and it seemed like a really good birthday present.'

'Did he like it?'

'I never found out. He dumped me the day before. And he seemed such an NJB.'

While Hannah kept an active look-out for what she called an NJB – Nice Jewish Boy – none of the many models she'd tested so far were up to the mark of someone as vivacious as she was. The situation was fast becoming, in her mother's words, a crisis of unimaginable proportions. 'Famine in Africa, Mum. That's a crisis of unimaginable proportions,' she later told me she replied.

'But they don't have to put up with patronising questions from their friends about whether their daughter is ever going to settle down, do they?' she asked, with what she considered unanswerable logic.

In the toilets, I had tried my best not to smile. 'I'm really sorry, Hannah. It's a terribly sad story. And now you can only ever marry a man called Simon. With your luck, he'll be the sort who keeps pens and pencils neatly lined up in the top pocket of his shirt.'

'It's not funny.'

'No. Not in the slightest.'

'And you can't tell anyone.'

'As if I'd want to tell anyone that you've got a bum note, so to speak.'

'Do you really want me to talk people through that night last Christmas with the Rudolph the Red Nose Reindeer Y-fronts? Flashing light and all?'

I didn't, and we shook on the deal.

So before Elly could tease any more out of either of us, I suggested that Hannah go and help Ash and Lucy. Ash was banging the machine angrily. 'Jordan's a place, not a person. Stupid bloody quiz.'

Alone again, my mood was only slightly lightened by recalling Hannah's bum. And that Elly would have had sex with me. Amazing. My teenage self would be so relieved to know.

She put out a hand on the table as some kind of peace offering. I ignored it. 'Look Charlie, we've got to get along. I had promised myself that I wouldn't react like I normally did, that I'd be mature. But you make that very difficult.'

'You did this deliberately. You knew things were going well for me here and you just came here to ruin it for me.'

'In Charlie-world, maybe people behave like that. But in the real world, believe it or not, people can function without thinking how it'll affect Charlie Fortune. In any case, it's your bloody fault I'm here anyway. Sort of.'

'You are so full of it, aren't you? How do you work that one out?'

'I only did law because of you.'

Now she was truly shaking my foundations and I wouldn't have any of it. 'Come off it, Elly, I only did law because of you.'

'No,' she insisted. 'It was you.'

'No, it wasn't. My mum kept on going on about how you were going to be this great lawyer while my big plan extended to being a stand-up comedian living hand to mouth.' The disbelief on Elly's face at that idea was not appropriate, I felt. '"How will you feel," she said, "when Elly's driving around in a Porsche and you're still driving that old Fiesta?"'

She looked amazed. 'And my mum said I was stupid to think of becoming a struggling artist when you were going to be this amazingly successful lawyer. "How will you feel," she said, "when Charlie's living in a luxury five-bedroom house and you're holed up in a pokey bedsit in Hackney?"'

We had a moment of mutual understanding. 'Crafty,' said Elly.

'I can't believe it.'

'"You can paint in your spare time", mine said.'

'Mine said I could be a comedian in my spare time.'

There was a more contemplative silence.

'Serves us right for listening to them, I guess,' I said eventually.

'I suppose so. I still paint when I can.' I saw a glimpse of the old Elly.

'I did one of those try-out spots at a comedy club a few years back.'

'I entered a picture into a competition a couple of years ago and lost to a ten-year-old.'

'The biggest laugh was when some bloke in the front row farted.'

'Must have been a child prodigy.'

'It was a terrifically funny fart, to be honest.'

For the first time in years, we regarded each other with a touch less hostility. 'It doesn't matter,' she said briskly. 'Law is what I'm good at. Bloody good at. And it still doesn't excuse you acting like such an idiot.'

'If you cut me open, you'd find my brain wrapped in the Companies Act 1985.' I paused. 'But that is so bloody annoying, isn't it? How our entire lives could be so easily manipulated. I don't quite believe it.'

'They must be so pleased with themselves.'

We looked at each other with more cool calculation than before. She was still a cow but we were here now and I could sense that the old Elly was still there. And also there remained the fact that she had been prepared – albeit quite some time ago – to have sex with me. So where did we go from here?

Lucy rushed over. 'Quick, do either of you know the names of any of the girls in SClub?'

Elly looked blank. 'What's an SClub?' I asked.

Chapter Six

Things felt a little different when I got to work the following morning, like something in my life had changed for the better. Elly and I hadn't exactly cleared the air but we'd continued to talk without resorting to physical threats, which was progress of sorts.

I began to realise she wasn't quite a devil woman and she began to realise that I wasn't a complete arse. I could tell she still suspected me of partial arsedom, but I was confident that I could dispel even that; after all, I no longer suffered from that compulsion – and, in my defence, it was brief – to wrap sweaters around my shoulders.

The evening had finished with last orders – even Lucy wasn't up for a club on a Monday night – and Elly saying she wasn't going to tell her mum that we'd had a civil conversation; she didn't want her getting any wrong ideas. 'Or you, come to that.'

I snorted. 'Fat chance.'

'She was so thrilled when I told her I was going to get a job here. The first thing she did was call your mum. That's why I didn't tell her until last week.' Mine, of course, had passed on the news instantaneously in a state of high excitement, and I thought better of explaining that

I already knew but hadn't told her.

'I'm surprised it wasn't their idea. The way they keep throwing us together was getting so embarrassing.'

'She just refuses to get it. She drives me mad. However many times I tell her that the sight of you made me physically sick—'

'Thanks for that.'

'No problem. I was exaggerating.'

'Good.'

'Only a bit, though.'

It was so easy to fall back into bad habits. 'Well, just hearing your name sends stabbing pains through my spine.'

'Yeah, whatever. However many times I put my foot down and say I'm not going to one of her stupid events because you're going to be there, she doesn't shout. She just goes very quiet on the phone and begins to sob, ever so softly. It's a brutal tactic.'

'But effective?'

'Totally. The hassle I've had off my mother because of you. So I'm not saying a word.'

'Mine offers bribes to see you. She irons all my work shirts for a fortnight.'

'But not your jeans.'

'No. I don't do that any more, you'll be glad to know.'

'You sure? If you do, I'd prefer to know now so we can agree never to speak again.'

'Quite sure. I'm more of a chinos man now.'

'Why doesn't that surprise me? Many Ralph Lauren polo shorts in your wardrobe as well?'

It was not reassuring to know I was a walking cliché. 'I may have one or two,' I mumbled.

'There's a shocker.' She laughed, but was there the vaguest hint of lingering affection in her voice? I could equally be deluding myself. 'Deck shoes?'

'Ha! You're wrong. I don't have any deck shoes in my cupboard.' Only because my last pair had worn out a couple of weeks before, in truth, but she was smug enough as it was.

There was a pause. 'So, where are we now?' Elly asked.

I couldn't bring myself to back down too far. 'Talking. You're still clearly something of a bitch, but not as fearsome as I'd expected. Bit of a pushover, actually.'

Elly balled her fists and visibly forced herself to relax. 'Look, you may be less of a tit than expected, but it doesn't mean we're best friends again. Let's just keep out of each other's hair for a bit and see what happens.'

'Fine by me.'

'And me.'

'So, that's sorted then.'

'Yes.'

And that was that. Not exactly a Camp David peace accord, but better than what had gone before.

My good mood was picked up by those around me at work, because a number of colleagues came up and asked how I was doing.

'Pretty good,' I told Mike, a lawyer a couple of years below me as we chatted by the coffee machine.

'You sure? We think you're terribly brave.'

Elly's reputation had clearly gone before her. 'Why? Elly's not so bad when you get to know her. Her bark's worse than her bite. But not as bad as her smell, of course,' I joked.

'Elly? Who's Elly? I mean your new trainee.'

Yes – today was new trainee day, when the latest victims joined the department to have their bright eyes dulled and bushy tails flattened. Rather than get one who had already been through the grinder at other departments, I was getting a fresh body straight out of law school. There was always more fun to be had with the new, wide-eyed ones.

'What's the problem? He's only pond-life sent here for our amusement.' I'd been sent some details by the HR department but hadn't really got round to reading them. About the only thing I'd noticed was that he was diabetic. Several trainees had shared my room over the years and they were all pretty much the same – arrogant know-it-alls who learn quickly enough that they know nothing and have less value than your average protozoa.

'You think? There is a fine line between bravery and acting like an idiot, you know. Take care, Charlie.'

The man was talking in riddles. 'I have absolutely no idea what you're talking about.'

'You don't, do you?' Mike was most amused. 'This is going to be great. Wait until I tell everyone.'

'What the hell are you—' I began, but he'd scuttled off, chortling.

Shaking my head, I went to my room to find what I presumed was my trainee, sitting in my chair. He was large in a rugby-player way, with well-tended hair which swept back and up dramatically. It looked like he had a wave coming out of his forehead.

'Hello, you must be Richard.' I held out my hand. That was about as much of his files as I could be bothered to read.

He just sat there and reached out. 'Well done, Sherlock.'

I wasn't fazed. 'Ok. First thing's first. That's my desk and my chair. That is yours.' I pointed to the desk by the door with what, in Babbingtons terms, was a very basic chair. Such things really mattered and I jealously guarded my padding. 'Second, if I was a client and you didn't get up to shake my hand, I'd probably have fired you by now. And third . . . that's my desk and my chair. Shift.'

Rolling his eyes theatrically, Richard reluctantly complied and sat on the hard-backed chair on the other side of my desk. Installed in my rightful place, I tried to make nice.

'So, into the big bad world of full-time work.'

He just sat there in silence.

'Everything you've heard about being a trainee here is all rubbish.'

'Yes?'

'Oh yes, it's an awful lot worse.' I leaned back with what I hoped was an experienced air.

'Goodness, I'm ever so scared,' he replied sardonically. 'Not.'

52

Goodness, I thought, what an original sense of humour. Not.

I pulled open a drawer and took out Richard's file. Westminster School, Oxford and then the College of Law; perfect Babbingtons material. Ash had an identical background – which is probably the only reason he was allowed through the front door in the first place – but only a few come out of it like him, arrogance offset by a dose of self-deprecating humour and ability to relate to those whose fathers don't tool around their estates in Bentleys. I suspected that Richard's father had a fleet of classic cars.

Richard had a look about him which said, 'So, when do I become a partner then? I've probably got room in my schedule next week.' There was never anything more fun than knocking it out of the truly arrogant ones, so I said, 'Presumably you've had your induction?' He nodded. 'We'll do the tour of the floor a bit later, but let's get straight to work, shall we? In those boxes in the corner you'll find a pile of old property agreements which need scheduling in chronological order for the takeover I'm working on.'

Richard didn't spring into immediate action. 'Come on then.' I clapped my hands.

He looked rather bored. 'I don't think so.'

'I'm sorry?'

'I said, I don't think so.'

'What?'

'Which bit didn't you understand?'

I couldn't believe his cheek. 'The bit where you're not doing what I asked. This isn't optional.'

'Don't you have anything more interesting?'

Quite astonishing, even by Babbingtons standards. 'Yes, plenty. But as you know sod all about the law as yet, I'm not sure you're quite qualified.'

'I wouldn't mind having a go.'

'No doubt and maybe, in about eight years, I'll let you loose on it. But for now, I think we'll stick with the scheduling.'

53

'Bloody hell. It doesn't sound much like fun.'

To think this guy was going to be with me for six whole months. And I hadn't told him yet about the very particular way I like my coffee. 'No, that's rather the point.'

He leaned forward. 'Look, I don't want to be rude or anything—'

I was getting fed up with his attitude. 'You're not doing too well on that front.'

'—but how am I going to learn anything doing scheduling?'

It was already time for the facts of protozoa life, a speech I usually reserved for later in a new trainee's first week and a casual drink in the pub. In an effort to soften the blow, I got up and moved round to sit on the edge of the table by Richard. 'There are ten golden rules about being a trainee here that they don't tell you during the induction. The induction, by the way, bears no relation to life at Babbington Botts. It is probably the last time you'll be able to leave here at 5.30 pm, for one thing.'

He tried to interrupt but I waved him off. 'Ok. Rule one, don't take the piss. I can't stress that enough. Indeed, rule two is that I really, really mean it when I say don't take the piss. Everyone, and I mean everyone, at this law firm pulls their weight. Three, you will be given, by me and others, some of the crappiest, tedious and life-sucking tasks your worst nightmares couldn't conceive of. You don't whine about any of them, not to me, at least. Save it for when you're down the pub with the other trainees. We've all been there – we had to do it, so you do too. And you do it because the crock of shit turns into the crock of gold at the end of the rainbow.' I was always particularly proud of that line.

'Four, always ask if you're not sure. Five, always ask if you have even a scintilla of doubt. The powers that be may overlook one screw-up, but not two. Six, don't embarrass me. It's just not worth it. Seven, do what I say. That's what I'm here for. Eight, be nice to me and I'll be nice back. I'm not a bad bloke, but, as you may have guessed,

I can't stand people who take the piss. Nine, be nice to your secretary. That's arguably more important than being nice to me, although I don't advise testing out that theory. And ten, and this is the single most important thing, I take two sugars and just a splash of milk – no more – in my coffee.'

I leaned back as Richard took it in. He didn't look as impressed as I'd hoped. 'Nice speech,' he said. 'But isn't there anyone else who can do the scheduling?'

I stood up. 'For fuck's sake, did you not hear a word of that? I mean, who do you think you are, the senior partner's son or something?'

Confusion creased his face. 'Well, yes, actually.'

'What?'

'Richard Greene? Son of Edward?'

'Excuse me?'

'Your senior partner? My father?'

I grabbed the file to check his name. Richard Greene, it confirmed. I hadn't made any connection. 'You're joking, right?'

He smirked. 'Oh no, boss. I wouldn't dare take the piss.'

I was really shaken. My partnership prospects flashed before me. How did they want me to react? Special treatment? But if so, why hadn't they warned me in advance? Maybe I was meant to treat him like any trainee. But then again, what if my little speech was dissected over the family dinner table that night? 'It doesn't matter . . . no . . . not at all. You've still got to do the crappy stuff. We all do it.'

He tried to look concerned for me. 'If you're sure it's wise . . .'

Oh shit. I hesitated and he played with his cuffs. More than anything, though, I wanted to wipe that smile off his face. 'Yes, I'm sure. Scheduling. Now.'

Richard didn't look happy. 'Can't do it right now, however. Pa wants me to pop in for a chat. Hope that's OK.'

What could I say to that? 'I guess, but I want you back here scheduling soon. I know all the hiding places, so don't bother.' Except the senior partner's office, of course. I'd never tried that one when I was a trainee. The kitchen was the best I'd ever found and that was only after an awful lot of sucking up to the in-house chefs.

Richard languidly rose as Elly stormed into the office, slamming the door behind her. She looked angry. I thought again. Perhaps 'spiteful' was a better description.

'I was wrong about you, Fortune, you are still a complete tit.'

Richard sniggered and I shot him a look which said scheduling was going to be the least of his problems over the next six months. 'Now what?'

'You had to call your bloody mother, didn't you? Like some child.'

'No, she called me this morning.'

'OK, big difference. But you had to blab, didn't you? Typical bloody man, you just couldn't keep it in, could you?'

'What do you mean?'

'About us. Talking. That's all we did. Nothing more, but even that's too much. My mum was on the phone just now, saying she was going to invite you over for bloody dinner.'

Mum had actually woken me up and caught me off guard. I hadn't meant to say anything, knowing the jungle drums would be beating before I'd put the receiver down. But then I'd needed something more to say than 'Been working hard, got pissed with my mates a lot', seeing as that summed up every week.

'So what?' Like I didn't know how much harder I had just made both our lives.

'Look, Charles. I don't know what game you're playing, but not with me. Not here. Not now. We're not kids anymore. I've got more important things to do. If you want to be a complete tit, and boy are you good at it, then fine. But do it far away from me.' And she stormed out, slamming the door again.

56

Richard looked at me, smiling, perhaps rehearsing the story for dinner. 'I'd better be going up to see Pa, I guess.'

I was now in no mood to be messed around. 'No. You'll stay and make a start on the scheduling.'

'I think I'd better—'

'Sit down and get started? Yes, that would be a good idea right now.'

Richard looked at me and, for the first time, seemed doubtful. I held his stare until he shrugged his jacket off and made for the boxes. 'I'd better call and tell him.'

I fell back into my chair. Things were still feeling different. Just for the worse.

Chapter Seven

I tried, for the first and only time, the subtle approach when Richard made to leave at 5.30. It was, after all, his first day, but did he have no idea? My eyebrows have never been so far north as I gave my watch a long, hard, disbelieving stare. Yes, it confirmed. It was only 5.30. In the afternoon, that is. Were it 5.30 in the morning, then I've said fine, another decent day's work done and off home for a well-deserved couple of hours sleep. But 5.30 pm? Did he think he was working in the postroom or something? Did he really imagine he was being paid £33,000 a year to work an eight-hour day?

But with a sketchy wave he was off, not knowing that his exit would be somewhat more difficult the next day. The overriding ethos of ensuring trainees suffered as we had done demanded it. The partner whose room I shared during my first six months at Babbingtons believed that I should never the leave office before he did, as that was the best way to appreciate what was to come. And to the extent that I spent hours at my desk wondering what on earth had possessed me to follow this career path, he was right on the money.

In any case, as his secretary had far more important

things to do, he could always find a use for me, whether it was picking up his dry-cleaning, buying presents for his wife, collecting dinner for the team (I single-handedly kept a nearby pizza takeaway in business), or even sharpening his pencils – he had this thing about having them all the same length. It was the kind of obsession and attention to detail that made him such a big swinging dick around the partnership table.

As the clock crawled by night after night, he would regale me with war stories: great contracts he had negotiated, deals he had worked forty-eight hours non-stop to complete, opposing lawyers he had screwed over, children's birthday parties he had missed and his inability to take more than a week's holiday. Even when he did go away, I would receive a call at eight every morning, wherever he was in the world, demanding that I tell him what was happening on his files.

Ironically, he dropped dead a couple of years back at the end of a fortnight-long second honeymoon which his wife had insisted he take. His trainee at the time told me later that she knew instinctively what had happened when the phone failed to ring that morning.

But I wasn't so bothered by Richard's indecently early departure this day, as I had my monthly session at Farringdon Law Clinic to get to. The clinic, despite being housed in a run-down shop, has an awful lot going for it. Geographically, at least. It has the great advantage of not being in too deprived an area and is also very close to a central tube station so I can get home quickly after a couple of hours helping what Graham always refers to as the Great Unwashed.

But just as I was packing up to leave, Graham called and asked me to wander over to his office if I had a moment. When the man who holds your future in his careless hands asks you to wander over, you find a moment. I took my jacket back off and navigated my way across the large, oblong-shaped open-plan office to his room. He waved me in while finishing up a phone call.

'They will pay that extra ten mill, take my word for it. They're desperate to close the deal.' He paused to listen. 'Yes, I'm sure. I'd stake every hour I've billed on it.' He listened again and then laughed raucously. 'No, you bloody well can't have that in writing. See you, Terry.'

Graham put the phone down, noted down the time taken on the call, then probably multiplied it by how many minutes late his train was that morning, and finally turned to me. 'That man would throw himself in front of a bus if he thought I'd charge him less out of sympathy.'

'Doesn't know you all that well then, does he?'

Graham grinned immodestly. 'Too right.' He then assumed a more serious expression. 'Now, Charlie, I hear you've had previous dealings with our fragrant new associate.'

Graham's network of snitches had worked well. 'You could say that.'

'She's quite cute, actually.'

Graham said that about any woman younger than his wife. 'You could say that.'

'Anyway, I'm told you two were shouting at each other this morning. That didn't take long.'

It felt like being up before the headmaster. 'Just a friendly exchange of views, Graham. We haven't seen each other for a bit.'

'A word to the wise, Charlie. She comes with a big reputation. And her partner is bringing an awful lot of work with him that will make our figures look just that little bit better. Might be best if you play nice.'

We'd all feared as much. 'Is there some kind of fast track going on here which the rest of us don't know about?'

Graham nodded. 'She's going like the clappers. You'll have to get moving if you want to keep up.'

'So it's not a done deal yet?' He knew I meant the partnership slots for next year.

'No. Not quite. You're all thought of very highly.' I felt a glow; that was pretty much the nicest thing Graham had ever said to me. 'But you know this place – even the fittest are hard pushed to survive. And boy, is our Eleanor fit.' He laughed dirtily.

This was all I needed to hear, and moved to stand up.

'And it's because you're so well thought of that—' Graham broke off to glance nervously at his watch. 'Actually, Charlie, I should warn you that—'

At that moment, the door flew open and in walked none other than Richard's old man. I jumped up, as if a fearsome sergeant-major had marched in. He was a tall, authoritative figure, with snow-white hair and small but sharp blue eyes.

'Ah, hello, Graham, old chap. Just passing. Thought I'd drop in.' He looked at me. 'You're Fortune, aren't you? Charles Fortune.'

The senior partner never just happened to be passing. And he didn't drop in. Anywhere. He also didn't have a particularly good recall of anyone he didn't play golf with. The closest I had got to him was a brief chat in the loo at the staff Christmas ball a couple of years back when he seemed to shake for an extraordinary long time – perhaps he took the big swinging dick thing a bit too literally, I thought at the time.

I turned to look at Graham, who grimaced apologetically. A carefully planned chance meeting to tackle the tricky problem of supervising the senior partner's son. How very Babbingtons not to face it head on.

He put his hand out and I took it in a state of total indecision. Should I display the strong grip I intended to take on his son, or would a looser, more relaxed approach be what he was after? In the event, he caught my hand painfully on the knuckles and squeezed hard. Did that mean anything? My paranoia was taking a similar hold.

'Well then, young Fortune, you're the chap who's got the task of bringing my Richard into line, aren't you? If you find a way of doing it, do tell me, won't you? I've been searching twenty-thee years for the magic formula.' He laughed throatily, and Graham and I duly joined in.

61

'I'm sure it won't be a problem. He seems a nice young man. Very bright.' If eight years in the law have taught me anything, it's how to state with conviction something I don't believe.

'Really? Then maybe you've got his double or something.' The boss laughed again.

I knew better than to be taken in by Edward Greene's genial demeanour. This man was a legend at Babbingtons – in his heyday he was known simply as The Fixer. The man to whom clients turned when they needed things done. He epitomised the saying that the secret of life is honesty and fair dealing. If you can fake that, you've got it made.

'As I've got you here, Fortune, I want to say that you mustn't treat him specially. Put him through his paces like any trainee. I'd expect nothing less.'

Did he really mean it? Or was he just saying this, in front of a witness no less, for the record? I just couldn't tell.

'So, next time he comes barging into my office at 5.30, I don't expect him to say he's going home.' Way to go, Charlie. One day, one black mark. Graham looked at me askance; while he wasn't in awe of the senior partner to the same extent as me, Graham was no more than a moderately experienced partner – he still had some way to get near the top of the tree. 'To be honest with you, Fortune, Mrs Greene's looking forward to a bit more time to herself without him laying about the place, getting in the way of the cleaner.'

I smiled. 'So I'm just some sort of glorified babysitter, am I?' Graham winced. Oops. I do occasionally have a problem with holding back those comments which should not, ideally, leave my mouth.

The old man looked taken aback. Then his gaze turned more thoughtful. 'You seem to have summed the boy up to a tee. His mother's babied him for far too long. It's time he learned what the real world's like.'

'Charles is your man for that,' Graham piped up. 'He's very down to earth.' It occurred to me that how I coped would reflect on Graham too. It gave me some rare leverage. And it could put me right on that fast track too.

'Of course, if you take advantage of the lad, then you'll be out of here quicker than a whippet with a bee up its arse.'

He stared at me menacingly, and my bowels took a dive. Then he dissolved into a hearty chuckle. 'Got you going there, didn't I, Fortune? Make the lad suffer. Should stiffen him up a bit. We all had to go through it. Do you know that the partner I sat with in my first seat made me learn off by heart the substance of each section of the Companies Act 1948? He was a stupid sod, but I can still tell you all about, say, section 109.'

I felt emboldened. Edward Greene wanted someone with a bit of bottle, after all. 'Go on then.'

'Excuse me?'

'Go on, tell us about section 109.'

I'd like to think his reaction was amused tolerance rather than silently ticking off black mark number two. 'If you insist, Fortune, it's about the certificate of a public company's entitlement to commence business, more commonly known as a trading certificate.' He looked terribly pleased with himself. The old boy's still got it, he preened. 'So, my lad, what section replaced that in the 1985 Companies Act?'

This was Babbingtons machismo at its most pronounced: show me the size of your legal ability. I glanced at Graham, who looked blank. He was a dealmaker who left it to others – me, more often than not – to get the detail exactly right.

It says much about the past eight years that I have regularly found myself with absolutely nothing better to do than browse through the Companies Act 1985. It is also a curious world I live in where this is seen as a virtue. 'It was replaced by section 117(1), although I believe the Act does not explicitly refer to it as a trading certificate.'

It was all Graham could do to stop himself giving me a round of applause.

Edward smiled and nodded with approval at Graham. 'Excellent. That's the kind of thing I expect my boy to be reciting in six months' time.'

How pathetic I am to feel so pleased by a display of supreme legal anorakdom. If only I had a more useful skill than memorising company legislation, I might be able to lead a more productive life. 'Don't worry, he'll have it off like his eight times table.'

Richard's dad looked a bit uncomfortable. 'Yes, well, hopefully not. He wasn't all that good with numbers, to be honest with you, Fortune. That's why we ruled out accountancy for him. And buying him a small business.'

Poor little rich boy Richard. You had to have some sympathy. But not too much, of course. Sentiment at Babbington Botts means remembering to buy your secretary a Christmas present to keep her sweet.

The senior partner finally looked ostentatiously at his watch and said he didn't want to stop us working a moment longer. 'After all, I've got a second home in Tuscany that you're all helping to keep up,' he chuckled. 'Good luck, Fortune. Remember – treat him mean and keep him keen.'

That just about summed up the firm's approach to management. 'Yes, sir.'

'See you soon, Graham.' He nodded meaningfully at us both and marched out.

There was a relieved silence as I fell back into my seat. 'How did this end up in our laps, Graham?'

He looked unusually apologetic. 'It was done while I was on that trip to Geneva last week. But it's a good opportunity if you get it right.'

'And if I don't?'

'Then you'll get to watch your friend Elly sail by.'

I stood up with real determination. That was all the incentive I needed. After all, if anyone could craft a lawyer able to bandy Companies Act sections around the dinner table at home, it was me.

Chapter Eight

Farringdon Law Clinic has a strange air about it, and that's not just because its users enjoy the rare privilege of free access to my and several other City solicitors' legal services. I think it's the punters' sense of powerlessness before the law, as well as a fear of the law, which my usual clients are far too rich to suffer from.

This is the other side of the coin. There is, obviously, more to the law and lawyers than corporate greed. For every timesheet padder, there is a legal-aid lawyer struggling to find enough money to pay the electricity bill. For every cross-border merger and acquisition, there are thousands of personal injury claims, unfair dismissals and divorce cases for people with nowhere else to turn except their high-street solicitor.

This is work which also provides thousands of reasons to stay safely cooped up in my ivory tower at Babbington Botts. I may have the steel to negotiate through the night over a sausage packaging company in Telford, but could I tell a divorcing father that he can only see his children once a fortnight? No thank you.

And, obviousy, not all corporate lawyers are overcharging, overworking, overbearing egomaniacs whose only contact with the real world is the black cab drivers who transport them around the City. I know of many who, albeit on the quiet, have slipped through the net with their consciences intact to some degree.

I like to think I'm one of them, and that would explain why I'm on the monthly rota at the clinic. Others in the City are less bothered by such things, though: the clinic is meant to be for the needy and only in the Square Mile could this definition be extended to include accountants, bankers, surveyors and sundry other well-paid professionals with a desperate need to find a bargain.

On more than one occasion I have found a pinstriped banker sort in front of me. They spend the first five minutes looking suspiciously for holes in the offer of free advice before getting all gleeful over the pot of gold they've found.

'It doesn't seem right. It's like me advertising two shares for the price of one,' a middle-aged, plummy-voiced stockbroker said a couple of months back, in near disgust at the abuse of my legal talent. 'Are you sure you're any good as a lawyer?'

'Actually, I'm an associate at arguably the best law firm in the world,' I said, offended. I upped my diction in a feeble attempt to press home my credentials.

'What is this then, some sort of day-release scheme?' He was genuinely puzzled; I had to be a legal retard.

I didn't feel the need to be polite. 'That's right. It's called the Lawyers Integration Scheme. They slowly send us back into the community to see if we can become useful members of society.'

Having accepted the idea of a lawyer providing free advice, he was seemingly prepared to believe anything. 'Are you serious?'

'Oh yes. I knew this one guy who they thought had reintegrated. Then he completely lost it and ran around like a madman, suing anyone he could find. It was very sad.'

He shook his head at a world gone mad. 'Still, it's free. That's the main thing. I guess I can take the risk.'

66

These people sometimes make me feel like a cheap week in Ibiza – they're so pleased with the price that they don't worry much about the quality.

But they are the exceptions. The punters who usually shuffle over from the plastic seats by the door to the row of four desks at the other end of the bare oblong room genuinely need our help, even though they present a very mundane collection of problems: difficulties with filling forms, benefits disputes, work worries, nasty letters from the council, that sort of thing. One of my favourite regulars is Julie, a tired, dirty-blonde street-walker better known on the kerbs of London over the years by the highly inappropriate name of Sparkle.

In her day, she assured me, she'd been a real looker – which I could believe, even though what I could tell was once a tall, slim body had become, as she put it, Sag City. 'All London's traffic problems started with blokes in cars stopping to look at me,' she once boasted. Sadly, her day was several years ago and I guessed she was now in her early forties. The only sparkle left came from a big mouth and a determination to dress as inappropriately as possible. And I thought that I had it hard.

Sparkle was always in trouble with someone, and she saw me as her guardian angel. The first time she came to the centre, she wearily offered payment in kind, and laughed unkindly when I said it was free.

'I'm sorry. Run that by me again.'

I was used to having to explode a hundred lawyer myths and explain myself very clearly. 'Free. Gratis. Without charge. At no cost. Complimentary. On the house.'

'Free? Really free?'

'That's right. Free.'

Sparkle mulled it over. 'Let me give you a word of advice about life. It's the golden rule. Never, ever do anything for free.'

Sparkle was a lot sharper than I'd expected and could be a real laugh. We got on well enough that we began going down the pub after the advice sessions. She came as welcome relief, so to speak, from the lawyers I was used to socialising with.

The fact is that the oldest profession has more in common with the legal profession than most lawyers are comfortable with. There's an awful lot of late-night work, we're not overly picky about who we perform our services for and we make sure clients know exactly what to expect for their money. That doesn't stop us bending over backwards to please, making the punters feel like the most important people in the world during their allotted time. And we charge as much as we think we can get away with.

Spot the difference was a favourite game of ours. 'At least my clients like coming to see me,' Sparkle said once.

'At least my clients don't come at all,' I countered. 'Not in the office, at least.'

The only real distinction, she went on, is that lawyers don't demand the cash up front. 'Biiiggg mistake,' she drawled.

There are others, I argued. 'Being paid by the hour rather than – how best to put it? – the orgasm—'

Sparkle looked hard done by. 'I should be so lucky.'

'—lawyers like to stretch things out, rather than get them over and done with as soon as possible.'

'Also, of course,' she guffawed, 'there are some things that even prostitutes won't do.'

The last time I'd seen her, we'd ended up in a nearby pub and she'd told me that I wasn't what she expected of a lawyer. 'I got to know a few in the old days,' she explained. 'Been arrested a few times, you know how it is.'

'Not really. About the most illegal thing I've ever done is park on a double-yellow line.'

She smiled. 'Have you ever slept with a client?'

It wasn't a question I could ask back. I thought back to the one time I'd been propositioned by a client, who had been far too old for my tastes anyway. And he had this terrible comb-over. 'No, I think there are enough people going around this world complaining they've been screwed by their lawyer without my adding to them.'

She laughed. 'Just want to make sure you don't get any ideas, young man.'

I feigned shock. 'Blimey, you don't have to worry about that. It'd be like propositioning my mother.'

'I'll take that as a compliment on the closeness of our relationship,' she said.

'Probably best,' I replied, grinning.

But I hadn't seen her since then; presumably the problem she'd had with her landlord had gone away.

I'd just finished filling in a benefits form for an elderly Asian woman towards the end of the latest session when Sparkle barged in, wearing a skirt that a woman half her age and dress size would struggle to look good in. She was followed in by three old men in scruffy tweed jackets, and instructed them to find chairs once she had settled down in front of me.

'I'm pleased to see you,' I said warmly. 'I was worried you'd found yourself another lawyer.'

'Nah. Us low-lifes should stick together, don't you think?' I smiled and she turned to the three men. 'These are some good clients of mine, the Bills.' I raised an amused eyebrow. 'No, you perv, not at the same time. I doubt they could cope with the excitement.' She shuddered. 'Wouldn't be a good experience all round, in fact.'

She introduced the smallest of the three, notable for an extraordinarily gnarled nose, as Big Bill; the tall, skinny one in the middle as Little Bill, and the third member of her coterie, whose impressively full head of hair looked suspiciously like nylon, as Billy Whizz. It looked like they'd come out of standard casting.

'Dare I ask where these names come from?' I asked.

Big Bill looked at me with pride. 'Well, it ain't because I'm tall, now is it?'

Sparkle flashed me a private smile, and said she'd brought them here because they had a problem.

'Some sort of counsellor is normally more appropriate for those kinds of problems, I'd suggest.'

'No, you idiot,' she said. 'A legal problem. I told them

that you're a bit rough, but you'll do.'

'That's funny. I tell people the same about you.'

We smiled sardonically at each other, and I then assumed my serious, 'trust me, I'm a lawyer' face. 'So, what's the problem?'

Billy Whizz looked troubled. 'We live in this house in the East End, see.'

'Nothing untoward, if you know what I mean,' Little Bill added, worried that a gay pensioner bordello was the obvious conclusion to draw. 'We met in the army and now our wives are all dead, we keep each other company.'

'It's actually my house,' said Big Bill. 'Lived there nigh on fifty years.'

'Which was the last time it saw a splash of paint, I reckon,' Little Bill grumbled.

'The whole area is like one bleedin' big building site,' Billy went on. 'Trendy flats popping up here, huge townhouses there. I mean, who wants to live in a loft? We ain't pigeons, are we?'

'You seem to shit as much as one,' said Little Bill.

'Now, now, boys.' Sparkle tried to keep them on the point. 'Let's just tell Charlie what the problem is. He's a busy man. Companies to buy, people to bill.'

'It started about a month back,' Billy said. 'We got this letter from some company saying they wanted to buy the land our house was on. But we don't want to move.'

'If you've been there fifty years,' I said to Big Bill, 'I'm not surprised.'

'We wouldn't know where to go,' said Billy. 'Even if we could afford them, one of them new flats ain't right for us.'

'Is it a good offer?' I asked.

Big Bill turned to Sparkle. 'It's not bad,' she said. 'It's a fair bit less than what it's worth, but then I did say to the Bills that the house isn't in the best of states.'

I rubbed my chin judiciously. 'I don't see that really matters if they're just going to knock it down.'

The Bills looked at each other. 'You know your bleedin' stuff, don't you, lad?' said Billy. Sparkle grinned. If only

70

all my clients were that easily impressed.

'It's just that we've heard stories, you see,' said Big Bill darkly. 'A few people being ... you know ... encouraged to leave their houses if they start kicking up a fuss.'

Billy explained that several of their neighbours had sold up with little argument. 'Most can't wait to get out, see. It ain't what it was, the East End.'

'But you don't want to?' I needed clear instructions.

'No,' they said in unison.

'Not even if they upped the offer?'

'Well, of course we would then,' said Big Bill.

'If it's enough,' Little Bill added.

'We ain't stupid,' said Billy. 'But it's criminal what they're offering.'

I smiled. 'How about I write them a letter from the clinic, asking them to negotiate. Throw in a few big legal words. Would that help?' They nodded vigorously and Billy handed over the original letter. 'I'll send a copy to you guys too, OK?'

The Bills got up to leave. 'See you tomorrow, Sparkle,' said Big Bill.

'I'm on for the day after, yes?' said Billy. She nodded.

'We'll make a time when I pick up my pension, if that's all right with you,' Little Bill asked politely. Sparkle graciously agreed.

They left and I started tidying up. The other lawyers were also packing up.

'Fancy a quick one?' I asked her.

'That's the fourth time today someone's said that to me.'

'I'll pay.'

'Fourth time for that, as well.'

I stopped putting files away to look at her. 'Last offer.'

'Yeah, why not? It's fun having a mate like you. Something different. I tell all my friends about you.'

Can't say I'd done the same, actually. 'What a combination we make,' I said, as we walked out. 'The lawyer and the tart.'

She shook her head vigorously. 'I think you mean, the tart and the prostitute.'

71

Chapter Nine

'Anthony Joy must be the most seriously misnamed lawyer on the cosmos,' Elly said. 'There are major trade description issues going on here. The only question in my mind is how come he isn't your Bastard Partner of the Week every time?'

The Partnership had, for the first time in eight years, grown in size. Without asking me first, Lucy had invited Elly along to our next Friday get-together a couple of weeks later.

'Is Charlie going to be there?' Elly apparently asked. Lucy confirmed that I would be, and told me that Elly went on, 'I suppose that if I get sufficiently drunk, I probably won't notice him.'

Since she had joined, we couldn't help but see each other regularly, whether in the corridor, the lift, the canteen, or team meetings. People had been asking me about her – nobly, I resisted the very strong temptation to spread wild rumours that would have made Catherine the Great blush – and more than one male lawyer had wanted to know if she was single. She had a heady mix of looks, intelligence and authority, which sent them weak at the knees. I could see the appeal but also knew the other side.

We spoke and had moments when we were almost friendly, but I still resented her being there at all. At the same time, I enjoyed a perverse thrill that we were in each other's lives once more.

'Joy's won the title on more than one occasion,' Hannah said. 'What you've yet to appreciate is how much competition there is.'

'We're talking a lot of bastards,' Lucy explained.

'There should be a collective term,' Ash said.

'How about a partnership of bastards?' I said and the others laughed except Elly, whose face just cracked slightly. At first this game had been boring, because there was one guy who won it on a near-weekly basis for calling Ash 'Chutney', albeit in the chummiest possible way. Hardly an isolated example of the things Ash has had to battle through over the years but undoubtedly the most consistent. He fortunately left, opening the way for the vile partner who would always turn to Hannah in meetings and say, 'So does the Jewess have anything to contribute?' He once did it in front of one of the firm's handful of Jewish partners and left within weeks. Since then, the field had widened considerably.

'Joy wins Dullest Man Since Creation on a weekly basis,' said Lucy. 'But why does he deserve this most coveted of titles? There's a high standard this week.'

I'd put forward Graham for landing me with Richard, while Hannah had nominated an elderly partner who always called her Helen and a couple of days ago asked her to make him some tea as his secretary was off ill. Hannah explained that she was rushing off to a meeting with a client and didn't have time.

'I didn't realise that they were sending off secretaries to meet clients now,' he said in amazement.

Elly acknowledged the challenge. 'OK, so I'm sitting in Joy's office as he's talking me through this file he wants me to help with.' She shook her head at the unpleasant memory; we all knew exactly what she was thinking. 'That room is incredibly gloomy, isn't it? It feels like it's going to rain in there any moment. And his voice is so monotonous that I could sense my life ebbing away by the second.

'Then the phone rang and I could hear this high-pitched, excited voice on the other end; it was clearly a child, presumably his daughter. He listened for a bit and then he said, get this, "Not bad, Susannah. Nineteen out of twenty isn't bad. But let's see if we can't make it twenty out of twenty next time." Then there was a long silence at the other end and he said, "There's no use crying, Susannah. Just because other people don't get twenty doesn't mean you can't. There's always room for improvement. Geography is a very important subject."

'And then he put the phone down and turned to me. "If I asked you the nature of a cumulo-nimbus cloud, you'd know that, wouldn't you?"' Hard though I tried not to, I joined in the laughter and Elly smiled, encouraged. I could tell that she was already starting to feel at home. 'And I was so tempted to say, "Of course I would, because actually I'm not a lawyer, I'm a fucking meteorologist."'

'It would have been a glorious way to go,' Ash chuckled.

'And after just two weeks as well – I'd have had a hell of a time explaining that one on my CV,' Elly said.

'You never hear John Kettley swear,' I mused, 'even if there's a cold front sweeping down from the North Sea.'

Elly ignored me. 'So instead I just waved my hands around in a vague cloud-like shape and he seemed to think I knew all about it. "Nice to see that somebody took notice in school," he said in this voice that was so depressing I thought I was going to start crying.' She looked around triumphantly. 'Come on – he's a bastard to kids as well as us. That has got to be a winner.'

The four of us exchanged looks and Hannah held up her hands. 'I give in. My guy's excuse is near-senility. He's actually quite sweet.' Naturally, I was prepared to argue, but Lucy ruled that while the Richard situation had its downside – 'Like being reported on daily to the senior partner, no pressure there,' I pointed out – it could as easily be my route to fame, fortune and the master key

74

which opened the drinks cabinet in each conference room (a responsibility unwisely reserved for partners).

So Ash began the drum-roll and cleared his throat. 'For insensitive parenting, asking an associate an even more ridiculous question than normal and showing greater interest in cloud formations that any regular person should, we duly name Anthony Joy as our . . .' we all chorused loudly '. . . Bastard Partner of the Week.'

Laughing, we began chatting amongst ourselves, and despite Elly and I making every attempt to avoid catching each other's eye, the way we were sitting meant she was included in mine and Hannah's discussion.

'I meant to ask you how the clinic went the other week,' Hannah said. 'Put the world to rights yet?'

'I do my bit,' I said. 'Which is more than the rest of you.'

Elly asked what we were talking about and Hannah explained about the clinic. 'He only goes because he loves the way the clients treat him.' She turned to me, with a mischievous look. 'What was the phrase you used once?'

'I was joking,' I protested feebly.

'Oh, that's right, I remember,' she said, having clearly never forgotten. '"They look up at me like I'm some kind of legal god," I think the words were.'

Elly was highly amused. 'That'll be a god in the sense that he's never there when you need him, is happy if others make sacrifices, and people only want to meet him when they're dead?'

Hannah giggled. 'And a legal god in the sense that it's a miracle he's a lawyer.'

I pouted. 'At least you haven't mentioned the time I gave that girl a burning bush.'

'Oh, pur-lease,' Hannah complained.

'That's disgusting,' said Elly, but bestowed a slightly less than chilly smile on me for the first time.

'So how have you found life in the hellhole we like to call Babbington Botts?' Hannah asked.

Elly looked enthused. 'It's pretty much what I expected. There's a sense of real purpose which I like. You just know

75

this is the top of the tree.' Which makes the fall even harder, I thought gloomily, but kept it to myself. 'My boss loves it here. "Playing with the big boys" is how he puts it.'

'Yeah, I guess this is a major step up for you,' I said.

Elly gave me an exasperated look. 'Just as well I've got your head to stand on then, isn't it?'

'You're right. I doubt you'll get anywhere without some help.'

Hannah laughed. 'Now, now, you two. Break it up. Have you not learned how to be friends yet? You're not at school any more.'

Elly and I pursed lips at one another. But there wasn't quite the same level of hostility. It had become just a little playful, I realised with a jolt.

'Please Miss, he started it,' said Elly, smiling.

Two could play at that game. 'I don't want to be her friend, Miss. Nobody else is.'

'He follows me around everywhere, Miss. Charlie's weird, Miss. Everyone says so.'

I could have sworn that the look she gave me was as flirtatious as it was spiteful, and it put me off my stroke in the insult game. 'Well ... well ... Elly smells, Miss.'

Hannah and Elly were unimpressed. 'Very poor, Charlie,' said Hannah, who got up to go to the toilet. 'Advantage Elly.'

'As usual,' Elly said.

Ash and Lucy were in the middle of an intense discussion about the firm's recent multi-million pound IT upgrade which meant that we could now have full access to all files and e-mails wherever we were in the world. And they meant it, too. Part of the deal was a state-of-the-art laptop computer for all lawyers.

'It'll be bloody useful,' said Ash. 'I've been meaning to get one for ages.'

'All it means is that we can now do lots of work at home,' Lucy said. 'Between the computers and our mobile phones we won't have a moment to ourselves. They'll put ankle tags on us next.'

'But at least you won't have to keep your CV on your computer at work, which is a plus,' I chipped in.

The pool table that took up half of the room then became free when a couple of guys in shirtsleeves and braces ran out of fifty-pence pieces. Mine was next in line and I nudged Ash to tell him it was our turn.

'Not now, mate,' he said. 'I've got to dampen the fires of Lucy's paranoia. She's convinced those pens they gave us last Christmas are bugged.'

'I'll play,' said Elly. 'I should wipe the floor with your oversized ego easily enough.'

I played hurt. 'Come on, Elly, let's try and have a friendly game, eh?' Her face softened. 'And it'll be good for you to get used to coming second to me,' I smirked.

'I'll have you know I'm a pretty mean pool player,' she said.

'You can be mean? Surely not.'

We got up with sharp looks at each other, and I did the honours with the money and setting up the striped and spotted balls. 'I'll let you break just in case that's the only shot you get,' I said.

Harumphing, Elly leaned over her cue professionally and slammed the cue ball into the pack. It scattered, with one striped ball flying into a top pocket. She looked up triumphantly, giving me a surprisingly clear and not unwelcome view down her blouse and of a very fancy bra. 'As a purely academic point of information, you're spots,' she grinned, before leaning over and tipping in another of her balls that teetered over a pocket. But her next go, a trickier shot across the table, saw the ball miss by a couple of inches.

Elly stood up and set about furiously chalking the end of her cue. With deliberate intent, I wandered around the table, weighing up my options. Letting her win might ease our relationship, but I couldn't do that. The balls were evenly spread, and I had the advantage of knowing the table, where it sloped and which pockets were particularly tight. I leaned down, got comfortable, and fired in my first ball, which was near a pocket. The cue ball stopped in an

77

ideal position for the next shot and I gave a satisfied grunt as if it was skill rather than blind luck which had arranged it. That ball went down and I gently snookered Elly by the top cushion.

'That was sneaky,' Elly said. 'How uncharacteristic.' But she was unable to escape without fouling.

'That was crap,' I said. 'How uncharacteristic.' I put down another of my balls before Elly could get back on.

Her next shot careered wildly across the table and left me in a good position. Elly stayed leaning over her cue for a moment, with a forlorn stare at the treacherous balls. She got up angrily without looking in my direction, but I took my time, surveying the state of the game, before I leaned down and potted my fourth, eventually leaving Elly with a difficult shot. Cursing me as a 'slippery, underhand sod with no sense of fair play' just loudly enough for everyone to hear – by this stage the others were looking on, with conspiratorial smiles – she skewed the cue ball badly and fouled again, leaving me to knock in yet another spot.

'It's looking bad for the new girl,' whispered Ash loudly into his glass. 'The pressure's on and the woman they call The Fortune Hunter is starting to crack.' Elly didn't look especially amused.

Lucy put her mouth to her glass. 'Charles "What's a Charlie" Fortune is on top. He's got his balls arranged and a strong grip on his stick. My, what a big break he's got.'

Hannah giggled. 'Joking aside, when you think about it, this is a very phallic game.'

'Bit of a surprise Charlie's so good with his cue then, isn't it?' Lucy said.

I stopped lining up my next shot to turn around and glare at them. They all stared back innocently and I returned to the table to pocket my sixth ball. Just one more and the black to go. Elly still had five on the table, but my next shot left her in a good position.

She took a wild swing and balls flew all over the place, with two somehow ending up in pockets. Elly smiled at me. 'As they say, "Fortune favours the bold".'

'No, I don't,' I said indignantly. 'That should actually be "Fortune favours the bald". It's a thing I have about shiny heads.' Hannah, bless her, laughed.

Face screwed up in concentration, Elly bent down – oh, how I tried and failed not to look at her backside – and managed to squeeze in yet another ball. She almost skipped around the table, but her next shot went awry and I was able to put my final ball close to a pocket for the next turn. Elly was so worried about trying to stop me getting to it that she messed up her own shot and left me to put mine down easily enough.

I stood up. 'Black in top pocket,' I nominated, and winced in pain as the winning ball rattled the jaws and bounced out, leaving the cue ball in a good position for Elly to pot her penultimate ball. And when she fluked the final stripe off two cushions and into the middle pocket, it was all she could do to stop herself running a lap of honour around the table.

'The tension mounts. Can Elly do it?' whispered Ash. 'Charlie's facing a lifetime of humiliation as yet another chuck of his masculinity is chipped away. That's almost all of it gone.'

'She's shown she can handle balls,' Lucy went on. 'But does she have enough of them herself to win the game?'

The black ball lay tantalisingly close to the top left hand pocket, but I knew just how tight it was. If the ball didn't go right in the middle, it would bounce out. I closed my eyes and prayed to all that's holy to me that she would miss – disappointing though it was to find the list consisting of my timesheet, an original 'Singing in the Rain' billboard poster and the May 1993 page from a car accessories calendar featuring a former girlfriend who overcame that handicap to become a glamour model. I opened my eyes to see her hit the ball too softly, meaning that it meandered slightly off course, bounced across the jaws and came to rest about four inches out.

'We know he's got a nerve,' a hushed Ash said. 'Now it's time to show if he has any others.'

'Elly's looking as grey as her name,' Lucy breathed. 'Buckinghamshire bragging rights are being won and lost on this table. It'll go down in history as the Battle of Babbington Botts.'

I leaned over with more confidence than I felt and slowly lined up the shot. It was, in normal circumstances, easy. I took a breath, pulled my hand back and then gently pushed the cue forward, hitting the cue ball low down so as to stop it rolling onwards and following the black into the pocket. My mind flashed up an image of Elly aged eleven, pulling with all her might on the other end of a skipping rope as we played tug-of-war in our garden. Then the black fell gently into the pocket, and Elly was pulled off her feet by the rope.

She stamped her foot in frustration, as she had done twenty years before, and I looked up at them all with a grin so awful that even I was appalled by the depths of my smugness. 'Winner stays on,' I reminded them. 'Who's next to the slaughter?'

Ash picked up a cue. 'Pardon me, ladies. This is men's work.' And that was all the excuse Lucy, Hannah and Elly needed to return to the table, where they started talking loudly about how much men liked rubbing their hands up and down their cues.

The night wound on with several more drinks and a violent disagreement over Ash's assertion that women could wee standing up but choose not to so as to make men hang around uselessly outside toilets. Then last orders sounded and Lucy cajoled us all into going for our usual bop. As none of us could be bothered with anything more elaborate than The Witness Box, we were off there again, with Lucy and Hannah persuading Elly to join their 80s music dance troupe. They'd been discussing ways to tease the men there even more and were considering adding a crude crotch-grabbing element to their routine.

'I'm not sure about that,' Elly said.

'Just imagine it's Charlie's and it really hurts him,' advised Lucy. 'That should do it.'

Chapter Ten

I knew exactly where I was the moment I woke. It was the sag around my bum, the awkward angle of my head, and the hard spring by my calves which told me it was Hannah's couch.

I recognised almost as quickly that the wise move was to stay still and definitely not open my eyes, so I dozed for some time, trying hard to recall how I had got there. I couldn't remember much after we got to The Witness Box, and Ash pulled me over so we could double up on two young blonde trainees sitting by the bar.

I usually let Ash do the talking in such circumstances, but was conscious that Elly might be watching, so I was keen to put on a performance. That I was considerably more drunk than usual might also have had something to do with it, I was willing to concede in retrospect.

Things were going pretty well with Clara, who was cute but a little dim, as Ash bought a third round of tequila slammers. He really should know me better by now.

As the liquid cascaded through my system, I felt suddenly inspired by the spirit of a Groucho Marx video I'd watched in bed the night before, as well as several other spirits from earlier in the evening. I had a fondness for the films because my dad would take me to see them whenever there was a revival. 'This is real entertainment, son,' he'd say, and refuse to take me to anything made after 1955.

I leaned over unsteadily. 'Do you know, I think you're the most beautiful woman here tonight.'

Clara smiled at me uncertainly, but pleased nonetheless. 'Do you?'

But before I could deliver the punchline – 'Actually, no, but I don't mind lying if I think it'll get me somewhere' – Ash cut across me, knowing full well what was coming because he'd heard me gurgle the line several times over the years, and never to anything approaching good effect. He'd taken the wise precaution of keeping half an ear to our conversation while he talked to Samantha. 'Charlie loves those old films, you know,' he said, in an unnecessarily apologetic voice. 'Charlie Chaplin, the Marx Brothers, that kind of thing.'

'I suppose it's trendy to be a lefty nowadays,' said Clara.

I sighed. 'That's Karl. We're talking Groucho. Big eyebrows, moustache and cigar?' I jumped off my stool and waddled around quickly in a rough imitation.

'I always liked Chico,' said Samantha suddenly. I immediately forgot all about Clara.

'Groucho had all the talent, if you ask me,' I said.

Then she mimicked Chico's faux-Italian accent for a famous line from one of the films: 'Buy your tootsie-frootsies here.'

'Don't tell me, don't tell me,' I said excitedly. 'That was from *Duck Soup*.'

Sam smiled at me encouragingly. 'Very good. Everything I learned about negotiating a contract came from *A Night at the Opera*,' she went on, referring to a famous scene where Groucho and Chico keep tearing bits off the contract they are discussing because they cannot agree.

With a lack of subtlety that only the truly pissed can

attempt, I clumsily pushed Ash out of the way to get closer to Sam. 'I have got to marry you, you realise,' I said. 'My dad would absolutely love you.' She laughed, fortunately.

We immediately become engrossed in 1930s films, and Ash seamlessly whisked Clara off to the dance floor. 'What do you think of Buster Keaton then?' Sam asked.

'Pretty good, I guess. He did a few clever things. But he wasn't exactly Groucho Marx, was he?' I was confident in my reading of film history.

Sam's demeanour changed instantly. 'Are you sure about that?' The question, ludicrously, sounded almost dangerous in tone.

I was suddenly worried. 'Shouldn't I be?'

What had started out as a pleasant piece of flirting turned into a lecture revealing boring fact after tedious revelation about the life of Buster Keaton. Like anyone cared.

'I remember my dad telling me that the Marx Brothers employed Keaton on one of their films when he was washed up,' I said.

'What do you mean, washed up?'

'Washed up? Unemployed. Not funny. Let's face it, he's hardly stood the test of time, has he?'

Sam was genuinely annoyed. 'Because some guy with a painted moustache and a stupid walk was the height of twentieth-century comedy, was he?'

I felt like I was defending my father. 'Let's face it. Keaton lost it after talkies were introduced. He probably had a voice like ... I dunno ... a girl or something.' I've come up with better insults in my time, in truth.

However, it was good enough for Sam. 'He had a good voice, actually. And this from a man whose greatest contribution to the world is comedy eyebrows.'

I pursed my lips. 'They named a famous club after him. Don't forget that. Not sure I've ever heard about the fashionable Keaton Club.'

It was the most bizarre disagreement I have ever had, and that's saying something for a lawyer who's faced some desperate arguments over the years. Like the lay preacher who refused to honour a court judgement to pay a debt to a client of mine because he said God was the only source of power.

In some ways, this made a pleasant change from the usual 'my firm flogs its lawyers worse than your firm' conversations I usually had with fellow lawyers, so I took a breath and instead tried to make peace.

'Let's compromise,' I said. 'We can surely agree on how good Chaplin was?'

'Chaplin?' Sam almost shouted, eyes wild. 'Chaplin? You mention Chaplin in the same sentence as Keaton? How dare you.' And with that, remarkably, she stormed off, grabbed Clara from the dance floor and left Ash to stare at me in disbelief.

He strode back to the bar. 'Bloody hell, Charlie, I was getting somewhere with her. What did you say?'

Her reaction had left me dazed. Just as well I hadn't told her I liked Harold Lloyd as well or she'd probably have put out a contract on me. 'I'm not sure you're going to understand. First it was Buster Keaton, then it was Charlie Chaplin and it suddenly turned nasty.'

Ash was not happy that celluloid had come between him and his conquest. 'OK, Charlie, you're on your own tonight.' He walked off in a huff as well, and that was the stage it all became hazy.

Some time later, the curtains were violently thrown open and light streamed into the room. I groaned heavily and could hear Hannah snort. The left side of my head felt particularly sore.

'Get up, you lazy sod.'

'And a very good morning to you too,' I croaked.

'If you're expecting a molecule of sympathy, think again.'

I tried slowly to raise my eyelids but found the effort beyond me and let them return gently to the closed position. 'Why? Do I need sympathy?'

'Don't deny that you were a complete berk last night.'

It was hard to confirm or deny in my current state, but I feared the worst. Perhaps my mind was doing me a favour by blanking out the rest of the evening. I sat up gingerly, eyes still shut. 'I'm sure you're right, but any chance you could fill me in on how I earned my berkdom?'

I could feel Hannah sit down next to me. 'So you don't remember the woman who poured a drink over you? Or the fight? Or what you said to Ian McPherson?' I wondered what he had been doing there.

'In no particular order, no, no and no.' A memory flashed through my head. 'Oh hang on. There was some woman.'

Hannah patted my knee encouragingly. 'That's right, by the bar. Where you'd spent far too much time, I should add.'

'And I said something extremely funny which she didn't laugh at. Is that right?'

'Kind of,' said Hannah, and I could hear that she was already softening. 'You were going on about Groucho Marx and Buster Keaton non-stop. You weren't making much sense. And then you remembered this stupid Groucho Marx joke – you kept saying your dad was always telling it – and staggered off to find someone to try it out on. It didn't end well, whatever it was you said.'

My mind was allowing me partial recall of some woman who talked to me while I was on about my sixth double vodka. 'Ah yes.'

'So what did you say?'

'Oh yes. Now I remember. I said, "You're a very good-looking woman, you know. Does it run in the family?" And she took the bait perfectly. "Yes, actually, I get my looks from my mother," she said. So I said, "Why, is she a plastic surgeon?" I seem to remember thinking it was the funniest thing I'd ever heard just at that moment.'

'I know,' said Hannah. 'I saw you fall off your stool. And then she poured your beer over you while you were down there. But credit where it's due, mate, it didn't stop you laughing like you were Mr Tickle's best friend.'

'Does that make me Mr Happy then?'

'Not after the fight it didn't.'

'Fight?'

Hannah took my hand gently and pulled me up off the sofa. She led me over to a mirror and ordered me to open my eyes. I reluctantly complied – it was not nice to look at. This really rough guy stared back at me with his hair all over the place, rheumy eyes and a bruise on his temple. I pointed to the bruise. 'Fight?'

'Fight,' Hannah confirmed.

'How?'

'Elly.'

'Elly did this to me?'

'No, Charlie, of course she didn't, tempted though I'm sure she was. In many ways, my friend, you did it to yourself.'

'I don't recall smacking myself round the head.'

'I was speaking figuratively, of course.'

'Of course. So who did it?'

'I can't believe you don't remember something like this.'

'I'm obviously suffering from trauma. I haven't been in a fight for years. My dad always said it was better to keep my looks rather than my dignity. So just a little bit of sympathy would be nice.'

'I've already told you, no sympathy.' Despite herself, Hannah couldn't stop a warm smile spreading over her face. 'But I'm prepared to compromise on tea and toast.'

I went to have a quick wash and put last night's clothes back on, and then we repaired to the kitchen where Hannah told me the story while she made breakfast.

'So you don't remember joining us on the dance floor?'

'Maybe that's the trauma my mind is blanking out,' I said, although it was starting to come back to me in horrifying segments. Did I really say that last night?

'Could well be,' Hannah grinned. 'You leaped in between us like John Travolta on acid. It was really embarrassing. Your dancing shoes are rather worn at the best of times. And this was most definitely not the best of times.'

86

'Enough with the abuse of my silky moves, just tell the story.'

'Anyway, me and Luce are dancing with you – or rather in the vicinity of you while you just whirled around like an idiot – and Elly's dancing with this cute guy.'

'This bit rings a bell. Rugby-playing sort. Big muscles. Yes?'

'Oh yes. Biiiggg muscles. As you soon found out.'

'Yes, yes, yes, I remember now. Tie Boy.'

Hannah smiled encouragingly. 'That's right. Not sure he liked the nickname, though.'

'But it was a disgusting tie. Elly is absolutely clueless about men, isn't she?'

At that moment, the woman herself materialised in the kitchen doorway, clad in pyjamas I knew were Hannah's. 'That'll be why I once fancied you, I imagine,' she said.

I opened my mouth in confusion. One part of my brain was pleased to be reminded that Elly had once fancied me – would have been happy to have sex with me, indeed – while the other was coping with her sudden appearance. 'What are you doing here?'

'She helped get you back here last night, don't you remember? Then she stayed the night in my bed.' I stared at her blankly, more than taken with the mental image. Hannah grinned at Elly. 'Memory's gone suddenly selective. I'm just talking him through the highlights of last night.'

Elly looked unimpressed by all things Fortune. 'Where have you reached?'

'We've got him on to the dance floor and he's just seen Tie Boy.'

'He really didn't like being called that, you know.' I fingered my bruise. 'Of course you know,' she laughed unkindly.

Their ganging up on me seemed unfair. 'What did I say?'

'You told me I couldn't dance with Tie Boy,' Elly explained. 'You can tell everything about a man from his tie, you said, and his looked like someone had just thrown up all over it.'

'I was right,' I said. 'Ties are very important. It was just this yellow and green monstrosity.'

'I told you to piss off, but then you stopped dancing and asked him if he always blew his nose on his tie.'

'Now, I don't remember that in the slightest. But surely he didn't hit me because of that. It was just a joke.'

'True enough,' said Elly. 'But then you told him that if he laid a finger on me, you'd kick his ass so hard that he'd be chewing your knee.'

Hannah shook her head sadly. 'It was nice that you were looking out for your friends, but that did rather upset him.'

'That was the point he hit you,' Elly confirmed. 'But Hannah's right, it was kind of nice that you were looking out for your friends.' She looked at me in a way I hadn't seen for an awful long time and something went off in my chest. 'Then again, it showed what a prize idiot you are. Ash laughed so much when he saw you on the floor that he almost wet himself.'

'So I didn't fight back, then?'

Hannah and Elly exchanged amused looks. Hannah tried to be gentle. 'Not unless you usually fight back by curling up on the floor whining "Don't hit me, don't hit me."'

'I could've taken him, you know,' I said.

'Of course you could,' said Hannah, as if to a small child.

'I just didn't want to make a scene.'

'Quite right,' said Elly. 'Because of course a drunken brawl in the middle of the dance floor wasn't a scene at that point.'

'Was that it?'

'Yes,' said Hannah. 'For some reason, they wanted us all out at that point. But not before we bumped into Ian on the way out and you told him that he had ... now how did you put it?'

'The best fucking associate in the world,' Elly finished. 'Nice endorsement.'

I tried to defend the drunken Fortune. 'It could have been worse.'

Elly agreed. 'Such as asking Ian if being a partner meant you got to shag lots of girls.'

'Exactly.'

'Then it's a shame you asked him that too. And gave him such a big wink.'

'Ah.'

'Ah indeed.'

'In fact, whoops. Sorry. That was a really offensive thing to say.'

Hannah left the kitchen, laughing, to go to the toilet. 'In some ways, Charlie, I'm glad you did it. I wouldn't have missed it for the world. I've never seen you like that before.'

Elly was happy to keep the narrative going. 'Fortunately, Ian was so pissed himself that I doubt he'll remember either. He had his hands full with some girl and they were going off to his casino. He seems to spend half his life there. I can never understand him – he's this guy who sounds like he gave the Queen elocution lessons and yet he comes to crappy bars and acts like he's still twenty-five.'

My memory kicked in at that point. 'Helena. It's coming back to me.'

Helena had smiled up at me from under Ian's arm as I gave her a leer. 'Hello, Charlie, remember me?' My fuzzy mind was genuinely blank. 'It's Helena, you arse. Surely you haven't forgotten that quickly?'

'Oh Helena, yes, of course. Helena. Second-hand knickers.' And then I giggled an awful lot.

Even in the noisy club, there was a silence. Ian looked appalled first at Helena, then at me, and then back at Helena.

'Time to go,' said Hannah, heaving one of my arms.

'Definitely,' said Elly, taking the other round her shoulder.

'See you then,' I said to Ian and Helena. 'Second-hand knickers. Yuck.'

I closed my eyes again at the memory and groaned. 'What happened to me last night? I've never been like that.'

'That wasn't all,' said Elly quietly.

'What else did I do? Are you sure I want to know?'

'No, I'm not, actually.'

'Go on, tell me. It can't get any worse.'

I had, not for the first time in the previous twenty-four hours, got it completely wrong. Elly looked me in the eye. 'Actually, you said that you'd always been in love with me.'

Chapter Eleven

'I've always been in love with you, Elly.'

I rolled the sentence around my mind for taste before spitting it out. No, it just didn't sound right. Not like me at all. I couldn't imagine those words finding form in my brain, taking shape around my teeth, and making such an ordered exit from my mouth. Marching off my tongue to battle with the battalions of derision and divisions of sheer disbelief sure to be lying in wait for them.

I've been in and out of love with the best of them over the years. Lieutenant Uhura from *Star Trek*, Isla St Clair from *The Generation Game*, Wonderwoman (both TV and comic book), Cheryl Baker during her Bucks Fizz phase (the rapid skirt removal being designed to provoke such a reaction, I've always presumed), and Carol Decker from 1980s pop group T'Pau – for the double whammy of naming her band after a Vulcan priestess in *Star Trek* and of wearing skirts that were inversely proportional to her tremendously long legs. Then there is the longest-lasting love: Randy Toff Charlotte in my first top-shelf mag, bought when I was sixteen. I knew my chat-up line should we ever meet. 'We must go out,' I'd say. 'We'd make a right pair of Charlies.' And she would laugh sweetly and fall into my arms.

I still have her in a drawer somewhere, sadly crippled by an ugly large hole in her superbly flat stomach, where a staple once was.

It took me many wasted months at university to realise that a law course – and probably law in general – was not the best place to find love. It was Jane who convinced me: a severe but beautiful Scottish girl I spent four months with due to swaggering and utterly misplaced confidence that I could defrost her. She was so gorgeous that I was desperate for us to fall in love, but she was the original law bore and, however much I liked being seen with her, nothing could mask the fact that she favoured *Chitty on Contracts* as a bedtime companion over me.

She liked nothing more – and by that I really mean nothing more – than spending our evenings discussing the division of property after divorce. I ended it after a night of unusual drunkenness (she'd got a good mark for a land law essay), when we stumbled back to her room, fumbling at each other's buttons. She'd got my trousers off and was just starting to tug with her teeth at my trunks when she looked up with a frown to ask about the operation of discretionary trusts.

My twenties were marked by an agreeably steady succession of one-night stands and slightly longer-lasting girlfriends. Whether my good looks, charm, devastating wit or earning potential was the catalyst, I neither knew nor cared. I only thought I was in love once – with Sandy, a doctor I dated for a year. She had a slightly over-clinical approach to my genitals, and the disconcerting habit of making me wipe my mouth with a Wet One before we kissed, but we loved spending time with each other.

That, though, is where it broke down. She was in the only profession that runs mine close in terms of working hours, and we just never saw each other. Ash thoughtfully calculated that in our year of dating, we'd seen each other for about three and a half months. It wasn't enough for either of us, and Sandy broke up with me after admitting that she'd started seeing another doctor in her hospital – seeing being the operative word, she'd said sadly.

92

Anyway, nobody has ever matched up to Randy Toff Charlotte. I spent so long memorising her write-up that I still have it down pat just in case we should meet, even after so long apart. 'Charlotte might look like the kind of girl who's lost most of her cherries, but there's still one that needs popping,' it began. '"I might not be a virgin," smiles the nineteen-year-old from Buckinghamshire' (this was the cause of much anguish – on the very positive side, we both came from Bucks, increasing the chances of our meeting; on the downside, someone else had got to her first). '"But I've never had sex with a virgin"' (choose me, choose me, my sixteen-year-old self screamed). '"I'd really like to take a young lad in hand, one about seventeen"' (no, no, no, Charlotte – sixteen is *so* much better) '"and show him all the tricks I know. Younger guys are more sensitive"' (that's me, Charlotte), '"more understanding"' (me again, I understand your need for a sixteen-year-old virgin perfectly), '"and they can keep at it all night"' (hmm, not totally sure about that). '"Now that's my type of guy."' And boy, was she my type of girl, although I spent a long time examining the pictures closely to determine whether she really was nineteen. Some people just have experienced faces, I decided.

Even if Charlotte and I were destined never to meet (and though I might not quite meet her criteria now, I was rather hoping they might have changed in the intervening years), I was confident love would come eventually. But there were other, more pressing things to achieve right now. Even if there weren't, Elly wouldn't make the shortlist unless it was about 556 names long.

So it seemed very unlikely that I had said such a thing to her. Was able to say such a thing, at least without a passing word on how much I've despised her over the years. No dash of spite? Not one hint of malice? Not even a sign of my lingering desire to bash her brains out – and here's the nice legal touch – with a gavel? No. It wasn't possible.

'I never said that,' I said flatly. It was my legal training coming to the fore – if you say black is white often enough and with enough vehemence, then it at least becomes a bit milky.

I couldn't read Elly's face across the kitchen table as she nibbled on toast. 'I'm afraid you did.'

I leaned slightly closer to her. 'Then I was drunk.'

'So much so that I was wiping dribble off your chin when you said it,' Elly went on, putting down the toast and smiling gently. 'You were quite sweet, actually. Haven't said that about you for a good twenty years.'

That distracted me into a brief moment of pride. Not even several pints and a dozen spirits could stop the Fortune factory manufacturing its charm. 'It was meaningless then,' I said, reaching over to the pepper pot and banging it down to emphasise the point. 'I was totally out of my mind.'

Elly's look was playful now, as she leaned over too. 'With love?'

'No, with enough vodka to incapacitate the Russian army.'

Her smile was steady but ambiguous. 'Don't be shy. I like a man who's prepared to say what's in his heart.'

'Good. You'll find "Sod off" engraved there, especially for you.'

That grin was becoming infuriating. 'In vino veritas,' she intoned.

'In vodka, vollocks.'

Elly shook her head in gentle disbelief. 'It's good to act on your feelings, Charlie.' I just couldn't tell if she was winding me up.

'So you won't mind if I shove this plate down your throat, will you? That's what I really feel like now. And it might shut you up for a minute or two.'

At that point, fortunately, Hannah returned and we both snapped back in our chairs. 'Do you mind? That's my mother's old china set you're threatening her with. She asks after it every time she calls, and counts it every time she comes.' Hannah's voice went up an octave, as it usually did when she mentioned her high-maintenance social climber of a Jewish mother. 'I'm just not a china-service person, my mum always says.' This was a woman who, after meeting posh friends for lunch in the West End, would gaily hail a cab, get in with a vigorous wave and air-kiss to her companion, and then get out when the taxi passed the nearest tube station. 'Don't look at me like that. I can hardly tell her that she'll find the missing plate in Elly's gullet, can I?'

'It's an entertaining image,' I said.

'Charlie World is an amazing place, isn't it?' said Elly. 'No wonder you prefer it so much to the real world.'

Hannah pulled a face. 'You two are getting along as well as ever, I see.'

I looked into Elly's eyes and waited to see whether she would recount my confession and enjoy a good old girly giggle at my expense. 'Just Charlie being Charlie,' she said eventually, looking straight back at me.

Hannah nodded in full understanding, oblivious to the undercurrents. 'If that's the case, feel free to throw my entire collection of soup bowls at him.'

'Tempting offer,' Elly said, 'but I think I'd prefer a shower if you don't mind.' They disappeared together so that Hannah could show Elly where everything was – I'd spent so many nights here that I had my own towel set in the corner of the airing cupboard – but Hannah returned shortly afterwards and sat down heavily where Elly had been.

'You doing anything tonight?' she asked hopefully.

'I do have a partnership meeting to go to,' I said.

'Yeah, of course, and I've got James Bond coming to dinner.'

We grinned at each other. 'So the diary's a bit blank, is it?' I asked.

'Yeah. I mean, when do I get the chance to go out and meet people, anyway? By the time I get home from work most evenings I have just about enough energy to put the microwave and TV on.'

95

I pulled a face. 'You're not working hard enough, if you ask me. I can't manage the microwave. It's tins of beans and hunks of cheese left festering in the fridge for me – and that's on a good day.'

Hannah always enjoyed this game. 'Hunks of cheese? I should be so lucky. I scrape a slice of green Dairylea out of the bin and eat it with a handful of stale Cornflakes.'

'You've got a bin? I should be so lucky. I just have a decaying rubbish tip in the corner of the kitchen. When nobody's looking, I throw it all out of the window.'

She grinned. 'You've got a window? I should be so lucky. You'd get more light and air living in a submarine than in this flat.'

I looked around the bright, spacious kitchen pointedly. I knew for a fact that the flat – in a very trendy warehouse development – was worth nearly as much as a submarine. 'You rent this flat? I should be so lucky. I borrowed a tent from a friend but all he had were the poles, with no canvas. Still it's a home, so I shouldn't grumble.'

'You've got a friend? I should be so lucky.' She paused sadly. 'I think that's rather where I came in.'

I put a reassuring hand on hers. 'What about last night? You're always meeting blokes on Fridays.'

'Yeah, and they're all hot-shot City lawyers who also have no lives. So we spend the whole time talking shop. It drives me nuts. And I've never come close to meeting an NJB.'

It's not impossible to have a fulfilling personal life as a lawyer, but so difficult when you are a slave to the timesheet. It's why City lawyers often end up pairing off – each understands the demands on the other and neither are back home early enough to sit around feeling lonely.

Her contracting circle of friends over the years has always hit Hannah especially hard. 'It's a Jewish thing,' she once explained. 'You're kind of judged by the number of friends you have.'

She often complains that many former friends went off and got married, happy to dispense with any thought of a career in favour of endless discussions about the comparative

96

absorption rates of nappies. They had no interest in her beyond trying to set her up with dull accountants from north-west London and bring her into their world, so both sides drifted apart. Those NJBs who weren't married by her age, she'd explained to me, were usually unattached for a very good reason. But her mother gamely refused to accept defeat. 'Even if you have a bad car, it still takes you further than having no car at all,' was her latest attempt to cajole her daughter along.

Fortunately for Hannah, as most of my childhood friends are still back home in Wycombe, most of my university friends are too caught up at their own firms to keep in regular contact, I'm far too busy to make any new friends and work also prevents me from maintaining long-term relationships, we were able to fill the holes in each other's social lives.

'Someone cancelled on me yesterday, so I think I'm free,' I lied, and wondered instantly why I had bothered. Hannah knew I was lying, and she knew that I knew that she knew. To think I'm sometimes clueless as to why some women won't share my bed for more than a night.

We decided to go to a film and were deciding which one when Elly returned in a fluffy white bathrobe, rubbing her wet hair vigorously with a white towel. There was a brief stirring in my groin, which I countered with the memory of seeing Elly chatting to our head of department last week and getting on like they were old friends – or worse, future partners.

'I'm going to pop out and get a paper with film times,' said Hannah, making to leave. I couldn't tell her that I didn't want to be left alone with Elly, so instead offered to go. 'No, that's all right, Charlie,' she said. 'I need some fresh air.' And she swept off with an 'I won't be long.'

The door slammed, leaving Elly and me to resume our staring contest.

'I really don't mean it, you know,' I said.

'Charlie, Charlie, Charlie.' Her mocking tone infuriated me. 'You can't fight love.'

97

I felt weary now. 'That's fine. I'm too busy fighting you.'

Elly stood up and put her fists up, waving them around in vague boxing style. 'Come on then, champ,' she said. 'Let's see what you've got.' She began hopping from foot to foot, her robe swishing open slightly to give me a flash of curvy leg.

'As ever, Elly, you know I've got too much for you.'

Elly started squawking. 'Charlie's chicken, a big feathery chicken.' It was something she used to wind me up with when we were kids.

I tried to ignore her by reading the margarine packet, but she bobbed forward and tapped me lightly on the shoulder, retreating back to the other side of the table.

'Oh look, it's Eleanor Ali,' I said. 'Floats like a cow and stings like a bitch.'

She started squawking again, and flapping her arms like wings. 'Look at me, I'm Charlie Fortune, Charlie Chicken.'

Irritated, I jumped up from the chair. 'OK, Elly, you want a fight? Do you?' I made a sudden move towards her and she shrieked, running out of the kitchen. I followed her into the small lounge where we grappled briefly, Elly handicapped by trying to keep her robe done up, before I tripped her over with a foot inside of hers. I pushed her down on the carpet and fell on top, pinning her arms over her head, my knees straddling her waist.

'Well, well, well,' she said, with an amused look. 'Looks like you've finally got me where you want me.'

I was about to tell her where I've always wanted her is hanging out of a top floor window with me holding on to her ankle, but didn't. I looked into that face and it took me back to when we were fourteen, and a fight I'd had on a field behind our school with this huge kid two years above. A big audience was watching in silence, but then Elly flew out of the crowd and on to his back with a scream. Between us we kicked and pinched and punched enough to force him to retreat, the other kids going with him, disappointed that I was only a partially bloody pulp.

Elly and I stayed on the grass, gasping for breath, until I rolled over and thanked her profusely. She looked back with the kindest, warmest smile, wetted her finger and wiped away a small trickle of blood from a graze on my cheek. Instinctively I climbed on top of her – much as I had just now – bent over and kissed her, eyes shut, afraid of the reaction. There being no immediate sign of rejection, I flicked open my lids to find Elly staring back at me with an intensity that nobody else has come close to matching since – not even Randy Toff Charlotte. It scared my fourteen-year-old self, and her, I think, and we never spoke of it again. Even when our lips resumed contact years later, there wasn't quite the same intensity as that very first moment.

'Do you know what I was just thinking?' I whispered.

Elly's gaze was steady. 'That fight. That kiss.'

I felt my eyes prickle stupidly that she knew. 'Yes. And you know something else?'

'You really did mean it.'

I was worried that my heart might pound itself out of my chest. 'You're right again.' I lifted a hand from hers and stroked her forehead. 'I've always been in love with you, Eleanor Gray.'

There, I had said it. The effort used up every molecule of oxygen in my body, and I began gulping in huge snatches of air.

Elly looked up at me just as before, no apparent change, unmoved by my words. They'd fallen out of my mouth, unplanned, unconsidered, unchecked.

Words as lemmings I'd seen on a National Geographic programme just a couple of days before – not depressed cartoon lemmings, queuing up politely to dive mindlessly off a precipice to instant splattery death. Not words that want to die. Real lemmings, little arctic rodents which rush into the sea, looking for a better life away from the lemming hordes. Real words, looking for a better life with a woman I have loved for as long as I can remember.

99

But in the hope of migration often comes forgetfulness. The lemming can swim, sure, but not as far as it thinks. It is not despair that sees the lemming drown, but hope. You can't blame a lemming for trying though, can you?

You'd think nature would guard against such persistent carelessness. Generation after generation. Man after tongue-tied man, rushing into the icy sea without knowing his limitations or thinking through the consequences.

Where is the race memory? The lemming which develops a fear of water doesn't realise how lucky it is, even while all its mates are laughing at it and dashing off into the depths. Would that something could stop men at the point they are about to make berks of themselves in front of women, time after time after time.

'I've always been in love with you too, Charlie.'

Then again, some lemmings make it.

Chapter Twelve

Are there any words which sound sweeter the first time they are said? 'I love you' may not have such a great ring to it when coming from my mother, or when Ash expresses his manly affection for me at the end of a long night down the pub, but the first time a woman looks you in the eye and says that she loves you is a heart-bending moment.

I was still wary, however. I recalled only too well this girl at university called Amy, who told me that she loved me after just a couple of weeks of dating. She then borrowed my ghetto-blaster on the back of my gratitude, and refused to give it back when she dumped me nine days later.

But I could see in Elly's eyes that she wasn't just doing it to get her hands on my Playstation. 'I do declare,' they said, 'that Charles Geoff Hurst Fortune is the love of my life.' (My dad is a huge football fan for ever indebted to Geoff Hurst for providing the best moment of his life – ever. The 1966 World Cup win eclipsed even the birth of his son, he is always a bit too ready to admit at dinner parties. Suffice it to say that I didn't put my full name on the application form for Babbingtons.)

'I take him to be my legally qualified boyfriend,' those

eyes went on, as full of expression as ever, 'to have and to hold for a quick snog in the stationery cupboard, for richer and for even richer, on crappy billing days and on healthy billing days, till partnership doth come to one of us. Then we'll renegotiate the deal.'

I smiled to myself and she smiled back with such tenderness that I could scarcely believe it was for my benefit, that anyone could feel this way about me.

I realised I was holding my breath and let it out raggedly. I'm not a huge fan of silence but such was the enormity of what had just happened that even I couldn't think of much to say. 'This is a turn-up for the books, isn't it?' was the best I could manage.

'Just a bit.' Elly smiled on, but her mouth then twisted into a grimace and she wiggled underneath me, uncomfortable with my weight. I looked down and slowly made the link between the look on her face and the lithe body connected to it. Suddenly, I realised how tremendously promising this was looking. Who could possibly have guessed that my tragic tale of fifteen years of wasted lust might actually have a happy ending?

I lifted myself up slightly to take more of the weight on my knees, and then ran my finger around her face. She closed her eyes and almost purred. Slowly, hesitantly, with deliberate care, I trailed my other hand down her face to her chest, where her right breast was partly exposed by the bathrobe. A hard nipple was peeking around the edge of the material. I half expected a lawyer to pop out from behind the curtains with a restraining order (two lawyers being company, three being a lawsuit), but there was nothing to stop me. I began to slide a shaking hand over her skin.

I tried to stop the shakes. I was embarrassed by them; they made me feel like this was the very first time I had – and this was a crude phrase that had stuck with me due to extremely regular repetition in the playground – got a bit of tit. For virtually every boy in my year, that was usually courtesy of Lisa Oakley, a thirteen-year-old who was so proud of her rapid development and regular bra-shopping trips that she would corner boys in the playground and order them to grope.

On a dare, I once told Lisa that I wasn't interested if she was wearing a bra, and so with that magician-like flourish which makes women the truly wonderful species that they are, it was off. And there they were, very possibly the pair on which Madonna's conical bra was modelled, defying gravity and ready to hang your hat on.

Elly's felt rounder and weighty, but more than anything I was overcome with relief. I'd spent so much time as a teenager watching them grow from behind blouses, dresses and T-shirts, wondering what they looked like, what they felt like, gazing at her cleavage, that I was just pleased to have finally got my hands on one of them. I may have found it erotic as a youngster to see her nipples thrusting against clothing, but it was a damn sight better actually to touch one. Elly moaned slightly and I started trailing my other hand further down her robe. It was a moment of deep intoxication.

'Bugger me,' said Hannah.

I looked up sharply to find her in the doorway, eyes wide, two newspapers and bottle of milk in either hand. Elly jerked upwards and unbalanced me, pushing me off to one side.

'It's not what it looks like,' I began instinctively, and Hannah snorted.

'It's exactly what it looks like,' Elly countered apologetically, pulling her robe tight around her body. A body that I had been on the verge of becoming much more familiar with. Sod it. Must show patience, must be cool, I told myself.

'I just dropped something down her robe,' I went on senselessly.

Elly flashed me with her old contempt. 'Like your hand, perhaps?'

I glared back and Elly just shook her head sadly – five minutes into this most astonishing of relationships and already I was a grievous disappointment. A record even for me.

'I . . . I . . . didn't realise,' Hannah stuttered. 'I thought, what with the arguing and everything . . . I just thought . . . you know . . .'

'That you could leave us alone in your flat without coming home to find us writhing semi-naked on the floor?' Hannah nodded. Elly sometimes displayed a most unlawyer-like directness.

There was a moment of silence as Hannah and I dealt with our discomfort, followed by our relief that Elly wasn't going to elaborate further. Then I said, for want of anything else, 'Since when did you read the *Daily Mail*?'

'I'm sorry?'

I pointed at the paper in her hand. 'You turning into your mother or something?' I laughed a little bit louder than I should have.

'Elly asked me to get it.'

I turned to her in mock horror. 'Don't tell me you're turning into your mother. That's all I need.'

The silence was somewhat longer this time, and Elly and I scrambled to our feet.

But then I thought I saw Hannah glance at me with new respect. As if she was looking at me as a man rather than a friend for the first time since we wrestled in the back of that cab all those years ago. And as a man able to seduce someone else who, less than half an hour ago, would rather have had a scorpion doing the hokey-cokey on her nipple than my hand.

Elly scuttled out of the lounge to get dressed – for once keeping my foot at a safe distance from my mouth, I didn't offer to help – but threw a backward smile at me that sent shivers down my spine and straight into my groin. Instead I followed Hannah into the kitchen, where she began fussing around with the washing-up, doing her best to behave like she hadn't just caught her best friend about to have sex on her living-room floor with her colleague.

After watching her clatter around a bit, I appealed for

her to talk to me. Hannah and I have always been able to share our feelings – which normally circle around a sense of legal inadequacy – and I was worried about what she was thinking. There had been the odd moment in the last eight years when I'd regretted our decision not to take our relationship beyond a grope in the back of the cab and wondered whether she had as well.

'It's none of my business, Charlie. There's nothing to talk about.'

'So you don't mind?'

Hannah stopped her furious attack on a cereal bowl and turned to face me. She looked at me closely and eventually her face softened; she seemed almost annoyed at herself for doing so and sighed theatrically. 'Actually, I do have one question.'

'Anything,' I said, but, being a lawyer, had to add a caveat. 'Within reason.'

Hannah burst into a grin. 'My new carpet. Wasn't too harsh, was it?'

'Top quality,' I confirmed, happy that she seemed cool about everything. 'Not a burn in sight. Feel free to roll about on it as much you want and with whomever you can.'

'The chance, my friend, would be a fine thing.'

The atmosphere noticeably relaxed. Hannah had clearly decided she could deal with this. 'This is a turn-up for the books, isn't it?' she said.

'That's exactly what I said.'

'And I thought you were in permanent mourning for me.' Now her look was playful.

'Tempting though it is to try and crack the only woman in the world who seems able to resist me, I decided that it was time to move on.'

'So Elly's just second choice.'

'Of course,' I said. 'How could anyone top my Hannah?'

Hannah switched her eyes to the door behind me. 'It's good to know early on where you stand, Elly,' she beamed.

Elly stood there in her crumpled work suit, arms crossed, grinning back at Hannah. 'It's not too late, Han. If you want him, I'm sure we can reach a compensation package. Be warned though, I'm a tough negotiator.'

'I did buy myself a KitKat just before. Will that do?'

Elly's brow creased. 'Four sticks or two?'

'Four.'

'Two should do. It's only Charlie we're talking about.'

'I see what you mean. Tough negotiator.'

They both looked at me with affection. I smiled sardonically. 'Ladies, in the word of confectionary, I am a king-sized Mars Bar. Big, tasty and totally satisfying.'

Hannah groaned. 'You are so welcome to him. I'll never look at a Mars Bar in the same way again.'

'More like a Milky Way,' Elly said. 'Small, cheap and unfulfilling.'

'D'ya wanna bet?' I said with a leer.

'Now I am going to be sick,' Hannah said, pushing me out of the kitchen and towards the front door. 'If you two insist on being like this, then all I ask is that you don't do it anywhere near me.'

'Or me, if you're going to make faces like that,' Elly said.

Hannah held the door open impatiently. 'Come on. Be gone with you. Some of us lonely singletons have empty lives to feel desperate about, especially now I have the feeling I won't be going to the cinema tonight with Charlie after all.'

'Thanks for everything, Han,' said Elly with genuine gratitude, giving her a kiss.

'Thanks for the floor,' I said, and they both hit me.

Out on the street, we walked slowly towards the tube station.

'So, what do we do now?' I asked.

Elly stopped and sat on a long wall outside a block of mansion flats. 'I can't quite believe this has happened at last.'

I sat down beside her, undecided whether to put my arm

around her shoulders. 'Me neither.' For once, Mr Take The Initiative With Women, I was not. Not with this particular woman, at least. I left my arm by my side, so annoyed by my timidity. I was just so scared about saying or doing something even slightly wrong.

She pointed at the station. 'What do we do when we get there? I'm going south, you're going north.'

'You could come back to my place for animal sex, I guess. That usually comes first in my experience,' I joked, but part of me was desperately hoping that she'd agree.

Elly looked at me in a way which hinted that she was seriously considering it. I held my breath. 'This is too fast,' she said.

I couldn't help but be disappointed. 'OK. So what do you suggest?'

'Let's each go home, calm down and then meet up again tonight.'

'Might have difficulty with the calming down bit, to be honest.'

'Me too,' Elly admitted, and for the first time that I could ever remember, looked shy. I'd never noticed how striking her eyelashes were. 'So we'll meet up tonight—' she began.

'I know this really nice Italian restaurant,' I said reluctantly. I wanted this to be different, special. Not your bog standard romance.

'And then we'll have animal sex.' She got up decisively and starting walking to the station.

A thrill ran through me. I ran to catch her up. 'Will that be before or after dinner?' I asked.

Elly stopped dead and turned to me. 'Will you stop asking me these incredibly annoying questions?' she said. 'Why can't you make the decisions for once?'

I put my hands to her face and brought her lips to mine. I watched her eyes close in bliss, and felt her hand grab my hair. I was glad we were out in the street. I wanted the whole world to see that I, Charlie Fortune, had finally landed the woman quite literally of my dreams.

Chapter Thirteen

The only time my dad plucked up the courage to talk to me about women, rather than the shortage of quality England left-backs, or the problems with growing sycamores in your back garden, or where it all went wrong for Charlie Chaplin, he imparted a piece of advice so valuable, so life-changing, so personal, that I want a son for the sole purpose of passing it on.

It was half-time of a game on the telly, and I was gabbling away about some date I had that night in an attempt to reassure him that his only child was out there, doing his utmost to carry on the family line.

'Son,' he interrupted. 'There's only one thing you need to know about women.'

I was agog. Out of nowhere, this was the paternal guidance I'd been waiting seventeen years for. The accumulated wisdom that had got him to the stage of conceiving and then, of a fashion, raising me. So if anyone knew his stuff, it had to be my dad.

He looked around nervously to make sure my mum wasn't earwigging as he handed down a priceless chunk of male lore, and leaned towards me. Licking his lips nervously, he then glanced at the television to make sure the pundits were too busy analysing the first-half action to catch this moment of supreme father–son closeness. 'My boy,' he said finally, when I could almost wait no longer, 'always take your socks off first.'

He sat back, satisfied at a job well done. I cocked my head as if I had missed something, and he responded by leaning forward once more. There was a lot more to come, thank goodness.

'After you've taken your shoes off, of course. Bit difficult otherwise,' he chuckled, 'unless you're the Harry Houdini of the sock world.' Dad shifted in his seat and grunted with pleasure as the game kicked off again.

At first I was furious with him for the most ridiculous advice I'd received since one of those career evaluation tests at school concluded that my respect for rules, punctuality, enjoyment of the open air and general vindictiveness made me ideal traffic warden material. But in the end, I appreciated what an enormous service he had done me. I've lost count of the number of times I've found myself in a race with some woman to get undressed, about to tug off my trousers, when Dad's voice floats through my head.

The mental picture that follows is always the same. She looks up for one final check that she's doing the right thing and sees me there, in my full glory ... and M&S pure cotton socks, with neat coloured triangles pixellating up the side. Not good. Not sexy. Just not right. Thank you, Dad.

But with Elly tugging urgently at my belt, I was having difficulty sticking to it for once. Awkwardly, I hopped on my left foot while trying to snatch the sock off my right. At the third attempt, I caught the end and yanked but didn't get enough of a handhold to pull the damned thing off. I stared at the dangly sock with dismay, hoping that it wasn't a portent of things to come. Why do they never go through this in the movies?

Elly was just about to pull my zip down, when she stopped. 'What the hell are you doing?' she hissed.

I mumbled something about itchy feet, grateful for a lull

109

in the action, and whipped off my socks. I then slid off my T-shirt, leaving me standing there bare-chested, breathing in ever so slightly. Elly gave me a quick once-over and was satisfied enough by what she saw to resume work on the trousers. I had an out-of-body moment, featuring me standing there almost naked with Elly on her knees working at my belt. I felt dizzy as fantasy and reality came together.

This was a moment I had daydreamed about extensively to the point of obsession in the old days, but it wasn't going quite to plan.

Fantasy:

Once finally united, the lovers cannot bear the thought of parting. Countless expressions of love pass between them.

Reality:

Elly had so many things to do at home that we had, albeit reluctantly, separated at the tube station and agreed to meet up at a restaurant near her flat in the evening. More than once on the way to the station, she'd stopped dead with her hand over her mouth, as if worried about what might come out of it next and land her in even more trouble. She wasn't taking back what she said, but expressions of love were in extremely short supply. She did keep on saying with little joy how pleased our mothers would be by this development.

'They'll be dancing around their kitchens,' I said.

'Baking celebratory cakes.' Elly was gloomy at the prospect.

'It's taken thirty years, but they've won.'

Elly looked at me through narrow eyes, reassessing the whole situation. I don't think either of us could stand the thought of our mothers' triumph. 'The deal is not exactly signed, sealed and delivered,' she said, but knew we had at least agreed heads of terms.

'We need to spend more time drafting the contract, for sure,' I replied. These are some jokes that only lawyers find funny – for good reason.

110

Almost against her better judgment, Elly smiled. 'That could be fun, I guess.'

Fantasy:
The lovers cannot keep their hands off each other. The fantasy goes into a lot of detail on this.
Reality:
As we waited for our respective trains, Elly gripped my shoulders and said, 'Are we doing the right thing? Are we just going to ruin everything?'

I wanted to tell her I knew she was right for me the moment, as ten-year-olds, she revealed that she had added a tank to an Action Man collection every bit as extensive as mine – this made my love unconditional. For years, we used her sole Barbie, a present from an aunt who then only bought the doll clothing which reached beneath her knees, as a hostage for our Action Men to rescue. Then, having daringly snatched her from the evil clutches of Mr Big (better known as a cuddly toy elephant called Harold), Barbie was so grateful that she gladly consented to our brave men, basically, indulging in one almighty gang bang.

I was weighing up the pros and cons of telling Elly that the way she egged her Action Men on sealed her in my heart for ever, when her train came. 'We'll talk about it tonight,' she said, stepping into the train, and then gave me a quick kiss, which lingered until the doors began to shut. With a look that melted me, she waved as the train moved off.

Fantasy:
My friends step back in awe at the strength of our love.
Reality:
I had been home less than twenty seconds when the phone rang. 'You are not merely a dark horse, my friend,' Ash said, without pausing to say hello. 'You are of the night.'

'And a good afternoon to you,' I said. 'Been speaking to

111

Hannah, have you?' The news, I had known, would spread in the time it takes to say 'Lawyers are trained to keep secrets.'

He was in a state of high excitement. 'You wouldn't catch me playing at home like this. Far too dangerous. When it all goes wrong it'll be terrible for all of us.'

'What do you mean, when it all goes—'

'Awkward conversations around the photocopier, the end to group piss-ups down the pub, insane jealousy when she becomes a partner and you don't.'

'Since when is she going to become—'

'You realise she'll tell everyone everything to humiliate you, yes? You won't be able to look your secretary in the face, let alone the senior partner, without them sniggering, just a little.'

'There won't be anything to tell, because it won't—'

'She'll make up a little nickname for you, mark my words. Something you'll hate and never be able to lose. I dunno, like Floppy Fortune.'

'You're just jealous, my friend.'

He had no reason to be, and I knew it. And he knew that I knew it. 'I know, I know. It'll be Champagne Charlie, because you always pop your cork too soon.'

'Ash. Mate,' I shouted. 'Shut the fuck up.'

'Ooh, touchy, aren't we?' he laughed down the phone.

'I appreciate that you consider a deep and meaningful relationship to be when the girl puts bread in the toaster for you before she leaves, but some of us are after something a bit more than that.'

'And you've found it with Elly, have you?' Ash was not convinced. 'What were the words someone used to describe her? Ruthless, was it? Deadly? Ultra-competitive? That's it – poison.'

'A schoolchild could see that I was only suppressing my true feelings through hostility,' I said, and then instantly worried that I was capable of saying something like that.

'Actually, that's what Lucy said. Or words to that effect. But she didn't sound like she'd just walked off the set of

112

Oprah. You're changing already, Charlie, and it's only been a couple of hours.'

'What did Lucy say then?'

'That it was clear you fancied the pants off Elly from the start. Hannah had thought you genuinely disliked her.'

'And what did you think?'

'Probably that you were feeling horny.'

'You may wonder why I rarely turn to you for advice, Ash. Don't.'

There was a beep on my phone to signify call waiting, so I told Ash to hang on. It was a triumphant Lucy. 'I knew it. I told them but they didn't believe me. I know you, Charles Fortune, and I knew you couldn't wait to make your move on young Ms Gray. This is great.'

I laughed, told Lucy to hang on a moment, and then went back to tell Ash that I was going to talk to someone who made sense. 'You want sense?' he said. 'You're not fifteen any more, Charlie. Remember that, if nothing else.'

I paused. 'Nope. Seems I'm still not turning to you for advice. Goodbye, Ash.'

I beeped back to Lucy. 'This is so romantic,' she said.

'Isn't it?' At last someone who appreciated what I was going through.

'It was always going to happen, you know. I'm really happy for you, Charlie.'

'Thanks, Luce.'

'Just don't bugger it up.'

Now that was advice I could take.

Fantasy:

The lovers are having a candlelit dinner, holding hands over the table and gazing into each other's eyes. The intensity steps up and they decide to skip the rest of the meal and head straight back to Elly's flat.

Reality:

Close enough for these purposes. The chef came out demanding to know why we didn't want our main courses, and I began a long spiel about how we'd had a late lunch

113

and were going to the theatre so had to have an early dinner. Elly gave me another of those pre-out-in-open-loving-Charlie looks of disgust. 'To be honest,' she told the chef, 'this is our first date after years of dancing around each other, and we can't wait to be alone.' He broke into a grin and we left with a free hunk of tiramisu in a doggy bag.

Fantasy:

Once in her flat, I push Elly up against the door and cover her with kisses. Our mutual passion mounts.

Reality:

I pushed her up against the door and we had our first seriously long snog. At first it was lovely, all soft, light kissing. But then her tongue travelled a methodical round trip of my teeth, like she was licking out a bowl of her favourite soup, finishing with a little bite of my bottom lip. I disengaged myself and pulled her towards the bedroom, where I encountered the sock problem.

Fantasy:

There may possibly be something in there about her eyes widening in delight as she takes in the full extent of my manliness.

Reality:

From my standing position, the best I could do was massage Elly's ears. I quickly worked out that this was not an erogenous zone, but rubbing my fingers lightly over the back of her head garnered more of a response; so much so that she stopped fiddling with the sole button that stood between her and overcoming the trouser obstacle. That was it for head massages.

After I shook the trousers off, Elly snapped the elastic on my trunks and had a peek before looking up at me with an earnest face. 'You know how for years you have a mental image of what something probably looks like and then you finally see it and realise you had it completely wrong?'

I rolled my eyes. Pleased though I was that she had given the issue some thought, the only two roads her sentiment could continue were signposted 'bigger' and 'smaller'. I wasn't prepared to risk it. I'd only let her down there at this stage of the proceedings in the hope of a blow job.

'I don't care,' I said, pulling her up so we were face to face once more. Better to suffer another tongue floss than start discussing what difference an inch or two makes either way. And my dentist would approve as well.

Fantasy:

At long last, I finally get free reign of her breasts.

Reality:

Now we were getting somewhere. Awkwardly, I undid the buttons on her blouse and slid it off with our lips still locked. I let my kisses drift down her chin and on to her chest, before coming to rest on her breasts, ably supported by a push-up bra. There was certainly no disappointment here. There is something about cleavage that simply does it for me, and explains why I spent much of my teenage years on the lookout for women bending over or sitting down, so that I could catch a glance down their tops. Cleavage simply holds out the promise of much more to come. The link seemed obvious to my younger self: rounded breasts, rounded woman.

My arms snaked around Elly's back and fiddled minimally with the hooks before the bra was released and it was bombs away. I pushed them back up and thrust my face in, losing myself momentarily in the smell of soap and realisation of exactly where I was. I licked her nipples, and then gently blew on them, and they promptly came up ever so well.

I was highly aroused at this point and took a step back. 'Take your trousers off,' I ordered, my voice catching slightly, but Elly complied without hesitation. I moved behind and pushed myself up roughly against her. She rolled her body into mine and I cupped her breasts again, nuzzling against her neck.

115

I let my right hand wander down into her blue panties, tracing lightly over her buttocks before I began pulling insistently at the silky material. With a bit of help from Elly, they went the way of her trousers, as did my boxers soon after. I pushed Elly on to the bed, and stood over her, unashamedly looking her up and down. Her body was everything I imagined it to be.

I used to have a good friend at school called Daniel Marcus, who compensated for his huge purple glasses, pudding-bowl haircut and permanently runny nose, by telling others why they had as little chance with girls as he did. Hard though that was to believe, it chipped away at my confidence every time we sat on a wall in the playground eyeing up the girls, and he would say, 'Elly Gray? Elly Sex on a Stick Gray? You wouldn't have a chance even if you were locked in a room alone with her when the three-minute warning goes off and she decides she has to have sex before she dies.'

I wanted to phone Daniel at this moment and say, 'Remember Elly Gray? Well she's lying naked in front of me. That's right, Specky, naked. And she's gagging for it. What have you got to say about that, Four-eyes?' He would probably remind me that he ultimately married the most gorgeous girl from school, who was even named Miss Wycombe one year, and now runs a highly successful chain of fitness centres. But I would still have made my point.

Then Elly smiled ever so slightly and other thoughts fled. With a bizarrely chaste expression and her eyes locked on mine, one of her fingers wandered down her chest and between her legs.

I was now beyond fantasy. We wrestled briefly on the bed and I emerged on top, holding her hands down above her head, and my penis just flicking the edge of her pubic hair, which I couldn't help but notice was trimmed to a standard a professional gardener would feel happy with. V for Victory, perhaps? I had a brief moment of panic that I had

116

not done the same – to be honest, it hadn't occurred to me to take a pair of scissors to my pubes for, oh, at least thirty years.

There was a look on Elly's face that said foreplay wasn't necessary, and I wasn't going to complain. Might as well call it for-her-play, I always thought. But then she started struggling against my restraint, and with a shove, pushed me up and then over on to my back.

She got up on her knees and looked ready to climb astride, when her eyes cleared. 'Shit. Condom.' I was about to point at my trousers and the wallet within, stocked before I came out in expectation rather than mere hope for once, but Elly was ahead of me and dived into a side drawer, from which she pulled out a variety pack.

She began sorting through them urgently. 'What is it with coloured condoms, eh?' she demanded, throwing one to the floor. 'Tell me what is remotely erotic about a man with a bright green cock.' Another one hit the deck. 'Or a curry-flavoured one, come to that.'

She finally found one she liked, ripped open the packet, and then gave me a smile so dirty that I knew for sure her mother would disown her if she ever saw it. 'Party trick,' Elly explained as she positioned the condom in her mouth – much as Sparkle told me she used to do in the days when she could be bothered – and then proceeded to roll it on. 'Look, no hands,' she giggled, when she had finished, having taken an agreeably long time to get it properly positioned. I didn't want to know where she'd learned it.

'Never been to a party like that,' I murmured, as, ever so slowly, Elly lowered herself on to me.

Memories tumbled through my mind: when we were fourteen and did our geography homework together. I got a detention for copying hers, she got off scot-free. I have never seen someone laugh so much. And when the detention was over, she was waiting for me outside the gates with a consolation ice-cream; when we were twenty-four and carefully avoiding each other at her mother's Christmas party. She looked so coolly beautiful in a grey polo neck that my heart flipped and I wanted to say something, get back to where we'd been. But then she was enveloped by some big trophy boyfriend with a chunky woollen sweater, huge dimples and a car so flash that his willy must have been about three millimetres long. Her eyes peeked mockingly over his shoulder at me, and I turned away, blinking hard; when we were eight and playing football in our back garden. I'd kicked the ball into a neighbour's garden and got no reply when I knocked on their door. Scared, I refused to go over the fence. With that look of contempt at male failings she was to perfect in years to come, Elly clambered over, retrieved the ball and was just starting to climb back when the neighbour's dog bounded into the garden, barking loudly. 'Help me, Charlie,' she screamed in terror and I reached out to pull her over. Lying in the grass together, Elly cried on my shoulder and I smelled her hair, which was sweet and summery; then I was back in the playground when we kissed, the most erotic moment of my life until, well, now; then I replayed the look on her face earlier today when she said that she loved me, at long last, the past didn't matter any more.

Heat began to burn the memories away. Watching Elly from below, the chin dimpled slightly with the effort, the flush to her skin, the way her mouth was slightly open, lips full, I could feel a lustful convulsing which meant I was about to come. I needed to come. I couldn't stand it much longer. I gripped her thigh with one hand and her backside with the other, and pulled her harder, faster on to me.

Fantasy:
    Elly is everything I'd hoped for.
Reality:
    At least I got something right over the years.

Chapter Fourteen

What I never expected about spending the entire day in bed is that it would be so totally exhausting. When I arrived at work the following morning, it was all I could do to lurch into Ash's room. But fortunately I summoned up enough energy to spread a look of triumph wide across my face.

Elly and I had woken late on Sunday morning. The only possible reasons we could then find to get out of bed were to go to either the toilet or kitchen. We lay there, curled up together, listening to rain thud against the window and luxuriating in the decadence of the day to come.

'It's raining,' Elly rationalised. 'I can't stand getting wet.'

'And there's nothing on at the cinema,' I said. 'In any case, we've got a telly right here, so what's the point?'

'I suppose we could go to an art gallery or museum or something,' she went on, but would have sounded more enthusiastic at the prospect of skinnydipping in lava. 'You know, something cultural.'

'I always feel I don't make the best of what London has to offer,' I confessed.

There was a pause. 'Then again,' Elly said, 'I've got a copy of *Time Out!* right here by the bed. We could read about all of the art exhibitions, rather than be so judgmental as to go to just one. That'd be ever so cultural. And we won't get wet.'

'Perfect. And then we can go to one we really like the sound of.'

'Not today, though.'

'Of course not. Maybe in a few weeks.'

'When we've had time to make a proper decision.'

'Exactly. You can't rush culture, you know.'

We pushed ourselves deeper into the mattress, satisfied that we were on the point of being extremely sophisticated and cultured.

'You know what I really fancy right now?' I said. Elly's hand slid across my thigh. 'OK, yes, I fancy that as well, but do you know what else I fancy?' Elly pulled my hand across her thigh. 'I think we've established I fancy that. But what I really, really want right now is a breakfast so big that by the time I finish eating, it's become my dinner. Sex always gives me an appetite.'

Elly licked her lips noisily and agreed that food was a good idea. But neither of us was willing to give up the warmth of the bed actually to action the plan, so I started to shove her out. To her credit, she didn't go easily, gripping the side of the bed hard, but at last she tumbled to the floor. I leaned over. 'Well, you're up now,' I said. 'You might as well make breakfast.'

Elly stalked out and I gathered the duvet back up around my shoulders and lay back to savour the moment. It was hard to decide what was the best aspect of this whole situation:

(a) That I'd seen Elly naked. It was childish, sure, but momentous nonetheless. I wished I could go back in time and reassure my fourteen-year-old self that it would eventually happen;

(b) That I was in Elly's bed, and hadn't needed to break into her flat to achieve it;

(c) That I'd had the most enjoyable night of sex in my

entire life, as much for who it was with as for its actual quality;

(d) That, to my silent amazement, I'd had by far the most prolonged night of sex of my life. It must have been the anaesthetising effect of the shock of seeing Elly naked;

(e) That Elly was now making me breakfast in the nude, although I'd begun to worry in case she was organising a fry-up; or

(f) That I'd seen Elly naked. There was no getting away from that. It was just ... how best to put? It was just such a huge relief.

After about ten minutes, Elly's face poked anxiously around the door. 'I think I've mentioned that I'm not the world's greatest cook,' she began.

'Oh goody,' I said. 'Burnt cornflakes.'

'No, because I'm also not an idiot,' she went on sternly. 'However, because I eat out so much—'

'You mean, dinner at your desk.'

'That's outside of my flat, isn't it?' Elly was getting testy. 'What I mean is that I don't go shopping all that often. So the cupboard's a bit bare.'

In the circumstances I felt I could be magnanimous. 'That's all right. If you made it, I'm sure it'll be lovely.'

She walked in with her breasts resting on the edge of the tray of food. 'I'll have those,' I didn't say, marvelling at her lack of self-consciousness, but didn't know whether her confidence was impressive or plain scary.

She set the tray down for me to inspect. 'Does opening cans count as "making" food, officially?'

'Lovely indeed,' I said, trying hard to be careful. 'Tinned asparagus. I haven't had that for breakfast in absolutely ages. Nor cream crackers. No breakfast table is without them, in my experience.'

'There's cake,' Elly said aggressively, pointing at a plate in the centre of the display. 'Perfect with a nice cup of tea.'

121

I stared suspiciously into my distinctly cool cup. 'This is tea?'

'No. It's orange squash, obviously. Look, I've already told you I hadn't been shopping for a bit, OK?'

I prodded the cake with a fork. 'It doesn't half look like wedding cake, you know.'

Elly tutted. 'Everyone knows wedding cake lasts in the freezer for weeks. Months even.'

I didn't want to ask the obvious question for fear of an answer finishing in 'years'. Carefully, I removed the tray to the floor and opened my arms wide. 'I think there are better ways to spend our time, don't you?'

Elly stepped back. 'Oh no you don't, buster. You're getting nothing until you eat that asparagus.'

Things returned to an even keel as we watched an old film in the early afternoon, Elly laying contentedly on my chest throughout while I gently stroked her hair. After it finished and Elly had gone to the toilet, the telephone rang. 'Get that, will you?' she shouted.

'Hello? Erm, Eleanor Gray's residence. I mean, house. Flat, rather.'

'Charles?' a voice shrieked in instant excitement. 'Is that you?'

I have, over the years, had some perfectly pleasant conversations with Elly's mum. This was not destined to be one of them. 'No, it's not. My name's ... Ash.'

'Don't be silly, Charles. I recognise your voice.'

I tried to go down an octave or two. 'No, really. I'm Ash ... Hannah. My name's Ash Hannah.'

'Your problem, Charles Fortune, so your mother says, is that everything's a big joke to you.' But there was warmth in her voice.

'Yes, Mrs Gray,' I said miserably.

The convenience of my marrying Elly in a wedding so big that virtually every resident of Bucks was likely to be invited overcame pretty much any negative feature I might have in her mum's eyes. 'So you're a mass murderer,' she'd say. 'Doesn't mean you can't make my Eleanor the very happy mother of three lovely children.' It was the cause of lifelong frustration to them that – until the past twenty-four hours, at least – we hadn't been so good as to get on and do what they'd wanted us to do for so very long. The last thing either of us wanted to do was encourage our mothers even more by letting on about last night.

'How are you?' she demanded.

'Fine, Mrs Gray. And you?' I felt about eight years old.

'Very well, Charles. Thank you for asking. How's your mother?'

A plainly ludicrous question. She was in near hourly contact with my mum since the excitement of Elly and me talking to each other. By contrast, I hadn't called for a few days so as to avoid encouraging her in any conceivable way when it came to Elly. 'Fine too, Mrs Gray. Thank you for asking.'

'Good. I'm pleased to hear that. Now, you're not over-exerting yourself, are you? Not working too hard, I hope?' I smirked with dirty thoughts. But the thing was that Elly's mum, presumably in an effort to ensure I was all ship-shape when the time came to pipe me into the family, had always treated me as if I was a species on the verge of extinction. There was nothing she wouldn't do to ensure I was happy, unbothered and generally favourably disposed towards all things Gray.

'No, everything's going really well at the moment,' I said.

There was then a pause. 'So, Charles, I must confess I'm a bit surprised to find you at Eleanor's flat answering the telephone. Is she all right? There's nothing wrong, is there?' The breathless hope in her voice sent me to pieces.

'She's fine, Mrs Gray. She just had to go—' For some reason, I couldn't say 'to the toilet'. At that moment, to my befuddled mind, it implied inappropriate knowledge of her private parts. And I knew Mrs Gray wouldn't approve of her daughter doing such an unlady-like thing in the vicinity of an eligible Charlie. You'd think negotiating multi-million pound deals through the night to impossible deadlines might help me think on my feet, but the best I could come up with was, bizarrely, 'She had to go the pet shop.'

At that point, with impeccable timing, Elly returned. I was momentarily distracted by the thought that I could accurately describe her as my lover.

'The pet shop?' Elly and her mother echoed with identical tones of incredulity. I put my hand over the receiver and tried to stay calm. 'It's your mother.'

Elly reacted with horror. 'She can't know you're here,' she whispered fiercely, her tits flapping from side to side as if they too didn't know where to put themselves.

I stared at her like she'd just decided to become a legal-aid lawyer. 'It's a bit sodding late for that, don't you think?' I hissed.

'Pet shop?' Mrs Gray repeated.

Eyes fearfully locked on Elly, I took a deep breath, put my mouth to the phone once more, and just let it get on with making something up. 'That's right, the pet shop. You see, I've been looking after this pet for somebody at work who's gone on holiday, but I'm off out for the day and I asked Elly to look after it for me. And it needed some food because I forgot to bring it. You know what I'm like, Mrs Gray. So she's gone to get some food.' Elly shook her head in distress at the hole I was digging with such speed. 'Let's hope, for its sake, that the food comes in a tin.' I laughed weakly and Elly made a face that didn't bode well for a repeat performance in bed.

'Extraordinary,' Mrs Gray said. 'What is it?'

'What's what?'

'The pet.'

'What's the pet?'

'Yes. What kind of pet is it?'

I looked wildly around Elly's bedroom, catching sight of a poster on her wall of the Beatles crossing Abbey Road. 'It's a zebra,' I said.

Elly smacked her hand to her forehead in disbelief. 'A zebra?' said Mrs Gray in disbelief.

'You fuckwit,' Elly breathed.

'A zebra . . . fish,' I added. 'In a bowl. Obviously not an actual zebra. How ridiculous would that be?' I laughed manically. 'But, you know, it's got stripes and stuff. Black and white. Up and down. Like a zebra, you see. Hence zebra fish, I should think.'

'Yes, I'd gathered that. Quite extraordinary,' Mrs Gray said again. 'Still, I suppose it's a nice thing for you both to look after it.'

'You know Elly,' I said, giving her a look. 'Heart of gold.'

Elly rushed out of the bedroom and slammed the front door. She came back into the bedroom with a loud 'I've got the food, Charlie. I can handle it from here. You better go.'

I held the phone out. 'It's your mother,' I said. 'We've just been having a good old natter.'

'That's nice,' Elly said. 'So thanks again. Bye now.'

I handed over the phone and stood there. 'I said "Bye now",' Elly repeated, gesticulating at the door.

I scuttled to the front door, opened it, caught sight of the neighbour in the opposite flat going out, wished I'd put some clothes on, shouted 'Bye now' again, and slammed the door. I then crept back in and flopped on to the bed.

'Mum, stop it,' Elly was saying, and scowled at me. 'We work together. We're contractually obliged to talk to each other. That doesn't make us friends so I wouldn't get your hopes up. It's not like we're jumping into bed together any moment soon.' Elly emphasised 'together' and then her mouth flicked up into a momentary half-smile. It was one of those glorious technical truths which any legal mind glories in. We couldn't jump into bed together any moment soon because I was already in it. We knew we had to tell them soon enough, but this wasn't the moment.

Mrs Gray gabbled away and Elly put her hand over the receiver. 'Zebra fish?' She still couldn't believe it. 'I mean, zebra fish? What on earth were you thinking?' But now she was smiling, ever so slightly.

125

The noise from the phone stopped. 'No, Mum. I don't think it would be nice for the two families to have a big Sunday lunch to celebrate. I've seen more of Charlie in the last few days than you could believe and I certainly wouldn't want to see even more at the dinner table.' I sniggered and Elly threw a pillow at me.

'Look, I've got to go,' Elly said, but her mum was one of those who was reluctant to say goodbye. It took at least five minutes of protracted farewells before Elly said, 'I've really, really got to go now, I think the zebra fish might be dying of hunger,' and finally put the phone down.

'If that's a taste of things to come,' she said, collapsing on to the bed next to me, 'then I think I might go and buy myself a bloody zebra fish, should such a thing exist. I'm going to need something to remind me of the very brief fun times before our mothers intervened.'

Come the evening, we voted unanimously to have a Chinese delivered. The only edible food remaining in Elly's kitchen were three more tins of asparagus, some chilli beans and half a tub of Marmite. Whatever way you put these ingredients together, we decided, would not make a great meal.

We'd both thrown on T-shirts and were sitting opposite each other on the bed, efficiently swapping cartons. 'I knew there was something I wanted to ask you,' Elly said through a mouthful of sweet and sour pork. 'It's been bugging me for years. Exactly who at school did you lose your virginity with?'

'I'm sorry?' Our relationship was on fast forward; this conversation came several dates earlier than it usually did in my experience.

'Come on. It hardly matters now. I'm just interested to know.' The fact was that however close the two of us were when younger, our relationship was still governed by the boy/girl treaty, so this was one subject that was off-limits. Add the frisson that existed between us – had we known what a frisson was, of course – and reports of Saturday

126

nights apart were limited to 'Did you have a good time?'
and 'Yeah, all right.'

'Was it Elaine Pinder?'

I frowned with the effort of trying to remember what
Elaine Pinder looked like. 'She was the one with braces
until she was eighteen, wasn't she?'

'That's right.'

'And carried around her pet mouse.'

'You've got her.'

'Maybe, but I can assure you I never had her.'

'What about Josephine Stubbs? She was more your
type.'

'Which was?'

'Feckless, brainless, pretty, available. A sophisticate
you were not. And don't give me that wounded puppy
look. You know it's true.'

'She had a very friendly face, that's all,' I said, unable
to defend myself any further.

'So it was her.'

'Sadly not,' I confessed. 'She told me I was a creep for
hanging around her so much. She got her brother to
threaten me to stay away.'

'But he was about three years below us, wasn't he?'

'I just don't like violence, OK?'

Elly laughed a little longer than was polite. 'So, who
was it then?'

I grinned. 'You'll never guess.'

'Shelley Ewart?'

'Smelly Ewart? Lived up to the nickname far too
vividly.'

'Martine Wilson?'

'She wouldn't let anyone go past her bra. She was
saving herself for love, she told me.'

'But she married that dreadful Barry Fenton, didn't
she?'

I could tell that Elly was reliving the same memory
of Barry's personal challenge to fart audibly in front
of every teacher. His *coup de grâce* was finishing with the

127

headmaster at the annual school prize day before a hushed audience of parents. 'It goes to show that love isn't blind, just plain ignorant,' I said.

'Veronica Dean?'

'Let's just say the boys called her VD for a reason.'

'Helena McDermott then.'

'I had thought I was in there,' I said. 'But there was this bizarre rubber knickers/bed-wetting thing going on that even I couldn't stomach, however desperate I was. We called her The Tap because all you had to do was turn her on, and out it came. I had ever such a job explaining it to my parents when they came home that night.'

Elly groaned in pain before demanding that I tell her. 'You'll have to pay the sex toll first,' I said in my most lounge-lizard voice, and though she rolled her eyes in disgust that someone she'd shared bodily fluids with could sound so slimey, she complied at once, removing her long T-shirt and exposing herself to me so casually that I was instantly aroused.

Some time later, I was fighting the inevitable urge to nod off. It says pretty much everything you need to know about men that our entire system shuts down post-orgasm. And I have yet to come across the no-doubt mythical woman who rolls over and says, 'You really put your all into that, Charlie, for which I can only thank you profusely. You deserve to go to sleep right now, so don't mind me.'

Elly, though, poked me in the back with a chopstick. 'Come on, you were going to tell me who it was.'

I smiled to myself. 'You're not going to like it.'

She was complacent. 'I think I'll get over it. We are talking fifteen years ago.'

I turned over so I could enjoy the full effect. 'Dana Davis.'

Elly put her hand to her mouth in shock and poked herself in the eye with the chopstick. She swore but the pain was little more than a distraction. 'No.'

'Oh yes. That'll be your best girlfriend at school.' I was

128

keen to rub it in; had waited many years to do so, in fact. 'Turns out she didn't tell you everything.'

'No.'

'Surprising, isn't it?' I grinned.

'But she hated you.'

'I know. All we ever did was have sex. It was a totally empty experience.'

'I just don't believe it.' I'd never seen Elly so dumbfounded. It was joyous to watch.

'But, as a great man once said, as empty experiences go, it was one of the best.'

Elly couldn't get her mind around it. 'She turned out to be a lesbian, though.'

I leaned back casually. 'You know, I wondered about that when I heard it. I naturally assumed that I'd ruined her for other men and that as she couldn't get better, she turned to women.'

'There are some things I refuse to believe,' said Elly, even more appalled than before.

'Sadly you're right,' I said. 'I bumped into her about five years ago in a bar in town. Turns out that she really fancied you, but as she knew you wouldn't go down that path, so to speak—'

'Charlie,' she growled.

I continued to smile contentedly. I could tell it was irritating her. 'Don't blame me. I'm just repeating what she said. As she couldn't have you, she thought I was the next best thing as we were so close.' Elly's head couldn't stop shaking in denial. 'It's ironic really, when you think about those boys who used to call you Elly Gay, all because you were so sniffy about boys.'

The revelations were coming too fast for Elly. 'They called me what?'

'Come on. It hardly matters now,' I said, mimicking her words. 'We are talking fifteen years ago.'

Elly seemed truly offended. 'I ... just ... can't ... don't believe it,' she said, before dropping her plate on to the bed, and stomping off to the toilet.

'If you want, I'll call them and confirm that you're not gay,' I shouted after her.

'Just . . . just . . . sod off' was the best she could manage. While not the most popular boy in the school, I was inoffensive enough to avoid a nickname.

A few minutes later Elly came back into the room with a rueful look. 'You're right. This is stupid. It was fifteen years ago.' She hesitated. 'But, erm, one thing.'

'Anything.' I wanted to be magnanimous.

'How old were you when, you know, Dana . . .'

'Sixteen. It was at your sixteenth birthday party, funnily enough.'

Elly put her hands over her ears. 'That's it. I don't want to hear any more. Confession over.'

I began trying to explain how we'd sneaked out to her dad's shed but she started humming very loudly and walking around the room. I fell quiet and Elly tentatively freed her ears. I opened my mouth to speak, so she put her hands back up and started humming again.

The next time she could hear me, I quickly said, 'I just want to say one more thing about it.'

Elly stared at me suspiciously, dreading more gory details.

'I only did it because she was the next best thing to you.'

Elly couldn't help but smile. Her voice was tender once more. 'And for the sex, presumably.'

'Yes, of course for the sex too. But I promise that it was you that I was imagin—'

At that point, Elly clamped her hands back around her head and started singing very loudly.

Chapter Fifteen

Elly and I had spoken of the need to keep our relationship quiet at work, at least in the first few weeks. It was a brief victory of delusion over reality.

Office romances are by no means unusual at law firms. Thrown together for so much time and often late into the night, eyes meet over a steaming photocopier and passions need to be directed somewhere; not everyone is so focused as to expend them solely on the drafting of an eighty-page contract.

Babbingtons boasts two married partner couples – bluntly, the best way to keep an eye on your lawyer spouse is to be one yourself. There are stories in the Babbingtons folklore of every other possible combination too: partners and secretaries, partners and trainee solicitors, assistants and library staff, and one particularly odd liaison a few years back between a very senior partner and a squat, surly and unsettlingly hairy Eastern European cleaner who was on a shift that began at midnight and whose command of English didn't extend beyond 'Clean office now. Bog off.' They were known behind their backs as the Hoover Twins, because from what one could hear by cupping an ear at his office door – and a favourite dare among assistants was running up and listening – there was an awful lot of noisy sucking going on.

But despite the long and honourable history of lawyers doing to each other what they practise so successfully on their clients, Elly was genuinely concerned that our relationship could harm both of our prospects if it became public – and especially hers. 'It just seems unprofessional,' she maintained on the Sunday night. 'I'm hardly through the door and already my knickers are down.'

As her knickers were down at that very moment, along with the rest of her clothing, it was hard to take her completely seriously. 'It's not totally bad from their point of view,' I reasoned. 'With an outside boyfriend, you'd be rushing off early all the time to see him. You don't have to do that with me across the floor.'

But Elly wouldn't be deflected and insisted that I swear I wouldn't tell. I was surprised, frankly, by her naivety. But then no law firm in the City is quite the hothouse Babbingtons is. She had still to learn that.

So it was no shock to me at least that within very little time on the Monday, I was getting knowing looks from partners, assistants and secretaries alike. Much of their day-to-day job is so dull that they all gobble up the tiniest mite of gossip and spread it with the efficiency of a firm-wide e-mail. It didn't much matter whether it was Hannah, Lucy or Ash who had let the word out, but I had my money on Ash anyway. I wasn't overly bothered. It would be a five-minute wonder and I didn't have the same concerns as Elly about the consequences. After all, Graham had told me more than once that he had no problem with playing at home. 'You always stand a better chance of a result,' he smirked.

Within an hour of getting to work, my secretary, Sue, rushed in with a pile of letters and starting making awkward conversation about the weekend. She was clearly dying to ask, but kept on glancing over her shoulder at Richard, who was moodily regarding a file I had asked him to work on and showing little sign of actually doing anything with it. I had explained more than once that you had to at least open the file before you could, in all good conscience, turn the meter on and start billing. I think it was the word 'conscience' that threw him.

'I bumped into Eleanor before,' Sue began hesitantly.

I didn't deign to look up from the correspondence. 'Really? Hope neither of you were hurt.'

Sue is a couple of years younger than me and has been my secretary since I qualified, so she knows to ignore my cheap attempts at evasion. 'She was looking ever so pleased with herself.'

'Probably had a great and momentous weekend, I should think,' I said, with a slight smile.

'I hear,' Sue said, 'that she's got a new man.'

I continued to flick through the post. 'A bit of a corker, by all accounts. Something of an Adonis. Leading contender for man of the year. Eleanor had to fight off a swarm of women to get him, you know.'

'Funny, that's not what I was told. Just another wet and wimpy lawyer, so the word is. All briefs, no trousers. You'll know the type all too well, I'd guess.'

'Wish it were me,' Richard piped up.

Sue swivelled around. 'I'm sorry?'

'Wish it were me. He's a lucky sod, whoever he is.'

Sue turned back to me with an air of some amusement. It was hardly surprising that nobody had told Richard. Even if he didn't have an attitude problem that would shock a few of the inmates at Strangeways, being the senior partner's son made him the legal equivalent of a plague-carrier. Few people had taken the risk and got too close as yet. I'd tried to extol the virtues of photocopier socialising to him – given the substantial amount of time trainee solicitors have to spend in proximity to one – but Richard refused to play the game.

We were standing by the copier as I talked him through how it worked a week or two back. 'I could play this like a violin when I was a trainee,' I said, conscious that law firms are about the only place outside of photocopying shops where this is actually a boast. 'They called me Yehudi.'

'And you're proud of that?' asked Richard, distinctly unimpressed as I whizzed through a series of double-sized, stapled A3 copies to prove that the old boy still had it.

'It meant that when the other trainees had a problem, they turned to me,' I explained patiently. 'Made me very popular.'

'I don't know who that says more about,' he said. 'You or them.'

'It says more about your job.' My tone was rougher. 'Get used to it, Xerox Boy.'

Despite his best efforts, I'd begun to feel a bit sorry for Richard and was working on his rough edges, even though, as Sue said, it would need sandpaper the size of Spain to smooth them out. And he was determined not to make it easy. My next attempt to keep him in the office past 6.30, I'd decided, would involve Superglue, several rolls of packing tape and a sawn-off shotgun.

The only time I'd seen Richard this animated was when we had a fire drill a few days back which had pulled us away from our desks for half an hour. As it happens, I've often been tempted to set a match to the office, because a real fire would do wonders for my partnership prospects. I could think of at least a dozen partners who wouldn't leave their desks and stop billing even if the flames were lapping at their timesheets. And it would segue nicely into their meeting with the Devil, who was reputed to have a special affinity with our profession. The old joke is told of how God once decided to take the Devil to court, and settle their differences once and for all. When Satan heard this, he laughed and said, 'And where do you think you're going to find a lawyer?'

So when it came to Elly, I felt I deserved a bit of inno-cent fun at his expense. 'Just your type, is she?' I asked.

'I should say,' Richard fairly licked his lips. 'Hundred per cent woman.' He nodded at Sue. 'No offence.' Even he had worked out that life would be intolerable if he got

134

on the wrong side of our joint secretary.

'None taken, I'm sure,' said Sue, swapping a look with me and, I knew, storing up the insult. 'And you're a hundred per cent man, are you?'

He was complacent beyond his years. 'No complaints as yet.'

'I think that's where I go wrong,' I said. 'I leave out little comment forms the morning after.' It raised a giggle from Sue at least. 'But you don't think you're a bit young for Elly? A bit wet behind the ears, perhaps?'

'Let's just say I'd be happy to have a go. I like them fiery. The way she tore you a second arsehole the other day was great.'

That wasn't quite how I remembered the encounter, but I let it slide. 'Why don't you then?'

'It would give you a lot of credibility around the office.' Sue was shameless.

'Do you think I stand a chance?'

I was starting to feel sorry for him again, but not sufficiently. 'As they say, if you don't bill, you can't get paid.'

At that point, Elly burst in, looking annoyed, and for the first time since I had found him in my room, Richard looked abashed. I couldn't fault him for getting more worked up about Elly than the law.

'I assume I'm not interrupting anything important,' she said aggressively.

'Richard was just saying how he's got the hots for an older woman,' I said, and he gave me a poisonous look.

It briefly deflected her. 'Anyone I know?'

'You're quite well acquainted with her, actually,' said Sue with an admirably straight face.

From her position dominating the room between our two desks, Elly turned to him. 'Let me give you a piece of advice,' she said, and he looked back at her adoringly, which in her irritation she totally missed. 'Messing around with someone at work is an instant disaster.'

His face fell dramatically, but I was put out myself. 'Messing around? And since when was it a disaster?'

Things had moved on rapidly since the day before.

Elly's look was pointed. 'Since the guy from the bloody postroom gave me a huge wink this morning.'

'What can I say? You're just a man magnet.' I cut a glance at Richard to ensure he didn't chorus his agreement.

Elly balled her fists in frustration. 'The point is that absolutely bloody everybody knows.'

'About what?' Richard was confused.

'Not everybody,' Sue happily confirmed.

'About me and Charlie? This is exactly what I wanted to avoid. I expect to see it announced in the bloody *Law Society Gazette* this week.'

'What about you and Charlie?' There was, bless him, fear on Richard's face.

She turned back to me impatiently. 'Was it you?'

For once I could genuinely plead innocence. 'No, of course not. We had an agreement.'

'He's been the soul of discretion, unfortunately,' Sue confirmed. 'The one time I actually want him to blab, and he hasn't.'

'About what?' Richard wailed.

'I'm not a blabber,' I protested.

'OK, put it this way. You do go on a bit.'

Elly fixed Richard with a glare. 'Was it you, having a laugh with your little trainee mates?'

Richard was terrified, yet ecstatic to be acknowledged again. 'I don't know what you're talking about.'

Sue was quick to jump in. 'Bit of a problem when it comes to mates, you see.'

'I bet it was bloody Ash then,' Elly growled, and on cue he walked in. This was warming up into a regular French farce.

'I do not go on,' I grumbled. 'I'm just naturally friendly and talkative.'

'Oh yes, blame me, why don't you? It's always Ash's fault.' He fell into one of the two chairs in front of my desk. 'What are we talking about, by the way?'

'Was it you who told everyone about us?' I asked.

136

Richard's eyes were wide. 'You and her?' he mouthed at me. I nodded and he looked, well, outraged would probably describe it best. I had been hoping for impressed, awestruck even. I needed something to help me connect with him.

'I find it offensive the way you always pin the blame on me, Charlie,' Ash said, indignant.

'Was it?' Elly's tone was steely. She would have been fearsome in court.

Ash looked shifty. 'I suppose I may have mentioned it to my secretary.'

We turned to Sue, who had no qualms about squealing. 'And she may have mentioned it to the typing pool.'

'My secretary told me before I had a chance to tell her,' said Lucy, wandering through the doorway and sounding disappointed.

'Come in, there's plenty of room,' I cried.

'It's made everybody's day,' Lucy went on. 'The trainees were running a book on it, so I'm told. The great love-hate relationship.'

Elly slumped into the other chair and put her head in her hands.

'Don't expect sympathy,' said Ash. 'You've made your bed. I just can't understand why you'd want to lie in it with Fortune.'

Elly looked up at me in resignation but with the hint of a smile.

Hannah's face poked around the doorframe. 'Absolutely everyone knows,' she said. 'Alan told me. He was ever so excited.' She was referring to her supervising partner, a man who found the intricacies of the takeover code so fascinating that by legend he had it by his bedside in case of a midnight call either from a client or to the toilet.

Hannah pushed Lucy further into my little room, which was getting crowded. I sat back, watching Elly talk to Ash, Sue trying to engage Richard, who was staring at Elly, and Lucy chatting to Hannah. Days often start off this relaxed. However much we try and get done between 9.30 and

5.30, we all know that we're going to be there until goodness knows when and so can't be bothered to rush too much at first, especially at the beginning of the week.

The social gathering was rudely silenced by Graham striding in. 'Ah, the Monday club. I thought I'd find you lot all here together,' he said. 'Especially you, Eleanor.' He grinned and I saw Elly tense. 'Sorry to break up the party, but I need all senior associates in meeting room three in five minutes. We've got some big news.' He disappeared as quickly as he came.

'It must be the British Pharmaceutical deal,' said Lucy, excited.

Hannah was more gloomy. 'Our lives, as we knew them, are over.'

Ash leaped out of the chair, energised by the thought that we had won an instruction for a deal that, so the rumours went, was a giant. 'Yeah, but think of the kudos.'

I was with Hannah. 'Think of the hours.'

'Think of the timesheets,' said Elly, and that shut us all up. 'And then think of the performance-related bonuses.'

The others scattered briefly back to their offices, leaving Sue – the only one of us whose prospects excluded partnership and so included keeping hold of her life whatever happened – to sit down and quickly go through some work I'd dropped on her chair on Friday evening.

I left Richard with an order to get some hours down on his timesheet for both our sakes, and walked over to the meeting room at the far end of the floor. The main area on our floor is oblong, with the lawyers' offices dotted along the light beige walls at regular intervals and the secretaries in four open-plan groups, each taking up a quarter of the light beige floor. Beyond this is a light beige kitchen and photocopying area, along with various other support staff and services, together with three functional light beige meeting rooms.

All we knew was that the partners had been working for some time on a potential deal involving British Pharmaceuticals, a mega corporation for which we jostled

138

with two other huge law firms to be thought of as its main adviser.

The small room was already packed, with more than a dozen associates crammed around the table (although my group was the most senior). At the top were four partners, including Tom Gulliver, the imposing head of the corporate department, Graham and Ian, Elly's supervising partner. Elly was already settled in the seat closest to them. I pulled up a chair at the far end as a couple of stragglers slipped in.

'British Pharmaceuticals,' Tom began, with the minimum of drama in his cut-glass accent, 'has begun negotiations for a recommended offer to the board of United Retail. The combined company will have a market value of about ninety billion pounds, and become the largest in the country.'

He couldn't halt a slight smile chasing across his face. 'I am glad to report that British Pharmaceuticals has instructed us to act for them in this matter.'

There was a gentle tapping of our approval on the table in true Babbingtons style. Tom smoothed down his Saville Row pinstripes, a traditionalist of the best sort – hard but fair. 'This will be the largest deal Babbignton Botts has ever dealt with. United Retail has at least sixty subsidiaries of note, and we are buying every single one of them. The timescale is not as long as we would want, meaning the due diligence exercise will be, I'm afraid, fearsome.' But there was relish in his voice; due diligence is the back-breaking process by which we would comb through each and every part of United Retail's business to make sure that our client knew what it was buying. It is so detailed, so laborious and so long-winded that I sometimes thought it was the reason lawyers were put on this earth.

Tom indicated the other partners. 'We will be the lead partners. We have begun breaking the team into groups to work on various aspects of the deal, and you will be told shortly what your responsibilities are to be.'

His voice dropped and a trace of menace entered it. 'I am

sure that I need not remind you how important this transaction is to Babbington Botts. We won the instruction because of our reputation for doing the job better than anyone. I intend to ensure that we maintain that reputation.' Make a mistake and it's 'drop 'em in the Thames' time, I knew.

There was a pause and I began doodling on the pad in front of me. 'Any questions at this time?' Tom asked, expecting none.

Momentarily distracted, I murmured to myself, 'Burp.'

'I'm sorry, Charles. I don't think I quite caught that.'

I looked up guiltily; all eyes – amused and amazed – were on me. 'Oh nothing. Just talking to myself.'

Tom's brow knitted slightly. 'Did you say, "burp"?' His tone was not encouraging.

I heard a stifled snigger from the other side of the table, and my career flashed before me. I glanced down at my jottings. 'Erm, yes. BURP. British United Retail Pharmaceuticals. Probably a name you'll want to avoid, when it comes to it.'

There was a horrid silence before, to my intense relief, Tom guffawed loudly. 'Burp. Oh yes, I like that, Charles. I must remember to tell Ronnie.' That would be Ronnie Stewart, the chairman of British Pharmaceuticals. 'OK, that's all for now.'

I exited quickly, shaking my head. 'That was a close one, you idiot,' Hannah muttered, and then Graham caught me up and asked me to join him in his office. Unusually, when we got there, he closed the door.

'Sorry about the burp thing,' I said, when we were facing each other over his desk.

'Don't worry. Tom laughs, we all laugh. That's the main thing.' He shuffled some papers around looking for the right one. 'I've got some good news, Charles. I know I said we'd review the whole partnership thing in a few months, but the partnership committee has asked the department to put people forward now.' My heart leaped wildly. 'And, as I told you, we always look after our own. So I'm proposing to put you up for partnership.'

It was all I could do not to lean over the desk, take his head between my hands and give Graham the most almighty kiss. Despite his broadmindedness over such matters, I wasn't sure our relationship had reached that stage. 'That's excellent,' I said, with admirable restraint.

Smiling, he handed me a sheaf of papers. 'This is an initial self-assessment form for you to fill out about yourself and your qualities. The partnership committee will take very wide soundings, so there's no point lying. They don't expect everything to be perfect. The main thing is that I think you're up to it.' The desire to give him a huge hug was almost overwhelming.

My chest flooded with warm happiness, but I tried to maintain a semblance of calm. 'What happens then?'

Graham leaned back. 'It's all explained in the covering letter. Interviews, presentations and so on. But it's worth the effort. I don't need to tell you that.'

He most certainly didn't. He got up and put his hand out. I stood and took it, and we shook for slightly longer than the Babbingtons code would normally allow. 'You're going to have a huge amount of work to do on the British Pharmaceutical deal,' he warned. 'It could make all the difference.'

I'd already worked that out. As Hannah had said, my life, as I knew it, was over. And I couldn't have been happier.

Chapter Sixteen

Ah, the sweet smell of approaching success. I had at long last locked my wheels on to the partnership track and it was off I go. I could barely stop myself skipping back to my room, whooping like a Red Indian deciding whether to start from the front or the back of the scalp. I was as high as a senior partner's billing target.

For too long it had felt like I was polishing the floor of a harem's waiting room with a toothbrush. The hours and the work may have been terrible, but I was still breathless with anticipation. Inside lay a world of temptation and satisfaction. And at last the door had inched open.

First Elly and now this. I felt like I had won the Cup Final, Wimbledon and the Grand National all on one day.

I've spent a lot of time wondering how it will feel when they call me into the imposing, high-domed partnership chamber for my anointment. Of course, there isn't any such a thing as an anointment, let alone a partnership chamber, so far as I am aware, but one can hope. Maybe they keep it really, really well hidden in the cellar or something. They must at least have easy access to a Masonic hall.

In any case, I have this regular fantasy set in the

chamber. As I make my way slowly up to the altar, all the partners are lined up against the walls, timesheets held aloft as a guard of honour, and lightly tapping their feet against the flagstones as a sign of approval. Before the altar stands the senior partner, flashes of light shooting out from his halo and magnificent in his royal blue robes (being the corporate colour).

I kneel before him as he reverentially places in my hand the drinks cabinet key. A cheer rumbles from the back of the hall to the front. Then a grinding noise from beneath heralds a small block of stone rising from the floor with a glass cover on top. With infinite care, the senior partner removes the glass and lifts into the air my new partnership telephone. 'All hail the BT XL54 conference phone,' the partners chant.

I then stand to rapturous applause, clutching the key high above my head with one hand and the telephone with the other, as doves spiral into the air, fireworks shoot upwards, confetti flutters from the heavens and a celestial choir sings 'Hallelujah'. For reasons I have yet to understand, the dream then usually ends with the choir switching suddenly to 'Wake me up before you go go' and the partners dancing around with bloated stomachs groaning over hideously brief swimming trunks, and gaily throwing assistant solicitors' severed heads to one another.

Then again, I would be equally happy with Graham popping his head around my door and muttering just two magical words: 'You're in.'

The last thing Graham had actually said was to warn me to keep the news quiet. No good would come from telling, he pointed out, and in any case it was not Babbingtons style to publicise such things.

That was instantly a major hardship. I left thinking that everyone should know I am officially considered partnership material. Why wasn't there a tannoy announcement for example? Or a special edition of the staff newsletter? It's important that people know they are dealing with someone who might soon have the right to make them cancel their holiday. Or collect my dry cleaning. There was even one partner – now fortunately retired – who once made his trainee work from the partner's house for a week. This was ostensibly to concentrate without distraction on a piece of upcoming litigation, but in fact was for the sole purpose of the trainee knocking the partner's garden into shape.

Still, the signs were there. For one thing, my mood had improved so much that everyone who spoke to me was instantly suspicious. 'You haven't got another job, have you?' one assistant whispered to me by the coffee machine.

For another, I began trying to perfect a partner's walk. This requires a mix of proprietorship over the whole firm, raging self-importance, a hint of sadism and yet a touch of kindly superiority. I didn't want associates sitting in the pub nominating me as their bastard partner of the week.

Back in my room, I sat back to survey my kingdom, wondering whether I could engineer a larger office while I was about it. Richard was scowling at the file which he had now managed to prise open. 'I don't get it,' he grumbled. 'Bloody timeshares. The same week every year, without fail, going to some God-forsaken hole on the Costa del Crap, seeing the same boring people trying to make the best out of their own ridiculously expensive holes.'

I had asked Richard to help on the sale of a timeshare company which had gone bust. It was sadistic really – which I now recognised as damn good training – because timeshares, surprisingly, are exceptionally tricky concepts from a legal point of view. Your lawyer telling you something is 'exceptionally tricky', or course, is like your plumber taking one look at some pipes and then sucking sadly through his teeth and muttering about the shocking state of your pipework.

But I was feeling recklessly generous. 'You need to do quite a bit of research on timeshares,' I told him. 'Feel free to spend time in the library.'

Richard didn't need a second invitation, and was up and out of the room in the time it takes to say 'cushy'. He already knew his way around sufficiently to recognise the library as the place where delinquent trainees slink off under the guise of doing research. That a newspaper might happen to catch their eye, or a fellow trainee may engage them in a vital conversation about the Unfair Contract Terms Act or a new foxy secretary, is the kind of unhappy distraction we all have to learn to cope with. It was particularly popular on a Friday afternoon, where trainees do their best to hide in the vain hope of avoiding any new work which comes in late and requires their presence over the weekend. We had all been there and had all been sought out by an angry-looking partner.

But it got him out of the room, and gave me space to play the game that has for some years whiled away hours on the tube: how would I go about telling people that I've been made a partner.

After a great deal of thought – and I really mean a humungous deal – I've reluctantly discounted telephoning everyone I have ever met as impractical. Even cutting it down to everyone I was at university and law school with presents formidable logistical problems.

I was just cycling through my advertising options, which are usually accompanied by the tune of the old advert – 'Hey there, Charlie Boy, looking really cool as a brand new partner' – when Elly came in and shut the door behind her.

She too looked excited. 'Have you seen the e-mail?'

I'd been far too busy with my navel, and so turned to my PC. There was a message highlighted by a little red flag entitled 'BPharm'. I quickly scanned it to see a list of assignments and team leaders. Elly, Hannah and I had been put in joint charge of the dataroom, where for the next fortnight we would supervise a huge team of assistants and trainees in going through every single contract United Retail had ever entered into to check whether there were any nasty surprises waiting for our client. It was a key task.

But I could barely concentrate. Should I tell her? What

if she'd had the same news? Think of the competition. And what if she hadn't? She'd be devastated. Either way, it could badly damage our relationship. But I so wanted to tell her because I knew she would understand the magnitude of what had happened. I gazed at Elly as she made a preliminary checklist of what we had to do, and realised I couldn't tell her. Not yet. It would be plain selfish.

'Looks like we're going to be seeing an awful lot of each other over the next few weeks,' I said.

Elly looked up. 'You realise we're not going to have much time for play with all this going on.'

I didn't much like the sound of that. 'After spending all day with you, the last thing I'm going to want is to spend the night with you as well,' I pouted.

Glancing over her shoulder at the close door, Elly leaned over my desk. My eyes couldn't help but be drawn down her blouse. 'You sure about that?' she said quietly. 'I didn't say we'd have no time whatsoever. Big deals really turn me on.'

If that was meant to be sensuous, she had badly misjudged me. When lawyers talk about doing sexy work, they are abusing the word terribly. Seeing Jennifer Aniston naked; now that's sexy. Working on some ginormous corporate takeover which has the ultimate effect of simply enlarging the trough into which the directors, shareholders, lawyers, accountants, stockbrokers and financiers can dig their snouts is not. Until they shove up and let me have a nibble, at least.

So I sat back from Elly lest the thought of having to draft the sale and purchase agreement later on made her too hot and sweaty. Yet I could feel a small flush of excitement too, and that's what reassured me that I still had it in me to fight the good fight. You cannot work these hours and at this intensity unless you get something out of it. For all my griping, a huge deal provided a thrill of challenge and ultimately achievement.

'I can see I'm going to have to work on you,' Elly said, rising to leave.

146

'Best not hang around, then,' I said. 'How about tonight?'

Elly pulled a face. 'I'm sorry, but I really want to clear a few things off my desk before we get into the dataroom. How about tomorrow?' I agreed with little grace and she left.

I was still dying to tell someone. I lifted the phone to tell my mum, but put it down as quickly. Telling her was like telling Elly's mum which was like telling Elly. And Dad wasn't an option. Mum never let him speak on the phone without listening in on the upstairs extension just in case he should say something embarrassing. It didn't take long to realise that everyone I was close to was either in competition with me for the same partnership, or would start spreading the news within nanoseconds.

Then I glanced up at my wall calendar to see today ringed in red and the words 'law centre' written in. In all the excitement, I'd forgotten that I'd swapped with someone and was due there again. I wiggled with joy in my seat. Sparkle would be my outlet; and it would be a lot less messy for her than with her usual clientele.

The day passed quickly. Like Elly, I needed to clear some smaller matters off my desk, while Graham had popped in early afternoon to say that I needed to prepare a briefing paper on why I thought I was partnership material.

'Isn't it obvious?' I said with a smile.

'Only to you, I suspect. You've got a week to do it and then about a week later you'll have to go before the assessment committee.' That was a body which by reputation could teach the Spanish Inquisition a thing or two about interviewing techniques. I couldn't wait.

Just before six, I went over to tell Elly where I was going. She was buried under piles of folders. 'You're going to the law centre?' she asked, in a tone which would have worked equally with 'you're going home to watch TV and scratch your groin for three hours?' She pointed to the boxes of files which lined her walls. 'Haven't you got a few things to be getting on with?'

'I have to go,' I insisted. 'I'm on the rota. There are people depending on me.'

She shrugged and refocused on the papers in front of her.

'I'm coming back after, you know.' I hadn't planned to until that moment, but ah well.

'Whatever. I'll see you later. Some of us have got real work to do.'

I happily left and walked slowly to the law centre. Would I still do this when a partner, I wondered? It might be a little undignified. Perhaps I could get my trainee to do it, so long as Richard had moved on by that stage. I wouldn't be doing the public a service by letting him loose on them.

As usual, Sparkle left her entrance to the end of the session. Conscious that Elly was getting a head start on me, I'd rushed through the clients and was waiting for the clock to hit eight before heading back.

She swept in, as before, with the Bills in tow. Billy Whizz won the battle to be the most chivalrous and settled her in one of the seats before me, while the other two grabbed more chairs. It appeared that one way Sparkle saved money was to cut back on buying clothes made with more than a few inches of material.

'Aren't you cold?' I asked, while the Bills were arguing who was going to sit in the other seat in front of the desk.

She shrugged. 'The quicker you can get 'em off, the quicker you can get 'em back on again.'

'Presumably you've never done much stripping then?'

'Used to. Then the bloke who got me gigs said my tits were too saggy, and that was that.'

'Everyone's a critic, eh?'

'Too right. If you want saggy, you should have seen his—'

'They ain't budged,' interrupted Little Bill, having won the right to be spokesman for the day and handing over a letter.

I scanned it. It was a standard legal negotiating position:

148

disagree violently with the other side, sound as if their request is not so much thoroughly unreasonable as criminally insane, and threaten to pull out if the contract isn't signed in three weeks. I'd written more than a few such letters myself.

'This is just the first stage,' I said. 'Nothing to worry about.' I peered at the signature, which rang a small bell.

Big Bill revolved his cap around his fingers nervously. 'But they said they'll withdraw the offer if we don't sign.'

'Maybe we should just sign,' said Billy Whizz, flicking a lock of nylon hair back into place. Wouldn't it be easier to use glue, I wondered to myself?

'It's a negotiation, that's all. They want your place, you said as much yourselves. They've got virtually every other building around you. They'll come round. It'll take a bit of time, that's all. You just need to keep your nerve.' I couldn't make out the scrawl. It was probably nothing.

'Don't listen to them,' Sparkle advised me. 'They won't pull out until the bitter end. Haven't yet, anyway.'

'We've already got our eye on a new place,' Little Bill confided.

Billy winked at me slowly. 'Really close to Sparkle's, as it so happens.'

'We're hoping to clear a profit on the house, you see,' said Big Bill. 'Have a bit more money for our leisure activities.'

'Oh yes,' said Billy with relish. 'Leisure activities.'

Only without much of the active, I presumed.

Sparkle looked at me. 'So you better get them a bloody good price on their house, OK?'

'That's what we call a conflict of interest, you realise.' I tried to sound my most lawyer-like.

'No conflict at all,' she said. 'I'm just interested in the cash.'

I said I would write another letter, but warned that I would be quite busy over the next few weeks. They all rose to leave.

'A big deal or something?' asked Sparkle.

'Just a bit. But you know what they say, all work and no play makes Charlie a rich boy.'

Big Bill asked, 'Is it worth it?'

There have been times, when I'm racking my brains for ways to manage my chargeable hours for the day without actually doing any work, that I've wondered just that. But then I thought of the BT XL54 conference phone. 'It's a living,' I said, which was both true and evasive.

'It's very good of you to do this for free,' said Billy, casting a sly look at Sparkle. 'Maybe you could consider something similar.' She snorted.

'How about some sort of reward scheme or loyalty bonus?' I said. 'Frequent flyer, that sort of thing.'

The Bills began to agree eagerly, but Sparkle gave them such a look that they rapidly filed out, duly chastened. She hung around as I packed up. 'Fancy a drink?' she said.

'Can't today. Got to get back to the office.'

'Christ, they're worse than my old pimp,' she said.

'Only a little less scrupulous.' We walked to the door. 'Oh, there's something I've got to tell you though. They've offered me the chance to become a partner.' I awaited my deserved shower of compliments.

Sparkle was less impressed than I'd hoped. 'That's good, is it?'

'Good? Good? Bloody brilliant, more like.'

She was still nonplussed. 'That's great,' she said, unenthused.

I stopped at the front door to the centre. 'It's like ... I dunno ... being promoted from salaried tart to the madam who creams the money off the top.'

Sparkle's expression was sardonic. 'You're clueless, aren't you? But obviously this is a big thing for you.' I nodded. 'Congratulations then. I'm really pleased for you. You must be really good at what you do.' And she leaned over to give me a hug and a genuinely warm kiss.

'You're the first person I've told,' I said. 'It's such a relief to get it out.'

'That, my love,' she said, 'is what I'm good at.'

Chapter Seventeen

When in years to come, my as-yet-unborn son comes to sit by my rocking chair, and with a serious frown asks, 'Dad, what have you learned about life?' I will pull the pipe decisively out of my mouth and tell him that there are only three things he needs to know:

1. That it doesn't make you blind;
2. Say 'You look lovely, darling', whatever the circumstances, and however much she claims to want an honest opinion; and
3. Never, ever spend an iota of a fraction of a microsecond in a dataroom.

Datarooms were dreamed up by a mind so twisted that only a legal training could be responsible. Locked up in a small room with no air and twenty people you don't want to be with for hours without end, the work is so boring that even being an accountant seems like an appealing career alternative.

Such are the levels of despair that it makes you yearn for the Bangkok Hilton – at least prisoners there have rats to keep them company. For two weeks, I just had a collection of witless trainees, gossipy, work-shy assistants and a hyper-ambitious Elly desperate to make her mark. Only Hannah provided a modicum of sense amidst the madness.

We arrived promptly at 8.45 am on the first day at the offices of Taylor, Shaw & Langley, United Retail's solicitors and a firm of near comparable size to Babbingtons. Sometimes, the other side's solicitors take pity on you – knowing all too well that it could be them on the receiving end next time – and set up the dataroom in a nicely appointed, light and airy meeting room, with ready supplies of hot drinks and choccy biscuits.

But Taylor, Shaw & Langley – known in the City as TSL or Totally Stupid Lawyers after the strongly held belief that a key condition of employment there was to have your brain, personality and all other traces of humanity removed – clearly begrudged the fact that they were about to lose a major client; Babbingtons was likely to assume the United Retail brief once the takeover was complete.

Elly, Hannah and I, as the dataroom managers, were met by the TSL associate charged with keeping an eye on us.

'This isn't good,' Hannah muttered to me. 'I had this guy on the other side of a deal once. Nasty piece of work. It was like he was in the running for Masochistic Machoman of the Year; virtually every e-mail I got from him was timed at between two and four in the morning. Typical male lawyer. I bet it's the bloody basement for us.' Or he'd learned how to alter the time on his e-mails, something I'd been doing secretly for ages.

We got into a lift and, sure enough, he pressed the basement button. But when we got there, he headed to a fire door and a flight of stairs descending into even further gloom. 'Sorry about this,' he said, without a trace of remorse. 'All our meeting rooms are busy and this is the only space we've got that's big enough.'

It takes much to offend thick-skinned corporate lawyers like us. But the room – a cold, bare, large oblong – was so awful as to be genuinely insulting. It was probably a storage room most of the time, but there was a sporting chance that TSL used it as a makeshift morgue when their assistants expired from overwork or were punished for not hitting their targets. It had been roughly converted with filing cabinets lining the walls, and a bank of cheap tables and chairs in the centre. Strip lighting flickered overhead among greasy, grumbling pipes.

Vindictiveness is not a hard emotion for most lawyers to summon up, but TSL had outdone themselves. And it was hard not to admire their style – a lot of effort and spite had gone into transporting everything down into this inaccessible cellar. I noticed that in the absence of any radiators they had put out three tiny fan heaters like my gran used to rest her feet on; it was the kind of attention to detail that made this law firm one of the best.

'It's a bit basic, but you'll find everything you need here,' the associate said with an admirably straight face. 'We'll have some sandwiches brought down at lunchtime.' He sounded so aggrieved at the thought of us feeding our faces that I wondered if he been told to make them himself.

'We could do with some tea and coffee to be going on with,' said Elly brightly. No amount of breeze blocks was going to ruin her first real chance to impress.

The associate looked at her, even more put out, as if she was asking for the key to the senior partner's private toilet suite. 'I'll see what I can do,' he said, although I was sure the sentence had ended in his mind with the words 'in a couple of hours, if you're lucky.'

Over the next ten minutes all the other assistants and trainees filed in – our hours in the room were a strict nine to five, so woe betide anyone who was late. They reacted with varying degrees of horror and resignation. For some of the trainees, including Richard, this was their first experience of a dataroom, and Hannah took them through the basic rules: they had to read every agreement in every cabinet, looking for obligations our client was about to assume and anything else that looked dodgy. Because life

153

wouldn't be unpleasant enough as it was, they were not allowed to photocopy anything or use dictaphones – they had to fill out manually special report sheets on each contract. The three of us split up our teams and off we went, and I took some pleasure from the look on Richard's face when he realised there was no way out this time.

Lunch lived up to expectations. The cheese and tomato sandwiches would have been great had they used cheese and tomato. Lettuce with a faint cheesy aroma and dripping tomato juice was hardly the same thing. In fairness, the crisps were only slightly stale, although the bowl of fruit was so ancient that Hannah was sure she'd seen a painting of it somewhere.

Later in the afternoon, Graham and Ian popped in to check how everything was going after a meeting they'd had in the civilised part of the building.

'Bloody hell,' said Ian, taking in the grim scene before him. 'Have you formed an escape committee yet? I'll leave with some soil in my pocket if it'll help.' Elly laughed with alarming sycophancy.

'You realise that nobody can hear you scream down here,' Graham mused.

'We've already checked that out,' Hannah reassured him.

'So they won't know if we kill you for putting us on this job,' I said.

'Yeah, but think of the smell if you did,' said Ian, and everyone sniffed. One assistant had described the room's aroma as Eau des Sour Grapes; something had gone sour, at least. 'OK, maybe that's not the strongest argument.'

The TSL associate was down at five on the dot to order us out. He saw the cabinet drawers we had marked as complete and tutted. 'Is that all you've done?' he asked. Here, and here alone, TSL stood for The Super Lawyers.

Hannah's nostrils flared. 'It's difficult with some of these contracts,' she complained. 'Do you get the tea ladies to draft them or something?'

'Actually, one of our tea ladies just became a partner at

your place, I think,' he sniffed, but nobody carries off an air of superiority like a Babbingtons lawyer.

'That doesn't surprise me,' said Hannah. 'I mean, it's not like any of your lawyers are up to it.'

I steered her out of the room before they started pulling at each other's hair.

Unfortunately, the dataroom may have closed at five, but our working day did not. We all trooped back to the office to get on with other work; Elly, Hannah and I also had to start work on the forms filled out during the day. They had to be collated into one huge due diligence report to be presented to the client virtually as soon as we finally closed the dataroom. An icy finger of hopelessness beckoned us towards a lot of long nights.

Still, it was fun working so closely with Elly. At first, she demanded that we keep our work relationship on an entirely professional footing, but on the second evening, after I called her for the twenty-sixth time in thirty minutes, she gave in and agreed to share as romantic a meal as you could hope for in a dark corner of the staff restaurant.

The restaurant – Babbingtons was far too posh to have an area as common as a canteen – was surprisingly good. Indeed, the firm looked after us extremely well; there was an in-house doctor, dentist, physiotherapist, travel agent, convenience store, dry cleaner and concierge service, with people who would take your keys and wait in for the plumber if necessary.

And, in a glimmer of corporate recognition of the wrecks we were becoming, a recent innovation was to employ a therapist. I've often wondered about her. Does she have a therapist of her own to whom she lies back and complains bitterly that if she hears just one more lawyer whining about his or her pathetic life, she's going to check into the asylum voluntarily? And I think I have a tough job.

The aim of all this? Let's just say that improving the quality of our lives was not high on the agenda. Unlike removing all distractions from fee-earning and giving us

155

virtually no excuse to ever leave the office. There was even a suite of bedrooms for those who needed a kip while pulling an all-nighter.

Still, it meant that even at nine in the evening there was a decent dinner to be had without resorting to greasy take-aways. The restaurant, bathed in soothing blue light, was reasonably busy given the hour, but it wasn't hard for us to find a secluded table.

'This is very exciting, you realise,' Elly said, as we supped some soup.

'Can't say tomato and basil really does it for me,' I said.

'Funny guy. This deal could take us places, you know.'

'I'm already on my way to an early grave,' I said. 'This is just prodding me along.'

Elly banged down her spoon. 'Can't you show some enthusiasm? Is it asking too much? If you're that unhappy, why don't you just leave?'

And let her grab all the glory? I don't think so. 'Ignore me,' I said. 'It's just the way I release the tension.' Or so the therapist had told me. 'I've got this whole self-pity thing going. It's really awful. I don't know how I cope some of the time.'

It took her a moment to get it, but Elly's face eventually relaxed into a smile. 'Look, I'm sorry we haven't had much time for us, but you know what this means to me.'

It means a chance to step over my still warm body to the next partnership meeting, I thought grimly, but fought the temptation to say it. 'Even you need to relax. What say on Friday night we go out, just the two of us?'

Elly pretended to hum and hah before extending her hand over mine. 'It's a date.'

It may have been a date, but no date I've ever been on has twenty other people tagging along to watch. But when it had come to it, everyone was desperate for some relief from the dataroom, and Elly said it would be rude for the two of us to slink off. 'Team bonding,' she advised. 'Very important.'

156

I was unconvinced. 'Because being stuck in an airless cell for a week hasn't brought us together?'

'Not in a positive environment it hasn't, no,' she said. I'd noticed a worrying selection of American self-help management books on her shelves at home, including *Believe Your Way To Partnership*, written by a super-rich US lawyer who had racked up two heart attacks, a gooey stress-related skin condition, around $25 million and three ex-wives. What was more impressive was that he'd found the time for three marriages; he once said that nineteen-year-old brides are like first-year lawyers: too young to know better. His book famously concluded with the line: 'The law isn't the be all and end all in life. But becoming a partner is.'

'I know it all sounds like bollocks,' Elly said with a grin, reading my mind, 'but a night out on the razz will do wonders for everyone, trust me.'

Elly was right, of course. The rhythm of every dataroom I've ever worked in is the same. For the first few days, the modicum of professionalism and enthusiasm to get the job done and done well helps everyone through a good amount of work. But hour by hour, there are signs that it is on the wane: slightly longer coffee breaks, regular volunteers to go out and buy chocolate bars, increasing volume of gossip about the partners. Eventually, on a two-week task like this one, things grind to a halt about halfway through. Friday night could not come quickly enough.

As we dallied at 4.30, demanding that our watches get a move on, discussion revolved around where people would rather be. 'At home,' at least three people chorused at once. 'With the phone off the hook,' one woman continued, 'my PC disabled, mobile phone switched off, door knocker stolen, curtains glued together, and Cary Grant film on the telly.' There was an appreciative silence.

'With Nicole Kidman on a secret island in the Pacific where the law prohibits women from wearing any clothes,' said a male assistant with a lost expression. 'The law can be a force for good, you know, if used right.'

157

'Make it Kate Moss and I'm there,' said another. 'I like to consider myself patriotic.'

'Make it Kate Moss and I'm there too,' added a female assistant, and everyone laughed.

'Make it Allison Heywood and I think every man in the corporate department will be there,' a trainee said, getting all wistful over a blonde female partner who carried off the mixture of power and sex to groin-stirring effect. I was sure that the stories told about her – all basically versions of her sleeping her way to the top and the way she had played off the childish rivalries among the male partners for her affections – were the product of nothing more than jealousy and male bigotry. No woman partner, unless she looked like Godzilla, could make it as far as Allison without similar stories circulating.

So the conversation quickly turned to partners you would sleep with.

'Any of them, if it'll help me become a partner too,' said a male assistant a year below me. 'Even Robert "Monkey" Tunkey.' Tunkey, a squat, pug-faced pig of a man, was renowned for instigating chest-hair competitions among all the male lawyers unfortunate enough to be put on his table at the Christmas party each year. And as anyone who came across him in the toilets at the wrong time could confirm, he was even the proud owner of a special chest-hair comb. After another couple of drinks each Christmas, he would then – wracked by giggles – start trying to put his hand down women's blouses to check whether they had any 'bosom hair', as he charmingly termed it. But he brought in some serious clients, so his exploits were just about tolerated.

'I'd draw the line at Brian Healy,' said a female assistant. 'No partnership is worth sleeping with a man who spends so much time with his hands down the back of his trousers scratching his arse.'

'I really want to get my hands on Darren Barnes,' another chipped in. 'I'm dying to know if it's a wig or not.'

'And then there's Joe Forbes,' said Hannah, to a wave of nodding female heads.

I tutted. 'You lot are so superficial. Just because he's good-looking, kind, powerful and a brilliant lawyer, you'd jump into bed with him just like that. Where are your standards?'

Hannah grinned. 'Not on his bedroom floor, sadly.'

Being Friday, Lucy and Ash tagged along, and at one trainee's insistence, we gave The Witness Box a miss for Mr Smiley. This was a newish club in town, and I was too busy chatting to Hannah to look closely at what was on offer before we were in. If I had, I'd have rather burned my timesheet than enter a circle of hell where my nightmares came true on a nightly basis: a place where not only have the 1980s never ended, but a place where they are to be worshipped, rather than packed up tightly in a box and shoved into the attic of memory.

The 1980s, to generalise, were something of a disaster zone for me as a relatively normal, straight teenager, with fashion and musical humiliation a distinct threat at virtually every turn. In fact, I can be more specific. I can just about live with 1980 to 1986, although 1982 and Dexy's Midnight Runners provided a blip in the shape of 'Come On Eileen' and a tragic but mercifully brief flirtation with dungarees. But 1987, in hindsight, is when it all started to go wrong.

Many things went tits up that year: not only was Maggie Thatcher re-elected (at the time, I didn't really get the 'Maggie, Maggie, Maggie, Out, Out, Out' stuff, yet of course I mouthed it when required), but I was persuaded to stand as the Conservative candidate in our school mock-election because nobody else would, a scarring experience if ever there was.

It wasn't enough that people laughed at me simply for wearing a blue rosette. Some idiotically enthusiastic young music teacher came up with the idea of each candidate performing a campaign song before the hustings that were held. The Communist candidate won a standing ovation for chanting 'Die Maggie Die' repeatedly until a teacher threatened to expel him, while I won nothing more than a duffing up from a group of pre-pubescent Chelsea fans for borrowing their song and warbling, 'Blue is the colour, Fortune is the name, Please vote for me, Because Maggie's not really insane.'

Fortunately, the silent majority of respectable middle-class kids at the school ensured a Thatcher-like triumph at the polls, which the other candidates tried to eclipse with a novel if politically difficult Labour–SDP–Communist–Green–Loony alliance that only excluded on principle the two-vote School Uniforms for Six Formers Party.

Then there was the big Stock Market crash, which sent my parents into white-faced huddles for several days and saw an early recession hit my pocket money. In fact, think-ing about it, 1987 was pretty rotten for them too: aside from my increasingly difficult, seventeen-year-old behav-iour, they also had to cope with the Great Storm, which uprooted an ugly tree in our front garden. That was good, because my dad had been meaning to do something about it for ages, but unfortunately the wind relocated it through the roof of his Austin Allegro. This was less good for him, because he loved that car – 'listen to it purr,' he would say as it chugged along, usually in the direction of a mechanic – but a moment of exquisite joy for me because he made me wash it every Sunday morning.

But now I see that 1987 was when Elly and I started becoming estranged. It was more stark than it seemed at the time. I – and the only excuse I can make for this is immaturity – got rather too far into the whole *Miami Vice* thing, with a varied selection of stripey linen jackets ('shall I wear the one with thin stripes, thick stripes or medium stripes tonight?'), sunglasses glued to my head and a metronomic obsession with rolling up my sleeves. Even now, in moments of extreme stress, I occasionally find myself trying to push my sleeves north. And hidden away at the back of my cupboard to this day is a narrow tie lined with piano keys. Some designs are so classic that I know it will come back into vogue eventually.

My hair was fashioned, in the loosest sense of the word, in what, if you were going to be unkind (which many people gratuitously were), was a poor man's mullet. That was always assuming there was such a thing as a classy rich man's mullet. An ill-conceived effort to grow a moustache foundered on what my mum – with a piercing glare at my dad – explained was genetically weak testosterone. But it was better than the other extreme: there was one girl at school nicknamed Permafrost, because she wouldn't let you do anything to her if it disturbed a perm so huge and out of control that her mother needed a whip and a chair to combat an outbreak of nits.

Music-wise, I tried hard to get into the classy teenage stuff like the Style Council – they were just so perfectly named for someone as stylish as myself – but couldn't stop myself bopping around to the likes of Belinda Carlisle instead. I loved nothing more than being at a party or disco when 'Heaven is a Place on Earth' came on, so I could use this joke I'd nicked from some comedian on the telly. 'No Belinda,' I'd declare to anyone who could hear, 'Carlisle is a place on earth.' It got the occasional laugh, and indeed there was one party where I actually pulled on the back of it. It was hardly a sound basis for a relationship though, and I was later back on the prowl three dates and a grope of too much hair in too many wrong places later.

Elly, by contrast, had gone all Goth. Where I was jigging forward at parties with a Bacardi and coke in hand to the strains of Mel and Kim, she was dancing backwards, eyes closed in rapture at The Sisters of Mercy, supping a pint of Snakebite. Where I sought any tan the sun could provide to give me that Miami/Sonny Crockett glow, she was caking her face in white foundation and making a passable imitation of the living dead. Where I was in bed early to maximise my energy for the following day, she was painting her eyes black as if to emphasise that she never slept unless forced to.

161

Mr Smiley encouraged fancy dress, and Elly got ever so excited when we spotted a couple of Goths in a far corner, looking suitably fed up with life and pining for a meaningful death, preferably immortalised in song or poetry.

Elly's face shined with nostalgia. 'Do you remember when I was like that?' she asked.

If course I did. It pushed us ever further apart. But the bizarre thing about Goths at the time was that none of them would admit to being one. Every Goth I met thought they were far too cool to be a Goth, even though they would happily – if one can use that word in the context of people who worshipped Morrissey – point at others dressed and made up identically, and sneer at them for being, well, Goths.

What I could never get over was the obsession with black. Black fishnet tights I could readily understand and welcomed Elly adopting them. But then there were the black skirts, trousers and jackets, while her hair – which fortunately was already the right colour – was duly crimped and backcombed, and ordered into place by blasts of hair spray so severe that Elly's part of Buckinghamshire still has its own little hole in the ozone layer. And as if they weren't depressing enough, Goths would then sit around for hours droning on about how deep Sylvia Plath was. 'Six feet deep,' I once joked and Elly refused to speak to me for a week until I agreed to listen to her recite endless, tedious poetry.

I turned to Elly, who had ordered Snakebite at the bar. A little corner of her soul would be for ever lined in black. 'What is it about Goths and the need for the definite article?' I said. 'The Cure, The Cult, Siouxie and The Banshees; what was that jolly little ditty by The Smiths?'

'Heaven Knows I'm Miserable Now,' Elly said without hesitation.

That was it, an entire movement summed up in one song title. You had to admire it really. There was no shilly-shallying with bands which were too polite to stake their claim. 'A Cure' just wouldn't have had the same ring to it.

At the same time, male Goths wore eyeliner, which was just too unsettling. My masculinity had already been thrown into confusion by the growing number of men sporting earrings. It was left ear, queer, wasn't it? Or was it right ear? Either way, it was queer, surely?

I once played a trick on my dad where I strolled into dinner with a clip-on earring. It took him a couple of minutes to notice it, another couple to look away and back again to make sure he wasn't seeing things, and eventually he said, in an absurdly dangerous tone, 'Lesbians are not welcome in my home.' Then he stormed out.

'That was such a cool time,' Elly said to me, tasting her drink and grimacing slightly. 'I was so damn cool.' She glanced at me with a grin. 'Wish I could say the same about you.'

It was a rare period in our growing-up where Elly and I went in opposite directions. So far as she was concerned back then, I was discarded as a Casual, which went for pretty much everybody who wasn't a Goth. The girlfriends that passed rapidly in and out of my life were, by contrast to Elly, a riot of colour, usually a bright cerise that was hard on the eye: puffball miniskirts, stilettos, handbags secured defensively across chests, of course, rolled-up sleeves. I recall one girl who would unconsciously mirror me every time I reached for my sleeves; it was a match made in 1980s hell.

I too went for colour, although even now I regret an unwise dalliance with a pink shirt and cardie combination that still stares out shamelessly from a wall at my parents' home, despite my very best efforts to knock the frame off and accidentally grind it into small pieces with my heel.

Keen though I was, fourteen years later, to pop Elly's inflated ego, I couldn't really disagree. I'd thought she was dead cool. I would watch her slouching around with her Goth mates and wish I could be there with her, although I'd have drawn the line at eye make-up. But she would sooner have done the Birdie Dance in a lime green puffball than let on to her friends that she was close to me. All our meetings had to be in private.

'And look at you now,' I said churlishly. 'Your seventeen-year-old self would be ever so proud that you became a solicitor.'

Elly looked melancholy and my heart thawed at the slight dimple that creases her chin when her mouth turns down. 'I do regret it sometimes,' she said. 'I never took time off after uni, never went travelling, never seemed to have much time for anything in the last few years except sale and purchase agreements.'

I knew how she felt, and a cloud of Goth-like gloom hovered over us as we watched several of the younger lawyers giving it their best on the dance floor. There was then a brief hiatus in the music as a group of five dancers leaped on to a stage at the far end wearing black T-shirts with yellow Smiley faces on them. 'Accciiiddd,' came the cry from the DJ.

The dimple disappeared as Elly smiled up at me. 'This isn't bringing back particularly happy memories for you, is it?' She put a comforting hand around my waist and gave me a kiss dripping with amused pity.

Ah yes, Acid House, another great 1987 invention. I tried so damned hard to get into this one, especially once Elly had cast off black and embraced yellow. Looking back, it was great preparation for legal life: spending hour after mindless hour gyrating to hypnotic rhythms segued nicely into spending hour after mindless hour ordering a thousand letters chronologically. But where my oh-so-brief relationship with drugs came to a snot-inducing, vomit-producing, faeces-excreting, head-near-exploding end, the drug of possible partnership had kept me going for years.

Elly disappeared on to the dance floor with Ash, who just had something about him that told you he had been cool as a kid. He had that unconscious ease of those who have never had to work hard to seek approval from their peers. It wasn't that I was especially square when I was younger – although my times as a Conservative candidate dogged me and made me more popular with the dorks than was comfortable – but I also wasn't especially cool. It was only when I went to university and put some physical distance between myself and Elly, that I relaxed and started to be myself, rather than the person I reckoned Elly wanted me to be.

Watching her gyrate on the dance floor with the enthusiasm that she brought to so much of her life, I felt warmth flow through me. We'd come out of the other side of our enmity, and I was overcome with relief, more than anything. I was reminded of the time we saw each other after our first years at university; with what I could only think was a deserved dose of natural justice, I'd heard through the usual sources that while I'd had an absolute blast, it had not been the easiest time for Elly. Our eyes had locked briefly and I'd known at that moment that I still wanted her, but that I could also manage perfectly well without. It was most liberating.

Interrupting Hannah, who was nattering away about these two male lawyers she had seen cutting amorous looks at each other in the dataroom, I strode on to the dance floor. I pushed Ash out of the way, but he was so with the beat that he simply kept spinning around with his arms in the air. Elly stopped with a smile so huge, so welcoming, so needy that I enveloped her and we kissed with the desire of people with years and years to make up for.

Chapter Eighteen

There aren't many forces in this world greater than the law. So the firms which wield it best are pretty powerful too, in their way. And then there are the clients, who expect both to jump to their command. Few can resist any one of these, so if the law, Babbington Botts and your client expects you to sit at your desk on a Sunday – and often they do – then that is where you will be, kitted out in your finest Ralph Lauren polo shirt and sharpest chinos (weekend casual wear has its very defined limits for partnership hopefuls; denim would sink my chances far quicker than any negligence claim).

But I know of one: the combined force of my mother and my girlfriend's mother. Crudely executed through their pincer movement on our Sunday afternoon was, a mixture of threat, bribery, guilt and shameless pleading saw us driving back to Bucks for a joint family lunch being held at my parents' house.

'I don't ask for much in life,' my mum had near-sobbed down the phone, ignoring my question about why then she'd made my dad buy her all that jewellery. 'Just the chance to see my boy happy—'

'I am happy,' I interrupted. 'Don't you believe me?'

166

'– with my own eyes,' she finished with steel in her voice.

She had been a good mother over the years; not overly protective, relatively unfussy and content to let me make my own mistakes, within reason of course and only once she'd steered me into becoming a lawyer. But it was just that she had yet to consider any of the many girlfriends who had faced a grilling while perched by the breakfast bar in the kitchen to be suitable for me.

They were, in no particular order over the years: too thick, too tarty, too skinny, too fat, too mouthy (unforgivably, she boasted that her mum had a dishwasher – ours was delivered within three weeks), too red-faced, too high-pitched, too Samantha Fox (something of a teenage highlight, that particular six-week relationship), too Swedish (Sam Fox lookalike followed up by a blonde au pair – not many people fulfil the majority of their life ambitions by the time they are nineteen), too keen, too grimy, too glum and one who was too good to be true (Mum was right about her – turned out that she had this piercing fetish that brought our time together to an abrupt end with her shouting, 'If you won't pierce your penis for me, then I don't see we have any future together.' It was then a race to see who could storm out first. Panic meant I won).

Whether the impossibly high standards she set were out of concern that my eventual wife should be perfect, or out of concern that my eventual wife should be Elly, was open to debate. If I had a pound for every time Mum had mentioned just how absolutely ideal for everyone a Charlie/Elly merger would be, as we lawyers might say, I could afford to buy Sweden and a whole land of willing au pairs.

Elly said her mother was always slightly more subtle. 'She goes totally overboard on any boyfriend she ever meets, like I've snapped up Jesus or something. But then she starts chipping away at him. "He's perfect for you, darling," she says. "Completely perfect. So long as you don't mind those teeth. And the way his eyebrows meet." That sort of thing.'

167

Elly had a thing about men who allow their eyebrows to grow the full width of their faces. 'They're either too lazy to do anything about it, which irritates me,' she would say, 'or they have something to hide.' I never received a satisfactory explanation as to why you couldn't trust a man with a single line of hair across his forehead, but unmanly though it made me feel – I mean, since when do men give two hoots about excessive body hair? – I now made sure I gave mine a regular seeing-to.

'This is going to be so damn awful,' Elly said gloomily as we trundled along in the slow lane of an empty motorway. One benefit of my super lawyer's salary was that I'd been able to buy the classic Morgan sports car I'd always lusted after – not that I ever got a chance to drive it – but this was one time when I was in no hurry. 'My mother'll be all over me. Your mother'll be all over me. If they mention the word "wedding" just once, I'm going to use the cake slice as a deadly weapon.' My mum always made a Victoria sponge for such events; ever since she'd won a third prize in a local cake competition, she'd been trying to perfect the recipe. 'It's all in the moistness,' she said with relish to anyone who complimented her on it. That rosette had single-handedly turned her into her personal vision of a domestic goddess, and she now played up to the stereotype with gusto.

'Like it won't be even more dreadful for me,' I grumbled. 'I don't know what's worse: your dad nudge-nudging me about women or your mum fussing over me non-stop.'

'The last time I was at your parents' house about a year and a half ago, they were already planning the dynasty,' Elly said. 'I overheard your mum say to mine that she was worried I didn't have child-bearing hips.'

My mum was still worried about it; more so, in fact, now there was a realistic possibility of it being her grandchildren fighting their way through the tiny opening. She'd mentioned it to me the other day on the phone, and was irritated when I seemed not to care much. So far, I had no complaints about Elly's hips. Nicely slim and smooth was as far as my opinion went.

'Don't you want a big family?' Mum asked.

Actually, I've always envisaged having something of a brood which I could then steer firmly away from the legal profession. But I wasn't ready for this conversation with her. 'Dunno,' I said in a teenager-like monotone perfected over many years.

'Well, your father wants a grandson to take to football with him,' she snapped, as if I now had no excuse to delay making up for what I had denied him as a child.

I hadn't thought to share the exchange with Elly; it would only have made my life more difficult.

'And like anyone apart from your mother says things like "child-bearing hips" any more,' she went on. 'And then your dad is convinced that I'm obsessed with petunias. For the last seven years, he's asked me every time we've met whether I've seen any with nice colours. I wouldn't know a petunia if I walked into Petunias R Us.'

I smiled with affection for my dad. 'It's only because you're the only person in either family to have ever shown the slightest interest in his garden.'

'I once poked my head out the window and said, "They're pretty, Mr Fortune. What are they?"'

'As I said, the only person to show any interest.'

We lapsed into a slightly sad silence on my father's behalf. 'The last time I saw your dad,' I reminded her, 'he asked me if I was getting much, now, what were the exact words he used? That's it, "jiggy jiggy". Your poor mum.' Unlike my own father, Gray senior took an active and somewhat voyeuristic interest in my life.

Elly was getting spiteful. 'At least my mum never tried to get me in the Girl Guides so I could get in touch with my feminine side at an early age.' She failed, fortunately.

'At least my dad never asked me if I could recommend a good make of condom.' Elly opened her mouth but no suitable retort would come or, let's face it, could come. The mental images had been bad enough for me all those years back; goodness knows what they were like for her.

Despite herself, Elly wanted to know what I'd said; I

169

decided not to mention the lengthy preceding monologue about the pros and cons of a vasectomy, and her dad's overly frank admission that he wasn't sure it mattered either way. 'I told him, "How would I know? You should ask your daughter. She's road-tested enough of them over the years."'

The Gray mouth turned steadfastly down. 'Funny guy. I'm not the one whose groin got all itchy a few years back, am I?'

Now that was low. Was there nothing my mother refused to share with her friends? Perhaps their children's sexually related problems were something to throw in when the conversation lulled at coffee mornings. I'd only told her because she found a variety of creams in the bathroom when I was home over Christmas. But I took a breath instead of firing back. 'You see what they're doing to us? And we're not even there yet.'

Elly stretched her hands over her knees in an effort to find some calm. 'You're right. We have to remember that we're not fifteen any more. And remember that we love each other.'

There was a silence and I suddenly pulled across on to the hard shoulder. Elly was alarmed, but I turned awkwardly in my seat towards her and took her hands. 'Bloody hell, I really do love you, you know?'

She smiled. 'I know. I'm so glad I took the job at Babbingtons. We'd've regretted not doing this for the rest of our lives otherwise.' We kissed. 'They offered me partnership to stay at my old firm, you know.'

'What?'

'Not immediately. But they said it would definitely be mine a year later.'

'But ... why didn't you take it then?'

'Why do you think?'

'To be honest, I can't imagine. Maybe you'd hit your head and had your entire memory and identity wiped.'

She put a hand to my cheek. 'Because of you. Because I wanted to be close to you again. Because I kind of hoped that this would happen.'

The car rocked as three massive lorries thundered by in convoy. For a moment I thought I might lose all manly pretensions and cry. Nobody had ever wanted me like this. 'I really, really, really love you,' was the best I could come up with.

'I know. It's great, isn't it?'

I looked at my watch. We were cutting it a bit fine. It didn't do to keep either the Grays or the Fortunes waiting past 1 pm for their weekly joint Sunday lunch. Their bodies soon fail if gravy is not liberally applied by 1.45 pm. Saying we couldn't make it for 1 pm would have been like asking the Pope to hold Christmas over a day or two.

I rejoined the motorway and we travelled on in warm silence. Before we knew it, we had reached the turn-off on the M40 and were there soon after, only five minutes after the asked-for arrival time.

My parents moved a couple of years back into a pretty bungalow on the outskirts of town. As we swung into the driveway, they were all there lined up by the door, as if in a dry run for the reception line at the wedding. Unable to wait, they rushed over to help us out of the car.

'Lot of traffic was there, Charlie?' my mum asked.

'We were getting worried,' said Elly's mum, her hand nervously holding a tall but brittle-looking pile of reddish hair against the effects of a breeze. 'I hope the drive didn't tire you too much, Charles.'

'We're five minutes late,' I said, instantly exasperated. 'It only took about forty minutes to get here.'

'Nice car,' said her dad, pulling me to one side. 'Look, Charlie, I just wanted to apologise to you for some of the more inappropriate things I've said to you in recent times. I realise they've made you feel awkward.' I blinked in surprise, the words sounding like they came out with difficulty, but then I caught him glancing over at an approving Mrs Gray. I doubted this was his initiative, somehow.

'Do you have any bags I can take, Charles?' she asked. 'Don't want you straining yourself even more after all that driving.'

'Bet the girls like the car,' Mr Gray whispered to me, watching carefully to make sure he wasn't overheard.

My dad had rushed round to help Elly out and steered her towards a flower bed. But for once he had forgone the vivid purple funnel-shaped flowers which I took to be petunias – it was to his eternal regret that I barely knew the difference between a buttercup and a cactus.

'What do you think of that, then?' he asked Elly, pride filling his smallish frame. 'Planted it specially for you when I heard about you and Charlie.' The bed was a jumble of coloured flowers that spelled out, just about, 'C' and 'E'. Clearly Mum's excitement had finally got to him.

He looked rather old, I thought. His hair had long given up the battle to cover his head, but his jowls were just a bit longer than the last time I'd seen him.

Elly smiled warmly at him. 'They're lovely, Mr Fortune.' Despite the families' closeness, this odd formality prevailed where Elly and I, like children, could not refer to the other's parents by their first names.

Meanwhile Mr Gray, who I always thought looked alarmingly like Jimmy Tarbuck, had put his arm around my shoulders and was walking me to the front door. 'Must be cramping the old style a bit, having my daughter around,' he said conspiratorially.

I played him with a straight bat. 'Not really, Mr Gray. Couldn't ask for much more than Elly.'

'I miss playing the field sometimes,' he sighed, and threw his wife a look over my shoulder. 'I've still got it, you know.' He removed his arm and squared up before me, making to pummel me in the stomach. 'There's life in the old dog yet.'

'There better be,' she said, sweeping past in her bright pink tracksuit, 'or I'll have you put down.'

Lunch passed at first without much trouble. It was as if they'd all had a rare moment of collective insight and realised that it would be better not to pressure us. That both Elly and I had spent a considerable amount of time the previous week imploring our mothers to keep off the subject might have helped, too.

So we instead talked at length about work, which received a wave of regular if uncomprehending nods around the table. They were of course genuinely happy that we were both solicitors, that we were doing well and that we were earning lots of money. These were the three key facts that sufficed for exchanges of news with their peers. They didn't want to know any more. The strange world of Babbingtons was beyond their experience and so even further beyond their interest.

When we ground to a halt, both mothers barrelled in with all the local gossip, in which they wrongly assumed both Elly and I had an iota of interest. It would be arrogant to say that we both felt slightly above the surprisingly racy goings-on down the post office, but it wouldn't be wrong.

But then, later in the afternoon, after we had removed ourselves to the lounge to watch a war film on TV, out came tea. My mum, her normally young-looking face creased with anxiety, hovered as slices of her latest Victoria sponge were handed out. Elly's mum nibbled a bit, and sat back with a satisfied sigh. 'Oh Sally,' she said. 'Your finest yet. Ever so moist.'

'Ooh yes,' my dad said with relish. 'Now that's moist.' There are few problems in a marriage, he'd once told me with all seriousness, that a natter over a good bit of sponge couldn't sort out.

Elly's dad finished chewing a large chunk. 'Some people don't get the idea of it, do they?' he mused.

'It's not easy,' Mum said, thrilled. 'It's taken years of practice.'

'Which we are the lucky beneficiaries of,' Dad said.

'A touch too long in the oven, and it's curtains,' Mum warned. 'Then it's Victoria rock cake.' She looked sad that such a fate could ever befall something that could have been so moist.

Mr Gray nodded knowledgeably. 'I bet that if you looked up the word "moist" in the dictionary, it would simply say, "Eat a slice of Sally's Victoria sponge."'

'Don't mind if I do,' said Dad in a rare effort of

humour, and reached for another piece to a tinkle of laughter from the mothers.

'So then, Eleanor and Charles,' her dad said suddenly. 'Where's this relationship of yours going?'

'I'm sorry?' said Elly, taken aback by the abrupt shift in conversation.

'You what?' I said.

'We're all friends here,' my mum went on, resuming her seat and staring at me anxiously. 'We just want to know where we all stand.'

'We all stand nowhere in particular,' said Elly, sounding dangerously calm. 'The only we of note is me and Charlie, and when we have some news for you, we will tell you.'

'So, you're planning an announcement, are you?' Her mum was trying to look on the bright side.

'No, we're not,' I said. 'What Elly means is that there's nothing to say at the moment.'

You'd think a lawyer would know to choose his words more carefully. 'So there might be an announcement soon?' my mum asked.

'No wedding bells,' Elly said firmly. 'No patter of tiny feet. No trips to buy rings. No news. No announcement. No nothing.'

'There's no need to be so aggressive,' Mrs Gray complained. 'You can see why we're interested.'

'Unite the Grays and the Fortunes and the kingdom of Buckinghamshire will soon be ours,' I declared, and everyone stared at me.

'I just thought,' said Mum, 'what with Charlie's partnership thingy, that you two might be making plans already. It's not like you don't know each other well enough.'

Elly's nostrils flared. 'Partnership thingy? What partnership thingy?' I'd finally given in and told Mum about it, but sworn her to absolute secrecy.

'You know,' Mum went on, oblivious to the warning signs I was flashing her. 'Being put up for partnership, isn't that what you call it?'

174

Elly turned to me, incredulous. 'You've been put up? When?'

'I was waiting for the right time to tell you.'

'That's right,' Mum said reflectively. 'I wasn't meant to say anything.'

'Waiting for the right time to tell me? When might that have been? Once you'd picked out your partner's chair? I can't believe you didn't tell me.' Her cheeks flushed with anger and more than a few regrets flew through my mind. I'd been on the verge of saying something so many times, but the moment never quite came.

'Look, I'm sorry. I was going to tell you tonight, actually.' A little white lie now didn't seem to matter much.

Elly was unconvinced. 'Really? Or might it have continued to slip your mind for the next few months or so until I saw it on an internal e-mail?'

I raised my hands in submission. 'I'm sorry. I cocked up.'

'Language, Charlie,' my dad said.

'I am totally, grovellingly, shamefacedly, abjectly sorry. What more can I say?'

'But Elly dear,' her mum said innocently. 'didn't you tell me that you were being put up for partnership too?'

There was a silence that in the movies would have been accompanied by the grandfather clock in the corner tolling and tumbleweed cart-wheeling across the back patio. Were our mothers conniving or just plain incompetent, I wondered. Elly and I gazed at each other, at once lovers and rivals. I couldn't read her expression.

'And you didn't think to say anything to me?' I asked far more politely than Elly had.

She had the decency to look abashed. 'I was going to. I only just heard.'

'Me too.'

Mum trilled how exciting it would be if we became partners together, but Elly and I knew better. It was possible, sure, but far more likely that only one or even neither of us would make it. I considered saying something absurdly

175

dramatic, like 'Let battle commence,' but wisely thought better of it.

'Stop looking so worried, you two,' her dad said.

'It brings out terrible lines on your face, Charles.' Mrs Gray was concerned for future family photos.

'I'm sure you've got nothing to worry about,' Mum added complacently. If only she knew. 'After all, didn't Elly's boss say how it was all part of a deal or something?'

My eyes widened. I knew it. Bugger. I was right. So there was an agreement after all when Ian brought Elly with him to Babbingtons.

'I knew it,' I said, kind of pleased that she'd concealed more than I had. 'Told them all down the pub, but would anyone believe me?'

'It's not what you think.' Elly was defiant. 'The only agreement was that I'd be put up, not that I would definitely get it.'

'We're ever so proud of you,' Elly's mum beamed.

'We think you're doing ever so well too,' my dad said, patting me on the arm. 'My son the partner. They'll like that down the pub.'

'Talking of the pub,' Mr Gray went on, 'did I tell you what Lager Len said about his wife entering a wet T-shirt competition when they were in Magaluf recently?'

The Charlie and Elly show had taken up enough of their time, it seemed. 'Isn't she about sixty-three?' said my mum, a hand over her mouth in horror.

'She won too. Apparently they created a special category for the saggiest boobs.'

They all laughed, although I noticed Elly's mum briefly put a hand to her bust to reassure herself.

Elly, though, didn't laugh.

'Come on, love,' her dad said, trying to jolly her along. 'Worse things happen at sea.'

There spoke a man who'd never sunk at Babbington Botts.

Chapter Nineteen

The dataroom on Monday morning was a hive of activity; it was just a shame that we got hardly any legal work done.

When we arrived, Hannah, bless her, failed to notice the frost that had formed between Elly and me, and huddled us together so we could discuss how to get things moving. 'I reckon we've got about eight days' work to do,' she said. 'And as we've only got five days left, we've got something of a problem.'

It was hard to concentrate as Elly and I were too busy glaring at one another. After our mothers had spent far too long deciding to hold a joint party when we became partners, we had finally escaped but still hadn't spoken properly about our newly discovered competition. In the car back from Wycombe there had been a good deal of tutting and sighing (that was me), a lot of fist-clenching (Elly is far more aggressive than me, I'd realised), and a tremendous amount of immature sniping.

'You should have told me,' I'd insisted.

'Me? What about you? Why didn't you share your amazing news with me of all people?'

'I really wanted to tell you, which is more than you did.' On reflection, that wasn't the strongest of arguments.

'This is typical of you,' she said. 'Overly secretive, overly argumentative and overly competitive. No wonder they've put you up for a bloody partnership.'

I was gripping the steering wheel so hard that I could feel my nails touching my palm. 'If they're the criteria, then I might as well give up now. You could teach the Krays a thing or two about being ruthless.'

Elly was oddly flattered. 'Do you really think so?'

'If you think that's a compliment, then I've just made my point.'

'Eleanor de Gangsta.' She tried it out and the tension, remarkably, eased. 'You lookin' at me?' she said with a vague New York accent.

'What?'

'I said, are you lookin' at me?'

'Not if I can help it.'

'Be careful, wise guy,' she said, 'or I'll set da boys on ya. Then we'll see how da cement jacket helps ya get ya partnership.'

I wasn't really in the mood. 'Whatever,' I said testily, forcing myself to relax my hold on the steering wheel, and concentrate on the dark road ahead.

When the rest of the team had arrived, we asked them to gather around so we could review how far we had got through the documents. However, top of the agenda was discussing Friday night. 'I think I'm still drunk,' groaned one pale-looking assistant. 'When I woke up on Saturday morning, I had all my clothes on back to front. Heaven only knows how that happened.'

Everyone had the decency to stay silent about the 'Reverse Monty' dance he'd perfected in front of us when we'd all fallen out of the club.

'I'm getting too old for all this,' said another, who was three years behind me. 'A nice cup of Horlicks, asleep by ten and in early for work, bright-eyed and bushy-tailed, that's my new regime.'

I smiled; I had made many a similar pledge over the

years which never lasted more than six days, when Hannah would persuade me to go out the next Friday night. She always said it wasn't the same without me, and that I had a duty as her best friend to make sure she was all right.

'You know I shouldn't be out on Friday nights,' she'd said the last time I'd vowed never to let alcohol pass my lips again, about three months ago. 'God may strike me down.' As if that had ever stopped her.

'Not much I can do about that, is there? I'm a good lawyer, but I don't exactly specialise in divine justice. You need a rabbi, I'd say.'

'But what about my mother? If she ever caught me ...'

'Hannah, from what I know of your mother, the pub is the safest place for you. Didn't you once tell me that she always locks the car doors when your dad drives past one?'

She tried again. 'My mum's relying on you to ensure I'm not corrupted.'

Amazingly, this was true. All the mothers I have met over the years have waved me through as an ideal chaperone for their daughters. Even as a teenager, despite my best efforts to project a bad-boy image – but then how many bad boys in the 1980s voluntarily wore sleeveless sweaters and thought, very wrongly, that they looked kind of retro-groovy? – I managed an air of respectability that reassured mothers the length and breadth of Buckinghamshire. That didn't mean I failed to get up to any naughtiness. It just meant I wasn't suspected of it.

Into my thirties, I am A-list material. I come from the Home Counties, I own my own flat, I earn a whacking great salary, my prospects are fantastic and I have this ability to make any mother love me. On at least two occasions have I prolonged a relationship with some girl simply because I got on so well with her mother.

'You wouldn't happen to be Jewish, would you, Charlie?' Hannah's mum had once asked me as we shared a companionable cup of tea at her flat. Hannah had earlier stomped off in an adolescent strop when her mother explained to me sadly that she doubted she would ever become a grandmother.

'Afraid not.'

Her mum sighed with graphic disappointment. 'Ah well, nobody's perfect.'

'I can shrug very expressively though, if that helps.'

'Not quite enough, sadly,' she said.

I glanced with affection at Hannah as Elly called for silence in the dataroom. With Hannah's back turned, Elly and I had called a day-long truce. 'We must talk about this properly,' she said.

'Tonight,' I agreed, fed up though I was with the female insistence on talking relationships to death. The moment Elly said to me, 'We don't talk enough,' I was going to leave. If only women counted all the conversations about cars and computers and sports.

Hannah then launched us into the warm-up she hoped would get everyone going.

'There are unconfirmed reports—' Hannah announced.

'—better to say unreliable reports,' interrupted Elly with a frown at Richard.

'That two of the trainees on the team were seen getting off with each other,' Hannah finished.

'I would suggest that nobody reads anything into the fact that they are the only two people not here on time,' Elly said with a slight smile.

'And I would like to apologise to you all if Eleanor and I have given you the impression that it is OK to get off with fellow lawyers,' I went on. 'I wouldn't recommend it in the slightest. Unless pillow talk about the Companies Act 1989 really turns you on.'

'Which bizarrely it does with Charlie,' Elly said, and everyone laughed. 'The moment I mention section 93, he loses all control.'

'Who can tell me what section 93 is?' I asked.

'Registration of charges,' piped up a keen trainee.

'Exactly. Now you see why it gives me such a thrill.' More smiles. 'The real problem is that your whole life becomes a timesheet,' I told them. 'Everything you do is apportioned into ten-minute segments.'

'Not that everything takes as long as ten minutes, of course,' Elly said to laughs.

'Or is worth recording at all,' I added with a grin.

As the group laughed, the absent male trainee came in, mumbling an apology for being late. You could almost set your watch by it: she came in exactly sixty seconds later, and made sure she was standing nowhere near him. They both tried to look anywhere but at each other and, of course, failed miserably, especially as we were all watching them for just those signs.

It was sweet that they thought they could get away with it. They had yet to learn that every trainee is contractually obliged to indulge in at least one unwise liaison with a fellow employee during their two years. I preferred not to recall my brief fling with an assistant from the banking department; my excuse was that I had only been at the firm for a couple of months and still don't know most of the people or the gossip. It was only at the firm's Christmas party, when I breathed a somewhat lurid suggestion in her ear, that she turned with an innocent smile and introduced me to her husband, who was a partner in the tax department. I was not the first, I later learned, nor was I the last to fall headlong into that particular man-hole.

'Right everyone,' I said, clapping my hands for some order at last. 'We fell behind a bit last week, what with one thing and another.' The one thing being boredom, the other being monotony. 'We've got five days left, so let's really get cracking.'

There was a murmur of comradely intent which lasted a good two hours. By eleven though, fatigue was setting in and the number of forms being filled out had thinned from a steady flow to an occasional trickle.

There was a ripple of excitement when a strip light flicked out, leaving one corner a little dark. It was like dealing with schoolchildren. Several volunteers came forward to go and tell our hosts, a few people threw stuff

181

at the other lights in an effort to knock them out of service too and render the room unusable, while Richard led the chorus of complaints about unsafe working conditions. 'All sorts of things could happen in the dark,' he said.

Surrounded by nothing sharper than a paper clip, I was pushed to see the danger spots.

'I dunno,' he said. 'That pen you're holding. It could have my eye out.'

'Unlikely,' I replied. 'I'll be too busy using it to write your performance review.'

The day wound on and throughout I felt uneasy about Elly, though she had suddenly started to flash smiles at me. Perhaps she realised she was in the wrong. She just had to go and ruin my run at partnership with one of her own. How totally selfish. I've worked so damn hard to get this far, but now she just waltzes in straight to the top of the pile. It wasn't fair. And what made it worse was that it was Elly. How can you love someone and yet despise them? It was like she had planned it when we were at primary school; that she had known she would have the last say. It was just so frustrating.

When we got back to the office, Elly marched straight to my room; I was about to let Richard go home but thought better of it. So I sent him off to do some pointless photocopying I would later tip straight into the recycle bin.

Elly closed and locked the door behind her before leaning up against it, arms crossed challengingly across her chest. I sought out the reassuring protection of sitting behind my desk. I'd expected more anger but instead there was weariness on her face. 'We can't go on like this for the next however many months,' she said. 'Neither of us is going to pull out, so we've got to just live with it. There's no point either of us worrying. There's nothing we can do. I can live with it. Can you, Charlie?'

I didn't want her to take the initiative. 'Let's wind back a moment, shall we? How would you feel if I made it and you didn't?' I was sure she flinched, ever so slightly, at the thought. 'Could you live with it then?'

She bounced against the door. 'In that highly unlikely event—'

'There you go again,' I said, slapping my palms angrily on the desk and revolving the chair 180 degrees so that I had my back to her.

The next thing I felt were her hands on my shoulders. 'I was joking, Charlie. You've got to calm down about this. I have. At first I was bothered, especially as you should have told me, but then I thought to myself: why? There really isn't anything we can do about it. And if I don't get it, then I hope you do. It would be almost as good for me. And it'll be good to have someone to share the anxiety with.'

This, more than anything, was what I hated about Elly. Her constant ability to throw me with the unexpected. Where were the narrow eyes? The spiteful tongue? The aggressive flick of the hair? I stared out of the window. In my memory, that's where. I was judging Elly against thirteen-year-old behaviour. She'd apparently moved on, and I hadn't.

She cared about me, I realised. It was a dumb realisation. But I was so hardened by my years at Babbingtons – for all the close friends I'd made in Hannah, Ash and Lucy – that I wasn't used to such a simple emotion. Girlfriends had come and gone, and only my ambition had remained.

Embarrassed, I swivelled back round. 'Do you mean that?'

Elly sat on the desk, humming and hahing. 'To be honest, I'd trample over your dead body if that's what it took,' she said, and then beamed a smile at me. 'You've really lost your sense of humour over this, haven't you?'

I forced out a smile. 'You're right. I'm cool about this. I know how much it means to you, Elly. I hope you get it.'

'That's my boy,' she said, and pulled me to her by my tie. The mood softened.

I fumbled at the hem of her long skirt and began to slide my hand up her leg but she pushed me away. 'We can't,' she said. 'No here.'

'The door's locked. The blinds are down,' I said, quickly pulling on the cord. 'Who's going to know?'

'Charlie, if we got caught ...'

That didn't sound like my Elly. 'We won't. Please, humour me. I've been hoping for this for years.'

She stood back. 'I think that is the most pathetic thing I've ever heard.'

'Please?' I whined.

Elly smirked despite herself. 'Out of pity and pity alone, I'm going to agree.'

My real ambition was actually to sweep everything off a desk in the throes of passion like they do in the films. But too much talk had blunted the emotion as I took in the desk. There was an awful lot of paper on it, stuff that would take ages to reorder if I just cast it to the floor. I glanced at Richard's desk, but didn't fancy having to explain that. 'Sorry old chap, a mini-tornado came out of nowhere and took your desk out. Never seen anything like it.'

Elly glanced at her watch. 'I don't want to hurry you or anything, Charlie, but we've got quite a lot of work to do.'

I started quickly piling up files and putting them on the floor. I tried to tell myself that the sweeping wasn't the important bit. When, eventually, there was nothing of consequence left, I pulled Elly to me with one arm and used the other to brush everything else off. Two textbooks on the side of the desk clattered loudly and satisfyingly against the bin, while I hadn't noticed a small glass which fell and shattered against the leg of the chair.

Trying hard to disregard the mess, I pushed Elly up against the desk and began unbuttoning her blouse. Is there a more exciting phrase in the English language, I wondered, idly, than 'unbuttoning her blouse'?

There was a knock on the door. It was Sue. 'Everything all right in there?'

Elly began work on my belt. 'Yes, fine,' I said loudly. 'Don't worry, Sue.' My trousers fell. 'I just dropped something.'

As Elly shrugged off her skirt, we became aware of a distant tone. It wasn't loud, but it was insistent and irritating. 'It's the phone,' Elly hissed. 'It's off the hook.'

I let go of her and, tripping stupidly over my trousers, scrambled around the floor. The phone was under some newspapers that had also been pushed off the desk. I returned the receiver and returned to Elly.

We were just rediscovering the mood when the phone began to ring.

'Ignore it,' I said and clamped my mouth to hers to stop further discussion. But the phone kept on ringing. I'd forgotten to put my voice-mail on, or the diverter to Sue.

'It might be a client,' Elly said, disengaging herself.

'And it might not.' I wasn't going to be that easily distracted.

'It might be important.'

'And it might not.' I made to grab her. Legal matters weren't high on my list of priorities right then.

'Please, Charlie. Just answer it.'

Irritated, I bent over and snatched up the receiver. 'Yes?' I barked.

'Hello, Charlie.'

'Mum, this isn't a good time.' Elly slapped a hand to her forehead.

'I just wanted to say how nice it was to see you both yesterday. You looked ever so happy.'

'Can this wait? I'm really busy right now with something.' With every passing second, the excitement was literally draining out of me.

'Like love's young dream you were, your dad said.'

'I've got to go now. I'll call you later.' Elly was wandering around the room now, blouse open, skirt off, gazing at the pictures on the wall. The image of her at that moment would stick with me.

'We just wanted to know what the two of you were doing the weekend after next. We're having some people around. It would be ever so nice if you and Eleanor could come along.'

'I'll call you back. Bye now, Mum.'

'Will it be today? Only you see I'm going to order some bridge rolls tomorrow.'

'Yes, I'll call later. I'm going now, bye, Mum.'

'Not too late. You know your father doesn't like the phone ringing too late.'

'OK, bye.' I put the phone down. 'Now, where were we?'

Elly regarded me. 'Somewhat further on than we are now.'

'Can we start again?'

Elly rolled her eyes. 'I'm only doing this because I love you, you realise.' It still thrilled me to hear that. 'I've got stacks of things to get through this evening.'

'It's much appreciated,' I said testily. 'Can we get on with this?'

Without interruption, things got going again. There was an unfortunate moment with some Blu-Tack on the edge of the desk – not that the packet warns it should be kept out of contact with pubic hair – but otherwise the event was starting to live up to expectations.

Then the doorknob rattled and there was another knock on the door, which we tried to ignore. I had just got over the embarrassment of having to double-check the sell-by date on the condom I'd secreted in my desk some time ago for just such an occurrence – I am, by nature, an optimist – but whoever it was wouldn't go away.

'Please, we're busy. Come back later,' I said loudly.

It was Richard. 'Charlie, can I come in?'

'No.'

'I've really got to come in, Charlie.'

'We're doing some very important work in here and we don't want to be disturbed,' I said.

'That's half-true at least,' Elly muttered.

'Have you finished that photocopying I asked you to do?'

'No, but—'

'By the time you've finished that, we'll be done too.'

186

'I presume it was a small pile,' Elly said.

I pulled a face at her. 'See you later, Richard.'

'Charlie, please. I have to come in right now.'

I was genuinely annoyed by his attitude. He was forever questioning my authority. 'For heaven's sake, why?'

'I really need my insulin shot.'

Elly put her hands over her face. 'Crap. We've got to let him in, Charlie.'

I was already pulling up my trousers. 'Just promise we can have another go at this.'

'Sure.' She smiled, but then her face hardened. 'When I'm a partner.'

Chapter Twenty

The need to get really motoring in the dataroom hit everyone at exactly nine in the morning on the last day.

It was inevitable. A week of dawdling followed by a burst of furious activity characterised every dataroom I've ever been in. Despite our best intentions – and Elly resisted hardest – the three of us found it all too easy to be drawn into the team's heated discussions, such as 'If you won the lottery, who would be the first partner you would tell to stuff his partnership up his arse?' (for me that was easy – it was an elderly sort who once called me into his office and warned me that if I ever wanted to make it, I should never again wear brown shoes) and 'Which superpower would you choose to make you a better lawyer?' (I went for invisibility so I could infiltrate the other side's offices and learn their tactics – and if that didn't work, I could always turn to bank robbery).

Collectively, we managed in the last eight hours as much as we had done in the preceding four days, and came in just under the wire. There was no choice. We couldn't extend until the following week, and even if we could, we wouldn't have wanted our hosts to think we were incapable. The danger was the quality of work done in the final push, but it was a case of fingers crossed – not technically a legal term, but one that lawyers employ far more often than their clients would think or hope.

We got back to the office and the three of us convened in Hannah's room, facing a huge pile of forms which we had to turn into a comprehensive report to the client by the following Thursday. Then there was the main sale and purchase agreement to effect the whole deal, which we had begun work on drafting, all subject to close partner-level supervision and scrutiny. As if that wasn't enough to be going on with, both Elly and I had to prepare for initial interviews before the assessment committee on Thursday – not that Hannah could know about that particular pressure.

There was no alternative but to work through, with regular joint meetings which also took in Ash and Lucy on the sale and purchase agreement. It was what being a City lawyer is all about.

We were at it until midnight on Saturday and back in by ten on Sunday morning. At eight in the evening, Elly and Hannah were in my room for the umpteenth time discussing a tricky part of the due diligence report when Lucy and Ash came in with the umpteenth version of the agreement; twenty-four hour secretarial support was one of the perks, such as it was, of being at a firm like Babbingtons. More than once had we toyed with the idea of chucking it all in and becoming one of the secretaries who worked on Sunday evenings. They were paid almost lawyer-like salaries for the inconvenience but didn't have the hassle of having to produce and check the documents they were typing. Nor did they have to spend the best part of a decade sucking up shamelessly to the partners and anyone else who could conceivably advance their careers.

The exchanges were pretty lacklustre, and Ash eventually called a halt. The Dunkirk spirit that such weekends engender was waning. 'Let's go home. Have a couple of hours in front of the telly to relax and be back here for eight tomorrow,' he said. 'The telly thing isn't compulsory, by the way,' he added, looking at Elly and me.

'Like I've got the energy for anything else,' said Elly, stifling both a yawn and the thought that had briefly grown in my groin. 'If it's all right, Charlie, I just want to go home, have a bath—'

'I'm sure Charlie's up for that,' said Ash.

'—on my own, read for a bit and then go to bed. On my own, if that's all right with everyone.'

'Not a problem,' I said. 'I'm sure you've seen enough of me the last couple of days.'

Elly was graceless enough to agree. 'It's like we're married. I spend day and night with you, I'm really relying on you to do your share, we spend a lot of time having arguments where I am in the right, and at the end of it all, I'm far too tired for sex.'

The others sniggered. 'What do you mean, arguments where you are in the right?' I said.

'What about clause forty-five?'

'An isolated example,' I grumbled.

'Uh oh, they're having a domestic,' said Ash.

'Tenner on Elly,' said Lucy. 'He thought she was Miss Right. He just didn't realise her first name was "Always".'

'We'll ignore clauses sixty-nine through to seventy-five, shall we?' Elly wasn't letting me off lightly.

'That simply sounds like seven more isolated examples,' said Hannah. 'Leave him alone.'

Ash looked thoughtful. 'But he's useful when it comes to operating the photocopier. You know women can't cope with electrical items that don't style their hair.'

Elly smiled and pushed herself out of her seat. 'I'm off. The problem is, Charlie, that I'm a perfectionist and you're just not.'

I grinned. 'That'll be why you're going out with me, and I'm going out with you, I should think.'

She paused at the door and couldn't help but laugh. 'There's another thing that really marks us out as a married couple. I will always get the last word.' And off she went before I could lamely shout, 'No, you won't.'

*

190

Monday, Tuesday and Wednesday came and went in a whirl of drafting and redrafting, and it was only on the third evening that we downed tools briefly. An elderly partner in our department was retiring and there was a three-line whip for us to attend, if briefly, his leaving party. We were all more than happy to go – if his departure opened up a slot in the partnership, we wanted to be there to ensure he was sent swiftly on his way.

We allowed ourselves an hour off for the party – enough time to be seen by the people we wanted to be looking. We made it up to the boardroom on the top floor at just after eight, and the party was in full swing; which in Babbingtons terms meant that a couple of assistants had loosened their ties. He was a popular man anyway, but there was always a wistful sense of 'I wish it were me' that attracted people to retirement parties. It also helps that Babbington Botts employs catering staff who are as aggressive with a champagne bottle as its lawyers are with a contract and a red pen.

The five of us were limited to one glass each, and it was while I was on the prowl for some peanuts – or lunch, as I thought of it, such had been the pressure of the day – that I made the mistake of going too near the overweight, red-faced partner from another part of the corporate department who was an infamous fixture at all firm parties. Were this a family do, he'd be known as the drunk uncle who took control of the drinks table and to whom nobody would lay claim to as he slid to the floor. To be charitable, he was of the old school of City solicitor, of whom even at Babbington Botts, there was a diminishing number.

'Bloody good for team bonding, this sort of bash,' he said in a plummy accent, wiping his bald head with a handkerchief. 'You're lucky or something, aren't you?'

It was an odd thing to say. 'I've had my share of luck over the years, I suppose.'

'No, no, the name's Luck or something, isn't it?'

'Fortune, Charles Fortune.' I'd only been on the same floor as him for the past six years.

'Luck. Fortune,' he spluttered in delight. 'D'ya see? God, that's funny.' He nudged me heavily and spilled some of his drink over his sleeve. 'Bugger. I better use some white wine to get that out, hadn't I?' His face then creased in concentration. 'But this is white wine. What the bloody hell do I do now?' He looked at me challengingly.

'Best to keep drinking it, I'd say.' It was like telling a pig that it should roll around in the shit some more, so he happily complied with my advice. After a long slog with Elly and Hannah throughout the day, I counted that a minor victory.

He rested his hand on my arm for balance, which cut off my prospects for escape, before launching into a lengthy monologue about some correspondence he'd been having with Companies House, which was brain-curdlingly dull even by the standards of correspondence with Companies House. He eventually drew breath and I prayed for his bladder to give way. Instead, he shuffled even closer to me and breathed unpleasantly into my ear. 'Do you wanna know something interesting?'

I smiled bravely as he coughed some of his drink back into the glass. 'Of course.'

'You see that filly over there?' His finger wobbled around.

'Erm, which one?'

'The one with the white blouse and pinstripe skirt, obviously. New girl but comes with quite a reputation.' He meant Elly.

'What about her?'

'Nice girl.'

'Very.'

'Nice legs. You can always judge a good filly by the shape of her legs.'

'If you say so.'

'And you'd certainly want to ride that filly.' The onset of more laughter brought on a strong coughing fit which I did nothing to ease.

I stayed silent. Then curiosity got the better of me. 'What kind of reputation?'

192

The partner withdrew his hand from my sleeve in disgust. 'What are you suggesting? A reputation as a very good lawyer, is what I meant.' He paused. 'You haven't heard anything else, have you?' There was a look of hope on his face that turned my stomach.

'No, nothing. Sorry.'

He was quickly mollified. 'Don't tell anyone this, Lucky, but she could be one of the chosen this year.'

My stomach was now revolving at speed. 'The chosen?'

'Don't be stupid. You know – become a partner.'

'Really?' Puking into his face was suddenly looking both a real and entertaining prospect.

'We've got to make at least a couple of women up every year, that's what the board says. I mean, so what that they only go off and have babies. We all know it. Just not allowed to say it any more.'

'Someone's got to do it,' I said. I was keen to say as little as possible; I didn't want to upset his flow.

'Sure they have. But then they want to come back on their terms. Three days a week, two days a week, work from home, work from bloody bed. That's discrimination against men, if you ask me. If I went up to Edward Greene and said, "Look here, old chap, I'd like to work from bed three days a week," he'd tell me to go put my head in a blender. And quite right too.'

'So she's not going to be made up because she's a good lawyer, but just because she's a woman?' That, at least, would ease my misery slightly.

He took a long pull of his drink, which I quickly refilled from a nearby bottle. 'Very decent of you, Lucky. Of course, it's not decided yet. And it does help that she's quite a good lawyer by all accounts.' He turned to me with sudden aggression. 'I mean, it helps, doesn't it? In a law firm? To be a good bloody lawyer? You might as well make my wife up otherwise. At least you'd get a decent cup of tea.' He calmed down just as quickly. 'And it's good that she's a pretty young thing. Not the wife, I mean. That's for sure. The girl Gray. I know that's rather old-fashioned of me, but there you go.' He gurgled some more wine down. 'If you'd seen some of the Helgas we've had to promote in the last few years, it would be enough to make you leave the bloody profession.'

There was a natural pause in the conversation. 'Next thing, we'll have to start making up a quota of pooftahs. Then it'll be time to leave once and for all.'

I grunted rather than trust myself to open my mouth.

He then glanced at his watch and banged down his glass. 'Bugger. Got to run for my train. Have to pick up my wife from her new art class. Any idea what macramé is?' He looked at me expectantly.

'Some sort of art with knots, I think.' That was the kind of vital information one gleaned from growing up in the Home Counties.

He shrugged, uncaring. 'Should come in useful on the boat, I guess.' He leaned up against me again. 'Remember. I never told you any of that.' And he moved unsteadily to the door.

'I wish you hadn't,' I muttered as Elly approached with a kind and warming look on her face.

'What was that all about?' she asked. 'You two were as thick as thieves. Not carving up the partnerships, I hope.' Her laugh was not convincing.

'Yes, actually. Apparently you're a shoo-in because they have a quota of women partners to fill,' I said lightly.

Elly scowled. 'That's not funny, Charlie. If you can't be mature about this, then just don't say anything.'

'You're right,' I said. 'It's not funny at all.'

Chapter Twenty-One

A key part of legal training is learning to cope when you feel totally, despairingly, gun-wrenchingly out of your depth. This happens a lot and the stress sometimes makes my scalp tingle. But it's one of those things they carelessly forget to mention as you pass through the law-school grinder. It was never a case of Tuesday afternoon, an hour of conveyancing followed by company law and then a class on dealing with a stomach ulcer at thirty-five.

In tacit recognition of this, the toilets at Babbington Botts are luxurious affairs, with careful, calming lighting, cool marble as far as the eye can see, and lots of cubicles. We all have our favourites; mine was at the far end, with a proper wall against which one can lean/smash one's head and a piece of graffiti on the back of the door that had defied all attempts to remove it because of the urgency of its advice: 'You don't have to be mad to work here. But you do have to be an insomniac workaholic willing to sacrifice your health, wife, children, spare time and ability to form meaningful relationships with anyone except a dictaphone.'

Friday lunchtime and I was ensconced there, trying to control my breathing. For all the times that clients had demanded an instant answer to a question I didn't even understand, or I had sat in meetings where I was suddenly required to show an intimate knowledge of a law I hadn't known existed until a nanosecond before, coming face to face with the assessment committee was by far the most bottom-loosening experience of my professional career. This time, I would personally face the consequences of getting it wrong, not the client. Worse still, there was no room for bluster; the one piece of advice I had been given some years ago about going before this committee was: 'You can't bullshit bullshitters. And this lot are the best.' The stakes were higher than I dared contemplate. The end. Kaput. Try again next year, they'd actually say, as if the passing of twelve months would make any difference to what they thought of me.

I fortified myself by thinking about the meeting I'd attended the day before at British Pharmaceuticals, where Tom Gulliver, Graham and Ian had made a presentation on the results of the due diligence exercise, after a lengthy briefing from the three of us. Elly, Hannah and I had gone along to provide back-up on the detail if required, and the three issues of concern that were raised all came under my supervision. I thought I acquitted myself well, and Tom gave me a pat on the shoulder as we left. I looked for signs of jealousy in Elly's smile of congratulation, but couldn't tell for sure. 'Rather you than me,' Hannah had said.

Elly had already endured her stint in front of the committee just before lunch, and flopped into the chair by my desk with a relieved sigh as I was dithering over whether to go out and buy a new tie. Having anticipated the dilemma as I dressed, I was wearing a dark suit and crisp white shirt that could be the canvass to any sort of tie I wanted. Did my plain plum effort say I was boring? I am not a superstitious person, but this was my lucky neck-wear, after all – I'd once pulled three weeks running at The Witness Box wearing it.

'That could have been a lot worse,' she said as I regarded the fetching racing green of her suit. That might work. 'An awful lot worse. They were actually rather nice to me.' I wondered whether that was because she was already home and dry. 'Except that Ivor Townsend. He kept scowling at me. I think they had some kind of unsubtle good cop, bad cop thing going.'

Townsend was the partner who'd spilled all the beans on Elly the other day.

'What kind of questions did they ask? Nothing about ties, I presume.' I sounded overly anxious even to my ears.

Elly looked at me quizzically. 'There was a lot of stuff about what I got up to at my old firm, what my ambitions were, that sort of thing. No hypotheticals, no case studies, and nothing, so far as I can recall, about ties. It was far more straightforward than I could possibly have expected. But it's a shame, because I'd really genned up on ties.'

'Sorry, I was just thinking about what tie to wear.'

Elly smiled. 'I know how you feel. My entire wardrobe is on my bed. Usual girly thing: tried this suit on first, then tried every single other suit, and ended up back at this suit, only by then I was late for my train. Clothes selection is one of the few times I envy men.' She mimed throwing open the doors of a cupboard. 'Shall I wear the blue pinstripe suit, or the blue pinstripe suit? No, I know, today I'll go mad and wear my blue pinstripe suit.'

I raised a trouser leg to show that I had a daringly different black pinstripe.

'But that doesn't mean I didn't have time to think about my Charlie.' She reached into the slim document case she was holding and pulled out a flat box with a small bow on it. She handed it over. 'I knew you'd be stressing about your tie. It's the kind of thing you do. You know, utterly fail to see the bigger picture. You might want to work on that bit before the interview.'

I took the box, feeling immensely guilty that I hadn't been so thoughtful, and pulled out a dark green tie with a raised swirly pattern. It was very striking.

'It sets your eyes off really well,' Elly said.

For the first time that day, thoughts of walking into the

197

room, tripping over a chair leg and pushing the coffee tray over the head of corporate's lap diminished. 'You're great,' I said. 'I don't stand a chance.'

'Maybe not,' she said, 'but at least you've got a nice tie for future job interviews.'

We chatted on about the questions they asked, and I felt a little calmer. It didn't sound too trying an experience at all. But once Elly had left to catch up on the latest version of the sale and purchase agreement, doubts crowded back in. Was I up to it? Really, honestly, truthfully, up to it? Or was I just a kid pretending to be a grown-up lawyer and about to be horribly exposed?

In the bathroom half an hour later, I spent about ten minutes tying and retying the knot of my new tie – couldn't be too small, or too big – before retreating to my cubicle. I sat on the seat, trousers up, trying to bully myself into calming down; after all, what kind of thirty-one-year-old was I that I couldn't face an interview with some partners, all of whom could plead guilty to some misdemeanour or other that makes them no less unsuitable for the position than me?

Take Tom Gulliver himself, who a few years back got into a childish spat with another partner over the affections of a female lawyer whose office separated theirs. Not only did Tom arrange at regular intervals for his rival's air conditioning to be turned off during the summer and heating turned off during the winter, but he even called in pest controllers to fumigate the poor sod's room, making it uninhabitable for two weeks, during which Tom made his final – and successful – move on the woman. At the same time, it showed an admirable deviousness that explained why he was where he was.

I then moved on to the 'What difference would it make anyway if I didn't become a partner?' phase of thinking. This involves massive self-deception that I wouldn't have wasted the last eight years and that my life would be just as complete were I to stay a senior associate for ever, or had to leave so I could become an inferior partner at an inferior firm. That was rapidly put to rest by the thought of my bank manager ringing to invite me to an exclusive cheese and wine do at his home after my first Babbingtons partner salary was paid in, together with a fleeting vision of Elly swivelling back and forth gaily on her partner's chair while beckoning a cowed Charlie into her room.

I spent a few minutes pumping myself up with the thought that actually, I am a perfect candidate for partner. I was convinced that I had it in me to become the most fabled of legal species: the rainmaker, the lawyer who brings in the work for the drones to do. I had the looks, presence and experience, a good way with clients, as well as a rudimentary knowledge of lap-dancing clubs that take corporate credit cards and ideas of how to get away with billing the money spent there.

It was a relief when the time finally came. I knocked loudly on the meeting-room door, waited for the shout to enter, and took a very deep breath.

It was just a regular oblong meeting room, with six partners ranged along one side of the table, and a lonely chair opposite them. There was Tom Gulliver, Townsend and four other very senior figures from different departments.

Tom gave me a look of encouragement. 'Do sit down, Charles. This shouldn't be too painful.'

'So the thumb screws are a myth then, are they?' I said lightly, and was met by a wall of blank faces. OK, so that was rule one: don't make jokes.

Rule two, I learned next, was not to gawp stupidly when the first question is a stinker. 'How will you feel, Charles, if you don't get made up?' Rule three was not to whine, 'You never asked Elly any difficult questions. So why are you picking on me?' I worked that one out before I had broken it.

Fortunately, the same went with rule four: think very, very carefully before you speak. My initial reaction – that I would go away and cry in a corner for three days if I wasn't made up – would not have impressed much. I fingered my tie. 'I'd think you'd all made a very bad mistake,' I eventually said with more confidence than I felt.

At least one mouth-twitch upwards as Ivor leaned forward aggressively. 'I'm always being told that we have more than enough corporate partners. Why do we need another one?'

A chill ran through me. Did that mean there was only one slot? But then I felt suddenly emboldened. There was something about this man that wound me up. Was it the mean spirit, the sliver of lunch on his lapel, his attitude to women, or the fact that, for no reason I have ever been able to divine, he thought my name was Lucky?

I leaned forward slightly to meet the challenge. 'No offence, but the average age of the corporate partners is around fifty,' I said. 'The corporate department is the engine of Babbington Botts and you need some more young blood to keep the fire burning. I am a good lawyer, with drive, ambition, an ability to get on with clients and the flair to bring in more.' I sat back, amazed by myself. I sounded, well, like I knew what I was doing. It just showed how I was a Babbingtons lawyer to the core – I had the unthinking aggression and bluntness that made our legal advice so valued.

'So I'm over the hill, am I, Charles?' Tom asked softly.

'No, I didn't say that. I just think you need a good number of lawyers who are still running up it, rather than surveying the scene from the top.' I hadn't meant to go in this brazenly, but knew I had to continue in the same vein. There was every chance that this was the best approach anyway.

But in response, the questions became increasingly aggressive. Had Elly lied or had I simply antagonised them? I was given a nasty hypothetical involving impossible deadlines, impossible clients and impossible legal hurdles, so I tried another breach of rule one. 'That would be the time I would undertake some positive upward delegation,' I said.

'What on earth does that mean?' Ivor spat out.

'That he would ask one of us,' said Tom, with a smile.

'If I've learned one thing in this job,' I agreed, 'it's "Never be afraid to ask."' That was a polite way of saying that actually, if I've learned anything in this job, it is to cover my backside as rapidly and comprehensively as possible. Lawyers never move more quickly than when there is a buck to pass on, so it is always best to bring in a more senior lawyer as he can ultimately take the rap.

'Now,' said Ivor, 'this pro bono work of yours. Tell us more about that.' He said pro bono in a way which made it sound like the practice of snatching young children from the streets and shipping them off to feed the white-slave trade.

'It's once a month for a couple of hours down at Farringdon Law Centre. Very run-of-the-mill legal problems. I enjoy it. It's an interesting break from what we get up to here.'

'I used to do something like that,' Tom reminisced. 'My client base seemed almost entirely made up of ladies of the night.'

I dived back in with way too much enthusiasm. 'Nothing's changed. My most regular client's a prostitute. She just keeps coming.'

Rule five had emerged. If you are going to continue breaking rule one, then don't do it in such a painfully inappropriate way unless you want to see a display of synchronised eyebrow-raising from a group of people you don't want to provoke like that. I stopped myself from compounding the error by joking that the work brought a whole new meaning to the idea of a rainmaker.

Tom looked at his fellow partners. 'It's actually not bad experience in some ways. I certainly learned a few things about client care, shall we say.' There was a sycophantic chuckle and that was when I realised just how badly I wanted to be in the club.

The interview wound down, happily with no detailed questions about the law of prostitution. Townsend seemed to glance at his watch every ten seconds or so, and soon enough I was sent on my way, with a promise that I'd hear shortly about whether I'd made it through to the next stage.

I returned to my desk to find the sale and purchase agreement with a list of things Ash wanted my opinion on. It was the last thing I could concentrate on right then, so I stared out the window and replayed the interview. I was concerned that I had been too aggressive and that had clearly put Townsend's back up. The others had given little away, while Tom Gulliver was a smooth sort who knew that you had to be behind someone before you could stab them in the back.

The phone rang and I picked it up, expecting Elly. Instead it was Sparkle. I was surprised. She'd never called me at work before.

'Hello,' I said. 'This is really spooky. I was just talking about you.'

She sounded agitated. 'Charlie, can I ask you a favour?'

'Not a sexual one, I hope.'

Sparkle was in no mood for jokes. 'It's just that Billy Whizz is in hospital. Somebody beat him up.'

I sat up. 'Is it serious?'

'It's not too bad, but he's an old man.'

'What can I do?'

'The other guys say it's something to do with the house and they're scared stiff. I don't want to ask you this, but do you think you could pop into the hospital tonight and have a quick word with them?'

Elly and I needed a break and some quality time together, and had planned to leave early. But I kept my sigh silent. I could be in and out of there quickly and we'd still have the night to ourselves.

'OK,' I said. 'Tell me where I've got to go.'

Chapter Twenty-Two

Elly was less than impressed when I explained how, before we spent a fun night together, I needed to visit a prostitute and three of her clients in an east London hospital.

'You don't need to see prostitutes now you've got me,' she said in a voice that dripped pity.

'Very funny,' I said. 'For that, you can come with me.'

'Where?'

I adopted a painfully patient expression. 'To visit a prostitute and three of her clients in an east London hospital. It's clear enough, isn't it?'

I started getting ready to go but Elly stayed resolute in the chair in front of my desk. 'I have so many questions beginning with "Why?" and "What the hell?" and "Never in a year of Sundays, buster" but I don't know where to start.'

I realised that my normal amnesia when it came to Sparkle had extended to Elly. I provided a brief history. 'We have this whole lawyer/prostitute thing going. It's quite funny,' I finished.

'Hilarious,' said Elly, still stuck firmly to the chair. 'We should amend your CV. Charles Fortune, specialist in general corporate matters, mergers and acquisitions, and keeping tarts out of the nick.'

'It's multi-skilling,' I grinned.

'It's multi-stupid,' she replied. 'No wonder you haven't told anyone. I can't think of a single person who would be impressed that you've formed a platonic relationship with a prostitute.'

I decided not to mention that it had kind of slipped out in front of the assessment committee. I hadn't stopped berating myself since I left the meeting and could do without another, undoubtedly caustic, dose from Elly.

She rose reluctantly. 'It is platonic, isn't it? If you've got something to tell me, Charlies, let's do it now.'

'Don't be ridiculous. Of course it is. Come on, it'll be fun, trust me. You'll love her.'

That, of course, was a lie wrapped up in a mere exaggeration. For one, the Royal London Hospital in Whitechapel is far from our normal sort of hang-out. Babbingtons provides top-notch private health cover to ensure that should we be struck down, the best doctors are on hand to get us back behind our desks with the minimum of delay. Illness, we were made to understand from day one, is for wimps with no hope of partnership.

The long ward smelled of decay and didn't look much better. I started checking the apathetic forms in the beds for Billy Whizz, but then Sparkle yelled 'Down here, Charlie' from the far end of the ward. She blended in as well as ever, with a rainbow-coloured top, scandalously short purple skirt and green leggings. Every patient seemed half-turned in their beds so they could watch her jump up and wave, as if we could somehow not notice her, although Elly won some attention as she wafted by in the expensive scent she'd lathered on beforehand like sun-block, only in this case it was NHS-block. She was hanging on to my arm in a very proprietorial fashion, feeling uneasy outside of her normal environment.

Billy, white bandages over the right side of his face, looked up at us with a smile, his head as smooth as one of Ash's chat-up lines, His nylon wig sat broodingly on a side table, not unlike something nasty from the Amazon that you see in the insect house at London Zoo. Big Bill and Little Bill scrambled up from their seats by his side and asked Elly if she wanted to sit down. Keen not to make physical contact with anything in the hospital – I'm sure she'd have let me carry her around, had I offered, to keep her shoes free from potential infection – she politely declined.

I made the introductions, leaving Elly and Sparkle to look each other up and down.

'You must be Charlie's young lady,' said Big Bill and Elly's grip on my arm strengthened.

'You've done well for yourself there,' Little Bill said. 'We think he's bleedin' great. Ever such a good lawyer.'

Elly wasn't overwhelmed by the testimonial. 'So he keeps telling me.'

I turned to Billy. 'So, what happened?'

'There was these three blokes, you see,' he began.

'The boss, in a really big suit,' Big Bill said. 'Must have cost a bleedin' bomb.'

'Then this guy he said he was his lawyer.' It was Little Bill's turn. 'Evil-looking. Typical bleedin' lawyer. No offence.' He nodded at us as if that would remove the stigma.

'And this really bleedin' big bloke,' Billy went on. 'As wide as he was tall, you know the sort, Charlie.' Billy clearly had some very odd ideas about the personnel at blue-chip City law firms.

'I could have taken him,' said Big Bill, puffing himself up to his full five-foot six.

'You couldn't have taken him down the bleedin' post office, you idiot,' said Billy, annoyed at being interrupted. 'Anyways, they was going on about how we should sell up and stuff, and should stop bothering them with all these silly letters.'

Little Bill fingered his hat nervously. 'They said there was no point us going down a tin-pot law centre when they had the best legal advice money could buy.'

I bridled. 'They don't know who they're dealing with. Maybe I'll sign my name next time.'

205

'Cos that'll do it for sure,' murmured Elly.

'I told them,' said Big Bill, 'we have such a good lawyer that they'll regret saying that.' I felt oddly grateful.

Little Bill picked up the tale. 'So these two idiots told them where to get off, like you'd advised us.' I suspected this wasn't going to be one of my most glorious moments in the legal profession.

'And they weren't happy,' said Billy.

'They was so unhappy that they knocked the mirror off the wall in the hall,' said Big Bill. 'Said it was a terribly unfortunate accident.'

'As was what happened to the bloody telephone table,' said Little Bill.

I could see the anger building up in Billy. 'Then they said, "oops, look, the phone line's come out of the wall. What a shame," and the big bloke pulled off half the bleedin' wall with it.'

If it wasn't so serious, I'd have laughed out loud at the cartoonish nature of the intimidation. And my advice had caused this; but how was I to know what would happen? Where I came from, if someone didn't like your legal advice, they'd write you a very stiff letter full of 'notwithstandings' and 'hereintobefores'.

Little Bill was shaking his head. 'So Billy here, all of a sudden he thinks he's that Superman or something, and rushed at them.'

'I was bleedin' angry, all right?' Billy protested.

'As fast as a seventy-seven-year-old man with a dodgy hip can rush, of course,' said Big Bill.

'It's fair to say they weren't taken by surprise,' said Little Bill.

Billy was getting restless in the bed. 'Fifty years ago, I'd have had 'em. All of 'em. Easily.'

'That's great, Billy,' said Little Bill. 'We'll ask them to take that into account next time they come knocking. Give you a two-minute head start or something.'

I tried to steer the conversation back to what happened and discovered that Billy's injury came from him being pushed away and hitting the corner of the telephone table, which knocked him out. 'There was bleedin' blood everywhere,' said Little Bill.

Big Bill turned to Elly. 'You don't know how to get blood out of a carpet, do you, dear?'

'Erm, no,' she said, nonplussed. 'Why don't you try some white wine? That seems to work with a lot of things.'

'Not sure we've got any of that,' he mused. 'Will beer do?'

Sparkle dragged us back to what the boys should do. 'I don't want to see the old buggers hurt any more,' she said.

'It's up to you,' I said, trying hard not to make my shrug look like I couldn't care less. 'It's not fair, but at least if you sell up you'll get no more aggro.'

Billy was now sitting up, arms crossed. 'Sod that. They're not getting away with it. I think we should behave like the awkward old sods they think we are anyways.'

'Don't be daft,' said Little Bill. 'Let's just sell up and be safe. The last thing I want is to have to start donating blood to a silly old fool like you.'

Big Bill hesitated and then turned back to Elly. 'I know we seem like daft old men, my dear, but we don't like being pushed around. Didn't like it in the war, don't like it now. I'm not moving just because some bloke broke my mirror.'

Sparkle pulled me aside as the three of them started discussing booby traps they could lay. 'I don't think they're doing the right thing,' she said.

'Hows about some landmines?' Billy was saying. 'That'll give the bleeders a shock and a half.'

'Of course,' said Little Bill. 'I'll just pop down to Tescos and buy some, shall I? Probably get loads of ClubCard points for them too.'

'It's their decision, Sparkle. I'll write one more letter and if nothing happens, then you and me'll get them out of there, OK?' She nodded.

Big Bill appeared excited. 'You know that guy Terry

from the pub? He was telling me the other day how there ain't nothing he can't get.'

Little Bill rolled his eyes. 'He's a rag and bone, man, you silly bugger.'

'We can ask, can't we? One of those Exocets would come in very useful.'

Little Bill laughed at the thought. 'Only if they happen to launch an air attack against us.'

We stayed a few more minutes and then said our good-byes. 'How's the partnership thing going, then?' Sparkle asked.

Elly, who had remained largely silent, swivelled round to look at me. 'She knows about it?'

'Yeah, he told me ages ago,' Sparkle said blithely.

'You told your friend the prostitute – no offence – that you'd been put up for partnership before you told me?' Elly was not impressed.

'It just spilled out,' I said.

'I get a lot of that,' said Sparkle. 'I can recommend some clinics.'

Chapter Twenty-Three

Every lawyer lives in fear of the Armageddon mistake. The blunder which wipes out everything, starting with your own career and rippling outwards to take down your boss, close colleagues and if it goes really, spectacularly wrong, the whole firm. It is of course a nightmare, and yet I would wager that every assistant solicitor at Babbington Botts has occasionally reclined at the end of a long day and thought of ways he or she could deliberately cock up and bring the entire engorged edifice crashing to the ground. The only problem is that you would find yourself at the bottom of the rubble and as yet there has been nobody quite full enough of Samson-like rage to do it.

It happens every decade or so that a law firm gets hit with such a horrendous negligence claim that its insurance doesn't cover it. And here's about the only sting in the tail of being a partner: it's fine and dandy when everything's going well, but should the insurance cover run out and the partnership find itself still owing, then all of its members have to dig deep into those overly capacious pockets.

And it gets worse: there is no end to the partners' individual liability. It's never got to the stage of leaving partners in a miserable line at the bankruptcy court – appealing though the image is, especially when you throw in some stubble, frayed trousers and wild, staring eyes – but in theory it could.

At law school there were tales like bedtime horror stories of one firm which got into sufficient trouble that the partners had to sell their fourth, third and even second homes, caused a week-long Stock Market slump by liquidating chunks of their vast holdings and then had to fly club-class rather than first-class for a period.

Of course, they were not the only people to suffer. The anguished cry went out, 'What about the children? Is nobody thinking about the children?' Trained counsellors were brought in specially to help teenagers in a certain part of Surrey, who threw the most terrible hissy fits because they couldn't understand why it was that their daddies couldn't buy them BMWs for their seventeenth birthdays like all their friends' daddies had.

As a junior lawyer, I was far too heavily supervised for any of my many mistakes to slip through the net. There was one time when, in a blue funk, I dictated a letter which began, 'Dear Dickhead, Your constant whining makes me want to vomit', and because I had a temporary secretary, it came perilously close to actually being sent, but you can't get sued for that kind of thing anyway.

But as I rose up through the ranks, I was given more and more autonomy to make my own uncorrected blunders. That I had lasted so long showed my ability to either (a) not make any mistakes, or (b) cover them up real fast. The test of your legal mettle isn't whether you can adhere to (a) – we're all human, after all – but whether you have the balls to cope with (b), especially when the shit is about to sail past the fan and land straight on your head and your head alone. There's nothing like the premature conclusion of one's career to focus the mind.

In a deal the size of British Pharmaceuticals, the probability of something going wrong escalated to a near certainty. One could only hope that first and foremost, it wasn't your fault, and second, that it wouldn't scupper the whole deal or the whole firm.

In any case, in the hurly-burly of it all, you have little time to consider this possible downside. I, along with Elly, Hannah, Ash and Lucy, was far too busy scurrying from one meeting to the next for a good four weeks as we tried to finalise the sale and purchase agreement. There were meetings with each other followed by meetings with the partners, after which we got back together again to prepare for our next meeting with the other side. After that we would meet with each other once more, meet with the partners and go back into our meeting room to prepare for our next meeting with the other side. Now and again we would enjoy the variety of meeting with our client, taking more instructions and beginning the whole wearying process once more. At least once every three days we had to have a meeting to schedule the meetings for the next three days.

This week, my parents had come up to London one day demanding to see me, and I had to block out an hour of my diary as a BPharm meeting to ensure I could make it. There was always the possibility that in going back through my diary to check what I should be billing, I would accidentally include that hour, but it wasn't like anyone would notice. Our fees would soar into the millions as it was; another £240 here or there wasn't going to bother anyone.

'I hope we haven't got you out of anything important,' Mum said as we squeezed into the plastic seats attached to the table at a nearby greasy spoon.

'Not at all,' I said, glancing at my watch out of reflex more than anything. As luck should have it, there was a momentary lull in work but I still felt anxious that things were happening which I needed to be in the office for. 'I try to make it a point every day to see sunlight. I always go out for at least twenty minutes; I'm seen as quite a rebel, in fact. So it's a treat to take a whole hour off. But I need to be back for a meeting at two.'

'Still,' Dad said, 'it's good money.' They had eagerly tracked my salary over the years, giving regular updates to their friends. It was like the Blue Peter Pound-ometer, or whatever they called it. As the plucky little gauge rose past the £50,000, £60,000, £70,000 and £80,000 mark, they had broadcast the happy news. The top level, which partnership would take me to, was marked 'Set up for life – all we ever wanted for our son'.

We chatted idly about their day out in London; it was something they did every couple of months, telling their friends mysteriously that they had a series of appointments in the hope that everyone would conclude they had a stash of gold at Coutts which they checked up on regularly.

Mum was playing coyly with her sausage, chips and peas. 'And, erm, how's everything going with Eleanor?'

They hadn't seen us since that Sunday lunch; even if we'd had the inclination – which we didn't – we simply had not had the time. 'It's all been work, work, work. Hardly any time for ourselves,' I lamented. 'But basically it's all going great.'

If it were humanly possible, I'm sure Mum would have glowed. 'Some things are more important than work,' she said, suddenly oblivious to a lifetime's ambition for me. I just caught Dad mutter to her, 'Eighty-five thousand pounds.'

'You try telling that to the chairman of British Pharmaceuticals,' I said and got matching blank looks in return.

'We had dinner with Uncle Tony and Aunty Hilary the other day,' Mum went on tentatively. That was the only permissible alternative to 'Mr and Mrs Gray' and 'Eleanor's parents' in front of me.

'I can't imagine what you talked about,' I said.

'It was funny, actually, because we were both talking about flats. I was telling Aunty Hilary about how you had that big old flat to yourself, and then she said that Eleanor was also rattling around in ever such a large flat.' So a score draw on the bragging, I thought. 'Then your father here starts grumbling about the ridiculous cost of property in London—'

212

'Did you know that a shed in Kensington went for £110,000?' It wasn't often that Dad interrupted, but property prices boil the blood of any right-minded Home Counties resident. 'A shed. A simple wooden shed like I have at the end of the garden, so it said in the paper. Madness. Absolute madness.'

Mum quelled him with a glance. 'As I was saying, we were talking about your flats and then together we said, "Why don't they move in with each other?" Both together, just like that. It was quite spooky.'

I was too amazed that my mother had hurdled a few decades of social mores in a few weeks to deride the contrived story. 'That would be quite a step,' I said. 'Are you sure you're ready for it?'

'Oh we are,' she confirmed readily. 'What about you, Charlie?'

It would be lying to say that the idea hadn't crossed my mind several times, but then, I'm a lawyer. 'Never really thought about it,' I said. 'That time I was going to move in with Mary, you were dead against it, as I recall.'

Mum was dismissive. 'Oh, that was different. We like Eleanor.'

Mary had been a sweet girl; we'd gone out for about seven months a couple of years back. But she made the fatal error, while admirably trying to ingratiate herself, of producing a far better selection of desserts than my mother ever could. Mary was particularly good at a luscious chocolate cheesecake, but to judge by Mum's face the first time she tasted it, the cake was full of the bitterest lemon rind.

I got busy with my watch as a way of bringing lunch to an end. 'Look, I've got to go. I've a meeting in a few minutes. I'll really think about what you said, though. But it's so busy at work at the moment that we haven't got time to talk about anything properly.'

Mum looked disappointed. I sensed she had Pickfords on instant call-out so she could go straight to my flat, pack everything up, and have me settled in at Elly's by teatime.

213

I wasn't lying when I said that we'd had little time for anything other than work, though. Frankly, the most erotic thing that had passed between us in what seemed like weeks was a couple of days before, when Elly had burst into my room and panted, 'God, I need you.'

Richard's eyeballs almost rolled out of their sockets so they could put themselves at Elly's service; he wasn't close to being over his infatuation yet.

I smiled modestly. 'Everyone needs a bit of Charlie now and again.'

'Oh, sorry. Was that your ego inflating?' Elly asked. 'False alarm, I'm afraid. Right this moment, all I need is your signature.'

It turned out that in the middle of everything, Elly had to handle a small matter for an overseas client she had brought over from her last firm. It was, she had proudly explained, the first good rain she had made and as she told it, they came out of nowhere, simply saying they'd heard many good things about her. She had set up an English subsidiary for them – 'They even trusted me to come up with a name for it,' she said with unreasonable pride – but house rules at Babbingtons meant that she needed another signatory on its bank account. 'It's nothing,' she said. 'Just form filling.'

With a shrug, I put pen to paper, thinking that the name of the company – Worthington Trumpet – rang the most distant of bells. As Elly was leaving, I asked whether she had any plans for that night after the last meeting of the day.

'I was hoping to go home, get a Chinese and curl up on the sofa in front of something mindless,' she said with a smile. 'I guess you'll do.'

In the end, I got back from lunch early, having sent my parents on their way with a promise to arrange another Sunday that I had no intention of keeping. I was weighing up what I could do in the twenty minutes I had spare before I was due to meet with the gang when the phone rang.

214

'Charlie,' a voice croaked.

'Who is this?'

The distress was palpable. 'Oh God, Charlie.'

'Hannah? Is that you?'

'I went for lunch and it was here when I came back. I was only gone fifteen minutes.'

I stood in alarm. 'What's happened? What was there when you got back?'

'Come quick, Charlie. Please.' And she put the phone down.

I hurried over to the other side of the floor and knocked on her door. There was no reply so I carefully opened it and poked my head around the side. The square room was virtually identical to mine except for the different pictures on the wall. Hannah was kneeling on the floor by the side of her desk, looking at the chair behind it.

'Oh God, Hannah,' I breathed, slipping in and closing the door.

She turned with huge watery eyes. 'I don't know what I did.'

The chair was calamitous. Awful. Appalling. Unthinkable. Tragic. A mistake, surely. Not Hannah, please. Not my Hannah.

What should have been there was Hannah's junior executive chair. She'd only graduated to it six months before and had been overjoyed. It told her she was going places far more than any bog-standard pay rise. Cool black plastic, smooth metal wheels and a well-oiled lever to bring forth the joys of reclining.

And now it was gone. In its place was the type of rigid fabric chair on bumpy plastic wheels that was standard issue for trainees. This was worse than insulting. It was catastrophic. With shaking hands, Hannah pointed to the memo on her desk, entitled 'Redeployment of reclinable resources'. She'd been Triple-R'd. The P45 was probably being processed as we gazed at one another. She looked so very desperate and I felt so very powerless. It was a brutal moment.

I got down on my knees and held her as she sobbed into my shirt. Shamefully, as I gripped Hannah tight, my first thought was for myself. Was this a group cock-up which could catch me or was it just Hannah in the frame? I couldn't think of anything specific that I had fears over, but then it is usually the little things that catch you out.

'Do you know what happened?' I asked softly.

Hannah shook her head against my chest. 'Got a meeting in ten minutes with Tom Gulliver,' she said, sniffling hard.

That made it worse. Definite. Were it something minor, her supervising partner would deal with it; that she'd been called to the head of department could only mean one thing. Another one was about to bite the dust.

We had enjoyed so many times together, so many evenings down the pub or just the two of us out on a Saturday night. Her sofa was like my weekend retreat. In some ways, she was my soulmate as much as Elly was.

I would miss her terribly, but there was a cold, selfish, if minuscule corner of my mind high-fiving and whooping for joy that it wasn't me and that the race for partnership had lost another runner. I hated myself that I could think like that. I hated Babbingtons for making me think like that.

There was a knock on the door and Lucy strolled in brightly. 'Wahey, what have we got here?' she said, grinning down at us. 'Caught in the act. And you a semi-married man, Charles Fortune. Shame on you.'

I simply nodded to the chair. It took a moment of incomprehension, but then Lucy's eyes widened in fear. She picked up the memo and clamped a hand over her mouth.

She fell to the carpet and relieved me of Hannah. 'Oh, Hannah. I'm so sorry,' she said. 'Do you know what happened?'

Hannah was crying again, so Lucy looked to me for an answer. I shrugged. 'She's seeing Tom in a few minutes.'

'Then we can't have you looking like this,' Lucy said decisively, and with my help pulled Hannah on to the chair in front of the desk. Lucy began tidying her up, digging into the desk for some make-up.

216

Five minutes later, we had Hannah as presentable and as geed up as we could get her, which wasn't very. 'Be confident and argue your corner,' I said, holding her by the shoulders and then pulling her into an embrace. 'It's probably an awful mistake on their part which you'll have to talk yourself out of.'

'That's what you're good at,' Lucy continued. 'You're a bloody great lawyer and don't you forget it.' She gave Hannah a big hug too and sent her on her way.

We promised to wait for her, me sitting in the hateful chair, Lucy in front of the desk.

'I don't believe it,' I said after a long silence. We all knew Hannah to be supremely meticulous.

'You don't believe it?' Lucy said. 'I don't believe it. Not Hannah. She's so meticulous. I could believe it of you. You can be very careless at times.'

Before I could react, Ash and Elly appeared at the door, Ash tapping his watch. 'We've got a meeting? Surely you haven't forgotten? What else do we do but have meetings? Charlie, you're always forgetting things, but Luce, I expect you to be the first one there every time.'

Elly tutted. 'Yeah, you slackers. Lazing around and yakking away like there's no work to be done. I expect it of you, Charlie, but Lucy, I'm very disappointed.'

'Guys,' Lucy said quietly. 'We've got a crisis. Hannah's in the shit.'

'Hence the chair,' I added. Ash looked at it and realisation dawned. I handed him the memo he immediately began searching for. I filled them in and they looked suitably horrified, Elly less so than Ash, but then she didn't have the history. 'I don't believe it,' Ash said. 'Hannah's so meticulous. Every morning she makes sure she has at least three pencils sharpened to her exact requirements.'

'I once caught her measuring them with a ruler,' Lucy said, and we all laughed nostalgically.

We continued 'I don't believing' it for a few more minutes until Elly, who had suddenly gone very quiet, said, 'I think I might know what's happened.'

217

But at that moment, Hannah returned. She was pale and shaking slightly. She gave Elly a brief, grim smile and came over to the desk. I leaped up so she could sit, and Hannah then went straight to the top drawer and began pulling out objects randomly.

'I want to keep my pictures of the 1999 fancy-dress party. They'll let me, won't they? Pictures of Charlie dressed as Wonderwoman aren't Babbingtons property, are they?' Her voice was thick and even the thought of the hideously drunk partner who had pinched my bottom and slipped me his mobile phone number that night did not lighten the mood.

'What happened?' I asked quietly.

'Do you think I can take my mug? I really hope so.'

It was her 'I've got the hots for Botts' mug, officially the worst campaign in marketing history. Some years ago, when marketing meant partners schmoozing at their Masonic lodges, the firm had run a staff competition to come up with a slogan. We dreamed it up one hilarious Friday night; less acceptable efforts included 'Where the law costs more,' 'Putting the illicit into solicitors' and 'My friend went to law school and all he bought me was this lousy Porsche'. But only in our bizarre little world could ours have actually won through the approval process – they probably thought they were being really trendy – and found its way on to other trinkets such as pens and T-shirts. The collectors' items were the handful of underpants inspirationally produced with the slogan to the rear before someone pointed out that it wasn't quite the image Babbington Botts wanted to project.

Hannah rummaged at the back of the drawer and produced a small metal trophy on a plastic stand with an inscription that read: 'Third place, Babbington Botts Mixed Doubles Table Tennis Tournament, 1996/97'. Finally, she looked up at me. 'Do you remember?' Her smile was fond.

Such was the lack of camaraderie at the firm that just four teams entered. In fact, we only came third because of a comedy accident involving Ash and Lucy. Ash had smashed the ball so hard that he fell on to the cheap table, which promptly snapped upright like a Venus fly trap. He was all right, but the edge of the table caught Lucy a knockout blow on the chin as it whipped upwards.

'You should have this now. It'll remind you of me.'

I took her outstretched hand and wouldn't let it go. 'Hannah. What happened?'

She blinked wearily. 'What do you think happened? He sacked me. Said it would be on notice, rather than instant dismissal in view of my loyal service over the years.'

Lucy put her hands over her face. I felt my eyes prickling. 'But why?'

'I didn't co-ordinate the submission to the Competition Commission seeking approval of the merger.'

There was a pained silence. The single thought circulating between the rest of us was, 'Not quite so shocked now'. That was an appalling howler, no two ways about it. Potentially an absolute disaster. If we ploughed ahead and then got hit by the Competition Commission, it could be very messy, not to mention expensive. It was the kind of issue you would think was too big to overlook, but there were so many things going on at the same time that it was far from impossible.

'I know what you're all thinking,' Hannah said, hackles rising. 'But it was never my job to organise it. I'm sure of that.'

'So why are you taking the blame?' asked Ash.

'Because apparently it *was* my job,' she said bitterly. 'There were bloody memos from Ian and Elly in the file about it. I just never saw them. Don't remember being told to do the submission in my briefing, but Ian swears blind that he told me.' She looked over at Elly. 'Don't feel guilty. It's not your fault. Somehow, I cocked up and now I'm getting what I deserve.'

Nobody had anything useful to say, and then there was a knock on the door. It was my secretary. 'Sorry to interrupt, Charlie,' Sue said, 'but Tom Gulliver wants to see you.' My throat contracted. Was I next? 'All of you, actually. And right now. Erm, except you, Hannah.' Sue was desperate to know what had happened. There would be maximum respect in the typing pool for information like this. I shook my head slightly and she reluctantly ducked back out.

We turned back to Hannah, who waved us away. The anger was building in her, I could tell. 'The world goes on. Babbingtons goes on. Don't worry about me. I'll see you all later. You better get off to that meeting.'

The others filed out awkwardly, but I lingered. 'If you want anything, if you need anything, just call, OK?' I said, concerned by the tension I could see building up around her eyes.

Hannah suddenly picked up the trophy and flung it violently at the wall. The cup flew off the base on impact and bounced back towards her. She looked up at me again. 'Sorry about the cup,' she said, tears beginning to fall. 'Sorry about everything.'

I knelt back down to her level and opened my arms. Hannah hesitated momentarily, dropped out of the chair and wrapped herself around my chest. And then she cried and cried and cried.

Chapter Twenty-Four

I had to go back to my office and collect my jacket before whizzing off to see Tom. Hannah's tears made it look like I'd just completed a five-mile run, and it wouldn't do for the head of corporate to see me like that, whatever the circumstances.

She had wept for about five minutes, before insisting that I leave and go to the meeting. 'There's no point you getting into trouble as well, especially over me,' she said, but her voice was so unhappy that all I wanted to do was hug her harder and try to make her feel better. But she pushed me away and got to her feet. 'Go, Charlie, please. I need some time alone.'

Reluctantly, I acquiesced, but made her promise eight times to call me the moment she needed anything, including a chest to cry on again.

At last I got a watery smile. 'You can count on it, Charlie. Nobody's chest beats yours. I've at least learned that over the years.'

I trusted that she wouldn't do anything stupid, much though the end of a career at Babbingtons is made to feel like the end of life itself. At least the windows were sealed: officially to ensure the air conditioning would work properly; unofficially, I was certain, to ensure no overly stressed assistant took the scenic route to the ground floor.

Several pairs of eyes were on me as I hurried over to my office, but I just kept looking straight ahead. The grapevine was humming, I was sure of that. I'd done enough to keep it going over the years myself, but it was the least of my concerns right now.

I stopped short. My door was closed; I could have sworn that I'd left it slightly ajar. I eyed it with mounting suspicion and fear. What if I was in the frame as well? What if I'd missed some memos? Had my chair already gone to a better place? Was some grey monstrosity lurking behind my desk, waiting to wheel me unevenly to the end of my career?

My hand lay on the knob for what seemed a long time. 'You OK, Charlie?' Sue said from behind me.

'Yeah, fine,' I replied, breathing hard.

'What's going on?'

'I'll tell you later,' I said, finding the courage to open the door.

My chair was there, just as I had left it. 'Stupid sod,' I breathed, scooping up the jacket and hastening off to Tom's room. I knocked lightly on his door and slipped in; the others were already there ranged around a small conference table. You know when you are in a senior partner's room: there are more windows than doors, and more spare chairs than windows.

Tom nodded me into a spare seat. 'I understand that you all already know what's happened. I don't have to tell you what a catastrophe has been averted. Well done Eleanor for spotting it. I won't forget that in a hurry.' Three sets of surprised eyes swivelled in her direction and I was at least successful in concealing my shock. Elly had squealed? Elly had dropped Hannah in it? Elly? My Elly? My Hannah? She looked back at me uncertainly. Tom either didn't notice or feigned not to. He had no interest in getting caught up in our squabbles. 'The fact is, though, that you four will have to soldier on without any more help. I think

222

it's too late to bring anyone new in, and in any case, I'm confident that you can handle the rest of the preparation before I step in and grab all the glory.'

There was the odd sycophantic smile. 'One day, the glory will be yours too,' he said to us all, but his gaze seemed to linger on Elly. 'Just not today or any day in the near future, I'm afraid.' He chuckled. 'Right, pep talk over. Let's get back to work, shall we?'

To him, the end of another associate's career was nothing more than the Darwinian order at work. He had risen so far partly on being a man known for having compassion – which marked him out among many of his colleagues and gave him a better rapport with the staff – but he tempered that warm emotion with a ruthlessness that would not broke anything coming between Babbington Botts and its rightful place at the pinnacle of the City legal establishment.

Without saying anything, the four of us returned to my room. I closed and locked the door.

'It wasn't my fault, you have to believe me,' Elly said instantly. She was leaning defensively against the wall with her arms folded; the rest of us kept our distance. 'Ian asked me to send the memos and then Tom comes to me about ten-thirty this morning and asks where we are on the competition clearance. You were all in that client meeting. I didn't know when you'd be back.' That was true; every time, one of us stayed behind just in case something urgent came up, and today it had been Elly's turn.

'I said I'd review the file to make sure, but he asked for a reply by eleven.' That sounded like Tom. His eminently reasonable streak meant he would give you twenty minutes to do something that would take a minimum of two hours; most other partners would give the time it took for the impulse to travel from your brain to your mouth.

'So I look at the file, see nothing's been done and panic. The last thing I want to do is drop anyone in it, but I could already hear them sharpening their blades.'

Lucy was hostile. 'So you ratted her in, did you?'

'No, I didn't,' Elly said emphatically. 'I told Ian confidentially, but he was the one who ratted. I promised we'd sort it, but he went straight to Tom.'

In a firm where untrustworthy, weasely, two-faced partners are the norm, Ian was setting new standards. If he wasn't careful, he'd put an end to our Bastard Partner of the Week award by claiming the crown indefinitely.

Elly looked so distressed that my heart went out to her. This was the woman I loved, yet I was doing nothing to defend her. 'I thought I could trust him,' she was saying, 'but he told me it was better to get a head start on the shit before it starts to fly.'

'You could have waited until we'd got back. Not told anyone,' Ash insisted.

She bristled with defiance. 'Who knew what time you'd get back? I could hardly call you at the client's and tell you there's a huge emergency, could I? What else could I do? Would you have waited?'

There was a thoughtful silence as we all wondered what we would have done in the same circumstances. Elly had simply adhered to the prime directive and covered her backside. Who wouldn't want to outrun the shit? There's no valour in taking a bullet for somebody else in this game – everyone thinks you're stupid and you just wind up getting killed.

'I hate to say this, I really do,' I said finally, moving over to Elly and squeezing her hand. 'But if Hannah cocked up, ultimately this is her fault. Not Elly's. However unhappy we may all be about it.'

'Thanks for that objective viewpoint.' Ash shook his head. 'She should have given us a chance to put it right. Hannah's helped all of us over the years, far more than we've helped her. It was the least she deserved.'

Lucy sighed. 'Charlie's right, Ash. This is the biggest deal in history. We can't cover up mistakes like that. You may have suddenly come over all masochistic, but group suicide's not my thing.'

Ash tutted violently, but he knew we were right. We all

felt crushed by what had happened, but the cold fact was that Hannah had only herself to blame. It wasn't up to us to cover her tracks. We may have all been firm friends, but in an environment like this, friendship has well-defined limits and they stop well short of self-sacrifice.

There was a sense of utter dejection in the room; then the phone rang. It was Hannah. The pain in her voice was evident as she said my name. 'I'm coming right now,' I said. I made to hurry out.

'We've got to get back to it,' Lucy said grimly. 'We can't afford to waste the whole afternoon. There's too much to do by tomorrow.'

We all moaned but Babbington Botts rolls on inexorably. There was reluctant agreement that the other three would plough on and I would join them as soon as possible. Frankly, I was relieved to be leaving them until I got to Hannah's room and found her angrily booting her bin across the floor.

'Bastard,' she snapped at me. My eyebrows shot up. 'Not you. Ken Bastard Sutherland. Bastard.'

Uh oh. Ken Bastard Sutherland – which was what everyone actually called him, as it so happened – was the firm's property tycoon and made a mint renting out decent-quality accommodation to young solicitors safe in the knowledge that they could afford it. Hannah thought this relationship would also guarantee regular pay rises and had been renting her flat from him for five years; she loved the place and once asked if she could buy it from him. You could hear the laughter on the other side of the building. 'What happened?'

She stopped pacing to glare at me. 'So I'm here alone, feeling pretty damn miserable what with one thing and another. One thing being I've lost my job, and the other being that I'll probably never find another one that doesn't involve wearing a pinny of some kind.' I smiled, but she pursed her lips violently at me. I assumed a grave expression at once. 'And then Ken Bastard Sutherland comes in to say he's heard what happened and that maybe it would be best if I moved out of the flat. Next bloody week.' She gave the bin an almighty kick against the wall. 'Bastard,' she yelled. 'I'll give him "inappropriate to stay".'

'Well, at least it's taken your mind off of getting sacked,' I said.

It would be fair to say that Hannah goggled. I'd never seen a person do that before, but there was no other way to describe the way her head shot forward, eyes widened and incredulity – of a dangerous rather than amused nature – spread across her features.

One of the few real problems with being a man, in my experience, is the inability to say the right thing when faced by a major female emotional eruption. Providing things to cry against is not the problem, but it just delays the moment when she looks up at you with tear-stained cheeks to say, 'What should I do?' and all you want to do is shrug and reply, 'I dunno. Why are you bothering to ask me? What do I know? Can we talk about last night's match now?'

'At least it's taken my mind off of getting sacked?' Her voice was rising fast. 'Is that meant to make me feel better?'

Don't say yes, don't say yes, don't say yes. 'No,' I said quietly. Phew.

Her eyes had taken on a manic quality. 'Because it hasn't, Charlie, I've got to be honest.'

The important thing, I knew, was not to start blaming anyone. 'Look, Hannah, you're just taking your anger out on me, which is quite understandable . . .'

'I'm sorry if I'm making you feel uncomfortable, Charlie, but my life is in ruins. FUCKING RUINS, GET IT?' As I began to advance slowly in an attempt to pacify her, she reached behind and randomly picked up a paper-weight from her desk. I retreated, fancying my chances better from a distance were I to say the wrong thing again.

'Hannah, I know it seems bad now, but there are worse things that could happen.' I wished at once that I hadn't said it, because I couldn't think of one.

'Such as?' She was tossing the paperweight from one hand to another like a shot-putter does before winding up to throw.

I wondered idly whether all men were as useless in these situations as me. I glanced at Hannah's *Octopussy* poster and recalled the many James Bond arguments we had enjoyed. 'Roger Moore is the most honest portrayal of a male character you will ever see,' she always insisted. 'A twitch of the eyebrow is your average male's entire emotional range.'

'Erm, erm, at least you've got your teeth.'

She was nonplussed. 'Teeth.'

'Rather than metal ones, I mean.'

'Metal ones? Are you deranged?'

I nodded at the poster and she turned. Then with a yell of 'fucking Ken Bastard Sutherland', she flung the paperweight at it, shattering the glass. She caught Roger in a place that took the 00 out of 007.

She turned back to me, face red. 'It's just so unfair. Why is this happening to me?'

Rather than point out that the fault ultimately lay with her, I wisely stayed silent.

'I know what you're going to say,' she said, more flatly. 'It's all my fault. I know that. I still don't understand how I did it, though.'

'It's a difficult deal,' I said. 'It's not that hard to over-look something.'

'Something this important? I don't think so. Anyway, this is me we're talking about, Charlie, not you.' Why did everyone keep saying that? 'I always double-check I'm wearing matching underwear before I leave the flat just in case I get run over.'

'I've always wondered about that. I mean, what do you think is going to happen? "Stop searching for that severed arm a moment, Bob, and come and take a look at this. Pink bra and yellow knickers? What on earth was she thinking when she got dressed this morning? Some people, eh?"'

227

She smiled slightly, the tension fading. 'Exactly. A girl's got to have standards.'

I moved towards her cautiously, palms wide to show I was emotionally unarmed. 'Hannah, there's nothing I can say to make you feel better, but I want you to know that I'm your friend and I'll do anything I can to help. If you want, you can stay with me while you sort yourself out.'

'Oh, Charlie,' she said, grabbing for my chest again. 'Thank you for being my friend.'

Once more, she began crying into my shirt and I knew exactly what she meant. We all had so few friends in this place, real friends at least, that the ones we did have made a huge difference to our lives. As I felt her body heave with sobs, the anger began to grow in me too. Why couldn't people like Ken Bastard Sutherland treat us non-partners like fellow human beings, rather than sub-species put on the earth for their entertainment and enrichment? Why couldn't people like Ken Bastard Sutherland see the misery they cause?

When I eventually disengaged myself from Hannah, and left her to go and sort out a few things with human resources – a highly appropriate name that always made me think of body snatchers – I was still steaming. I had decided to make my stand. Ignoring all attempts to intercept me, I marched to the lift and waited impatiently for it to transport me up six floors to the property department, home to the evil Sutherland.

A speech was forming rapidly in my head. It was Churchillian in its call for human rights, even for trainee solicitors. It was biting in its analysis of Sutherland's arrogance and rudeness. It was humbling in the way it showed just what people thought of him. 'I am not just a walking timesheet,' I would finish, passion cracking my voice. 'I am a person with as much right to dignity, respect and the odd early night as you. A person who has the ability to love more than just his stapler. A person—' And here my voice would drop, laden with exhaustion. 'A person who just wants to be free.'

228

It was everything I'd ever wanted to say to a partner without resorting to a stream of expletives that would make a Mafia hitman blush.

I stormed past a surprised secretary and straight through his open door. Sutherland was sitting with his feet on the table, writing on a legal pad. After carefully finishing his sentence, he looked up at me. 'Something I can do for you, Mr Fortune?'

'It's about Hannah Klein's flat,' I began aggressively.

He threw the pad on to the desk. 'It's only been on the market about ten minutes. I'm impressed, Fortune. Talk about get up and go. You got up and the flat went. It's a thousand pounds a month single occupancy if you take it now, eleven hundred if you wait a day.'

I was just about to launch into my speech when I noticed his pen. A pen so magnificent in its sparkling shininess (could that nib actually be made from gold? It seemed possible) that it said everything about being a Babbington Botts partner.

I tried not to be shallow. Tried really, really hard. I didn't want to be shallow and in very many ways, I wasn't. I wasn't just interested in the money, the status or the power. But put it all together, and I wanted to be the kind of person who wielded a pen like that. I wasn't proud of this realisation – and hoped desperately that it wasn't really me, but rather the person Babbingtons had moulded me into – but that still didn't make it any less true at that moment.

My speech, for all its absolute truth and magnificence, was also about to deprive me of my job, home, prospects and future. A glorious end that would be passed down as legend by one generation of assistants to the next, I was sure, but an end nonetheless.

Sutherland tapped the pen against his left thumb impatiently. 'The price is going up every minute we wait here, you know,' he said.

Yet my friend had been dumped on and there was nobody to stand up for her, nobody willing to tell Ken

Bastard Sutherland what a bastard he was. I braced myself to take the highly novel approach of putting principles before profit. 'I don't want the flat,' I began.

He threw the pen down. 'Why didn't you say? You're wasting my time, Fortune.'

The words teetered on the edge of my tongue as I watched the pen roll across the table and off the edge by me. I leaned down and caught it neatly, avoiding the ink. It felt like it could write a thousand extravagant cheques. 'But I know someone who might be interested,' I said quietly, hating and congratulating myself at the same time.

Sutherland was suddenly my best friend again. 'Why didn't you say? Send them round pronto, will you? This one'll go quickly, I suspect.'

I mumbled my thanks and retreated. What had I been thinking? Who would gain from a martyr's sacking, except my partnership rivals? It wouldn't make the slightest difference to the firm, and soon I would be on the lookout for new digs as well. I just wanted to help Hannah, and the best way to do that was to avoid following her out the door.

I walked back to the lift, relieved to have caught myself in time. But a small part of me wished with all of its might that I'd had the courage to see it through.

Chapter Twenty-Five

The next few days were miserable: miserable because we were staggering under the most appalling amount of work, and miserable because Hannah was leaving.

While her sacking was on notice, it was thought prudent to get her out of the office sharpish. It was a super-refined version of the black sack, burly security guard, don't talk to anyone about anything and don't darken our doorstep again method of dismissal. She was frozen out of everything and advised not to come into the office except to take her belongings and finalise her departure.

The following weekend, the rest of us downed tools on Sunday afternoon to help her move out. Some of her stuff was coming to my flat, for which Elly, Lucy and Ash were responsible, but a lot of the larger items – including my beloved sofa – was going to her parents' garage, for which she hired a small van and asked me to help.

She cried once more when leaving the flat for the last time. The memories were good and she'd gone around every room, telling me a story about each. When we glanced into the airing cupboard, she just giggled.

'I refuse to believe it,' I said. 'There isn't room to swing a cat.'

'I wouldn't know,' she said. 'Cat-swinging wasn't top of the priority list when we were in there.'

I didn't bother asking why they squeezed into the airing cupboard when there were plenty of more spacious and comfortable locations. It's one of those things that seems a good idea at the time until you fling out a hand with the passion of it all and tip a heavy pile of towels on your head.

'That doesn't sound like the normal NJBs you go out with,' I noted sternly. 'You didn't tell me about him. Was this one not an accountant then?'

'He was, but I got him drunk,' she said sadly. 'It was the only way to stop him talking about double-entry book-keeping.'

We moved into the empty living room. 'Where it all began,' she sighed.

'Eh?'

'For you and Elly, I mean.'

I shrugged. 'Oh yeah, so it did.'

'Do you remember how I walked in on you? That was so embarrassing.'

'You should have seen it from my angle.'

She turned to me and hugged me again; she had become very touchy feely of late, needing reassurance all the time that I wasn't going to turn my back on her. 'Still, I'm glad you're happy, Charlie. It's important to me. I've got all my partnership hopes riding vicariously on you now. I really hope you get it ahead of Ash and Lucy.'

My attention had wandered slightly to memories of grappling with Elly on the floor, but I was flooded at once with that horrid sense of panic. 'Ash and Lucy?'

'I shouldn't say anything, but I don't really care now. They've been put up for partnership. I saw a memo on Lucy's desk about going before the assessment committee when I was in her room. And Ash was chatting up this girl at another firm who I was at law school with, telling her he was going to be a partner.'

My heart sank further still. 'They've been put up? Oh no.'

'I had my interview with the committee a few weeks back.'

'You did?'

'Yeah. It went really well, ironically enough. It was quite funny actually. After Gulliver fired me, I said to him "Will this count against me with the assessment committee?" He laughed so hard he almost had a hernia. "Good to see you're taking it like a man," he said.' She smiled. 'He got all friendly after that. Told me that I had the right attitude and that he was really sorry he had to do it. Said I would have made a fine partner. It was nice of him.'

There was a silence as we contemplated how success had been snatched from her.

'What about you, Charlie?'

Could I trust her? She'd spilled the beans on the others easily enough.

She knew what I was thinking. 'I won't tell anyone. Promise. You're the one who's been a real friend through all of this.'

'Well then, yes. I've been put up. So has Elly. You've got to promise not to tell.'

She put her hand to her heart solemnly. 'Promise.'

'Not that it matters. Lucy's bound to get it. And Elly, now she's got all the brownie points over the, erm, you know.' I trailed off awkwardly.

'You can say it, Charlie. I'm not going to start crying again.'

'Sure?'

She looked sad. 'I'll try, at least.'

'Yeah, well, since she picked up on your competition thing, she's been so flavour of the month that virtually every partner has been in to give her a good old lick, so to speak.'

'Don't worry. You'll get it.' Hannah was confident.

'Why do you say that?'

'Because I'm going to help you. It's the least I can do for you putting me up rent-free. Combine your charm and my legal ability and we're more than a match for anyone.'

233

'What about my legal ability?'

'As I said, your charm and my legal ability.' And she gave me the most genuine smile she had managed for days.

Five dos and don'ts of suddenly finding yourself living with a female friend:
1. Don't nuzzle your girlfriend in bed and press your groin up against her backside while your new flatmate is noisily moving around next door in the spare bedroom.

'You are joking, aren't you?' Elly hissed.

'What's wrong?'

Her back stiffened, the opposite of what was happening to me. 'Hannah's next door. We can't.'

'We can be very quiet,' I said, in such a wheedling way that even I would have refused to have sex with me. And I love myself with a passion.

'There isn't a discussion to be had on this. No means no means never in a decade of Sundays, buster.'

'But she might be here for ages.'

'And who's fault is that?' Elly was trying very hard to be cool about the whole 'Hannah in Charlie's spare room' business, but sometimes her frustration leaked out. 'Looks like you've got quite a problem on your hands, doesn't it?'

I sat up grumpily. 'We'll just go to your place.'

'And leave Hannah alone in such a fragile state?' She mimicked my words of concern from an hour before. 'What kind of friend would do that?'

'You're not being very sympathetic.'

'Sympathetic to Hannah? Yes. Sympathetic to your need for sex? No. Seems I'm all out of sympathy all of a sudden.'

2. On no account say that you'll go next door for the sex you're being denied.

'Calm down,' I said. 'It's a joke.'

'It's not funny, Charlie.' Elly had turned round and her

look was fierce. 'We're not in a good place right now.' She had extended her American-style reading matter to relationship books since Hannah had moved in, in an effort to figure out whether it all had a deeper meaning.

'You don't have to tell me,' I grumbled. 'This bed used to be a great place when you were in it.'

'It's just a bad arrangement,' she said earnestly. 'I want to be supportive, especially for Hannah, but we get so little time together and this is ruining what we do get. And then you make your stupid jokes about Hannah and it just makes me angry. And worried.'

I put my arm tight around her. 'Don't be ridiculous. If anything was going to happen between us, it would have happened eight years ago.'

'You say that, but she's really vulnerable right now. I see the way she looks at you.'

I was surprised. 'What way?' This was one of those men/women things where women see things that aren't there, while men can't see anything but hope it's there anyway.

'I understand that you want to be a good friend and everything, but this can't go on for much longer. It is not doing you and me any good, Charlie.'

'It's only been a week or so.'

'Ten days, actually.'

'So?'

Grumpily, Elly turned her back on me once more, yanking seven-eighths of the duvet with her. 'Whatever.'

I poked her hard, alarmed that she'd resorted already to one of the deadliest words in the female dictionary. When the syllables say she doesn't care but the tone tells you viciously that she does. 'No, no, no, no, no. You can't leave me on a "whatever".'

She was remorseless. 'I'm going to sleep now.' And for all my quiet groaning, forehead-slapping and other general signs of distress designed to pull her back from the far edge of the mattress, Elly was having none of it. Not that she was asleep. Who could even close their eyes when

235

they're lying in bed so rigid with irritation? Exhausted by the emotion, however, I dozed off in a couple of minutes.

3. Don't be embarrassed when you catch each other in your underwear.

The only surprising thing was that it didn't happen until evening thirteen. It had been a very long day, and Elly had gone to her flat 'so I can get some peace and quiet', as she put it, trying to be pointed. I was going back to my room after cleaning my teeth. As I opened the bathroom door, Hannah was approaching in a short, plain nightdress and had lifted it to scratch her stomach. I was in a T-shirt and boxers.

She'd seen me in my boxers enough times as I rose groggily from her couch, but I'd often wondered about her choice of undies.

'Tanga, just a short hop away from an all-out G-string,' Ash had always insisted during our many discussions on the issue, rolling the word around his mouth like fine wine. He was strongly of the opinion that you could tell most of what you needed to know about a woman from her choice of underwear. 'Was ever such a small amount of material put to such outstanding use? I can see Hannah as closet-Tanga. Just a bit racier than you'd expect.'

I was pleased to see that I'd been right instead; she was, as I'd confidently predicted, regular panties (a word that was, by comment consent of Ash and me, the finest in the English language – it was the inspired inclusion of the word 'pant'), but quite brief ones.

Hannah pulled down her nightdress and blushed. 'I guess we better get used to this.'

'I didn't realise you hadn't been to the bathroom. I've just filled the sink.'

'Charlie, I've been bothered by this for years. Why do you soak your boxers in the sink? What's wrong with the washing machine?'

'Do you know how much Calvin Klein underwear costs? They need loving, not an impersonal spin.'

Hannah's face was a picture; I expected her to start backing away from me very slowly while scanning the walls for the nearest escape route. 'I have to be honest, Charlie. Sometimes you say and do some very odd things.'

'At least I wash them every day,' I said, recognising this as a very male point of view. 'You should be thankful.'

'That's nothing to be overly proud of. You do realise that, don't you?'

I pouted. 'This is about the first time I can recall a woman criticising me for being too hygienic.'

She put her hands out, palms down, and slid by me. 'Not criticising. Just interested. This is the first time I've lived with a bloke and it's interesting in a David Attenborough kind of way.'

'Nice knickers,' I muttered to her retreating back.

4. Don't play silly drinking games.

Unable to think of a more mature way to pull Hannah out of her funk, I resorted to a large bottle of vodka, a half-full tequila bottle, my private stash of whisky and whatever else I could lay my hands on to do the job for me.

It was Saturday night and in a fit of conscience, Tom Gulliver had told us to take the afternoon and evening off. We scarpered, knowing he could have second thoughts at any moment. Elly had gone home to see her parents, but fortunately mine were away on a weekend pottery course because my mum had seen a rerun of *Ghost* and thought it looked like fun. Whether it was the pot-making or the sex that appealed, I didn't dare ask, but I prayed that she would return with a new flower vase for me.

Elly had suggested that it would be easier for both of us if I didn't join her, and I wasn't going to put up much of a fight.

Sat in the living room with glasses and bottles filling half the table, nibbles lying around in their packets, and an enormous pizza taking up half the floor, our improvised drinking game was based on children's television.

237

Hannah had to drink her first vodka shot for failing on the names of Trumpton's fire brigade, which I'd lobbed her as an easy starter. 'It's not fair,' she grumbled, having left out the brothers Pugh. 'I always thought the "pew, pew" was a whistle. Then Barney McGrew, Cuthbert, Dibble and Grubb.' I then made her down another because technically she'd forgotten two names and for thinking that any fire-crew could safely consist of just four people.

I then got her on Doctor Who. 'What do you mean, Colin Baker?' she demanded. 'It was Tom Baker. Everyone knows that.'

It helped me win the game, but not any social credibility, that I knew the names of each Doctor, and that two Bakers had filled the role. I had been an active and proud member of the Doctor Who Appreciation Society when younger, but had buried that fact deep in my past when one potential law firm employer told me they had seen it on my CV, laughed themselves silly and immediately threw my application in the reject bin. 'Call us again if you make it to the fourth dimension,' the callous but surprisingly well-informed HR person had giggled down the phone at me.

I told Hannah and she laughed herself off the sofa. I joined her on the floor as the drink flowed, and we soon found ourselves sitting on opposite sides of the table, passing bottles and drinks to each other. I was into the tequila for forgetting that Choo Choo was a member of Top Cat's gang. 'That's two names,' she shouted happily. 'So two shots.'

I started a legal argument that I should only have to consume one drink because he was a single cat with a double-barrelled first name; alternatively because both names were the same anyway and so should only count as one; and because in any case, Top Cat usually called him 'Chooch'.

But Hannah was having none of it. 'I'm not a lawyer any more, so shove it.'

I got her back immediately – and big time – because she could only name Bingo from The Banana Splits. 'Fleegle,

Drooper and Snork,' I yelled. 'That's three.'

But Hannah was nothing if not a tenacious battler. 'Penfold didn't have a first name,' I said, outraged. 'It was like Dangermouse himself. He wasn't called Bernard Dangermouse, was he?'

The argument got heated, and although she tried to play on my pity – 'There are some things that I don't forget, you know', said in an overly miserable tone – I refused to believe that it was Ernest Penfold until we powered up my laptop and found it on the Internet.

I was further penalised for identifying Penfold as a mouse as well, rather than Dangermouse's faithful hamster pal.

More than half of the vodka and most of the tequila was gone when Hannah launched an uprovoked attack on Mr Benn. 'The man's a raving queen,' she said. 'Lives alone, dresses well and has this secret life where he goes to a shop, and an older queen lets him dress up and act out all sorts of fantasies.'

I made her drink some whisky for being judgmental about Mr Benn.

She then stood up in excitement. 'How could I have forgotten?' she cried, before running off into her room. She came back with a slim, gift-wrapped box.

'Hannah, you shouldn't have. It's just nice to have you here.'

'It's not for you. It's a birthday present for my brother,' she replied, ripping off the paper. It was a video which she thrust into my face.

I was awed. '*Monkey*,' I breathed. 'I haven't seen that for years. This is too exciting. You're the best, Hannah.'

We quickly cleared the food wrappers and pizza crusts off the sofa to Oriental cries of 'Monkey' and 'Pigsy', turned the lights low and settled down companionably to watch Monkey, Pigsy and Sandy battle with demons and bad lip-synching in their efforts to protect Tripitaka.

'Tripitaka actually lived and really did go to India to get Buddhist scriptures,' I murmured. It was one of those things I'd picked up over the years that never went down well at dinner parties. It was just plain unhealthy.

Hannah, though, rubbed my arm and shuffled up closer to me. 'You surprise me sometimes, Charlie Fortune. You're a clever bloke, do you know that? Not interesting, but clever.'

The episode was huge fun. 'What does that mean?' Hannah asked, after the narrator delivered one of his regular snippets of bizarre Buddhist wisdom, in this case 'Even a starving camel is still bigger than a horse.'

'It means, obviously, that if you have a camel and it hasn't had anything to eat for ages, then it's still bigger than a horse. Seems clear enough to me.'

Hannah took a thoughtful gulp of wine. 'And that applies to life how?'

'If you're not deep enough to understand, then I'm not sure I should tell you.'

She pinched me. 'Go on. Humour me.'

'Well, it means that you should get a bigger horse. Or keep your camel well fed.'

'Profound, that. Must bring it up if I ever get a job interview.'

We watched on in silence before the narrator asked gravely, 'Does love mean labour even for the carp-hearted?'

'Yes,' I responded at once.

'So you're wise as well as clever,' Hannah laughed. 'Who'd've thought it?' She then shifted on the sofa to face me. I turned my head but kept my eyes on the screen.

Out of the corner of my eye, I saw Hannah's head moving towards mine. Dulled by the drink, I thought nothing of it and our lips touched softly.

After a few seconds, I realised where I was and what was happening. I pulled back violently. She leaned further towards me, eyes closed, but I pushed her away. 'What are you doing?'

'Nothing,' she said, hand over her mouth in horror. 'I slipped.'

240

'Slipped? Whilst sitting still on the sofa?'

Hannah put her head in her hands as Monkey's extendable staff was growing in a blatantly phallic way after a randy dragon princess urged him to 'make it bigger'. 'Oh God, I'm so sorry. I don't know what came over me, Charlie.'

Inspired by Monkey, there was a double entendre to be had there, but I was just able to resist. 'Hannah. We can't. We shouldn't. We mustn't. We . . . we just can't.'

She had turned away from me and begun to cry again. 'I know, I know. I'm so sorry. It's just that you've been so good to me and I'm feeling so low and crap and worthless and everything, but you make me feel better about it all, and suddenly I just wanted to kiss you.' She took a big gulp of air.

It was hard to blame her for that, but we both knew it was wrong. Another time, another place, another girlfriend, another everything, and who knew? 'It was the drink,' I said decisively.

She nodded vigorous agreement. 'Yes, that's right. I can't remember the last time I was this pissed. It must have been the drink.'

We were both shaking slightly but tried to carry on as though nothing had happened. But Monkey didn't seem quite so funny, all of a sudden.

5. Don't tell your girlfriend about what happened.

Chapter Twenty-Six

What would you do with £168,960 over a space of eight weeks?

Fly first-class around the world every weekend?

Hire Richard Branson's private island, and Richard Branson as your butler, perhaps?

Go into your bank with 16,896,000 pennies, ask for them to be converted into two-pence pieces, and watch the reaction?

Maybe get every lawyer in the City pissed on 67,584 bottles of Budweiser, using 21,120 pizzas to line their stomachs beforehand?

Or spend it on Charles Fortune plugging away for 704 hours at his desk at a bargain-basement £240 a throw. An average of eighty-eight hours a week during the eight weeks of the British Pharmaceuticals deal, I was horrified to see.

Couldn't I have made it ninety? A nice round, impressive figure? If only I hadn't been so stupid as to leave by nine a couple of times in the fourth week. Damn my mother for making me believe when I was younger that 'all work and no play makes Charlie a dull boy'. If only she'd kept on saying 'all work and no play makes Charlie a rich partner with shallow yet beautiful women swooning at his feet' then

242

maybe I'd have hit the ninety mark. And then perhaps the professor who once told an entire lecture theatre that I was a legal Ronnie Biggs – that is, untouched by the law – spontaneously combusts with the humiliation of it all.

Indeed, what's wrong with a few hundred-hour weeks, I could hear some sadistic partner muttering to himself as he checked over my billables. Never did me any harm. I knew I needed to be more ruthless still with my timesheet. Sure, when I made all those cups of coffee, I didn't have the file in front of me, but I was thinking about it, wasn't I? And even if I wasn't, the coffee was to keep me awake so I could work on the file, which was virtually the same thing.

The deal was finally winding to a close. The sale and purchase agreement was agreed, almost all the checks had been completed, and we were just left with one final day of misery. United Retail had to make a series of warranties in the agreement as to the state of the company, and, as is usual practice, would wait until the last moment to dump a huge amount of documentation on us which disclosed anything that might be relevant. It was the kind of thing that makes the chairman of Xerox sleep well at night while depriving the likes of me of any sleep whatsoever. Perhaps one last all-nighter would tip me over the edge – but whether to a ninety-hour average or the Epsom Home For The Legally Insane was hard to tell.

Hannah and I hadn't mentioned what had happened again, except to agree forcefully the following morning that we wouldn't mention it again. I was sad in a way, because under different circumstances Hannah and I would have made a great couple, but I loved Elly and knew there was nothing more or less to it than that.

Nonetheless, Hannah and I had started developing something of a married couple routine. She slotted into the housewife role easily enough after seeing one recruitment consultant who, with his hand more or less over his nose at the reason for her sudden appearance on the job market, had suggested that Hannah might want to give it a bit of time before she started applying to other firms.

'Time's a great healer,' he said, ushering her out quickly. 'And maybe you'll decide that the law's not for you after all.' Rather that than have the decision made for her, ran the subtext, by a hundred firms who wouldn't touch her even if it came down to Hannah or the hand-painted, bewigged and gowned gnome who sits in wise judgment over my father's garden in honour of my legal qualification.

So with nothing better to do, she found furiously tidying the flat to be an ideal displacement activity; she even found my long-lost work palm pilot under my yukka plant, compacted with soil. I remembered then that I had hidden it for safekeeping in the days after someone tried to break into the flat. And she ironed my shirts, collected my dry cleaning and even on occasion made dinners which proved why she was a lawyer, to the despair of her mother, who had said sternly that Hannah really wasn't helping in the continuing search for an NJB. These dinners were made even better when Elly started joining us. I'd been over-compensating wildly with her – not that lavishing love and praise was the hardest task in the world – and she soon realised that she had nothing to fear from Hannah being in my flat.

The day when the deal was done and the work finally over was simply wonderful. 'Now I know what Mandela felt like after being released from that jail,' one partner said to me in all seriousness. There would be plenty of little things to tie up in the aftermath, but for the time being, it was a chance to stand back and admire a bloody hard job exceptionally well done. And, more to the point, the many millions of pounds that Babbington Botts would be paid as a result. The owners of deluxe Caribbean hotels declared it a day of national celebration, I am led to believe. 'We can soon retire early,' one was heard to say, as he ratcheted up his room rate another token 10 per cent to make his regular legal customers feel at home.

There was champagne in the boardroom, back slaps all round and even, courtesy of Tom Gulliver, the offer of the

244

last two days of the week off in recognition of the work we'd all put in. 'Go have fun, enjoy yourselves, forget all about us,' he said to Elly and me. 'But don't forget to take your pagers, just in case.'

Fortunately, Hannah had discovered my pager the day before under the sink, jammed in to hold up a pipe.

Elly and I retreated to a corner where we discussed what we would do with our brief freedom. I suggested seeing if it was possible to spend four days in bed but then Elly clapped her hands in excitement.

'Let's go to Disneyland Paris,' she said.

I pulled a face.

'Come on, a bit of mindless fun is just what we need. And the hotels are right next to it. There'll be plenty of time for everything.' She fluttered her eyes at me.

'But it's my birthday on Saturday,' I complained. 'We should do something exciting that night and we're not going to find it at Disney.'

'How about we come back for Saturday evening and go out just the two of us somewhere special?' There was more eye-fluttering and a subtext so unambiguous that it was impossible even for me to misunderstand, so I nodded agreement.

'And Anita and Melinda will be there as well. They're going with their husbands this weekend and asked me ages ago but I said I wouldn't be able to.'

I groaned. The Mogadon Twins were old school friends of Elly's who had enthusiastically adopted her attitude towards me when our relationship went sour. I never understood why she kept up with these two, but Elly claimed that she enjoyed being one of the girls now and again; the only saving grace was that she didn't see them all that often. She said it was important to keep in touch with friends like these.

'I thought that was what barge poles were for,' I grumbled.

The only possible connection I could ever see between them all was that they had all married or were dating lawyers. Anita and Melinda were tied together even more

245

closely. Both their names ended in 'a', which stood for astoundingly annoying.

I suspected that in reality they appealed to Elly's vanity. They looked up to her as the leader of the gang, while Elly was a little too impressed by their money – Anita's through her family, Melinda's through her marriage – and the great comfort it brought them. It was the middle-class, 'make something of yourself' girl in her. It wasn't like she wasn't doing brilliantly as it was, but she had a nagging urge for more, I fancied.

In any case, guilt is a great motivator. I believe in life dealing with things through a rough and ready, reward and punishment approach, and felt that my punishment for a brief drunken kiss with Hannah was a long weekend surrounded by the Mogadon Twins and surly Frenchmen cavorting in Mickey Mouse costumes.

I stretched my mouth wide in forced appreciation. 'That would be great,' I said. Lingering hopes that a needy Hannah would force me to cancel were dashed when she waved me off with an 'It'll be nice to have some time alone without you under my feet.'

And so, two days and one exceptionally early start later, we were facing each other at the Eurostar terminal at Waterloo. That it was 6.30 am didn't stop Anita and Melinda – who are both smaller than me – still managing to stare down their carefully powdered noses at the rehabilitated Charlie Fortune, unable to see what had made Elly change her mind.

Anita was quite tall, slim, gorgeous and utterly stupid. It was typically male of me to assume that she'd got her part-time job in marketing at another large law firm simply through her looks or because she was married to one of the lawyers there, but for sure it wasn't down to her wit or wisdom.

'I haven't seen you for ages, Charlie,' she said. 'I'm sure you've shrunk.'

I was prepared to give tolerance a brief go. 'I don't think so.'

'No, you're wrong. You've definitely shrunk. Like old people do. Don't you think, Robbie?' she asked her husband, who had never laid eyes on me until that moment.

He nodded vigorously. 'Somebody's half-inched a half-inch, I bet,' he said, and set about laughing wildly.

But the woman had style, I would give her that. Unlike Robbie, sadly, who clearly didn't get out of the office all that much and whose idea this whole trip had been, apparently. While his right hand shook mine, his left pulled a string which brought together in a clap two further hands attached to the front of his baseball cap.

'Good to meet you,' he said, bobbing around like a hyperactive puppy. 'Don't mind me. I'm mad. Everyone'll tell you.' His cap applauded the confession wildly, while Anita watched indulgently.

There's no quality control in the legal profession any more, I thought. 'I guessed as much,' I said, nodding to his T-shirt, which was emblazoned with a cut-out of Robbie's head surrounded by the words 'You don't have to be mad to be me, but it helps!!!'. Why three exclamation marks, I wanted to ask. Does that mean you're really, really, really mad, or just really, really, really irritating?

'You two are going to get on brilliantly,' Anita said. 'Robbie's such a scream.'

'I can see him making me scream,' I agreed, but it passed them well by.

All sorts make up the legal profession, including those who try so hard not to be boring lawyers. I felt sorry for him, in fact. Robbie was at a firm known for a galley-ship approach to assistants while a few partners held on to the cash. It didn't matter much so far as he was concerned though; Robbie was as much partnership material as my dad's gnome.

Melinda was smaller than Anita and attractive too, with raven hair and a red theme to everything she wore. She was, if anything, marginally more stupid than her pal and had the charming inability to distinguish between comments that should stay inside her head and those which society deems acceptable to come out.

She introduced me to Henry, her husband, who was around five years older than the rest of us. 'He's a property partner at Franklin Arnold & Tipton,' Melinda reminded me proudly. 'Earns absolutely pots of cash.' I knew Franklins well – it was their salaries, rather than initials, it was said, which put the fat into fat-cat. 'Elly says you're trying to become a partner as well, but we all reckon they'd be stupid not to choose her ahead of you.'

Henry winced slightly. A stiff, grey sort, he looked like he'd be as at home in Disney as Donald Duck would be at his desk at Franklins. They didn't seem the most likely of couples, but he certainly had the income to keep Melinda in a style to which she was very keen to become accustomed.

'You're not mad as well, are you?' I asked with a game smile.

'Only for the law,' he replied. I prayed he just had a very dry sense of humour and a poker face. Further proof, I later learned, that there is no God.

In a desperate move, I deliberately dropped my passport, hoping to be denied entry to France, but Robbie galloped up from behind us and bashed me on the head with it several times. 'What are you like?' he asked.

'Sane, for the moment,' I muttered to his retreating back.

The seat allocations put us directly in front of Anita and Robbie, and made me doubt my reward/punishment theory; it's not like I had killed anyone, after all. But why else would I have to put up with three hours of Robbie bouncing up and down behind us, periodically appearing above, leaning heavily on our seats.

'This is so exciting,' he was saying. 'Normally, I'm Mr Boring Conventional Lawyer who sits behind a desk all day. So when I get a chance to be myself and all mad, it's great.'

'And this is the real you, is it?' I asked, the sarcasm far too faint for Robbie to notice.

'Too right. A hundred and twenty three per cent mad,

that's me. Robbie Hunter the Madman, they call me. Honestly, they do. I'm just so wacky, I can't stop myself.' He laughed manically, which made other passengers look at him, fearing that they'd been landed with a train loony.

I leaned over to whisper to Elly. 'Tell me again why you are friendly with these people?'

She patted my arm and switched on her full-beam smile, which always flipped my heart over. 'Because they're my friends, that's why. Have been for, like, for ever.'

There was a brief moment when we were going through the tunnel and Robbie was showing me in painstaking detail how his hat worked, that I hoped for the Channel to break through and swallow us up, but the feeling reluctantly passed and we eventually found ourselves drawing up at a Disneyland bathed in a chilly but bright winter sun.

I'd anticipated maybe going to bed for a bit, having a bath, an indoor swim and generally relaxing. Robbie, who seemed to have swapped his feet for springs, had other ideas, however. Within thirty minutes of checking in, we were lined up at the gates of the park, fully prepped for the fun he promised would engulf us.

Faced by Main Street, Robbie – now topped off by a cap with Mickey Mouse ears sticking out the sides which wiggled in excitement as his head went to and fro – didn't know what to do. There were too many things to look at, and it seemed to overload his system. He kept jerking in every direction, on the verge of steaming off, but couldn't decide where to go. Henry, meanwhile, was studying the park map with the frown of a property lawyer used to more professional cartography.

I turned to see the girls nattering away, and sighed. This was hardly how I envisaged our precious time off, and my mood blackened further when my suggestion that we all split up for a bit (I had twenty years in mind as a decent period of time) was rejected for being boring.

'Everyone at school used to think you were boring,' Melinda said. 'But Elly swears blind that you're not any more.' The odd thing was that she wasn't being deliberately malicious; if something came into her mind, she would automatically repeat it out loud, perhaps as unexpected proof of brain activity.

Eventually, Henry decreed that we would start in Frontierland and cover the park in a methodical anti-clockwise motion. Robbie skipped off ahead of us with Anita, which was useful to the extent that it gave the rest of us a brief break and meant he was already in the queue for Big Thunder Mountain when we finally arrived.

After a fifteen-minute wait, we found ourselves strapped into the roller-coaster, done up like a Wild West train. Robbie and Anita were right at the front, with us behind them, and as the train slowly cranked up a steep incline, all I could see and hear was Robbie waving his hands in the air and shrieking 'Oh my God, oh my God, oh my God, here we go, here we go, here we go'. The train then paused for us to look around and plunged back down at speed. Elly gripped my hand and couldn't stop laughing, which I joined in with, further entertained by the thought of Robbie and Anita's safety bar giving way and seeing them splat, Wile E Coyote-style, into the rocky Wild West outback.

Robbie, of course, had the right attitude to this place, and we slowly all got caught up in the childishness about us. It wasn't brilliant but it was, as Elly had predicted, mindless fun. So we shrieked in concert with Robbie up and down Space Mountain, were jiggled about senselessly by Star Tours, and yo-ho-hoed along with the Pirates of the Caribbean.

At one point, as we hurtled around a sharp corner in Indiana Jones and The Temple of Peril, I felt Melinda touch my hand. I glanced at her in surprise. 'You're not as awful as I remember,' she shouted.

I wasn't sure what to say, so I lied. 'Neither are you.'

Later in the day, we did finally break off on our own, and Elly and I headed straight towards 'Le Pays des Contes de Fées', which sounded to us like the country where they count fees. 'Otherwise known as Le Pays de Babbington Botts,' Elly said.

250

As it happened, it was a gentle cruise through a fairytale landscape, and Elly lay back against my chest, catching her breath.

'I love you so much it sometimes panics me,' she said quietly. 'I worry that something will go wrong and this will all be snatched away from me.'

My whole body tingled. I couldn't comprehend how much I loved her. She'd been my perfect partner in my mind for so long, and now it was reality. Some moments, I still couldn't believe it. 'I worry too,' I said, and felt her stir anxiously. 'Who wouldn't when things are this perfect?'

It was corny but for once, rather than put her finger down her throat in disgust, she twisted around and kissed me lusciously. 'I know exactly how you feel.'

We were still entwined as the boat emerged at the end of the ride. I could hear Robbie far closer than expected or desired. 'Wahey. I didn't know this was the love boat.'

Anita looked around anxiously. 'Is it? It doesn't say that anywhere. I thought this place was for families. A love boat is hardly appropriate when there are children around. There isn't even a height restriction.'

Smiling, we climbed out and talked about the evening. Robbie wanted to go back to the hotel, freshen up and then come back to the park so he could see it at night. Henry and Melinda had already left, but apparently couldn't wait to get back out there. 'That Henry,' Robbie said. 'Makes me laugh. Said this place made him want to lobotomise himself with a rusty fork.' He rolled a finger at his temple. 'And they say I'm mad.'

However, Elly and I had other plans and cried off, citing the need to do a little bit of work back in our room. That wasn't entirely untrue – we had been asked to take a laptop with us to check e-mails just in case anything came up – but there were things higher on our agenda than that.

Robbie tried to shame us out of it with an overly loud chant of 'Boring', but there were some peers whose pressure we were able to withstand.

Feeling the need to treat ourselves after six difficult weeks, Elly and I were spread out in a junior suite and had no intention of leaving that night. After a gloriously slow and measured bout of lovemaking, we ordered room service, and returned to the bed for seconds.

Elly then disappeared off to the shower, telling me to switch on her laptop and check the e-mails. We had it arranged so mine would be diverted to her account.

Lying on the bed naked, I went through the messages, none of which were important or even interesting. I then started idly flicking through other folders on her desktop. I got to 'BPharm', of which I'd had more than enough, but noticed a document called 'Hannah'. The shower was still on, so I clicked it open to find the notorious memo from Elly to Hannah. I couldn't think why she'd called it that; there was no sign that she gave all her documents pet rather than functional names.

I closed it, thinking of Hannah and wondering whether I should give her a quick call to make sure everything was OK. I was about to shut down the machine when something in the dialogue box caught my attention.

The computer had to be playing a cruel practical joke on me. This was a memo that was dated and supposedly sent several weeks beforehand. But it had, apparently, only been created the day before Hannah was sacked.

Chapter Twenty-Seven

There had to be a rational explanation.

The computer could be on the blink, for one. Part of the Microsoft conspiracy to destabilise the world.

My eyes could be playing tricks on me, for another. I've never totally trusted them – they've always looked slightly weasely to me.

It could be my mind, overwhelmed by the pressure of the BPharm deal and comforted by the sticky embrace of paranoia.

I closed my eyes and mind tight for some seconds and then pushed them back open. It was all still there.

This could be a twisted joke by Elly; not that she had a record of jokes like this, but that might be what made it so clever.

Then again, it could be a test. That was it. To see how I would react when faced with what turns out to be her mock betrayal. To discover whether my love would conquer all. Her insecurity was such that I had to be tested.

There was also, I knew, however much I wanted to deny it, an utterly impossible explanation: that there had never been a memo for Hannah to overlook. It had been written the day before Hannah was sacked to ensure that the very same event occurred.

Maybe it was a complicated set-up. Someone who wanted to get rid of Hannah, considered her competition that had to be pushed out of the way by framing her for some terrible misdeed.

Who would benefit from Hannah being exposed like this, thrown out of the firm and the competition for partner? Well, me, for one, but I was as sure as I could be that I hadn't done it. Ash and Lucy as well, but would they do something like this to ease their path to partnership? Just to keep as many non-Elly suspects in the frame as possible, I added them to the list. We would often joke that all of us would step over the others' still-warm corpses while holding the Uzi, if that was what it took, but didn't really believe it.

Perhaps it was a cunning plot by Hannah herself. Maybe she hacked into Elly's PC, found the file, named it to catch my attention and then somehow changed the date for me to discover and expose a fantastic conspiracy against her. So it may even be Hannah trying to push Elly out. I hadn't considered that possibility.

Or perhaps she had trained an otter which infiltrated Elly's flat, powered up the computer and made all the necessary changes with its rapier-quick nose. I should ask Elly if the keys ever felt a little wet, perhaps snotty.

I shook my head in distress at the effect all those National Geographic programmes I kept watching late at night were having on my mind.

I stood up confused. Then sat back down on the bed and opened up some other files but there was nothing incriminating there. Nothing which confirmed that Elly had set up Hannah in a manner so underhand that it at least deserved praise for its audacity.

I got back to my feet, grabbed a dressing gown and started pacing around. Should I confront her? Should I pretend nothing had happened and try to work it out for myself first? I should at least calm down before I did anything.

Elly came out of the bathroom, wrapped in a short, fluffy white towel with her wet hair hanging straight, already combed. She looked very horny. 'I suppose it's a bit early for third time lucky, is it?' Her smile was of randy hope.

Ten minutes ago, I'd've been all for giving it a very enthusiastic go, but it was a measure of my despair that now the offer left me cold. 'Why does the computer say that the original memo to Hannah about the Competition Commission was created the day before she was sacked?'

Several reactions flashed across her face, but the only one I caught for sure was guilt. My insides curdled.

I'd seen that look often enough not to mistake it. Maggie Brown, who'd been seen kissing Simon Denton behind the bike shed – I mean, cheat on me if you must, but not in such a clichéd way, please – before meeting me at the swings. I was not sorry when Maggie suffered a minor industrial injury through reckless use of the see-saw with Simon a few days later.

Elly sat down on the edge of the bed with a hand to her chest, whether to calm her heart or hide it from me, I wasn't sure. 'I don't know what you're talking about,' she said.

Sandra Morton at university, who'd spent the night, whipped my land law essay and passed it off as her own. Last laugh on her as well, though. She got a D and then had the cheek to take it out on me, claiming that I was – and I am still able to quote – 'an intellectual amoeba who's as much fun in bed as a burning cigarette'.

Both hurt me, but I didn't believe her and I didn't believe Elly. I pushed the computer in her direction. 'It's clear enough, Elly. Tell me what's happening here.'

She didn't bother to look at it. 'It's a mistake, it must be.' Her eyes widened. 'You're frightening me, Charlie. Stop it.'

Penny Freeman, a one-time assistant solicitor who even said she loved me, wanted to move in and all the time was shagging the forty-two-year-old wart-infested head of the postroom. Still, she too got her come-uppance, right at the time he was giving her his come-uppance. They were caught by the managing partner in an executive toilet that was hardly ever used. 'My word,' he is reported to have said with remarkable cool. 'I never realised the postroom still did personal deliveries.'

My voice was flat, almost disinterested. 'Tell me what's happening.'

'Nothing,' Elly said, voice rising with anger. 'I don't know what you're talking about. It sounds like you're the one with the problem.'

Caroline Greenway used to share a violin class with me when I was twelve, and we would always go home together on the bus. The other boys always teased her for having teeth that would shame Bugs Bunny and a stammer that would embarrass Foghorn Leghorn, and though we got on famously on those bus rides, I never had the courage to ask her out. Then Elaine Stanton joined us in the class, and on the first ride home, I chose to sit next to Elaine – all blonde hair, freckles and pop socks. The crushed look on Caroline's face has stayed with me for ever, and nothing I could ever do would make up for it. And I think about it every time I see her now, which is often as she is a well-known, glamorous soap actress, while Elaine Stanton, according to the most recent update from my mother, manages the local dry cleaners. Would that it was an isolated example of my poor judgement.

I moved gently towards Elly and knelt. She looked down at me and there was fear in the face I found so beautiful. The fear looked ugly there, disfiguring. It had to be removed. I held her hands. 'Elly, you know I love you. But I know you're not telling me the truth.'

I could feel her body tense for a return to the attack, but then it seemed to subside.

'You do love me, don't you?' she asked. This was a side to Elly I'd never seen.

'You know that.'

'Whatever?'

Oh dear. She wanted absolution before I'd heard the confession. It must be bad.

'Charlie. Say you'll love me whatever.'

I couldn't. I tried, but I couldn't. The lawyer in me hates blanket promises like that. 'Just tell me what happened.'

'It was all Ian's idea,' she said miserably. 'I've been feeling so awful about what's happened to Hannah. You have to believe me. That why I've hated her being around your flat all the time. Please believe me.'

I could, but I wasn't ready to forgive and forget. Elly took a ragged breath.

'He was meant to be overseeing the competition clearance but he'd got so caught up in other bits of the deal that it had somehow slipped through the net. I was in his office one day and mentioned it. He went mad. Told me it was all my fault. That we'd both be fired for it. So we cooked up a plan to get us off the hook.'

I let her hands slip from mine, and rocked back on my haunches with the shock of it all. 'But why Hannah?'

There were tears forming. 'Ian told me that she was the favourite to become partner out of all of us. Said we might as well clear some of the competition out of the way while we were about it.'

I was momentarily distracted by the revelation that Hannah had been top of the pile; that was a turn-up for the books. 'How could you, Elly?'

'What else could I do?' Her voice was rising again, but this time with hysteria. 'You don't know Ian like I do. He has this awful temper; you don't see it often, and most of the time he's great, but he can be an absolute bastard. He told me that I'd get the sack if I didn't help him, that I'd never work in the City again, that he'd done this before and knew exactly how to get away with it.'

So many questions – like why didn't she come to me for help – but only one really mattered. 'How could you, Elly?' I felt horribly ill. Elly wasn't the person I thought she was. The person I wanted her to be so much that nothing else had mattered. I'd been wrong all along, thinking that there was nothing left of that eighteen-year-old girl who'd turned my insides out so cruelly.

Yes, our world was fantastically competitive, and yes,

we all wanted to get to the top ahead of the others, but I couldn't believe that when it came to the crunch, Lucy, Ash, Hannah or I would have done the same thing. We were good people at heart, all of us.

'You have to come clean, try and make this thing good,' I said, giving her one last chance.

Elly bowed her head and nodded in slight agreement.

Silence settled until there was a knock on the door. I rose, thinking it was room service picking up the trolley, but the moment I pulled it open, Robbie pushed his way in.

'Did you see the fireworks? They were *absolutement fantastique*, as they say over here.'

Anita and Melinda were hot on his heels. 'So this is what a junior suite looks like,' Anita said. 'Thought it would be bigger.'

I stole a glance at Elly, who was still sitting on the bed, looking disconsolate and pulling the towel tighter.

'They're not partners, you know,' Melinda said. 'So they probably can't afford a senior suite.' She looked back to see Henry loitering just outside. 'We could, obviously, but Henry said he'd prefer to flush our money down the loo rather than spend it on a big room in this place. He's ever so funny, my Henry.'

Robbie had been darting around the room, running his hands over everything, but stopped to throw me a look about how unfunny both Henry and Melinda actually were.

I'm not sure my raised eyebrows conveyed the weight of the irony bearing down on me.

Eventually, Robbie's circuit brought him back to me. 'I can't believe you missed it all. The park's closed now, you know. That's all folks,' he said, in a voice trying to mimic Donald Duck, I think.

'That's Warner Brothers,' I said, eyes on Elly and not really listening. 'Not Disney.'

'Oh no it's not,' he replied in the same voice, lunging forward and catching me on the nose with his latest cap, which had a yellow Donald beak protruding from the front.

'Ow, bugger,' I said, clutching my face.

258

Robbie put his hands up in mock-horror. 'Wooh. Sorry about that. But that's what happens when you're up before the beak.' Anita and Melinda stared while he chortled to himself. 'Beak. D'ya get it?' He pointed to the hat but the stereo blankness remained. 'I don't know why I bother sometimes.'

'Me neither,' I said, but he was oblivious, bouncing over to Elly.

'Come on, princess, cheer up,' he said. 'Worse things happen at sea. They're bound to do the fireworks again tomorrow night. Nice towel, by the way. Hope we haven't interrupted anything. Eh? Eh?' He giggled.

Elly shot me such a woebegone glance that I immediately started trying to push them all out.

'Say no more, say no more,' said Robbie, resisting as hard as he could and trying to poke me with his elbow. 'A nudge is as good as a wink to a deaf man.'

'Blind man,' I said.

Anita was puzzled. 'How can a blind man see a wink?'

Robbie shook his head in exasperation and gave me another look. 'It's Monty Python, surely you know that, Anita? They were almost as mad as me.' It was a boast I wasn't sure John Cleese would be proud of.

'Do you mean they're about to have sex?' Melinda was catching up at her own pace.

'Melinda Forrester,' Robbie shrieked, as I pushed the door shut. 'You are sssooo embarrassing.'

Relieved, I turned to see Elly clicking away at the computer. I rushed over and snatched it away, only to find the incriminating documents permanently deleted. Her face displayed fear and defiance. There was love there too.

'I do love you, Charlie,' she whispered. 'I'm sorry. But I can't go through with it.'

Dazed, I dropped the laptop carelessly to the floor, went to the wardrobe and pulled out my suitcase. I went around the room, throwing everything in, and zipped it up.

Without a backward look, I walked out, closed the door quietly and went down to reception to get another room.

Chapter Twenty-Eight

I left on the Eurostar the following morning without saying goodbye to Elly; she would be on the one we'd reserved later in the day. I was relieved to leave the hotel, especially as I was pursued from the lift to the reception desk by an oversized Goofy upset by my reluctance to join a breakfast conga around the lobby with him, six hyped-up pre-teens and, inevitably, Robbie.

Regrettably, Robbie was kitted out in Donald Duck shorts that didn't do any favours to a duck, let alone a human. 'How mad am I?' he asked breathlessly, and tweaked one of Goofy's ears.

Anita strolled up. 'Robbie just loves kids so much,' she said, shaking her head in amused tolerance. 'Loves mucking around with them. He'll make such a great dad.'

Not my first choice for a role model, I thought. And the sacrifice on Anita's part, and the long-term consequences of bringing the spawn of Robbie into the world, both struck me as too high a price to pay. 'He seems to empathise with them,' I said.

She nodded vigorously. 'He's really in touch with his inner child.'

'In touch?' I asked. 'Seems like they're sleeping together on a regular basis.'

Anita's face bunched in confusion, but before I was forced to explain that he wasn't actually sleeping with someone else, the man himself congaed by, stopping long enough to say that they'd be leaving for the park in five minutes, so she had better 'be there or be square'. She happily left me to get ready.

I'd almost made it out the doors when Melinda floated by. 'You're not leaving, are you?' she asked.

'No,' I said. 'I'm just taking my bag for a breath of fresh air.'

Melinda nodded and wafted on. 'See you later then.'

The four hours it took me to get back to the flat went by numbly. I burned with anger on Hannah's behalf, felt sick that Elly had so readily stitched her up, and consumed to my core with despair that things had come to this.

I'd been sure that Elly had changed, that she was a force for good in my life. But she hadn't changed. I felt betrayed. It was a truly shitty day to be celebrating my thirty-second birthday.

As I unlocked the front door, I could hear loud disco music and when I got to the lounge saw Hannah with her back to me, dancing around in pyjamas singing along. I pulled back out of sight and watched her through the crack by the door hinges. It was 'I Will Survive', but she was after a different kind of empowerment. I could hear Hannah warbling the words we'd written several years ago for a Christmas revue.

'Oh please, BB,' she sang at the chorus. 'Put your trust in me. I'm the one who's going to be this law firm's greatest ever trainee. I'm going to work till it's so late and never take a holiday, and when you need to know the law, just walk up and knock on my door . . .'

Smiling, I padded back out of the flat and waited for the song to end before making a very loud entrance. The music was hastily turned off as the tape wound on, alarmingly, to 'Do Ya Think I'm Sexy?'

261

She came out to the hall to confront me, face pink with embarrassment and exertion. 'What happened to the rest of my Charlie-free weekend? You can't just waltz in here and ruin it, even if it is your flat.'

I'd decided not to tell her the truth quite yet. She deserved to know, to have the consolation of discovering that she'd done nothing wrong, but first I needed more time to process everything that had happened. I couldn't face talking it through right now.

'I was feeling really ill and just wanted to get home as soon as possible,' I explained.

Her face creased with concern. 'Anything I can do? Nurse Hannah can wear a pinny and wield a plaster with the best of them.'

The image appealed. 'Thank you, Nurse, but I'll be all right. You can go back to preserving the memory of Rod Stewart's career.'

She looked decidedly shifty. 'I don't know how that song got on the tape. It's an absolute mystery. Anyway, what are your plans today?'

'I thought I'd catch a Downtown Train and then go Sailing with Maggie May.'

Hannah harrumphed. 'God help me, but I've always found him one of the sexiest men alive.'

I reeled theatrically. 'Even though he's, like, eighty years old?'

'He's not eighty, he's about fifty-seven, and a very young-looking fifty-seven at that.'

'I'm not the one who's ill, I'd say.'

'I got fired so I'm allowed to be difficult. Now sod off and leave me to dream of tartan.' Hannah went back into the living room and turned the music back on, louder if anything.

The smile sloughed off my face the second her back was turned and I retreated to my bedroom while Rod belted out several tributes to various women. It was all I could do not to beat the walls in a frenzy.

*

Rod eventually ran out of steam and went quiet – as you would expect of a fifty-seven-year-old man – and Hannah pottered around quietly while I lay on my bed, hoping that something might emerge from the cracks in the ceiling that would provide an answer to everything. The phone rang once and I could hear Hannah speaking into it with hushed urgency, but couldn't summon up the interest to find out who had called.

A bit later, she knocked softly and came in. She perched on the edge of the bed. 'How's my poor little soldier then?' Her sympathy wasn't overflowing.

I tried to hide everything I was going through. 'Not too bad.'

'So you're feeling better? That's great. It means we can go out tonight for dinner.'

I groaned and said I didn't want to go anywhere except possibly the kitchen, as I'd stashed some Toblerone at the back of the fridge.

Hannah's face assumed a shifty look once more. 'You might suffer a little disappointment on that front,' she confessed. 'I couldn't sleep last night and kind of finished it.'

I sat up. 'What do you mean, finished it? I hadn't even started it. And it was about the size of a small mountain, anyway.'

Suppressing a smile, Hannah lay a calming hand on my arm and said she'd make it up to me by taking me out to dinner. 'My treat. To thank you for everything you've done.'

I felt guilty at her spending money when she no longer had an income, but then I had been really looking forward to the chocolate, and so grunted my assent. She got to her feet. 'Good. We'll leave in an hour, so chop chop. You know how long you spend in the bathroom. Goodness only knows what you get up to in there, you big girl.'

'At least I don't spend the time eating other people's chocolate,' I grumped at her retreating back.

Exactly sixty-eight minutes later, we were ready to go,

although Hannah refused to reveal our destination, saying it was a surprise. I'd showered, shaved and spent ages, as usual, dealing with my nose hairs (embarrassed, I hid the trimmer under my bed even when I had the flat to myself, and sneaked it into the bathroom; by the end of every other day, it's like I've had Alan Titchmarch up my nostrils with a large bag of fertiliser).

We took the tube into town, and bowled up at a posh wine bar and grill with soft red lighting and the promise of jazz later in the evening. We were taken to the back of the dining room and rounded a corner to find a single large table containing Ash, Lucy, a couple of other people from work, my old school friend Mike 'Cookie' Cookson and Elly. While the others stood up at once with a chorus of happy birthdays, she sat, staring steadily at me, awaiting a reaction. I averted my eyes and turned to Hannah.

'You shouldn't've,' I said, meaning it.

'It was all Elly's idea,' she replied, laughing, 'but you coming back early meant we had to change the plans around a bit. She was meant to bring you here for a romantic meal.'

Rather than deal with Elly, I turned instead to Mike, about the only friend I had left from outside Babbingtons. While others drifted away after countless cancelled evenings due to the pressure of my work, Mike remained, the kind of friend you don't see for ages but still get on with brilliantly when you do.

Anyway, he knew what it was like for me. We went through university and law school together, and he too joined a huge law firm. Cookie – we always wondered whether we became friends just so we could enjoy the Fortune Cookie joke as often as possible – says he knew after ten minutes of the induction at his firm that it wasn't for him; it was something to do with a heavy warning that his preference for buttons over cufflinks wouldn't endear him to the senior partner. Frankly, it was something everyone else already knew. It was too structured for him; a tall, gangly sort with untameable hair, he was a man unable to

264

wear a suit with anything approaching conviction.

But it still took him another five long years to pluck up the courage to do anything about it, during which time he built up such hate for the law that it is the only other man-made construction visible from space. Eventually Cookie quit, after a drunken partner had told him at the firm's Christmas party that they were more likely to make up Genghis Khan to partner than him. 'So long as he dresses a bit better than you, at least,' he supposedly giggled.

Cookie retrained as a social worker, had time to indulge his passion for electronics in his spare room and earns about half as much as a Babbingtons trainee. I admired – albeit from afar – his determination to help people who would be escorted from the BB building via the thick boots of a security guard.

In the first couple of years as trainees, Cookie and I lived together and had a great time until my father – supportively concerned that I would be found out at any time in the legal profession – finally wore me down with his endless nagging on how important it was to get a foot on the property ladder. But at the time I could only afford a one-bed flat, leaving Cookie to take the split with an admirable lack of both grace and animosity.

I felt guilty that we hadn't spoken for ages. We'd exchanged some e-mails of late, but I'd wanted to tell him about Elly face to face; he'd happily joined in my hate campaign after Elly had told some girl she really liked that she'd find a better-quality boyfriend in the local sewer than go out with Cookie. 'Then again,' she said reflectively to a group that included us on the periphery, 'you'd probably find him lurking down there already.'

We embraced warmly. 'You do know who's here, don't you?' he asked out of the corner of his mouth. 'Only Elly Bloody Gray.'

We grasped each other's forearms. 'Yeah, Cookie, there's something I've been meaning to talk to you about.'

'Don't tell me, you two are suddenly best pals and are sleeping together on a regular basis.' His humour was high. His eyebrows went higher still when I confirmed that that was exactly what had happened.

'Oh. My. God. When? How? Why? I've got so many questions.'

I glanced around at the other expectant faces. 'Not now, mate. Later.'

'There's only one question that I really need answering now,' he whispered. 'Is it what we always expected?' The idea of Elly in the bedroom had been about our number three topic of conversation after Samantha Fox in the bedroom and Madonna in the bedroom.

Despite everything, I couldn't help but grin. It may have been delayed by fifteen years or so, but I was at last a successful teenager. I looked Cookie in the eye and said 'pretty much'. He collapsed with laughter.

When all the greetings were done, everyone sat down again. They had, of course, reserved a seat for me next to Elly, with Hannah on the other side and Cookie next to her. Hannah and Cookie – who had met each other several times over the years through me – were yakking away at once, and everyone else seemed suddenly absorbed in each other, leaving me with Elly. But I just couldn't look her in the eye.

'There was nothing I could do,' she said softly. 'It was all arranged ages ago.'

I contributed silence.

'Can't we just enjoy this evening and sort everything out tomorrow? Please, Charlie.' Her voice had a desperate note to it.

'It's not that easy,' I hissed. 'I still can't get over what you did.'

'I'm truly sorry, you've got to believe me.'

At last, I faced her. 'So go and tell Tom Gulliver what happened first thing on Monday.'

She hesitated, mouth half-open to say no, so I pushed my chair back violently. 'I can't believe that you're able to sit here so close to Hannah,' I whispered violently, and headed for the toilet.

It was one of those fancy marble affairs that I hate because there was a middle-aged guy notable for an apparently self-performed haircut sitting on a stool by the sink. He was watching sadly over an extensive collection of aftershave bottles and a small wicker basket containing a handful of coins. Things could be worse, I knew. At least I didn't have a job where the main perks were an endless supply of quality paper towels and an industrial-strength loo brush.

I stood by the urinal wondering what he tells his friends that he does. Personal grooming consultant, perhaps? Sanitation counsellor? Towel-dispensing agent? Basin buddy?

It was the servile attitude that made me feel so awful, and it always worked too from a financial point of view, because I felt duty bound to share with these guys my good fortune at having a job that doesn't require me to operate taps for careless men with urine on their fingers.

Still mightily confused, I stared at myself in the mirror above the sink for longer than was decent when there is someone watching you with a financial interest in your hand-washing. Despite the lure of wiping them against my trousers and making a rapid exit, I gave in and took the proffered towel, hoping I had something smaller than a fiver in my wallet. Taking change from the basket just looks so cheap.

'Bloody women, eh?' the man spat suddenly.

'I'm sorry?'

'Bloody women. I know that look. It's the "Shall I tell her it's over now or wait until later?" look.'

'I'm sorry?'

'When you're a male hygiene co-ordinator, you get to know looks like that. Just dump her. It's not worth it. She'll just do it again. Whatever it is.'

It seemed strangely sound wisdom. 'How do you know?'

'The bitch in the ladies. The so-called female hygiene manager. She gave herself the title, you won't be surprised to know. Keeps saying she'll share the quilted paper every time it comes in, but she never does. I know she has a stash hidden away in there somewhere.'

I backed away slowly towards the door. 'Well, thanks for the advice.'

'Last night's the last time I sleep with her, mark my words. That little trick won't work again.' He began furiously straightening his row of bottles and I slipped out. As I did, someone was leaving the ladies opposite and I caught sight of a shrivelled Oriental woman perched by the sink there. She looked about ninety-two. 'Pig,' she hissed at me.

The evening dragged, but I held my end up so well that nobody noticed that I would rather have been one of those idiots spending three weeks lying in a tub of baked beans than tripping the light fantastic with them. Elly and I barely spoke; I could hardly bring myself to look at her. It broke my heart to see her looking so gorgeous and so sparkling when she was talking to the others that I just wanted to forgive her and forget it ever happened. But then I looked at poor Hannah, laughing away when she was so sad and desperate, and I knew that inside Elly was hollow, a mockery of everything I'd thought she was. I considered making a dramatic declaration at the table, but knew it wouldn't help anyone.

Later in the evening, as people danced to the band, Cookie dropped into the seat vacated by Hannah. 'Bloody hell, mate, you look awful.'

I stiffened. He knew me too well. 'What do you mean? I'm fine.'

'Right, of course you are. You can't fool me, Fortune. I know when something's wrong.'

I looked around. 'Not here. Come to the bog with me.' We exited together, eliciting a cry from Hannah that Elly should watch out, she had competition. She just looked at us suspiciously.

The toilet was empty but for my new friend the co-ordinator, and I filled Cookie in as quickly as I could.

He rubbed his chin. 'This isn't just a leopard that hasn't

268

changed its spots. It's one that hasn't filed its claws, either.'

The co-ordinator slammed his fist down so hard on the sink that the bottles rattled. 'If you don't show them who's boss from the start, they don't stop taking advantage of your good nature,' he said in a constrained shout, eyes bulging. 'Oh no. You'll never get a new soap dispenser unless you get down on your knees in front of her and actually beg like a dog.'

Cookie began seeking the nearest emergency exit, but I reassured him blithely that this was just another example of the male/female divide.

Bewildered, he asked me what I was going to do.

I sighed. 'I don't think I've got much of a choice and it's killing me. What do you think?'

'You know what I've always thought of Elly. I'd say you've had a lucky escape.' I bowed my head in pain, wanting it all to go away, and Cookie put a reassuring arm around my shoulders. 'Come on, mate. Chin up.' That was almost loving as male bonding goes. 'You've got a birthday cake due any minute.'

I dug into my wallet again and dropped more coins in the basket.

'She actually makes you bark,' the co-ordinator confided, in a tone so low and menacing that I had a mental image of him pushing his former lover down the bowl and inflicting on her endless bog-washes until she drowned.

Smiling manically, we escaped. 'And you think you've got problems,' Cookie said.

Chapter Twenty-Nine

The evening had been pretty crap all round, but I got through it with the help of those industrious Danes and their breweries.

I'd spent a fair amount of time reassessing Elly. More than anything, I couldn't get over how she smacked her lips when she ate. I'd never noticed before, but now I had, it was driving me bonkers. Was it so hard to keep those full lips shut while chewing? And the way she attacked her food, sucking it down at speed like someone was above to snatch it from her tongue let alone her plate, was very unpleasant.

And her ears were tremendously pointy, I realised. Forget Venus, it looked like this woman was from Vulcan.

She looked quite tired, now I was looking. Dark smudges etched above her cheeks, grooved with lines.

And she'd overdone it with the blusher.

There was a big, angry red spot on her back which you could see when she leaned forward.

And was that a tiny bald patch I could see right in the middle of her head?

Just past midnight, with the wine bar winding down, the end was in sight until Hannah invited everyone back to the flat. She caught my glare, swayed slightly and giggled. 'Treat it like your own place, you said,' she reminded me with a beaming smile.

The other two work people cried off, explaining with virtuous smirks that they had to pop into the office later in the day and wanted to go home first. For a mad moment I considered escaping to the office myself, but didn't think that being caught drunk under my desk would do much for my partnership prospects; it was perfectly acceptable behaviour once you had reached the top – there were some partners who, when sober, couldn't advise a client how to cross the road – but not before.

The others were keen to keep going, and before I knew it we were back in the flat, with Lucy and Ash dancing drunkenly to Oasis in the middle of the living room, Cookie and Hannah busy in the kitchen slopping vodka down the sink in an effort to make unusual cocktails from a book Lucy had bought me as a present, while Elly and I sat on opposite ends of the sofa, glaring at one another.

'This is almost as much fun as your seventh birthday,' she muttered.

She'd never let me forget it. I've had birthday parties every single year of my life. My mum just loves celebrating things. If I hadn't put my foot down, we'd still be filling our glasses annually in honour of Harry The Hamster Joins The Fortune Family Day (she used to buy him special nuts to mark the occasion). Of course, it would actually be more appropriate to commemorate Charlie Learns The Value of Seatbelts After Harry The Hamster Suffers A Fatal Collision With A Lamppost While Perched Atop A Speeding Remote-Controlled Car Day.

Mum was always trying something new. It didn't do my popularity in the schoolyard much good when, as a new seven-year-old, I celebrated my birthday at a posh local eaterie with a strict table plan, printed menu and specially prepared songbook with which my soon-to-be-ex-friends were meant to serenade me into my eighth year. 'Next you'll be eight, but everyone already knows you're great' was the show-stopping line. Dad prodded away gamely at a tiny Casio electronic organ in an effort to get the sing-a-long going, but the silence was stonier than Brighton beach, even from Elly.

This led to a rethink the following year, when Mum hired out a cinema. Whether it was because it sounded to her like the kind of thing Jonny Morris would be behind, or simply because they got the wrong reel in the projection room, me and twenty mates sat bug-eyed as *Animal House* paraded before us. What we learned in that hour and a half informed our relationships with women for the next twenty-plus years, which in its way explains much. Fortunately, Mum stayed outside in the foyer gossiping with a couple of the other mums – by chance she only popped her head in during the few innocent moments and nodded with approval at how quiet everyone was being – while mine and two other dads were put in charge of supervising us. They were as transfixed by the swearing and horny women as we were, so said nothing. For years after, if someone was acting lamely in my group of friends, we would quote the film and demand: 'Greg, honey? Is it supposed to be this soft?'

Such was the massive success of the event that Mum repeated it the following year. This time, almost fifty people from school and elsewhere turned up with hopes high for a showing of *10*, in which we would apparently see Bo Derek's tits bounce up and down at regular intervals. But Mum had done a modicum of research this time, and my reputation as a man who brought naked girls to the masses plummeted when the credits to *The Black Stallion* began to roll. Promising name, but totally let down by the horse.

It might have been all right had Mum provided copious amounts of popcorn and chocolate as a diversion, but sadly the afternoon deteriorated into a competition to see who could hit the screen front furthest away first with apples and then, to increase the challenge, with the cucumber sandwiches she had supplied.

And so it went on. I'd rather forget birthday number thirteen (cousin Arnold pretending to be Kevin Keegan), number sixteen for the innovative if ultimately alarming 'Come dressed as someone in your class from the opposite sex' theme, number eighteen was simply embarrassing because of an Elly-organised boycott, while twenty-one was arguably the most successful birthday ever because I got off big-time with Carrie Lock, who my fellow male law students agreed – and we'd had organised polling to determine this – was among the top five prettiest girls on the course. When, later in the evening, I expressed disappointment that we hadn't hooked up earlier, she just shrugged and said: 'I couldn't think of a present to buy you.' I refused to allow that to ruin the evening, though.

But my thirty-second birthday was right up there with the worst of them, even number twenty-four, when a fellow trainee – known, in fairness, as a very nervous sort – projectile-vomited across the entire dinner table while we were discussing who the firm was going to keep on after qualification. It turned out that he was right to be worried; an especially mean supervising partner advised him to take up a less pressurised profession, such as unemployment. But a mouthful of puke rather took the edge off my sympathy.

Elly took a deep breath and shuffled along the sofa. 'Charlie,' she said in that no-nonsense tone that so impresses partners. 'Can't we put this behind us?'

'You just don't get it, do you?' I was saddened by the realisation that she genuinely didn't.

'Oh, grow up, Charlie.' Now she was irritated. 'If you don't look after number one in this business, nobody else will. I'm sorry about what's happened to Hannah – truly I am – but that's in the past now. Let's move on.'

I was about to explain, forcefully, why she was so utterly wrong when Hannah and Cookie returned bearing a tray laden with odd-coloured drinks. 'Cookie's had the best idea,' she said. There was a wary silence. 'Let's play truth or dare. I haven't done it since I was in school. It'll be a real laugh.'

I tried to protest but was shouted down by Lucy and Ash, who thought it hilarious. Hannah busily arranged the room so we were all sitting on the floor in the circle, each sipping our curious drinks. 'We got kind of bored with the book so we started making our own,' Cookie explained.

At first, it was relatively anodyne if not that pleasant, especially when Lucy said she would willingly abstain from sex for a year in return for a night of passion with John Prescott – it's the jowls and earthiness, apparently.

Ash confessed that he would gladly act as the senior partner's footstool for half an hour every day for the rest of his life if that was what it took to become a partner and Hannah broke it gently to an excited Cookie that she had never kissed another woman.

I chose a dare, which involved going into the bathroom and arranging myself so I was wearing my underwear on the outside, justifying the five minutes of agonising earlier that evening on which pair of trunks to go with.

'Sex on legs.' Lucy was not impressed as I returned. 'But you're still welcome to him, Elly.' The look that passed between us went unnoticed.

Then Elly declared that she would take a bullet if it came to a choice between her or me, and everyone went 'aah' and gave me a look which said how lucky we were to have found such love. Except Cookie, who said it was possibly the most pathetic thing he'd heard in his entire life – and that included my nineteenth birthday party, where eight people bought me law books as presents – and that we should all go into intensive therapy at once.

Things soon got more raucous, mainly due to the lethal nature of the cocktails. In the second round, Lucy, who now looked so pissed that she'd fall off the floor if she could, called on Ash to choose.

'I'm an open book,' he said. 'I'll go for truth.'

She giggled uncontrollably for a few seconds before composing herself. 'If you had to snog someone in this room, who would it be?'

He gazed around the circle with a calculating eye. I

would have been abashed by the question, but it takes a lot more to make Ash blush. 'Sorry girls. And boys. It's got to be Elly. It's something about those lips.' Elly smiled at him, equally unembarrassed.

Ash turned to me to choose. Terrified of a question that would expose anything that had happened with Elly, I went for another dare. 'To keep with the theme,' he decided at length, 'I'm going to blindfold you and each of us is going to kiss you. You then have to guess who's who.' Lucy clapped her hands in excitement.

So I sat there in the dark to a soundtrack of ceaseless giggling, while lips were pressed to mine. The first was utterly revolting, mainly because it was a bit bristly but also because the giver seemed confused with the kiss of life. The second, however, was lovely: soft, moist lips touching mine with gossamer lightness. The third, I knew instantly, was Elly. There was an urgency in the touch, a desire, I thought, for forgiveness. The fourth was work-manlike and not unpleasant, but you wouldn't in normal circumstances be unbuckling your belt immediately with the passion of it all. There was a pause before the final one, and then a beautiful hesitancy in the initial contact, before warmth flooded in. It seemed to last far longer than the others, before the kisser slowly withdrew.

The blindfold was removed and, warily, I began my list.

I got number one right. 'Cookie, my friend. Those five seconds of contact have answered for me a twenty-year question as to why you don't hang on to your girlfriends,' I said.

The appealing gentleness of number two made me sure it was Hannah; I could tell by the hilarity of the reaction that it was, in fact, Ash. The five seconds of contact with him told me why women fell under his spell so easily. 'You kiss like a girl,' I told him. 'And that's not a compli-ment.'

Oops. Big oops. Number three wasn't Elly. She wasn't pleased, Lucy – who in fact it was – wasn't pleased, and I was hardly cart-wheeling for joy either. It turned out that far from seeking forgiveness, Elly's was the joyless fourth kiss, which I'd assumed was Ash.

We stared at each other. Elly looked ... I wasn't sure how she looked. But was it fear I saw? Or just shock at everything that had happened? There was love there, I could still see that. I searched for regret but found nothing. I felt empty. It was over. Why couldn't she be my Fantasy Elly of the last fifteen years? Why did she have to ruin everything?

My God, what an awful feeling. I'd never thought it would come to us getting together in the first place, but for us then to fall apart felt absurdly tragic.

So it only registered slowly that number five was not Lucy, as I had imagined – there was something about the heat and vibrancy that made me think of her – but actually Hannah. I glanced at her; she had her hand over her mouth, as if to withdraw what her lips had done. But there was an intensity in her eyes that we had never shared before. I didn't hold her stare.

'I'm a bloke,' I wanted to shout at them all. 'I don't do complication.'

An awkward silence slowly permeated the alcoholic fog in the room. The hilarity of the evening was now just an echo. Ash looked at me curiously, but I couldn't bear it a minute longer and started making noises to get everyone out. Cookie was staying the night on the sofa, so Ash hoisted himself to his feet, pulling Lucy up.

'The walk with do us good,' he said. 'I'll make sure Lucy gets home.'

'Can you see Elly back too?' I asked.

He laughed. 'What? All the way to your bedroom?'

But Elly had leaped up and was already buttoning up her coat. I could tell she was restraining the tears. 'I need to be up early, so I'm going back to my flat,' she said quietly.

Cookie, Hannah and I lined up at the door to see them out in a flurry of goodbyes. Ash and Lucy were already walking down to the lift, while Cookie and Hannah had disappeared back into the living room. We faced each other.

276

Elly put her hand to my cheek in the way she knew I liked. 'I love you, Charlie.'

Words I'd spent so long not even daring to hear were now as nothing. I gently removed her hand. 'Goodnight Elly.'

Chapter Thirty

I was spitting mad. Heartbroken, upset and incredibly sad as well, but more than anything, so mad that I suddenly felt empathy with Dr David Banner, the guy who turned into the Incredible Hulk at times of great emotion. How satisfying it would be right now to go around mindlessly shouting at people and propelling them through walls.

But how was it, I wondered, briefly distracted, that there was never anyone around to see his trousers split and his body turn green. Even that made me angry. How ridiculous was it that a man could turn into a monster and yet in a planet as overcrowded as this one, not a single person ever clapped eyes on Dr David Bloody Banner in mid-transformation.

Mind you, even if it happened in the middle of the canteen at Babbingtons, the most there might be would be a slight cough from someone at the impropriety of it, but nobody would actually say anything. It would, though, be noted on my record: 'Turns inappropriately green, doubles in body size and roars incoherently with rage when under stress. Recommend no promotion.'

Bloody Elly. She'd screwed everything up.

When agitated, I tend to pace and Hannah didn't have to

be at her most observant to guess that something was up. She'd been avoiding me since the night before, scurrying around, and darting in and out of the kitchen for provisions, but finally dug up the courage to confront me. Cookie had alredy sloped off, giving her his number. 'Take it from someone who's kissed him,' I'd advised as he handed over a scrap of paper. 'Burn it.'

If there was a choice, what would be the best way to execute Elly for crimes against Charles Fortune? That was a toughie.

I think Hannah was put out when I told her flatly that it had nothing to do with her and nothing to do with the night before.

'Oh, well, that's good,' she said. 'Cos of course it meant nothing. Just messing around drunk, you know the thing.'

Probably the axe. Greater chance of something going wrong, causing excruciating pain. I wasn't totally concentrating on Hannah. 'The thing, that's right,' I said vaguely. 'That was a lovely kiss, though.'

Hannah went a cute pink. 'Did you think? What exactly did you like about it?'

Tutting to myself, I wandered off to resume my pacing.

Hannah followed me around, nagging me to reveal all, but I would only tell her to piss off. She nagged some more, and I told her to piss off more. She said, testily, if I would please tell her what was wrong. I replied, easily out-testying her, 'Will you please piss off.' She said she wouldn't shut up until I told her, to which I went for the lowest blow I knew and said that if she didn't piss off at Olympic speed, I'd call her mother and say I was worried about her daughter being single for ever and maybe now was the time to introduce her to that Jewish friend of hers she was always going on about who has a matchmaking business on the side.

Hannah – to her credit, as this fate was a mortal fear – was not so easily deterred. 'Do that and you won't have anything to worry about at all because you'll be trying to cope with a saucepan through your head.'

I went into the lounge and fell on to the sofa. 'Elly and I split up.'

Hannah became a study in concern. 'What happened?'

I needed to say something but couldn't face telling Hannah the whole story quite yet. I wasn't ready to deal with her anger and upset as well. 'She cheated on me,' I said. It was entirely true in the broad sense of the word.

Hannah put her hand to her mouth, the thrill of the shock revelation bringing a smile to her lips, which disappeared as quickly as it came. 'Who with? Was it anyone we know?'

'I don't want to talk about it.'

'No, no, of course you don't. It wasn't Martin Montgomery, was it? I always thought he looked at her strangely. And he is so good-looking.'

I felt a flash of paranoia but then remembered that Elly, for all her voluminous faults, was truly in love with me. 'No, it wasn't Martin. I don't want to talk about it, OK?'

'Sorry, of course. Andrew Hill?'

'Hannah, shut up.'

'Just tell me it wasn't Walter Flint. I know he's the legal profession's answer to Einstein, and that Elly finds big brains really sexy, which of course seems rather odd what with her going out with you and everything, but the whole business of his head being wider than it is long is just too freaky.'

'I'm going to count to five and if you say another word, I'm calling that matchmaker myself just to get you out of my hair for the next forty years.'

She sat on the arm of the sofa and slowly sneaked an awkward arm around my shoulders. It was the most unconvincing effort I had seen since I was fourteen and tried the classic cinema yawn, stretch and 'whoops, look at that – my arm just felt around your shoulders' manoeuvre. Caroline Beeson, who was acerbic beyond her years, just said, 'Charlie, you seem to have dropped something,' and I vowed never to listen to my late grandfather's advice about women again. 'Works like a charm,' he'd said with a wink.

280

Hannah pulled me back to the pain of reality. 'Sorry, Charlie. Is there anything I can do?'

I sighed. 'No, I just need some time to myself.'

'I'll get out of your way, go to my mother's or something.'

I looked up at her for the first time. 'You'd do that for me? Matchmaker and all?'

'Yeah. I reckon I'm damaged goods anyway. The shame of it all. My mother told me I'd be much harder to shift after all this. "So what does your wife do, Mr Cohen?" "She's the woman who almost brought down Babbington Botts through her own staggering incompetence. But I'm hoping that she's capable of bringing up our children under strict supervision."'

Laughing, I grabbed at the hand draped over my shoulder. 'Don't go home. I want you around, you know, just in case and stuff.'

She smiled broadly and got up. 'I know,' she said. 'Why don't I see what wonders I can rustle up for lunch.'

I smiled back. 'Aha, so you can cook after all.'

'Well, I did go to Sainsbury's yesterday specially,' she said with a modest grin as she disappeared off into the kitchen. 'All I need is my trusty fork, and you'll see that nobody pierces the film of those wholesome microwave meals better than me.'

It was one of those times when I had to talk it out with someone – even if I didn't know exactly what I was going to say – but I couldn't find anyone to listen. Hannah was obviously out, and I didn't feel it was right to burden Lucy and Ash with what Elly had done. My mum would just cry a lot, say 'How could you do this to me?' and accuse me of ruining her detailed plans for my future, while my dad would suggest that mowing the lawn for him would be good therapy. I thought of talking to Cookie again, but he reckoned I was well out of it and couldn't understand what all the fuss was about.

In desperation, I fiddled around with my rarely used, office-supplied personal organiser and found Sparkle's telephone number.

'Hello there.' The voice was huskier than normal.

'Sparkle? Is that you?'

'Yes, lover. How can I help you today?' I was neither convinced nor turned on.

'Is that any way to talk to your legal adviser?'

'Charlie? Is that you?' The voice was suddenly far more welcoming. 'What are you doing phoning me? There's nothing wrong with the Bills, is there?'

'No, no, nothing like that,' I said, and gave her a rough outline of what had happened.

The laugh down the phone was long and throaty. 'The only thing worse than bloody men, in my experience, is bloody women,' she said, adding that of course I could come over, but she still had a couple of appointments to get through. She gave me directions and I set off at once, pleased to be out of the flat, leaving Hannah – whom I had to reassure several times that I was not going out to throw myself off a bridge – to work on some job applications.

Sparkle may have been a pal of sorts, but that didn't stop me mentally filling in the details of her life with the broad brush of stereotype. I'd assumed that she lived on the top floor of a dingy council block, with lifts that had given up the will to be repaired, smackheads reintroducing the concept of community by shooting up together on every stairwell, and kids juggling flick-knives, handguns and knuckle-dusters. So I was surprised that she actually rented a neat if small terraced house in a reasonably respectable neighbourhood. There was even a hanging basket by the door, which itself was painted a cheery orange.

There was a long pause after I rang the bell. I rang again and had my finger on the bell for a third and final time when the door opened slightly to reveal a balding middle-aged guy in a suit.

He blinked nervously. 'Erm, yes? Can I, erm, help you?'

I was quickly double-checking the address I'd written down. 'Sorry, I must have the wrong house.' I turned to leave.

'Are you, erm, here for, erm, Sparkle?'

Maybe this guy was some kind of minder, or even her pimp, although I was sure she'd said she was long past needing that kind of help. And if he was a pimp, then somebody should have pulled him aside and explained that an M&S suit didn't project the right image. I nodded and he opened the door to let me in, before carefully closing it and leading me into the front room.

The square room wasn't big but it was busily furnished, although it was easy to be distracted by the television in the far corner, which was showing two naked guys silently but energetically getting it on with a naked woman whose breasts were so large it was little wonder that she couldn't get up from the floor. At either end there were dark patterned chairs framing a sagging sofa, covered by a huge patchwork throw, against the near wall. It was flanked by small tables that were piled high with porn mags. The largish bay windows were covered by opaque nets, with thick dark red curtains ready to conceal further any of the goings-on inside. Opposite the sofa was a nice period fireplace with shelves on either side. On the left was a very eclectic collection of books, while on the right was an equally diverse mix of videos.

'Hope you don't mind waiting. Sparkle's running a bit late, you see. Just like the doctor, eh?' His laugh was more confident now he had tagged me as a fellow punter. 'And I don't know about you, but I find that her hands are just as cold as well.'

I nodded again as I wandered over to the mantelpiece. Sitting proudly between a wrought-iron candlestick and a photo of a much younger Sparkle in leathers smiling happily atop a motorcycle, was an obscenely large and knobbly bright purple vibrator. Curious, I picked it up and pressed the button at the base. The head started whirling at a dizzying speed. Scared it might put my eye out or something – that would be an easy one to explain at work – I quickly put it back on the mantelpiece but it flapped around manically like a fish out of water and fell to the floor, where it brought a whole new meaning to the idea of carpet shag until the man came over, picked it up and turned it off.

'First time here?' he asked. I nodded once more. 'It won't be the last. Sparkle has a very loyal client base.'

In other circumstances, that was the kind of reference that helped you on your way to partnership. I smiled to myself and picked up the cane that was propped up against a chair. I flicked my wrist and it swished satisfyingly through the air. I could have sworn that a look of some pleasure crossed my companion's face at the noise.

'So I'm in for three o'clock,' he said. 'How about you?'

I went slightly red at once. 'Oh no, I'm not here for that. I mean, I've got a girlfriend and everything.'

He looked offended and pushed back his shoulders. 'So what? I've got a wife. But she's less fun than having sex with a mincing machine soaked in sulphuric acid.'

The pleasing thought of Elly naked flashed into my mind, but I forced it back out with a regretful farewell. 'Sorry, mate, no offence. What I mean is that I'm a friend of Sparkle's. But this is the first time I've been here.'

Slightly mollified, he dropped on to the sofa and reached for the pile of magazines. I wandered over to the videos, doing my best to ignore the muffled cry which struggled through the ceiling. There were some westerns, a good smattering of classic Bette Davis, a long line of *Star Trek* movies, and quite the most impressive range of pornography you could ever hope to find outside of Amsterdam.

Mr Three O'clock was totally engrossed in a copy of *Jugs* to judge by the way he was rotating the magazine to view it from different angles and his hushed comments, such as 'goodness me, would you only look at the size of them.' Between that, Sparkle's own asset base in that region, and the video – where the plot had moved on apace with the entrance of a top-heavy blonde neighbour holding a small empty bowl who would clearly do absolutely anything to get her hands on some sugar – it was clear where his preferences lay.

284

But once he realised I was browsing the videos, he got up to give me a guided tour. 'There are some real classics in here,' he said knowledgeably. 'If you see one you like, I don't mind putting it on. Sparkle always has this one on for me because she knows how much I like it, but variety's the spice of life and all that.' I carelessly fingered one. 'Aha, a spanking man, I see. Every time you come here they're arranged in a different way. One of Sparkle's clients is this guy who does dictionaries and he gets a real kick out of ordering porn videos, sometimes by name, sometimes by genre, sometimes by lead actress, that sort of thing.'

'No, no, not spanking.' But the idea prompted another fleeting image to speed through my head, although this time it starred Hannah and her peachy bottom. I pushed it away with alarm. 'I was just, you know, looking.'

He stood back, now condescending. 'Of course you were. But don't worry. It takes all sorts. I'll just go back and continue what I was doing.'

I moved over to take in the books, which, I was relieved to see, were of the sort that only contained sex demanded by the context. Once again I was surprised. I'd expected trash and while there was a historical romance strain in her reading, there was a surprising amount of modern Irish literature. I chided myself for being such a bloody snob.

Mr Three O'Clock was halfway through *Big 'n' Bouncy* to a muttered chorus of 'talk about gravity-defying' and 'they'd blot the sun out from the right angle' when finally there was noise on the stairs and Sparkle appeared wearing a green kimono.

She looked genuinely pleased to see me. 'Hello, Charlie. I hope Fabien here has been keeping you entertained.'

'I think he's been too busy entertaining himself,' I smiled and Mr Three O'Clock proudly showed her his magazine.

She turned to Fabien. 'Have you got some time to spare?' He nodded. 'Good,' she said, and ushered in Mr Two O'Clock, who looked in his early forties and to judge by the cut of his suit, fairly prosperous. 'This is Maurice.'

Fabien and I looked at each other quizzically. I suspected this wasn't usual brothel decorum. 'I know this is a bit strange, but I'd like Fabien and Maurice to hear about the whole Elly thing. They can probably help more than me. Maurice has been married, what, three times?' Looking faintly embarrassed, Maurice raised four fingers. 'But I've always been faithful to you, Sparkle, don't forget that.'

She nodded regally as if she expected nothing else. 'And Fabien here is a relationship counsellor. It's absolutely perfect.' I looked at Fabien with wild surmise, but decided I just didn't want to know.

I was sceptical but Sparkle persuaded me, especially when Maurice settled down and said he'd love to help. Fabien chuckled: 'I'll call it a freebie. You don't get many of those in this house.'

So, reluctantly, I told them the tale at some length, and when I finished there was a thoughtful silence.

'Screw her,' Maurice said decisively.

Sparkle was sardonic. 'That's your answer to everything.'

'No, I mean it. Give it to her with both barrels. Use every dirty trick in the book to get that partnership ahead of her.'

Fabien steepled his fingers. 'In my job, I have to advise people to be careful and calm. I have to try and take the sting out of these terrible emotions that are swirling around a relationship. It's difficult to accept, but it is usually better to turn the other cheek.' Maurice snorted. 'But in this case, in my professional opinion, she's clearly an absolute bitch, so, as Maurice so eloquently put it, screw her. Go for the jugular, boy.'

I frowned at Sparkle, not sure I was getting the best advice here. 'Charlie, it's your decision. But it strikes me that this woman's been walking all over you for twenty-five years. It might be time to get your own back.'

The words hit home. I was suddenly seized by a rush of emotion. I could almost hear my trousers ripping and skin turn green. 'You know, I think you may be right.'

Chapter Thirty-One

Every great figure needs a nemesis: Nelson had Napoleon; Sherlock Holmes had Moriarty; Big Daddy, of course, had Giant Haystacks. There was Kennedy and Castro, Superman and Lex Luthor, Barbie and Sindy.

And then there was Charlie and Elly.

I went into work after the weekend determined to hit Elly where it hurt the most: in her partnership ambitions. I would be SuperLawyer, faster than a speeding bill, able to leap tall legal problems in a single bound. Or Lawyer Barbie, although without the dress and constant interruptions from Ken. I might throw in a few ill-founded rumours as well, just for the heck of it. Remind her of one of the less mature aspects of our teenage rivalry.

But I had reckoned without my nemesis. She had all the attributes: the strategic nous of Napoleon and the guile of Moriarty, mixed up with an Haystackian ability to flatten people. She also boasted the staying power of Castro and the ruthlessness of Luthor, all wrapped up in the body of Sindy.

I stood impatiently in the lift to my floor, hopping around the empty car like a boxer limbering up. 'In the red corner, we have Charlie "The Buckinghamshire Bruiser"

Fortune. Weighing in at £240 an hour, he brings grace, wit and a cheeky but winning smile to the ring, together with an ability to bluff his way through that may yet see him reach the very top.'

'In the blue corner, we have Elly "The Wycombe Waster" Gray. Already with one broken heart on her record, she has the killer combo of great brain and great legs, sure to send any partner wobbly with one flash of her perfect teeth.'

Elly didn't know the meaning of gentle sparring. I'd been at my desk all of ninety seconds when she steamed in, projecting a detached, professional air. She dropped a file on the desk. 'This is the bill for the Norton Fisher deal. I just need you to quickly check over it.'

I glanced up but there was nothing to read in her face, so I scanned the bill. We both knew that we had to maintain a cordial working relationship. 'I think there's some kind of mistake,' I said. 'It's got you down at £250 an hour.'

Elly's face was slightly contorted. She was trying to conceal the fact that she wanted me to see that she was trying to conceal a smile. 'Ian thought I should go up a notch and the other partners in the group agreed.' She waved a hand airily. 'Ten pounds here or there doesn't really matter.'

She knew it did. And she knew that I knew it did. I wanted to control my extreme jealousy, but failed. The last time I'd seen her smile victoriously like that, neither of us had any clothes on. Now it was just our desire to do the other down that was laid bare.

Within just a few short months she'd waltzed past me. I'd been stuck on £240 for about a year and a half now, and my frequent requests, jokes and begging to have it pushed up had fallen on deaf ears. You'd have thought Babbingtons would be only too happy to ratchet me up to the highest level they could possibly get away with, but there were even greater issues than profits at stake. This was a firm where your charge-out rate was your status and your status was everything. It gave you an incentive to work harder still. It had been suggested to me so often that I just needed to put in another 5 per cent that by now I must be up to about 685 per cent of my capacity.

The phone rang and I snatched it up. It was Graham. 'I was hoping you could pop your head round my door in, oh, say the next thirty seconds or so,' he said gruffly.

I hid my alarm as I replaced the receiver. 'Sorry, Elly. Gotta go. I've a meeting with some partners.' It was her turn to look worried.

I scooted over to Graham's room. He waved me in and told me to close the door, which in itself was a bad sign. He had embraced an open-door policy, he had readily explained, so he could check who was wearing what skirt and how short it was. 'The trouser suit is the worst thing ever to happen to women's clothing,' he often maintained.

'A couple of things. First of all, are you doing anything the weekend after next?' Before I could even form the words to say 'I intend filling my now-empty life with so many chargeable hours that you'll be able to retire to Barbados next year', he barrelled on. 'Good. I'm pleased to say you've made it through to the next round. There's this new partnership assessment centre thing going on at some hotel in the Midlands over the weekend. You are, as they say, cordially invited.'

I returned his smile. 'I assume I don't need to RSVP.'

'If you can't make it, there's always next year, I suppose. Or the year after, or the year after that. You could be going for many years to come, in fact.'

'I get the idea.'

'Good. Well done, anyway. You should be proud of having got this far. Although it might be a good idea to put a bit more effort into being seen as a heavyweight presence. Be seen around the office a lot over the next few weeks doing important things, that sort of thing. Be here a bit more than usual, perhaps.' Short of ordering fitted wardrobes for my office, it was hard to know how I could, but I just nodded. 'Like your friend Miss Gray. First in

289

and last out yesterday, so I'm told. Nothing like Sunday working to impress. You should know that by now.' OK, I told myself, trying to be cool, the SuperLawyer thing starts this moment.

It seemed as good a moment as any to bring up my charge-out rate. He looked faintly embarrassed that I knew about Elly's rise, but said he couldn't recommend another one so soon after hers. It begged the question of why he didn't recommend it in the first place, but I stayed my tongue. 'Maybe just try and up your game by 5 per cent and I'll put it to the next corporate partners' meeting,' he said.

He leaned back in his chair. 'The lovely Miss Gray leads me on to the other thing, Charles. I don't wish to pry but I understand that you've done the dirty on her.' I gaped. 'I don't care what happened and want to know even less.' Damn her. She'd got her retaliation in first. 'But already people are talking. Charles did this, Charles did that. Of course I don't believe any of it, but it's not good having that kind of thing going around the office.'

'What kind of thing?'

He looked at me with fatherly disapproval. 'I think you know. Just deal with it, Charles, will you?'

I thought of pouring out the truth. For all his many faults, Graham was just about fair, and I could see him doing what was necessary. But there was no longer any proof since Elly had deleted it from her computer: this was a firm where if it wasn't written down, photocopied eight times, distributed across the department and then carefully filed, then it didn't exist. And worst of all, Elly knew this.

As I rose to leave, Graham said, 'I did warn you against playing at home, didn't I?'

I admired the blatant hypocrisy – another perk of being a partner. The most recent story doing the rounds was from the other week, when Graham propositioned the temp who was standing in for his holidaying secretary.

He is supposed to have sat on her desk chatting late one evening, then switched on his full cheesy smile and asked, 'Are you as good in bed as you are with a keyboard?'

And she reportedly replied: 'Are you as boring in bed as you are in this bloody dictation?'

I noticed a scowl or two on my way back to my room, where Richard, still chairman of the Elly Fan Club, ignored my good morning. Then Ash strolled in and fell into a chair. 'Charlie, mate, that was a bit rough, what you did to Elly.'

I slapped the desk in exasperation. 'I didn't do anything.'

'But leaving her in the rain miles from home, without a coat or an umbrella. That's just not on.'

'I'm sorry?'

Richard chipped in, looking angry. 'And without any money. There's no need to be vindictive.'

'What?' There was a horrid buzzing sound in my ears.

Ash shook his head. 'And chucking her keys down a drain? What's got into you, Charlie?'

'I genuinely have no idea what you are going on about.'

'Ash stared at me in doubt. Then Lucy appeared in the doorway. 'Charlie. Be honest with me. Did you really slash Elly's tyres?'

I gripped my head in my hands for fear that it would explode. 'Where have you been getting this from? Has Elly actually said all this to you?'

The three of them looked at each other. 'Not exactly,' Ash conceded.

'I was told by a friend in the property department,' said Lucy. This was a fast-moving Chinese whisper even by Babbingtons' standards.

Richard was unabashed. 'Someone said they'd heard it from someone who got it from Elly's own secretary.' That seemed to be enough for him.

I was trying hard to keep calm. 'It's not true, OK? We've split up but none of it happened like that.'

Ash and Lucy looked equally amazed. 'I can't believe you two have split up,' he said. 'Why?'

'You two looked so happy on Saturday night,' Lucy said.

I wondered whether she was mad or had just been pissed, before saying, 'I don't want to go into it now, but let's just say it was the right thing to do.'

They pressed me and even sent Richard out of the room so I could talk more freely. But what was I going to tell them? Some fantastic tale of conspiracy carried out by a woman who everyone else thinks could walk on water but is too modest to prove it and too nice to scare the ducks? These were good people who wouldn't believe that one of our number could do such a thing without thick files of evidence and a jury intoning 'guilty' after a ten-week trial.

I pleaded with them not to believe what they heard and to ask others to do the same. 'You know I wouldn't do all that stuff, don't you?' I said, wondering if our eight-year friendship could falter so easily. 'You do believe me, don't you?'

Ash shrugged. 'Of course we do, mate, but there is a bit of history here, isn't there? And you were so into her. It can send you a bit loco, know what I mean?'

'Ash. Lucy. I didn't do anything. We broke up, that was it. No tantrums, no slashed tyres. For pity's sake, it hasn't even rained this weekend. Tell me you believe me.'

Lucy's stare was straight and honest. 'Of course we do,' she said.

Ash nodded. 'It doesn't sound like you at all. But there's something you're not telling us.'

'Hopefully, I'll be able to soon,' I said, and ushered them out. More than anything, I knew I had to stay calm. Elly had come out all guns blazing, but I was determined not to be bothered by wild rumours that would die a death within a few hours. I flipped open a file decisively and was just starting to get my head around a distribution agreement when the phone rang once more. It was the receptionist saying she had a Mr and Mrs Stanley Fortune for me. It always made me laugh that when faced by anything approaching formality – and a receptionist at a pukka City law firm certainly counted – my mother's voice would rise a plummy notch or three and she would introduce herself officially as Mr and Mrs Stanley Fortune.

'OK, put her through,' I said.

'Erm, no,' came the reply. 'I mean that Mr and Mrs Fortune are down here in reception for you.'

I looked at the receiver in surprise. 'What? Why?'

She was getting a little testy now. 'I'm really not sure. Would you like me to ask?'

'Well, if you wouldn't mind.'

There was a tut, the sound of a hand going over the receiver, and muffled noise. 'Apparently they happened to be passing. And they've never seen your office, even though you've worked here for eight years.'

Unhappy at the collision of my work life with my family, I rushed down to reception and dragged them away from the receptionists. 'I'll bring in those photos next time,' Mum was promising one of them. 'He looked so adorable in that matching tie and shirt. Goodness, what a time the seventies were.'

Mum was wildly overdressed. 'You haven't been invited to tea by the Prime Minister, have you?' I asked.

'Now, Charlie. What have I always told you: a smart appearance marks out a smart person.'

I smiled at my dad, who was looking unhappy in a blazer and a tie imprinted with dancing lawnmowers. 'Could do with a few plants in here to cheer the place up,' he said.

'So, you were just passing, were you? Where were you going?'

There was an awkward pause. Bloody Elly. This was one step too far. Impressive, I conceded. But one giant step too far. She should have kept our families out of this. No doubt she'd called her mother who'd called mine, who'd decided – or been asked, perhaps – to take immediate action. I'd once been given *The Art of War* by Sun Tzu, staple reading for any aspiring lawyer. How I suddenly regretted having tossed it into a drawer.

'We came up to do some shopping, go to the bank, that sort of thing.'

'Well, there aren't any shops around here and the nearest bank is the Bank of Malta. I didn't realise you had an account there.'

'We've been reviewing our financial arrangements,' Dad offered weakly.

There was another awkward silence.

'Well, it was great to see you,' I said, clapping my hands with finality and moving towards the front door. 'I'm really busy, so what say I give you a call tonight?'

Like bad luck, the awkward silences came in threes. Mum didn't move. 'Now we're here, we'd love to see where you work.'

I waved a hand around. 'Well, this is it. Not much to see, really. Just an office.'

'No, your room and so on. And then maybe we could catch up, have a little natter about things.' Even if I could charge it at £500 an hour, this was a little natter I could do without.

But she's not an easy person to budge when she puts her mind to it. 'We're not allowed to take people actually into the office. We have loads of meeting rooms for visitors. How about I show you one of those before you go?'

But Mum started waving at her receptionist friend. 'Do you mind if Charlie takes us up to his room?' she said loudly. 'We won't be a few minutes.'

'No problem, Mrs Fortune,' she yelled back.

Defeated, I led them to the lift and took them up. We almost made it to my room without anyone saying anything to us, when Mum stopped in the typing pool. 'Which of you is Sue?'

My secretary stood up and Mum introduced herself. They knew each other well enough from all the times she called. 'Here's that strawberry shortcake recipe I always said I'd give you,' Mum said, digging in her handbag, and a memory of intense pleasure passed over my dad's face. Mum and Sue then began nattering away about how difficult I could be.

'Tell me about it,' Mum said. 'When he was a boy, he

refused to go near me when I was using a letter opener. Said he was scared.'

'That's so amazing,' Sue said. 'He still says the same. Every morning I have to open his post like I'm his slave.'

'I'm just nervous around sharp things,' I snapped. 'You never know who you're going to want to stab.' And I glared at them both.

Dad had wandered over to the stationery cupboard. 'Goodness,' he said, amazed by the wonders within. 'I didn't know you could get blue Post-It notes. Have you seen these, Charlie?'

With impeccable timing, Graham then walked over to hand in some typing. His curious gaze turned into something more hostile in my direction when he learned who the visitors were. Barely minutes after he'd counselled me on the need to look like a heavyweight presence in the office, here I was holding a family reunion in the typing pool.

'Great office you've got here,' my dad said, shaking his hand. 'Do you know you've got orange Post-It notes in there. Always thought they only came in yellow.'

'Lucy, Ashok,' Mum suddenly shouted, waving at them across the other side of the room. 'Come and say hello. I haven't seen you for ages.' By now, most of the floor was watching as they sheepishly complied. It was turning into a right old party.

More and more people wandered over, and then Mum caught sight of Elly striding purposefully from the lift. 'Eleanor,' she cried happily. 'How lovely to see you, dear.'

Elly came over and embraced Mum, giving me a wicked wink as I watched. 'I'm so sorry to hear what happened.' At this point, Mum shook her head at me violently. 'I'm sure we can do something about it. Charles never knows what's best for him.'

'Mum, do you mind?'

'So it's just as well we're here to give him a nudge in the right direction, don't you think?' Elly nodded gravely. 'And we'll pay for those tyres, dear, don't you worry.'

I was fit to explode but was grabbed by Lucy and pushed away. I stood to the side and watched moodily while the entire floor appeared to stop work and join the fun. The babble was getting louder, but I heard Graham – who was trapped against a desk by Mum – say that she must be very proud of me.

Mum glanced over with affection. 'Oh, despite everything, we're very proud of him. And it'll be even better when he becomes a partner this year.'

It was like one of those moments from the films where the entire room falls silent and turns to look at one person. I broke into a lunatic grin, which didn't seem inappropriate given that I seemed to have stumbled into an asylum.

'Well, I never,' my dad said from the crowd. 'Pink ones as well. Never seen anything like it in my life.'

Chapter Thirty-Two

Things had been going badly with Elly. I'd been trying hard to get my own back, but in the fortnight or so since our break-up, she seemed to be getting the better of me at every turn, and I was starting to think that I'd do well to get a job in the postroom, let alone a place at the next partnership away day.

I worked and I moped, then worked some more, and seeking variety, tried pining for the happier, less complicated past. Hannah was absolutely wonderful, just being around when I needed, making me laugh and offering hugs at especially dicey moments. The last thing I could do was tell her everything and ruin what little happiness there was in both our lives.

The assessment centre weekend was forty-eight hours of sticky palms. After Lucy, Ash and I got over the embarrassment of not having told each other that we'd been put up, Elly joined the fray as if nothing had happened. She was, as they say, in the zone: once again, I was largely an irritating irrelevance in her go-ahead life – roles we were at least both familiar with. Making the right impression was all that counted to her. She was kind of impressive, kind of frightening, kind of annoying.

'I love you, Charlie,' she said to me quietly in a corner. 'Nothing's changed that.' My treacherous heart reacted to the words. 'But this weekend is business, you know that, don't you?'

But the rural peace of the hotel, not far from Stratford, comforted me. I was no country boy – I barely knew one end of a cow from the other – but could see the appeal of a third home bathed in this. It was hard this weekend not to make plans for how I would spend my partnership wonga: a family home outside London, perhaps somewhere like Oxford, with a flat in central London for those nights when it was just too hard to go home for reasons of work, alcohol or amorous assistant solicitors. Then the third place could be in the Cotswolds perhaps, so the kids could enjoy the full benefits of country air.

Around forty associates were there from across the firm and across the world – those from Babbingtons' several overseas offices also had to attend. Throughout the two days, I couldn't escape Oskar, a massive, sharp-faced guy from the Frankfurt office who took an immediate liking to me.

'I'm from Barcelona,' he said to me when we were first introduced at the welcome reception, and laughed heartily. His accent, though, sounded distinctly Germanic.

'Do you work in the Madrid office then?'

'Que?' He grinned.

'I'm sorry?'

'Que?' The grin widened alarmingly and I saw a lot of gum.

'Do you work in the Madrid office? I didn't think we had a Barcelona office.'

'Don't mention ze vor.' He wagged a finger at me, giggling hard.

'I'm sorry?' The man was making so little sense I wondered whether in fact he was talking to an invisible friend.

'I mentioned it vonce but I theenk I got avay vith it.' And he laughed until he wheezed.

298

I presumed the pressure was getting to him already. 'Look I've got to, erm, go somewhere to, erm, do something, so, erm, please excuse me.'

But Oskar seized me by the arm. 'I'm from Barcelona.' He said it really loudly, like I was slow.

'So you keep saying. Strangest Spanish accent I've ever heard, I've got to say.'

'Don't you know it?'

'Never been there.

'You started it.'

'No, I didn't.'

'Yes, you did. You invaded Poland.' Oskar was doubled over by the hilarity of it all. By this stage, everyone was silent and staring at us in a way that could only be described as not career-enhancing. I gestured to indicate that I was an innocent bystander to this utter loony. Elly's face was a picture of pleasure, like she had just firmly struck off two names from the competition.

'*Fawlty Towers*, what a programme,' he sighed happily. 'Vhen I was growing up, ve used to vatch your sitcoms all ze time on British forces television. I love ze British sense of humour. Zhat's vhy I joined Babbingtons. So funny. I know, I'll do ze funny valk.'

To my horror, Oskar seemed to be winding up for a brief goosestep around the room, taking both our futures with him. I grabbed an arm and yanked him over to the bar. 'Better not.'

I soon discovered that it wasn't just that Oskar liked *Fawlty Towers*, knew every line and introduced himself to any English person by saying 'I'm from Barcelona', but it appeared that 1970s sitcoms were his entire early education in English.

Why do you want to be a partner, Oskar? 'I just vant to keep ze riff-raff avay.'

Do you like the hotel, Oskar? 'Vhat vere you hoping to see out of a Torquay hotel bedroom vindow? Sydney Opera House perhaps? Ze Hanging Gardens of Babylon?'

But put him in one of the mock meetings that were held

299

as part of the assessment, and suddenly he was more fearsome than one of Sybil's putdowns. He just didn't have a single social skill, which hardly disqualified him from partnership. I tried to teach him that there were times to do his impressions and times when he should goosestep quietly in his room, but I don't think it got through.

Elly in the meantime went about the weekend with calm efficiency. It wasn't that she had it in for me as her sole purpose, but she didn't miss an opportunity when it arose.

I'd begun chairing a mock meeting of a group she was also in. 'Right then, guys,' I began, and caught her raising an eyebrow in the direction of one of the external moderators, a woman who began the weekend by earnestly assuring us that she was here 'to empower you all and cultivate your positive legal forces'.

It wouldn't have worked in a real Babbingtons meeting, and she knew it, but the moderator gravely made a mark on her clipboard and asked me politely if I would mind refraining from such exclusionist modes of expression.

But we were constantly shifted between groups, and though I got distracted when Elly made her groups laugh or I saw her in serious discussion with the moderators, I felt I acquitted myself fairly well. I impressed myself – not the hardest of tasks, admittedly – by how confident and competent I sounded in what were difficult, if simulated, situations. Clearly something had rubbed off over the years.

The weekend finished on the Sunday evening with a buffet dinner joined by the partners on the assessment committee. This would sort the men from the boys – sorry, Elly, the adults from the children – because it was one of those stand-up affairs law firms specialise in, where you have to eat, hold your drink and speak to a partner all at the same time, ideally without spitting chicken in his face. Putting your glass down was tantamount to saying you were a worthless lawyer.

I had found myself in a small group with Oskar, Elly, Lucy and a couple of others. The banter was light and Elly was at her charming best, making people laugh, making

300

them feel good about themselves. I felt a stab of regret at what I had given up.

But as one of the partners wandered over, she turned her full beam, mischievous smile on me. 'Back on the sauce, Charlie?' she asked loudly, nodding at my beer. 'Do you really think that's wise?'

'It's the effect you have on men,' I replied, and Lucy rolled her eyes.

'Hello. I'm not sure we've all been properly introduced. I'm Nigel Coates, head of shipping. And you are ...?' Coates, a diminutive, slightly nervous sort with a bushy beard, nodded at me in a friendly way.

'Don't tell him your name, Pike.' The Teutonic comedian was at it again, but had moved on to *Dad's Army* for variety.

I blanked him out. 'Charles Fortune, corporate,' I said, trying to convey in the way I said that one word that I was both businesslike and approachable. We went round the group and he seemed to linger longer on Elly; she flashed him her 'Yes I'm gorgeous – what's a girl to do about that, eh Nigel? – but that doesn't mean I'm not a bloody great lawyer too, how's that for a knockout combination that any law firm would want in its partnership' smile.

'I don't envy you people,' he said. 'We never had anything like this centre in my day. One day they just called you in and congratulated you on becoming a partner. Didn't even know you were being considered.'

'A bit like *Blind Date* then,' I said, and immediately realised it wasn't. There was a pregnant pause, one that was about to give birth to half a dozen smiles from the others at me saying something stupid.

'Only without the, you know, dates. Or Cilla Black, come to that,' I said.

Oskar tried to help out. 'Don't panic, don't panic, Captain Mainwaring.'

Why stop digging when everyone's having so much fun, my mouth clearly decided. 'More of a blind marriage, I guess.'

Coates peered at me uncertainly. 'Well, yes, thanks for that, Charles. I'll bear it in mind next time I look at my partners. Insist on my conjugal rights, perhaps?'

There was some enthusiastic laughter and then a pained silence as everyone furiously thought of a way to continue the conversation.

Sensing the mood, Oskar tried out a Scottish accent. 'Ve're all doomed, ve're all doomed,' he hooted.

'Well, lovely talking to you all,' Coates said, panicking, looking up at the German man-mountain, 'but I need to go and talk to some other people about something.' And he was off before you could say 'We buggered that up good and proper.'

'The problem vith people like him,' Oskar confided, 'is zat zey don't like it up 'em.' And he fell about again.

I tried to catch up with Coates again, but he seemed to be keeping his distance, and conducting very loud and animated conversations whenever I moved in his direction. And, of course, later that evening, I saw him having a good old laugh with Elly.

I came back depressed, and resisted Hannah's efforts to cheer me up. Nonetheless, I welcomed the distraction on offer the following week, not long before Christmas. Hannah had begged me to help out a friend of hers who was moving into the dating business for over-thirties with one of those daft speed-date nights. She was short of one man and one woman to make up the dozen on each side she had promised her other punters, and Hannah had agreed on behalf of us both only on the basis that we would rather hand over all future children into slavery than give anyone a telephone number.

I soon discovered, however, that it was largely a Jewish event. 'Won't it be a bit awkward?'

'Not at all. I've got quite used to being seen out with you over the years.'

'I'm laughing inside, honestly.'

Hannah giggled. 'Don't worry – we promise not to

laugh at you just because you've got a foreskin. Though it is kind of funny.'

'No way,' I said. 'It's bad enough having to put up with one Jewish princess without spending the evening with another eleven.'

She stored up the insult for future payback. 'Come on, it'll be fun and take your mind off everything with Elly,' she said, and she nagged and nagged and nagged until I said yes just to shut her up.

'Maybe we'll find you an accountant to settle down with and get you off both my hands and your mother's. That'd be a result. I'll call her if you like, let her know we're going.' I smiled evilly.

'You do that and maybe I'll have a crack at a DIY circumcision.'

She was right. I needed to think about something else and imagined the evening might produce some ghoulish entertainment.

Ten minutes is a long time with someone whose sole interest outside of work is Shakin' Stevens, I learned that night. I also discovered that he'd started in a band called Shakin' Stevens and The Sunsets, first had a top forty record in Australia, and had thirty top thirty hits in the UK. Despite myself, I felt a stirring of detached interest. 'Thirty hits? You mean he didn't just do "Green Door" and "This Ole House"?' I was ashamed enough to know that.

The woman on the other side of the table didn't stare at me through gargantuan purple-framed glasses and a huge mop of frizzy hair as one might have uncharitably assumed. Karen was an extrovert with cheekbones to die for, a job at a top merchant bank, a flat not far from mine in Hampstead and a Persian cat called Shaky. 'And I bet you never knew that he brought out a compilation album just a few years back that reached number twelve in Norway and, get this, number one in Denmark.'

I sat back wondering whether the little clock on our table had expired with boredom. 'Big in Denmark, eh?' I said,

303

and smiled a lot because I couldn't think how to follow a sentence like that.

There was then a merciful ping around the room and all the men got up to move clockwise to their next date. We were in a large room that doubled as a nightclub at weekends and had plenty of dark corners for the various tables.

The next woman, a pleasant if brisk brunette with perfect teeth, was holding a clipboard. One thing I'd learned that evening was that women in their early thirties were pretty clear on what they wanted in a man.

'Let's be adult about this, shall we? We both know why we're here. So we'll dispense with all the "I'm Maggie. I have a good sense of humour and like cinema and Chinese food", yadda, yadda, yadda, OK?'

'Erm, yeah, whatever.'

She held out a pad and a pencil for me to use, but I shook my head. Frowning, she made a mark on her clipboard. I strained to see what she had written, but she held the clipboard at an oblique angle.

'I do have a sense of humour, by the way,' she said sternly. 'Actually not so keen on Chinese food, as it so happens.'

She busily wrote down my age, occupation, parents' occupations and make of all our cars. She smiled across at me sweetly; I was clearly shaping up satisfactorily, although she pursed her lips slightly at the news that I wore contact lenses and had a few fillings. My genes weren't totally up to scratch, but she shrugged as if you couldn't have everything in circumstances such as this. She then pushed over a piece of paper and a pencil. 'Obviously you don't want to reveal your exact salary, but if you could just tick one of these bands, that would be ever so useful.' For the hell of it, I marked £150,000-plus and I caught the slightest intake of breath.

'I've always had a thing about lawyers,' she said. 'That Kavanagh QC, ever so sexy.'

'But he doesn't have a second home in Monte Carlo,

304

does he?' I asked suggestively, and then the ping sounded. It looked like her world had collapsed.

The next woman sat back in her chair with her arms folded and told me to make her laugh. So I told her my best joke, which unfortunately also happens to be my filthiest. Nonetheless, it is funny enough usually to get away with it.

She regarded me dispassionately, as if I had only confirmed her view of mankind. 'Lowlife,' she said, and then simply stared at me for the remaining nine and a half minutes.

With a heavy heart, I moved on to Nicky, a sweet-looking woman with short black hair and the cutest dimples. 'Look, I'm sorry to waste your time,' she said. 'I've just come out of a messy end to a long relationship and I shouldn't be here.'

I rolled my eyes. 'Tell me about it.'

She took me a little too literally, and I discovered that she'd just been dumped by a guy she was best friends with at school but only started dating three years ago. I sat up. 'That's spooky,' I said, and explained that my situation was similar.

She broke into a watery smile. 'What pisses me off more than anything is that he ran off with my best friend. We were all best friends at school. How bloody clichéd is that?'

We were leaning towards each other with mutual interest. 'So what happened to you?' she asked.

I waved my hand around vaguely. 'She did the dirty on me too but I don't want to go into the detail.'

'I know how you're feeling. Can't bear to think about it. Can't understand how it's all gone wrong. Can't believe that years of fantasising about this person as your perfect partner could come to such a horrible end.'

I leaned back in surprise. Here I was thinking that I was the only person in the world feeling like this. Nicky tentatively put her hand out, and after a moment I covered it as a sign of support. 'It's good to know I'm not alone,' I said.

'Me too,' she replied, staring deeply at me. 'And it's good to know that there's at least one normal guy here. The one before you spoke fluent Klingon and said that if he ever got married, not that it's likely if I have anything to do with it, he wanted to have a Betazoid wedding, whatever that is. Apparently it's some *Star Trek* thing and he just giggled a lot because I didn't know what he was talking about.'

I looked a bit shifty. 'Now don't think badly of me, but I can kind of enlighten you.' Nicky looked amused. 'Look, I had my appendix out last year and watched a lot of telly while I was recovering, all right?'

'So what's a Betazoid wedding like.'

'I think it's, erm, this race of people who get married naked.' An inappropriate image of Nicky flashed through my mind.

She mulled it over. 'I guess it would save on a wedding dress.'

'You'd want to be careful when you cut the cake, though,' I said, and we both laughed.

The clock pinged, and we looked at each other with regret. 'See you later,' she said, eyes crinkling with good humour. 'I hope.'

I smiled back. 'Or as they say in Klingon, k'pla.'

With reluctance, I moved on. The noise in the room rose with the bar takings. There was the woman with Tarot cards who flipped over three identical love cards and made big eyes at me. Sadly, in her excitement she dropped the rest of the pack on the floor and I saw that they were all the same. I came across an accountant called Melanie who confessed that 'Girl Power' had changed her life. 'Call me Mel VAT,' she giggled. 'Or Balance Sheet Spice.' I might have assumed she was joking had she not begun virtually every other sentence by saying 'I'll tell you what I want, what I really, really want in a man.'

Finally, after surviving the woman with the squirrel phobia – 'It's the tails,' she shuddered. 'So bushy' – and the woman who was so nervous that she coughed her dentures on to the table, I was hugely relieved to reach Hannah as my last port of call. I started to tell her about the last two hours and especially Nicky, but she seemed strangely keyed up.

'Hello, I'm Hannah,' she said suddenly.

I rolled my eyes. 'Do we have to do this?'

'I'm a lawyer, kind of.'

I sighed. 'Me too. But without the kind of. So what happened to you then?'

'I had to leave. My employers wanted to relocate me.'

My face was a study of concern. 'I'm sorry to hear that. Where to?'

'The dole queue.' We smiled at each other. 'So, Charles. Where do you live?'

'In a flat in Hampstead.'

'Alone?'

'No, I've got this really annoying woman squatting in my spare room at the moment.'

She pulled a face at me. 'Still, you've done well to find anyone who'll put up with you in a confined space. She must be pretty amazing, if you ask me.'

'You're right. There's been even less room since her ego moved in as well, but she's ever so useful to have around the house. The other night she made dinner for me and it was this amazing feast. There were golden flakes of corn, covered in frosted sugar, and she topped it off with the juice of a cow. It was inspired.'

'Maybe she forgot to go to the supermarket that day,' Hannah suggested drily.

'At least she couldn't burn it for once,' I said, 'so it wasn't too bad. Anyway, how about you?'

'I'm lucky,' she said. 'I'm living with this great guy.'

I sat back. 'Really? What's so great about him?'

Her gaze was steady but there was an abrupt burst of electricity. 'He's kind and funny, laid back and intelligent, great company and an absolute rock in my life.'

I felt my cheeks going red. 'It, erm, sounds, erm, like you don't really need to be here then.'

Suddenly, Hannah's eyes were filling up. 'Problem is, I can't tell him how I feel. What with everything that's happened in the last few weeks, it's totally the wrong time for both of us. It's bound to be a horrible mistake which will ruin everything. What do you think I should do?'

There was fear in both our faces. This had come out of nowhere and my basic rule of only coping with one huge emotional confrontation every decade was in tatters. Ever since Hannah kissed me I had kind of known, and had given the idea more than a passing thought myself. But I felt sick with the enormity of what might happen in the next few seconds. I wasn't ready, I hadn't prepared. Where was my legal pad so I could make a few notes? Where were my books to research the law of falling for your best friend? What about the Beware of Being on the Rebound Act 2002? There must be a precedent in the Babbingtons library to help me cope with this situation. Was I ready for what could be the biggest merger and acquisition of my life?

I smiled grimly at myself, frustrated that I was now the sort of man who thought in those feeble terms. Hannah looked at me, uncertain what to read into the expression.

There was a sudden noise from elsewhere in the room, and all heads turned as Karen leaped onto the dance floor and broke into a wobbly-kneed jig with some flushed-looking guy in a suit. They began crooning in unison – and not particularly well, it has to be said – about the Green Door, before dissolving into fits of laughter. I suspected it was as much to do with all the Bacardis I'd seen Karen knocking back as with a desire to recreate Shakin' Stevens' greatest hits in the middle of an empty nightclub.

There was an embarrassed silence from the rest of us as we tried to return to what we were doing. Hannah was right about this being totally wrong. I was mere days from the ruins of my fantasy relationship and under huge pressure at work, and yet compared to Hannah, my mental state was tickety boo.

'Come on everyone,' Karen yelled. 'It's Shaky time.'

She was back to back with the man, still wobbling away with brio. Apparently they'd seen an eyeball peep in through a smoky cloud behind the green door.

This was my best friend, not my girlfriend. We'd put the whole mutual attraction thing behind us countless years before. Yet Elly was a dream that had become reality only briefly before I was forced to appreciate that it is hard for dreams to make the transition.

Karen shook her way over towards our table on the edge of the dance floor, pulling the guy playfully behind her by his tie. I glanced at her and she beckoned me towards her with her free hand. They laugh a lot behind the green door, she reassured me tunelessly.

I shook my head violently and leaned towards Hannah, taking the hands that were nervously grappling with each other. The stare that came back at me was uncomplicated, and I was then sure of the way forward. 'You were probably right to tell him,' I said softly, and my breath caught in my throat. Slowly, I leaned further in. 'This could be the best mistake I ever make,' I said, reaching out for her face and pulling it towards me.

I then heard a ping and the event ended in the cold light of fluorescence. But I wouldn't let go of Hannah. Our lips touched and my cares suddenly fell away, and the Shakey revival thankfully dried up in Karen's throat. Was I fickle, desperate, compensating or just lucky? At that moment, I couldn't have cared less if Chris Tarrant had repeated the options with a million-pound cheque in his hand.

There was a strangled cry. 'I don't believe it,' someone said. It sounded like Nicky. 'I've been cheated on within half a sodding hour.'

'Oh for pity's sake,' said another. There was the sound of a clipboard hitting the floor. 'That was the one I wanted.'

Hannah pulled back and smiled at me ever so slightly. 'Too late.'

Chapter Thirty-Three

It has never been hard to draw eerily close parallels between working at Babbington Botts and being locked up in jail, except at least they let you out for an hour of exercise in prison and try to make you into a useful member of society.

I was now gripped by the fear that all the lessons I had learned at Babbingtons that stopped me being screwed by my colleagues would take on a far more practical use in chokey.

But if you had told me just twelve hours earlier that my world was going to go completely pear-shaped, I would have laughed in your face like a villain with a particularly dastardly plan up his sleeve.

The previous few weeks had been absolutely euphoric. Nothing could displace the memory of our return from the speed-dating. Of my spare room becoming spare again, and a night of such gentle passion that it made my toes curl just to think about it.

The heat of the moment had lasted through the cab journey back to the flat. 'Déjà vu,' I murmured, recalling out brief grappling in the back of our first shared taxi all those years before. 'Are you sure?' I'd used the same words then, but this time my smile was relaxed.

Rather than, as she had that time, sit back, look worried and eventually think better of it (I learned a life lesson that night – never give 'em time to weigh up the pros and cons), Hannah put her hands around my head and pulled me back towards her. 'Talk about delayed gratification,' she said.

We made it through the lounge in classic movie style, pulling off each other's clothes with every step, before we were standing by my bed in our underwear. Finally, far later than a neutral observer might have predicted, I panicked.

'Bloody hell. Should we be doing this?'

Hannah put a finger to her cheek in brief contemplation. 'Yes, we should,' she said decisively and fell backwards on to the bed. She beckoned me to join her.

Instead, I paced the gap between the bed and the door. 'Hannah, I've just come out of this whole thing with Elly and I've got all sorts of issues to deal with right now. And you're in a really bad place at the moment, and . . . and I'm sounding like I've just walked off the set of a soap opera. God, what's wrong with me?'

Hannah laughed her sweet laugh and my heart melted. 'I'm sure about what I'm doing, Charlie. But if you're going to regret this in the morning, then perhaps we shouldn't do it.' She made it sound like that would be a really bad idea for all sorts of appealing reasons and showed no signs of moving.

'I don't usually make it this hard,' I explained, and moved to kneel above her on the bed. I could see she was breathing harder and it wasn't a secret that I was pretty aroused too.

Her hand was on my thigh, awaiting the green light for a deeper incursion. 'So, are you going to regret it?'

'You know, I think I will regret it in the morning,' I said with mock sorrow and Hannah looked shocked. 'If we don't do this, that is.'

It was strange a first; not exactly like seeing your sister

311

naked, but not the abandon of a normal first night. I knew
her so intimately as a friend, and no good friend puts his
hands where mine were going, surely? Hannah was less
abashed and took me firmly in hand. 'Oh shit,' she said.

I stared down at my groin. 'Not the reaction I was after,
to be honest.'

She stared at me anxiously. 'Well, you know how some
people have only driven automatic cars, and wouldn't
really know what to do with gears?'

'Yeeees.'

This confession was coming at a price. 'You know the
whole Jewish thing isn't all that important to me, but it just
so happens that I've only ever slept with Jewish guys
before. It's kind of a conscience thing. My mum hates the
idea of sex before marriage, so in my mind it's always
been slightly better if I do it with Jewish men. But, erm,
as a result I'm not entirely sure how to deal with the ...
erm ... whole foreskin issue. I mean, what do you do with
it?'

Smiling, I gave Hannah a beginner's guide to the foreskin to a chorus of 'ooh' and 'aah' and 'I see' and 'I've
always wondered'. She experimented to my own chorus of
'ooh' and 'ouch' and 'not too hard' before finally it was
'that's a bit more like it'.

We made leisurely progress, knowing it would never be
quite as thrilling again and realising along the way that in
fact our relationship had long been ripe for this. I was just
about to seal the deal – but could I not think in any terms
other than corporate transactions? – when I hesitated.
'Final chance to change your mind,' I said, looking down
at Hannah. 'Think of your mother.'

'No way to both,' she smiled, and pulled me on to her.

The Christmas period disappeared in a Hannah-induced
haze. Having breached the dam, so much came flowing out
and we stayed up late into the night just talking, before
retiring to bed and having the most enormous amount of
fun. Hannah and Charlie. Who would've thought it? Just

312

as well she got sacked, all in all. Elly had done me a favour. I laughed at the harsh irony of it all.

I felt dizzy with the speed of how quickly everything had changed, but calm in the certainty that Hannah didn't have it in her to do what Elly had. We'd had the most wonderful New Year's Eve in the flat, with good food, good drink and good sex. We needed nothing more.

I wouldn't be a man if I hadn't spent some time idly comparing the two, but I found the exercise surprisingly pointless. Elly was my first love and whatever she had done, a tiny portion of my heart would always remain with her. Hannah made me feel calm and whole.

While I was busy feeling tremendously pleased with myself, Elly had been busy being tremendously lawyer-like. It was the second week of January. She'd been in the office since seven-thirty and already completed a legal update report of some recent court decision which she had then distributed to the whole department by the time I arrived. I'd wanted to throw a sickie and spend the day gazing at Hannah, but she insisted I go to work and show everyone what a great partner I would make. 'I don't want you to ruin your career as well,' she said.

I was trying and comprehensively failing to work on a variety of small matters – punctuated by a series of telephone conversations with Hannah that were so sloppy she said I could always find a career writing greeting cards should I ever leave Babbingtons – when Sparkle called. The Bills had got home the night before to find that a brick had been thrown through their front window. They were getting really frightened, she said, and it was time to consider whether there was anything left to do but give in. I was worried for the Bills in a 'but isn't my life great?' kind of way, and agreed to meet her outside the office at lunchtime as I had a two o'clock meeting. 'Please wear something normal,' I pleaded.

I left the office at the same time as Ian McPherson and we were forced to engage in desultory and slightly awkward conversation. He then raised his eyebrows further

313

than they should safely go when he caught sight of Sparkle, dressed from head to toe in PVC, waving and yelling at me from the other side of the street. 'It's, erm, my sister,' I explained quickly. 'She's allergic to natural fibres.'

Bidding Ian a hurried goodbye, I rushed over to her. 'Wear something normal I said.'

'For the last lawyer client I had, this was normal,' she replied blithely. 'I just hope you don't all do the nappy thing. And it had to be cotton with plenty of safety pins. How can a man be aroused by safety pins, eh? Not that Pampers would have fitted the fat old sod.'

I caught Ian staring at us and pushed Sparkle to get her moving away. 'There's a crappy sandwich bar down the road that I doubt any of my colleagues go to. We'll eat there.'

But Sparkle refused to move. 'I know him,' he said thoughtfully, staring back at Ian. 'I'm sure I do.'

'I doubt it. It would be a great bit of gossip, but I doubt it. Now come on, I haven't got much time and there's something I've got to tell you.' The image of Hannah lying sleepily on my chest kept popping into my mind and I was keen to share my good news. I had told Ash and Lucy on the understanding that this was one piece of gossip they really couldn't share around, but otherwise had thought it prudent to keep to myself.

'I don't forget a face.'

'Yes, yes, I know, especially when you've sat on it.'

Sparkle glared at me, offended. 'Do you mind? I know what I do is one big rude joke to you, but it's bread, heat and rent to me. You public school boys are all the same when it comes to sex. Never got over your nanny giving you a bath.'

'Didn't go to public school,' I grumbled. 'And I never had a nanny.' But I have just had sex, I wanted to add.

'Anyway, he's not a client.'

Ian was walking off, so I turned to watch his retreating back. 'You've probably made a mistake. Look, there's something I've got to tell you.'

I could almost see the lightbulb ping above her head.

'That's it. I was round at the Bills about ten days ago when some official-looking blokes knocked on the door to make them a new offer to leave. He was one of them, I'm sure of it.' I looked at her doubtfully. 'I'm telling you, it was him. They said he was a lawyer and that he had papers right there to sign. But Big Bill said he wouldn't sign anything without his lawyer checking it first.'

I frowned. 'I'd be surprised. He's not a property lawyer. It's probably just that all middle-aged men in suits look the same. Not that you see them in their suits all that much, I guess.'

Sparkle thankfully ignored me. 'He had this lovely slim black briefcase with his initials on. That was it. They were IBM and Billy Whizz asked him if he'd stolen it from a computer store. Nobody laughed except for Billy.'

I stopped dead. 'That's too weird. Let me go back and check this out while he's out of the office. We'll have to talk about the Bills later.'

Sparkle looked triumphant. 'So you believe me now?'

'It's probably just a coincidence, but I happen to know his full name is Ian Bruce McPherson.'

For all that computers have made a lawyer's life harder by allowing closer scrutiny of what we do, they have made some of it better, in particular research. Within a few minutes, I learned a lot about the property company that was buying up the Bills' area: it was not a Babbingtons client, but was recently bought by the English subsidiary of an overseas company with the oddly familiar name of Worthington Trumpet. That was a Babbingtons client, and the initials IBM indicated the lead partner. Unfortunately, access to the computer file on Worthington Trumpet was password protected, so I sat back and thought a moment. If Ian was working on something, Elly was almost certainly helping him. And Babbingtons was still sufficiently distrustful of new-fangled technology to keep everything in paper form as well.

I wandered over to Elly's room nonchalantly, ready to

315

stroll straight by if she was there, but it was empty. I asked around in the typing pool outside her office and learned that she was out for a client lunch. I mumbled something about needing a file and went in, but such was the office policy at Babbingtons that I couldn't dare close the door. I pulled open cabinet drawers and scanned the contents as quickly as possible, but found nothing relevant. There were various piles of paper but they threw up nothing either. All that was left was her desk, on which I was sorely tempted to carve 'Charlie loves Hannah. So there', but managed to resist. Wary of who might pass the door, I dropped a pen and, heart thumping, knelt down behind the desk. If someone found me now, I wouldn't have much of an excuse.

The top drawer was brimful with girly stuff; if a national tampon shortage is ever declared, I and I alone will know where to point the emergency services. Elly was paranoid about such things making her look less macho in front of male lawyers and so was fully prepared just in case.

The middle drawer seemed equally unenlightening, but then I caught sight of a piece of paper covered in a variety of efforts to sign the name 'Eleanor Fortune'. I rocked back on my haunches, and momentarily forgot about everything that had happened. I had a similar piece of paper in my drawer until recently that was full of amateur calligraphy of 'Eleanor and Charles Fortune'. You would find it on a few childhood pencil cases as well.

I shook my head to push such traitorous thoughts away and opened the bottom drawer. Just one file was there: Worthington Trumpet. The first client Elly had brought in under her own steam and for whom she'd set up this English subsidiary. Which was, I recalled with a jolt, the company which had me as a signatory on its account. And then, at last, I realised why the name was so familiar. It was what Elly had called a toy monkey she'd had when she was about seven. She went everywhere with it and I always had to factor Worthington – or Mr Trumpet, as she insisted I call it for weeks until I was deemed to be on first-name terms – into any games we were playing.

316

There was something about all this that was itching my antennae, but the file was thin – aside from details of some bank payments which in themselves did little to ease my mind – and clearly not what I needed. Presumably, the main file was in Ian's office.

As I was considering my next step, there was the sound of someone clearing their throat. Alarmed, I looked up to find Elly's secretary in the doorway, giving me an evil stare. It wasn't hard to guess where she stood on the whole Charlie/Elly break-up.

'Can I help you?' she said in a way which sounded like the sentence should end with the words 'run yourself through with an envelope opener?'

I smiled sweetly, as though sitting on the floor of my ex-girlfriend's office was the most obvious place in the world for me to be at that moment. 'No, thanks. I'm fine.' I held up my pen. 'I was passing and I just dropped this.'

It didn't escape her notice that I'd have needed to throw it like a javelin to wind up in this position. 'Does Eleanor know you're in here?'

I held her gaze while I placed the file back in the drawer and inched it closed. I stood up. 'Do you know, I'm not sure she does. I'll just go off and tell her, shall I?'

The woman eyed me with such loathing that you'd have thought I'd impregnated Elly with snakes. 'Why don't you do just that?'

With as much grace as I could muster, I swept out muttering, 'See you later. Don't fall down any flights of stairs or anything.'

I had to wait until nine-thirty before Ian left. I was desperate to go home, see Hannah, take her to bed and forget about everything. But something felt very wrong and I knew I had to get to the bottom of it. I'd made regular excuses to sweep by Ian's room, and finally it was empty. Even better, he had closed the door on his way out. His coat and briefcase – which I'd noticed on a lunchtime pass was slim and black and had his initials on – were gone, and the computer was dark. On my way back from the toilet, I quickly tried the handle and found that it was unlocked.

I then had to sit at my desk for a good fifteen minutes while I psyched myself up and also allowed for Ian to pop back for anything he'd forgotten. I was no James Bond. Far from it. I had nothing more than a licence to bill, but knew I had to discover what was happening. Feeling totally conspicuous by my attempts to appear inconspicuous, I waited until there was nobody within sight of his door and slipped in. It was larger than an associate's room, obviously, but this just meant Ian had more places to dump things. Files were piled high against the wall, next to stacks of law books and magazines. But this time, I went straight for the desk, stopping to admire the sleekness of the wood that denoted partner status. I pulled on a drawer but it was locked, and my stomach flipped unpleasantly.

One thing about lawyers, however, is that they are reliably unimaginative. I looked around quickly and my eyes settled on the plant on the window sill. I felt around the earth but found nothing until I lifted the plastic pot out of the fancy ceramic: two small, identical keys attached on a small ring and with a little soil on them. It was exactly where I would put them. I wiped a key clean and it went straight into the lock. Like Elly's, the bottom drawer delivered up what I was looking for: a thick manila file with a sticker on the front denoting a number and the client name.

I hid behind the desk and was about to begin flipping through the file when the door handle creaked sharply and the door opened. 'Ian, old chap, I was just wonder—' The voice of another partner stopped short as he found the office empty. I crouched as low as I could, holding my breath and utterly petrified. My career could be over in seconds. Surely he could hear my heart thudding against the floor? 'Gone home already, have you? Bloody part-timer.' He chuckled to himself and then said, 'Oh, I haven't read this one.'

I heard the rustle of paper and it sounded like he had begun reading a magazine. I'd noticed a pile of *Law Society Gazettes* by the door, and was sorely tempted to

318

jump up and suggest that now wasn't the time to catch up on the hot legal news of the day. But I was too busy trying to let out my breath as quietly as possible.

There was a moment when it sounded like he was wandering towards the desk, where he couldn't fail to see me, but after what seemed like hours, he said, 'Oh, is that the time?' and finally retreated. I heard the door close and let out a ragged gasp.

I still didn't move for another couple of minutes, but eventually I forced myself to focus on the file in front of me. I'd come this far, I told my jibbering limbs.

It was a lawyer's nightmare: a holding company registered in a South Pacific island where financial probity meant that your bribes only rose with inflation; pitiful client identification made up of blurred photocopies of passports of people who couldn't have looked more dodgy if they'd been carrying bags with 'swag' written on them; transfers into Worthington Trumpet's account of serious amounts of cash that were then pushed back and forth through other accounts for no obvious reason.

Some of the money was also being used to buy up the land around where the Bills lived. From what I could tell, theirs was the last piece of the jigsaw and there was already a developer lined up with a fat wallet in hand.

All lawyers at the firm were required to go through training to spot suspicious transactions, and this was the kind of thing that would have the fraud squad high-fiving. Circulating money endlessly was one classic way to sanitise it. Buying property was another. And, for whatever reason, Elly had made me a signatory on its account. That would teach me not to read what I was signing.

This was the kind of company that eschewed pencils inscribed with its name for a supply of branded horses' heads. My career was about to take an iceberg and Titanic-like turn for the worse.

There was something that could spoil the Hannah-induced glow, I realised. Just two innocent words on their own that together spelled money laundering.

Chapter Thirty-Four

'Why didn't you tell me earlier?'

Simple question. Buggered if I could think of an answer that would pass muster when Hannah came to ask it, as she inevitably would. I grimaced at the woman sitting opposite me on the train in frustration and she squinted back, trying to work out if I was a rapist, a mugger, or just an alarming but harmless tube loony. She looked a no-nonsense sort who would assume that whatever I was, it was nothing that a face-full of pepper spray wouldn't sort out sharpish.

In an ideal world, I wouldn't have had to go home after my snooping around and tell Hannah everything. In an ideal world, she would have worked it out for herself, Miss Marple-like, and already sorted the entire situation, brilliantly exposing Ian and Elly in front of an amazed policeman who would then lead them away in cuffs as they cursed her name. And she would totally understand why I hadn't mentioned earlier what I knew.

There was no easy way to break it to her. Those stomach acid-creating words 'There's something I've got to tell you' never bode well, especially when they are followed by words such as 'Ian McPherson and Elly stitched you up over the memo and now I'm stuck in the middle of a money laundering conspiracy.'

I wondered if there was a way to distract her from the news. 'Hannah, there's no easy way to tell you this. Your parents have been attacked by a pack of ravenous jackals.'

In my mind, she threw her hands to her mouth in horror. 'Since when were there jackals in north London?'

'I know, you'll probably laugh about it later, it's so unlikely. But the good news is that they survived the attack.'

'Oh, Charlie, thank goodness.'

'Sadly, by complete chance, a gang of white-slave traders were going by and shipped your parents off to Asia on a boat.'

Her eyes were wide. 'White-slave traders in Hendon?'

'Incredible, isn't it? How unlucky can two people be? It's the kind of thing you hear happens to the other people, but you never imagine it'll happen to you. But in any case, they survived that too, fortunately.'

'Thank God. We must go and see them at once.'

'There may be a problem with that. Unfortunately, while they were at sea, they were scooped up by a flying saucer full of aliens with sharp probes and a deep fascination with human anatomy.' Hannah would be white with shock. 'Oh, by the way, you'll never believe this either but I've uncovered a whole money laundering thing at work and also, as it so happens, you are completely in the clear, but let's not worry about all that right now and see what we can do about those aliens and their pointy sticks.'

That was about the level of both my desperation and inspiration. But when I reached the flat, the approach became entirely untenable. Hannah's parents were sitting in apparent comfort on my sofa. If they had met the aliens, one could only assume they'd left before the probes came out.

You can put her in front of the rudest partner, the most uncooperative client or the most leering of men down The Witness Box, and nothing fazes Hannah. Put her in front of her parents, and you can almost see the pigtails descend from her expensive hair-do and long white school socks slide up her calves. As I opened the door, Hannah rushed into the hall to warn me. She rolled her eyes theatrically – fifteen years ago she'd no doubt have been scowling and chewing manically on some gum as well – as she gave me the bad news.

'I am so sorry, I just couldn't stop them,' she whispered.

I smiled with total forgiveness in the hope of setting the mood. 'That's all right. Sorry I'm so late.'

'Why didn't you tell me earlier?' she asked, looking irritated. My stomach lurched. 'You could have called and told me you were going to be this late. I've been stuck here with them for ages.'

'Oh, yes, of course. Sorry. Really sorry.'

Hannah glanced at the living room. 'I'm the one who's got the most to be sorry about.'

I wouldn't bet on it. 'There's something I've got to talk to you about. It's really important.'

She pecked me on the lips and took my hand to lead me into the living room. 'Not now. If we're lucky, we'll get rid of them quickly. They've only hung around this late to see you.' Hannah saw my puzzled look. 'I kind of told them that we're together now. My mum's ever so pleased.'

I could imagine. Whenever I had seen her of late, Hannah's mum would embrace me warmly, and I could always sense her thinking, 'Do you realise that you're now the number one choice in the "Get our embarrassing unemployed thirty-something daughter married off already campaign"?'

I stood still for a moment. 'But what about the whole Charlie not being Jewish thing? Don't force me to provide them with the physical evidence. Because I will, you know, if I'm cornered.'

She laughed. 'Charlie, I'm thirty-one. Her exact words earlier this evening were: "At your age, we can't afford to be so choosy. At least he's a nice boy and has a good income."'

Estelle and Larry Klein were enjoying their late middle age, as my own mother described it. Expensive-looking jewellery jangled from various bits of their bodies, while Mrs Klein's golden/orange glow hinted at a closer relationship with a sunbed than was strictly healthy. A petite woman who was fighting hard against the demands of gravity, she dressed in a way which suggested she was at least twenty years younger in her mind. Mr Klein had embraced a Mafia-style patriarch role with gusto to judge by the chunky chain partially obscured by a forest of grey chest hair, fat ring on his wedding finger and a stomach spilling a good distance over his belt.

Mrs Klein bounced up from the sofa to greet me. 'Lovely flat you've got here,' she enthused. 'So big.' Was she already sizing it up for her grandchildren to run around in?

Mr Klein pumped my hand with manly congratulations. 'So you've got your hands on our daughter at last, eh?'

'Mum, Dad, stop it,' Hannah hissed. She had long suffered a love/squirm relationship with her parents.

Mrs Klein steered me to the seat next to her on the sofa. 'We've always liked you, Charlie. You're a nice boy.'

'Bloody hell, Mum, why don't you just ruffle his hair and give him a lollipop as well?'

Mr Klein leaned forward slowly in his armchair, trying not to show what a struggle it was to redistribute his weight. 'All we're saying, darling, is that we're pleased you've found yourself a nice man after all these years.'

Money-laundering? Oh God. I could go to jail.

'You should see some of the frights she's been out with,' Mrs Klein confided to me. 'I'm convinced that no more than half of them have had a pulse.'

Hannah was clutching nervously at her hands. 'That's because you bore them to death, Mum.'

Mrs Klein regarded their daughter lovingly. 'The fact is that the shelf Hannah's found herself on is getting more and more dusty.' Hannah slapped her head into her hands. 'It's about time she settled down with a nice man who's going to look after her.'

323

Mr Klein was now on the edge of his seat. 'You are going to look after her, aren't you, Charlie? Especially now she hasn't got a job.' The tone was vaguely threatening, but I couldn't imagine how he would enforce it. Cut me out of their social circle, perhaps?

'Actually I'm probably going to jail soon for fraud, so there may be something of a problem here. Excuse me while I ball myself up in that corner and cry,' I didn't say. I ordered myself to concentrate on something other than bars and prison showers. It was bad enough that Graham had sometimes, with a big guffaw, told me that I was his bitch, but that was nothing compared to a lifer nicknamed Marilyn who has 95 per cent of his body tattooed.

I forced myself to smile. 'You know I've always thought the sun shines out of Hannah,' I said truthfully. 'From all directions.' The Kleins laughed. 'It's just a shame that it's taken what happened to her for us to realise how much more there could be to our relationship.'

Hannah peeked through her fingers at me, and there was love in those eyes. My heart swelled and the bars briefly disappeared. 'I'm now almost glad it happened,' she said quietly.

'You wouldn't be saying that if you had rent to pay,' Mr Klein told her sternly. 'Thank you for looking after our little girl, Charlie.'

Hannah took an exaggerated look at her watch. 'Goodness,' she said. 'It's long past eleven. Time to go, I think.'

Fearful of the 'why didn't you tell me earlier?' question, I wanted to delay their departure for as long as I could, even though I was sick to death with interfering parents, whether my own or others. But Hannah quelled me with a fierce look. And after much fussing around coats and extended farewells, they left. Do please come and visit me in jail, I almost shouted after them.

Hannah slumped onto the sofa. 'Why is it,' she wailed, 'that I always feel about eight years old when they're around?'

I sat down beside her and held her hand.

'Hannah, there's something I've got to tell you.'

She turned to me, alarmed by the words. There was nothing else to do but explain it all from the beginning.

I have never seen anyone look quite so dumbfounded. Her mouth opened to expel words at various intervals but then closed again. She didn't know where to start: the personal betrayal, the vindication, the money laundering, the threat to me, the unbelievability of the entire situation.

'I've been kidnapped and left in the middle of a John Grisham novel, haven't I?' she said eventually. 'This cannot be true.'

I held her hands tighter and told her gently that I didn't want it to be, but it was. Surely Ash and Lucy would visit me, I thought.

'Money laundering?' Her look was incredulous. 'Money laundering? At Babbingtons? They're greedy bastards, sure, but crooks? Never. It's just impossible, inconceivable.'

I'd had the same thought. 'My guess is that this all started before Ian and Elly joined us. Maybe by bringing it over as work in progress, there weren't the usual checks or something.'

There was a long silence. 'So I didn't cock up then.' Her tone was not of exhilarated relief. She just sounded exhausted.

Maybe my mum could smuggle a file in one of her cakes. 'Elly saw you as a big threat to our partnership hopes. Apparently you were the front runner. It seemed like an opportune moment to get you out of the way.'

Hannah smiled. 'Front runner, eh? I always thought you'd be the first one to make it. Might still be, I suppose.' The silence stretched even longer this time. 'Why didn't you tell me earlier?' she asked quietly.

I was still no closer to a convincing answer. 'I dunno,' I said. 'It never seemed like the right time. And I really wanted to have some evidence before I started telling people. But I never dreamed that there would be anything this dodgy going on.' It sounded feeble even to my ears.

She thought about it for some time, and then said, 'That's a really crap excuse, you know. You were my best friend. Did that count for nothing?'

'Hannah—'

'You didn't do anything. You didn't try and do anything. You ... you ...' Her voice was rising with horrified disbelief and she pulled away from me. 'And have you got this evidence?'

'Not exactly.' I could hear the prison door slam shut.

'Does that mean you hope to get some evidence but haven't yet?'

'This is why you were going to become a partner,' I joked weakly. 'Always asking the right question.'

Hannah was unmoved. 'Does it?'

'I'm working on it.'

'That means you haven't got any evidence and have no prospect of getting any, yes?'

At least Marilyn wouldn't ask me lots of bloody awkward questions like this. I imagined him as a man of few words. 'I'd agree it's not looking totally positive on the evidence front right now.'

The laugh this time was bitter and the voice far louder. 'A lawyer right to the end. Why can't you just say I'm screwed?'

'Hannah, please stay calm.'

Now she was standing. 'I should be calm about my job being stolen from me, should I? Or maybe I should be calm about my partnership hopes and entire bloody career going down the toilet? Calm that this little thing which you didn't quite get round to mentioning might have ruined my life?'

I gazed up at her, seeking forgiveness. 'Sorry.'

There was none to be seen. 'Sorry? That's it, is it?'

'This isn't easy for me either, you know.'

You'd think someone with my professional training would know to engage his brain just a touch before saying something that idiotic. Maybe I was too stupid for Marilyn to bother with.

Hannah had marched to the other side of the room, where she was standing with her arms firmly crossed. 'You're right, Charlie. I haven't looked at this yet from your point of view. Now let's think about this.' She bunched her eyebrows and put a thoughtful finger to her jaw. Her expression was not unmocking. 'Oh yes, you've still got a job. Oh yes, you haven't been thrown out of one of the best law firms in the world because you're supposedly incompetent when actually you're not. How awful of me to think of myself first.'

I was not feeling great either. 'And you're not stuck in the middle of some frigging ridiculous money-laundering conspiracy either, don't forget.'

She glared at me. 'OK, let's look at that for a second, shall we? You just signed something without looking at it?' I nodded in pain. 'Without thinking about it?'

'Kind of,' I agreed miserably.

'Without asking a single question about it?'

'That's one interpretation,' I mumbled.

'What kind of lawyer are you, Charlie Fortune?' She threw up her hands. 'And they called me incompetent.' There was a charged pause. 'You didn't do anything. You didn't tell anyone. Did you care so little for me? Does making partner mean that much to you?'

I was bang to rights and bowed my head. 'What can I do? Just tell me.'

There was no love in the look this time around. 'I don't know,' she said, and abruptly exited. I heard the prison door slam. It could have been the spare-room door.

Sleep didn't come easily that night. Even if I could persuade myself briefly that the money-laundering thing would work itself out because my only real crime was gross stupidity – which in itself was only a minor consolation – I was immediately assailed with fears that I would lose Hannah no sooner than I had found her. This was no feisty argument that could easily be patched up the following morning. I eventually fell into a fitful sleep.

I awoke to an angrily beeping alarm. To judge by the

time, I'd slammed the doze button several times, and it was already gone 8.45, more than forty-five minutes after I normally woke up. I climbed out of the bed at once and stumbled to the spare room. I knocked softly but there was no reply. I hummed and hahed over the ethics of going in anyway, but the need to see Hannah overwhelmed me and I pushed the door slightly.

The curtains were open, the bed made and the room empty, her stuff gone. On the side table was a piece of paper and a pen. Hannah had begun writing 'Charlie, I just had to,' but for whatever reason had not finished.

I rushed around the flat but there was no sign of her. I had the Kleins' phone number and called it, but it just went on to the answerphone. I left a message with no hope of hearing anything back.

No hope of anything much, come to that. The women in my life hated me. I could end up in jail for fraud. Marilyn was probably lathering up already. I had been found out for the small person that I was.

I sat staring at Hannah's unfinished note, feeling utterly bereft. Throughout my adult life, I'd always had a plan of sorts. Always known what to do next. Until now.

Chapter Thirty-Five

There was only one practical thing I could do at that moment, even though it was hardly advised for an aspiring partner. I lifted the phone to call Graham and throw a sickie, but then thought better of it. It was a toss-up between a day at home feeling miserable and a day at work feeling miserable, but at least I was more used to the latter and the office would also provide some distraction.

I spent the train journey trying to work out how deeply Elly was involved. It seemed stupid to have an outsider as the co-signatory on the Worthington Trumpet account if something dodgy was going on. She'd said it was urgent when she'd collared me, but it still seemed an unacceptable risk to take. The only explanations were that she didn't know what was happening, or that, as a perverse loving act, she wanted to pull me into the web as a co-conspirator. It also wasn't impossible that Ian was getting Elly to put her and my name to everything so as to keep him officially well away from all things Worthington Trumpet.

It occurred to me that Elly may have thought I was incapable of discovering what was happening. I dismissed the idea uneasily.

The feeling that the world was against me intensified

when I finally reached work. I'd barely had time to skim through my personal e-mails and order Richard off to the library on a vindictive research task when Graham popped into my room. Graham rarely, if ever, pops without purpose.

'Half-day, Charles?' he asked pointedly.

This was the first time I'd been in late for something like three years – and that included the mornings after the 4 am finishes – but to judge by the arched eyebrows and sarcastic comments I'd picked up on the way in, you'd think that it was cause for celebration that I'd made an appearance before midday. It wouldn't be so bad if people could come up with something more original to say than 'Half-day, Charles?' but not a single supposed comedian had.

I'd probably not hear the end of it from Graham for the next six months. 'Pleased you could make it,' he'd say to me at afternoon meetings and the like.

Reason number 236 to be a partner: you can make crappy jokes at the expense of your staff without rebuke and without limit.

'You may not have heard yet, what with your late arrival and everything, but Ian McPherson's been causing a bit of a fuss this morning. Apparently someone was seen leaving his room late last night after he'd left. And he reckons that someone went through his desk.' He paused. 'Do you know anything about it?'

I tried to control my panic. Was now the time to confess all? Throw myself on Graham's mercy? I almost laughed out loud at the thought. By nature, Graham favoured the lion over the Christian every time.

'Me? Why should I know anything about it? I've got no reason to be in Ian's office. None whatsoever, I can assure you.' My indignation was rising in concert with my alarm.

Graham looked at me strangely. 'You were here late last night, Charles, that's all. The security records show you were one of the last people out. Apparently, you didn't leave until ten-fifteen. Did you happen to see anything, that's all?'

'No, nothing. Too busy working, Graham. You know me, all work, work, work for that partnership.'

Graham smiled with the security of a man pulling in well over £300,000 a year. 'That's the spirit, Charles. Are you sure you're all right? You seem a bit jumpy given that you've just had a massive lie-in.'

It was only ten o'clock, for heaven's sake. 'I'm fine. Can't wait to get cracking. Make up for all the lost time this morning.' Graham missed the faint sarcasm.

'Excellent stuff. I'll leave you to it. You know by now that in my book, there's only one good reason for being late.'

Of course I knew. Graham's book only had one chapter, entitled 'My life as a sex god'. I dipped my eyes knowingly at him. 'Then I guess you'll have to forgive me for being late this morning.'

He laughed. 'Good to know you've learned something from me. Anyone I know?'

I measured my words. 'Nobody who works here.'

Graham looked disappointed that he didn't have any fun gossip to spread around the partners' dining room. 'Still, well done. But not too many late mornings, eh? Can't have my assistant enjoying a bigger reputation with the ladies than me, can I?'

'Not much chance of that,' I said with a smile, and amazingly he just lapped it up. The randy old goat lost all perspective when his libido hijacked his brain, which was reassuringly often. Not that he turned any of it into action, however. I recalled the firm summer party not long after I started working with Graham where I first met his wife, a tall, striking redhead with a deceptively pleasant smile. As she downed Pimms after Pimms, she took a caustic knife to every partner and wife she could see.

She pointed at one group of property partners. 'In order, drunk, pervert, drug addict, and, thanks to the wonders of Viagra, womaniser.' She then moved on to their respective wives: 'Little Miss Prim; new second wife, doesn't yet

331

know he's a pervert; drunk by lunchtime; partnership slut. Matches made in Babbingtons heaven.'

By now, more than a few Pimms had passed my lips too. 'What about you and Graham?'

She glanced at me reprovingly. 'What a terribly indiscreet thing for a young solicitor to ask his boss's wife.' Then she smiled. 'My Graham talks a big game, but doesn't play a big game. He knows I would clean him out, humiliate him and then clean him out some more. He's no fool.'

I found her incredibly sexy at that moment; just as well that not even Babbingtons could monitor your thoughts. 'And you?'

'I want to be the senior partner's wife. So I hope you're not having inappropriate ideas right now.'

Oh, maybe they could after all. 'Not all all.'

She patted my shoulder and began to move away. 'That's all right, Charles. I'd've been insulted if you hadn't thought about it, just this once anyway.'

Although I hadn't dared to move within three feet of her whenever we had subsequently met, we now got on famously, and always enjoyed a ready exchange of gossip.

This brief diversion ended with a movement in the doorway. It was Elly, mouth etched with anger. 'What were you doing in my room yesterday? My secretary said she found you scrabbling around on the floor by my desk.'

I was fed up with being on the receiving end. Was it Give Charlie A Good Kicking Week or something? 'I'm tired of this, Elly. Please go away.'

She stood glowering at me, looking very appealing in a tailored beige suit that gave enough away to remind me of those perfect thighs. It wasn't hard to remember why I found her so irresistible. She had a small mole two-thirds of the way up on her left thigh, like an island surrounded by a vast creamy sea and only populated on occasion by a tiny curling hair. That mole was possibly the sexiest thing I have ever seen and kissed.

'No, I won't go away. Why were you crawling around

my room?' She barrelled on before I could reply. Despite what I felt about her, I couldn't help but find her sexy when she was like this – so dominant, yet masking a very feminine frailty I alone knew was there. 'I know you found this, you sneaky bastard, because it wasn't where I left it.' She waved around the piece of paper covered with her attempts to sign 'Eleanor Fortune'. 'How dare you? How dare you poke about my desk?' She tore the sheet down the middle. 'This, Charles Fortune, is my lucky escape.' She carefully sliced it into quarters.

Now seemed as bad a time as any to take the plunge. 'I was just looking for details of that bank account you had me as a co-signatory on.'

That stopped her mid-tear. I watched her reaction carefully: I had clearly rattled her more than I should have were it all entirely innocent, but there was nothing that shouted 'I'm a money launderer, I'm a money launderer, arrest me now.'

'Why were you looking for that?' The question was posed in a suddenly mild voice, but there was stress beneath it.

'It occurred to me the other day that I'd just signed something without really looking at it. Talk about love being blind, eh?' And I hated the fact that when she was in front of me like this, I would realise that I did still love her to some extent. But I felt something different for Hannah – different but stronger.

She didn't return my smile. 'There's nothing to worry about.'

'You're sure about that?' My tone was light.

'Very.' Hers was not. But it could easily have been paranoia that I was going to try and steal her client.

'Maybe if I could just have a quick look at the file, it would ease my worries.'

Her face softened, and so did I. How could Elly be involved in fraud? Then I remembered what she'd done to Hannah, and realised I simply didn't know what Elly was capable of. 'Charlie, I told you, there's nothing to worry about,' she wheedled. 'The file is probably stuck under some huge pile in Ian's office and it'll take me ages to find it. Especially with Ian so paranoid now about people being in his room.' Oh Elly, how can you just stand there and lie to me? She heard herself speak and peered at me suspiciously. 'That wasn't you last night, was it?'

I hoped I could fib more convincingly. 'Of course not. Why should I go into Ian's room?'

She appeared unsatisfied, but what more could she do? 'Look, Charlie, I'll get you that file sometime, OK?' Yeah, right, like hell you will. 'Just keep out of my room and my drawers.' She walked around my desk to the bin, and the fragments of her signatures fluttered to earth. 'This could have been all yours, you know.'

'I know.' But there was no emotion in my voice and she walked out. Bugger me, she has the sexiest bum too.

I sat back, no closer to working out the level of Elly's complicity. But if she was prepared to screw Hannah like that, then I had to be prepared for the worst.

I struggled on at my desk until after lunchtime, but just couldn't hack it a second longer. I had to work everything out and this was not the place to do it. I tried an old schooldays trick of holding my breath for as long as possible while outside Graham's room, and then burst in panting and looking terribly distressed. Going home ill during the day is such a rare event at Babbingtons that he acceded to my request with alacrity. The last thing he wanted was some kind of comeback because he had made me work on, especially if it was the first sign of the heart attack that was the due of most Babbington Botts lawyers.

The flat, though, offered little respite. Too many memories of Hannah and Elly, and too little to do except watch boring television – one day, I must try and get myself a life, I decided – so I climbed into my car and pointed it in the direction of Wycombe. Mum would be thrilled by a surprise visit.

I caught the first stirrings of the big rush home on my way out of London, but drew up outside my parents about an hour later. I couldn't park in the drive, though, as there was another car already there, which I recognised as Elly's parents'. That was the last thing I wanted to cope with – Victoria sponge laced with parental fury – so I gently pulled away up the street.

I drove around aimlessly for a bit, before happening upon the road which led towards where we lived when I was growing up. I motored on and stopped outside our old house; on a whim I rang the bell. It pinged away merrily to a tune I thought might have been by Black Sabbath, and the door opened to reveal a little old lady in a pink house-coat, with no fewer than three cats winding their way around her legs.

'Can I help you?' she asked, looking suitably kindly.

'It's just that I used to live here years ago, grew up here and all that, and I was passing and thought it would be nice to have a look around for old time's sake. Do you mind?'

She gave it a moment's thought. 'Yes, I do,' she said, and slammed the door.

Clearly little old ladies weren't what they used to be. I went back to the car, but decided instead to have a wander. I walked down the parade of shops, which had stayed largely unchanged, buying a chocolate bar from the newsagents. But the tall Asian man who had run it for donkey's years and had let me run up a huge tab on penny sweets in my first unsuccessful foray into debt management didn't recognise me, and I couldn't be bothered to explain.

Eventually I reached the park where much of my youth had been spent. You had to walk up an unpromising concrete path lined by stunted trees, and cross an ugly bridge over a railway line. But then the park opened up into a veritable Buckinghamshire Eden, with a very pretty walled garden at the centre which had been Make-Out Central for generations of kids.

I bathed in the easy nostalgia of it all. This way the singularly huge oak tree where a running Elly had tripped over a massive root and broken her arm, and made me promise that I would tell people she had fallen out after climbing to the very top; that way the hidden bench where Maddy Faulks had allowed me into her training bra in return for a chance to ride my brand-new Chopper bike.

Oh Elly. What have you done? I yearned for the girl who would race me up and down this park, tell me with tantalising enthusiasm that she didn't need any other friends, and then blow a kiss at me before shooting off again.

Then Hannah's face appeared, and I realised how much we'd shared as adults, how much she'd given me over the years, the signs of love that I'd been too stupid to see.

I went into the walled garden. There was one young couple at the furthest bench from the entrance busily sucking each other's face off. I sat at what had been my favourite bench on the other side of the small pond in the centre. At long last, I felt able to think clearly: about Elly, about Hannah, about money laundering and about what I wanted for the future.

The couple left, and others came, wondering, no doubt, about the strange man taking up a valuable bench with such blatant non-kissing activity. This was very much a place where doing took priority over thinking. Much later, I left to reclaim my car, finally certain about the way forward.

The following morning, when I awoke, I felt calm and focused for the first time in ages. The figure beside me stirred and shuffled over to claim a place on my chest.

'Morning, Charlie,' said Elly.

Chapter Thirty-Six

Elly pushed herself up on her elbows so she could look me in the face. 'I didn't think we'd be doing this again,' she said, with a smile.

We were less than twelve hours into 'Charlie and Elly Part II – Return to the Bedroom,' and she was right, there was no sign that two days ago we'd have happily scooped out each other's heart with a teaspoon.

Having determined my plan of action, I drove straight to Elly's flat. I rang the bell and fell to my knees in supplication as she opened the door.

Elly regarded the scene dispassionately. 'You might want to start wearing a hat,' she advised. 'That's not the most flattering of angles any longer.'

Ash believed that women found his full head of hair a turn-on. 'Just shows I'm carrying around more testosterone than you can shake a pair of knickers at,' he would say. By contrast, the front and the back of my hair were starting an undignified race to see which could reach the midpoint first.

I scrambled to my feet. On the way over, I'd tried out countless forms of words but none of them did the job. There was that whiny, desperate little boy buried deep in my character for whom I cared little but equally couldn't stop from making his presence felt during many of the big emotional moments of my life. No words came which conveyed simply how Elly had been at the centre of my world since I was a child beyond 'Please, please, please, please, please take me back, Elly, I'll do anything you want' in a feeble voice.

It looked like she was ready to go to bed. She was wearing a bobbly old green cardigan and her long white T-shirt featuring a big yawning duck in a red-striped nightcap. Whatever had passed between us, I hadn't stopped thinking how gorgeous she was. I put a hand to the face which had been in my mind's eye for so many years. 'Elly, I need you. Have done since I was five, but never more so than now.'

'You, Charles Fortune, are more full of shit than a shit factory at full capacity.' But there was no note of gentle mocking in her voice and her mouth was set grimly.

'What?'

'You're screwing with me in some sad, pathetic, little way. I know it.'

I considered returning to my knees, but these were my favourite chinos. 'Honestly, Elly. I want to get back together. Go on like nothing's happened.'

She made to close the door, but I put a foot in the way. I rather hoped she wouldn't slam it because these were my favourite shoes as well. Instead, she stared at me incredulously. 'Like nothing's happened? What's going on here, Charlie? Last thing I heard, you were going round telling people at work that I was some kind of devil woman.'

I smiled apologetically. 'Devil bitch, actually.'

'And what was all this about a harp?'

'It was a harpy. I called you a harpy.' It was like a bad game of Chinese whispers.

'I don't have time for this, Charlie. Or you and your feeble games. You're pathetic. You can't even come up with good insults.' She was so much better at this than me, as one of the secretaries had helpfully pointed out the other

338

day while asking whether it was true that I had offered Graham sex in return for becoming a partner.

There was a tense silence. 'I mean it, you know,' I said. 'I've always been in love with you.' Doubt flickered across her eyes. 'Remember my sixth birthday at school?'

I'd sat at the doors after the end of school, with a box of Milky Bars, a cardboard Milky Bar Kid hat, a plastic pistol, nerdy glasses and the promise of eternal gratitude from my classmates as they passed by (at an age when eternal lasted two days if you were lucky). But Mum had fatally under-bought and ugly mob scenes developed which white chocolate should never warrant.

'You hid the last bar and gave it to me on the way home,' she said, her eyes dazzling me with their intensity. 'You were probably keeping it for yourself.'

'You know that's not true.'

'I hate this. I hate you, Charles Fortune.' She made to hit me.

'You know that's not true either.'

'I just don't understand why you're here.'

I took her raised hand. 'There was never anyone else,' I said softly. 'Just give me another chance to prove it.'

'Why should I?'

'Actually, I think we both need another chance, don't you? After everything that's happened?'

Elly looked so frustrated. 'I knew on that walk home that you were the man for me.' She smiled, defeated, and her voice was husky. 'Just took me another twenty-five years to realise it, that's all.'

'Nah,' I said, hugging her hard. 'You're simply a sucker for a guy in a uniform.'

Before I stepped over the threshold, I had to promise that I wouldn't be seeking sex until she had sorted everything out in her mind. With the caution of a good lawyer, Elly then redefined the promise to include sexual contact of any nature or any behaviour that could reasonably be identified

339

as having sexual content. She was a step away from putting it down in writing.

Though the very idea of agreeing to such a thing would have appalled me just a few weeks ago, I did so readily. There were too many other things going on to let sex get in the way. I had some very specific goals from the resumption of our relationship. And then there was Hannah. The memory of her flushed face beneath me was too fresh.

We would sleep together, I agreed, with the emphasis on the actual sleeping, pyjamas and the rest. 'I just worry that nobody can resist me for long,' I said. 'Especially you.'

'I don't think you need worry. Remember, I've seen your underwear drawer. It's like some kind of early-warning system for unwary women.'

Some time later we were curled up together in bed, sufficiently clothed for our mutual comfort. 'What made you change your mind?' Elly asked softly.

'All sorts of things,' I murmured.

'Such as?'

'Let's not over-analyse,' I said. 'Live in the moment.'

Elly made to turn round and face me, but I held my arms tighter across her chest to prevent it. She struggled briefly but it was simply too comfortable for both of us, and she gave in. 'I'm not over-analysing. I just want to know why you changed your mind.'

'I told you. I need you.'

'Can't you be a bit more specific?' She sounded a bit irritated.

It was both the woman and the lawyer in her that required detail. It was a challenging combination to say the least. 'You've always been the one for me,' I said. 'You know it, I know it, our parents know it, everyone else knows it. So why fight the inevitable?'

I could sense Elly's smile and she pushed herself even deeper into the curve of my body. 'Why indeed?'

This time there was no reluctance to tell the world, and the world was more than happy to listen. 'We're ever so pleased,' one secretary told me. 'We've had nothing interesting to talk about since you two split up.'

'Apart from all the bitching both of you were doing,' another chipped in. 'That was very entertaining. That Eleanor's got a real mouth on her, hasn't she? And she seemed such a nice girl.'

I made a particular point of getting chummy with Ian again after Elly had vouched for my restored credentials as an acceptable member of legal society.

Lucy and Ash insisted I join them down the pub that evening to quiz me in detail.

'I can't keep up with your life,' Lucy said, having secured a discreet table. 'First there was Elly, then there was Hannah, and now it's Elly again. I've got to be honest, Charlie, I'm feeling a little left out here.'

Ash raised his print in my direction. 'Me too. I mean, good luck to you and all that, but I'm feeling discriminated against on the basis of my sex.'

I took a thoughtful sip. 'In the words of our esteemed head of litigation, just try and sue me, you bastard.'

Lucy puckered her lips cartoonishly and grabbed my hand. 'Charlie, you know I've never fancied you,' she said, which was never a way I liked to start conversations. 'But I am now really curious to find out what the fuss is all about.'

'It's the Charlie factor, Luce. You should never reckon without it.'

'Oh please,' Ash snorted.

'Maybe we should just have sex and be done with it.'

'For the sake of clarity, I shan't be making the same offer,' said Ash.

'Which saves me the trouble of saying no to both of you then. This will no doubt come as a crushing blow to you, Lucy, but I'm going to have to decline your beautifully phrased offer. My heart belongs to another.' I looked at my watch. 'And I'm meeting Elly in thirty minutes, so I better be going.'

'I think you're being very selfish,' Lucy said mildly, coping with the rejection without much trouble. 'I shall now have to turn to Ash for consolation. That's how desperate I feel.'

Ash looked interested. It's not like he hadn't thought about it over the years. 'There's something about posh girls that does it for me,' he'd said more than once. It was almost his life credo. Sometimes I wondered if he only became a City solicitor so he would be surrounded by them.

Lucy caught the expression and laughed. 'For the sake of clarity,' she said, 'that's consolation in the shape of dinner, fully clothed, followed by escorting me as far as the tube station.'

I left laughing, and met Elly outside the office before grabbing a cab to the cosy Italian restaurant near my flat where the husband and wife owners constantly pour out their troubles to you – in turn he's a letch, she's a harridan, but I've never met a better-matched couple in their way – and they then ask in offended tones why you haven't eaten the food. But they also make a trifle which I hope will be the last taste in my mouth before I die. There would then be no worry about reaching heaven as I'd already be there.

We spent more time marvelling at the resuscitation of our relationship, chuckling at our parents' united reaction – relief mixed with ecstasy and a sizeable slice of frantic anxiety that I'd find a way to bugger it up again – before moving on to the hot issue: rumour had it that the partnership announcement was imminent.

'I know it'll be you,' Elly said, just beating me to the shameless display of false modesty which was required at a time like this. 'You've been there far longer and that'll be what swings it.'

'But you and Ian have been billing hugely,' I said, shaking my head. 'That's what really counts at the end of the day. I don't know how you do it.'

'What can I say? Our clients appreciate what we do for them.'

342

I almost felt physically ill. I'd been doing more sleuthing, mainly courtesy of a girl in the accounts department with whom I'd long had a mutual *Upstairs Downstairs* kind of flirtation that amused both of us lightly but had gone no further than a brief kiss at the firm's Christmas party three years before. It had been her decision to leave it at that. 'My friends would disown me if they knew I was seeing a lawyer,' she explained apologetically. 'My social credibility would go through the floor.'

Through her and more than a bit of snooping around some of the papers Elly brought home from work and sometimes even left lying around, I uncovered just how much activity there had been on several Worthington Trumpet matters; money coming in and out of Babbingtons' accounts on a regular basis and hey presto, it was clean. One final rinse through buying a property, and new Babbington Botts Automatic washes your dirty money right through.

Then Elly told me that she was very excited because her big client was coming over to the UK the following week. 'You know, the one I told you instructed me based on my fantastic reputation? He's coming over here because he might have some more business for us. Some big property deal with a developer. If it had come through a bit earlier, it could really have helped my partnership chances.'

I tried to control my breathing. It had to be Mr Worthington Trumpet. 'Like you need any help,' I said as lightly as I could. 'Stop bragging, will you?'

I moved us on to more general office gossip – there was a fantastic e-mail today announcing that mild tax partner Samuel Carter would in future be known as Samantha – until over coffee Elly began stirring her cup with such concentration that I knew there was something she wanted to ask me.

'About Hannah,' she said lightly. 'I've been hearing stuff about you two.' She left the question hanging. Ash or Lucy again. It had to be.

'She's gone back to live with her parents,' I said,

343

looking embarrassed. 'She was vulnerable, I was vulnerable, nothing much happened and even that should never have happened anyway. I don't even know if we'll see each other again.'

Elly looked troubled at thoughts of Hannah, as well she might. 'Did you, erm, ever tell her about, you know . . .'

I looked Elly in the face. 'Can we just drop the subject? Hannah's gone. I'd prefer not to dwell on it, because it makes me feel exceptionally sad.' Regrets, she had a few, I was pleased to see. But not enough.

The silence was lengthy and awkward until my hand snaked out across the table as a peace offering. Elly grabbed it gratefully. 'Do you remember that holiday in Bournemouth when we were eleven?' she asked.

'The one where I fell into the pool fully clothed and you dived in and told everyone you had saved my life?'

'That's the one,' she said, holding my hand harder still. She stared at me in such a way that I knew I was seeing a rare glimpse of Elly's own needy little child. 'Now we're even.'

The next few days whizzed by, but all my efforts to get in contact with Hannah were in vain. Would I ever see her again? My heart went cold at the thought that I wouldn't. But at least I was occupied. I had plans to make, more drawers and briefcases to go through at Elly's flat, some very unusual conversations to have, and finally arranged to meet Sparkle and Cookie on Thursday evening by Tottenham Court Road tube. We sat in a cheap pizza place over slices which had been steadily curling under a hot light as I explained what was happening and what I needed from Sparkle. 'You're a crafty so and so,' she said eventually. 'No wonder you make such a good lawyer.'

'Thanks for that. I'll feed it into my next appraisal at work.'

We wandered into the first electronics store we liked the look of and explained what was needed. I flashed my gold-tinged credit card and with Cookie's help, left some time later laden with boxes and bags. 'I feel like that Julia Roberts out of *Pretty Woman*,' said Sparkle.

'I wouldn't get used to it,' I said. 'That's as close as you're ever getting to my credit card.'

'Shame,' she grinned. 'Gold's my lucky colour.'

We jumped into a cab over to the Bills, who were all too eager to listen to what I had to say. I had to move an hour later, leaving Cookie to take Sparkle through the ins and outs of our purchases, happy at what I had achieved so far, but miserable at what was to come. I then whizzed over to Ash's flat where I explained and asked for a few things which left his eyebrows stuck to the ceiling.

I greeted the following Monday at Elly's flat and bounced out of bed nervously. The sex thing was fast moving up the agenda as Elly because increasingly convinced that we were fully back on track, but our agreement was holding on the grounds that it seemed a rather daringly adult thing to be doing – or not doing, as the case may be.

In all other respects though, things had quickly returned to normal. She stubbornly refused to get up quickly, and grabbed a passing leg as I headed towards the shower, demanding 'Charlie Time'. That was once a request that wobbled my knees, but not today.

We struggled with brief intensity before I fell back on to the mattress, grumpily pushing her away. 'Don't you have a long meeting out of the office to prepare for?'

'Do I? How do you know?'

'Because I've been peeking in your diary every day to make sure,' was probably not the answer she'd appreciate most. 'You told me last night, remember?'

'Just another five minutes. Pleeeease,' she said, echoing many a childhood plea, and I couldn't help but relent. The number of times as kids she'd got her way by wheedling 'Pleeeease Charlie, it'll be fun' was only matched by the number of times we – or, to be accurate, usually I – then got into trouble.

And now was unlikely to be any different but I eventually

345

extricated myself and got us to the office. The clock did its best to be difficult, but at long last it reached the appointed hour and Elly left for her meeting. I hurried back to my desk and called Sparkle. The plan was for Big Bill to call Ian and say he was finally prepared to sell, but that he had to do it as soon as possible as he was acting behind the others' backs. I sat impatiently but in due course Ian came in.

'Charles, old chap, need a favour. Could you just authorise a payment out of this account? It's one of Eleanor's files but she's out of the office at the moment and it needs to be approved sharpish.'

He handed me a piece a paper with the Worthington Trumpet account details on it, and feigning disinterest, I scrawled my name where indicated.

'Many thanks,' he said and smartly turned heel.

I counted to a hundred with as much patience as I could muster – which wasn't much – grabbed my coat, and headed off after him.

Chapter Thirty-Seven

It was over.

Eight bloody years. In my darkest moments, I had feared being exposed, the world seeing how inadequate I was. But still I never realised it would feel quite this awful.

Two thousand nine hundred and twenty pointless days. Would etiquette deem it unacceptable to throw up over Graham's desk?

Seventy thousand and eighty wasted hours, an astounding number of which were chargeable. One part of me wanted to grab the next flight to Brazil and hide out for the rest of my days among noble Amazonian Indians of the non-cannibal variety, another part wanted to grab the managing partner and chin him.

A quarter of my life in which I could have done plenty of more fun and less stressful things which didn't end up with becoming a partner at Babbington Botts, rather than slog my guts out throughout and achieve exactly the same result.

'Cheer up, Charles. There's always next time. Several people over the years have made it second time around.' Graham realised he didn't sound all that reassuring. Profits had never been bigger, the time never more ripe for sharing them around an enlarged partnership. I had done everything asked of me, countless other things they would have asked me had they thought of them, plus several things you wouldn't ask a lab rat to do. And still they hadn't wanted me in their club.

Even worse, they wanted Elly and Lucy.

'You know how PC it is to have lots of women partners these days, even the likes of Samantha Carter,' he said. Then a thought struck him. 'If you knock young Eleanor up sharpish, that'll be her out of the way.' He laughed heartily at the suggestion. This was Graham trying to help and went some way to explaining why he specialised in company rather than family law. 'On reflection, best not to mention I said that. I would probably be misunderstood by the feminists.'

By feminists, he meant any woman who wouldn't sleep with him.

I sat dumbly, trying really, really hard not to cry.

It had been early that morning and I had been staring blankly at my PC, trying to recall the events of the afternoon before with something approaching calm. I only hoped that my plans would come good. I was doing my best to control my breathing when I caught sight of Elly moving rapidly towards my room with the gait of someone who wanted to run but knew it wasn't the done thing.

She burst in and turned to Richard. 'Out. Now.'

Richard looked devastated that the object of his undying affection had spoken to him so roughly. 'Why?'

'Because I said so.'

That was the kind of reasoning any Babbingtons employee could respond to, and he left with a sloppy smile in Elly's direction. She closed the door behind him and leaned against it, breathing heavily. I could think of no other way to describe her than to say she glowed.

'I've made it.'

She could only mean one thing. I stood up in shock. Thoughts of everything else vanished. 'Oh my God.' My first thought was for myself. What about me?

She skipped over and threw her arms around me. 'I've made it, Charlie. I've made it, I've made it, I've made it. I can't believe it.' She kissed me with such force and passion that I feared she had permanently flattened my lips. 'I love you, Charlie.'

I was reeling. 'How ... when ...?'

'Just now. Ian called me in and Tom Gulliver was there. I almost peed my pants, I was so scared when I realised what it was about. But then Tom said, "I'm pleased to report that you have been elected to the partnership" and it was like fireworks going off in my head.'

My phone rang as Elly performed an intense little dance of joy that looked like she was trying to stamp out a small fire. It was Graham, asking me if I could just pop into his room for a second. Shaking, I replaced the receiver and stared at Elly. 'It's my turn,'

She pulled me into another embrace. 'You've got nothing to worry about and remember: I love you, Charles Fortune.'

At that moment, Lucy steamed into my room. This time, I recognised the glow. She and Elly looked at one another and gave a little shriek of joy each. Lucy turned to me. 'I'm going to find out now,' I said, with an attempt at a brave smile. 'You deserve it, Lucy.' In that, I was sincere.

I left them excitedly comparing notes about how the news was broken. I made my way over to Graham's office, which involved walking past Ash's room. Unusually, the door was closed and I stopped briefly to gaze through the small head-high rectangular pane of glass laid in the otherwise solid wood. Ash was sitting slackly in his chair, staring into space, with his left elbow on the desk and his fingers against his temple. He caught the motion at the window and glanced up at me. His vacant expression told me everything I didn't want to know. I laid my palm on the glass as a meaningless gesture of support, and moved on.

I paused outside Graham's room and tried to compose myself. Think good thoughts, I told myself, and a picture

349

of Hannah popped up, casually leaning over the breakfast table to kiss me. With a final blow of my cheeks, I walked into Graham's room.

I knew instantly. There was no glow to be had here. They looked suitably funereal at the death of my Babbingtons career.

'Sit down, Charles,' said Graham from behind his desk. I complied, my head already filing with white noise. Everything I had done the afternoon before suddenly seemed utterly irrelevant.

Tom was perched on the edge of the desk. 'I'm sorry to tell you, Charles, that you haven't made it through this year's partnership selection.' His mouth moved some more but about the only words I heard were 'very difficult decision' and 'next year'. Yes, there was next year, but the chance was far slimmer second time around, and the brutal up or out system was about to push me through its unforgiving grinder. I had no desire to be second-class Charlie anyway, whatever the rewards.

Tom had stopped talking, I noticed, and stood to leave. He patted me awkwardly on the shoulder as he passed, leaving Graham with the task of dealing with any aftermath. The partners lived in fear of a repeat of the time one overlooked assistant – who on the plus side had great computer skills but on the downside occasionally exhibited near-psychotic tendencies – had managed to prove both simultaneously by wiping the department's computers. There were back-ups, but it caused chaos for days. Unsurprisingly, he wasn't given a second chance to join the partnership and two security guards were detailed to escort him from the building and stop him touching absolutely anything before he did so.

Graham yakked on for longer than I could stand, so eventually I said I needed some time to myself. A normal boss might have told me to take the day off, but Graham was not overburdened in the sensitivity department. 'Sorry to ask you this, Charles, but I really need that Burgess contract by the end of the day.'

I felt justified in goggling at him for a bit, and he did have the decency to look a bit shifty. 'The client's really shouting at me, you see.'

I understood the impulse but said I would see what I could do.

I kept my head down on the way back to my room and closed the door behind me when I got there. Elly was alone, sitting at my desk. One glance and she threw a hand to her mouth. 'Oh, Charlie, no.' She rushed over to hug me long and hard, mouthing the same useless platitudes Graham had, only she meant them.

We've loved, we've loathed, we've argued, we've shared everything, but until that moment we've never felt awkward with each other like this. It was hateful, all the more so because I detected – and I could be entirely wrong about this but don't think I was – the tiniest part of Elly that was rejoicing at her victory over me. Worse still was the knowledge that I would probably have been exactly the same.

We talked and I tried to put on a brave face. She looked at me with love, concern and an unmistakable air of 'rather you than me', for which I could hardly blame her but did anyway. Eventually I said I wanted to be alone, and she left reluctantly, saying that she'd come running the moment I asked. 'I love you, Charlie,' she repeated for the umpteenth time, 'come what may.'

I forced the corners of my mouth upwards. 'Just as well, I guess.'

The walls seemed to close in on me as I sat there for ages, swamped by anger, regret, emptiness, crushing disappointment and any other horrid emotion that I could dredge up.

Eventually the phone rang. 'Hello, Charlie,' said Mum, with such overwhelming joviality that I knew she knew. She was probably collecting the ingredients for a consolation Victoria sponge as we spoke.

'Hello, Mum.'

'How are you?' She definitely knew. Elly would have

351

told her mum who would immediately have been on the blower to mine.

'OK.'

'Anything, erm, interesting happened in the last few days?'

I thought about prolonging her suffering, and even though there was a point – if it hadn't been for my parents I would never have become a lawyer in the first place and would have been spared all this – I couldn't bring myself to do it. 'Actually, Mum, I've just had some bad news. I've been passed over for partnership.'

'Oh dear,' she said, far too quickly. 'There's always next year, isn't there?'

My dad was on the upstairs extension. I could imagine him sitting on the floral print bedspread, uneasy at an emotionally difficult situation. 'They don't know what they're doing,' he said gruffly. 'Remember those chaps at Decca Records who turned down the Beatles because they thought guitar music was going out of fashion? Well, this is just the same.'

For the first time that day, I smiled. 'Thanks, Dad, that means a lot.'

'Oh, really?' I could sense him going slightly pink – he wasn't used to good-parenting compliments.

'It's only work,' Mum said, renouncing the years of ambition she'd been carrying on my behalf just like that. 'Don't forget that there are more important things in life. Like Eleanor.'

That didn't cheer me up. 'She made it to partner, by the way.'

Their effort to sound surprised was feeble. 'Lots of women earn more than their husbands nowadays,' Mum said at length. 'It's nothing to be ashamed about.'

I couldn't be bothered to pick off the battery of assumptions swirling around her head. 'Look, I've got to go. I'll speak to you later.'

I sat for some time deep in a blue funk. Lucy came in to console me in such a kind and genuine way that I did feel better for it, while I eventually dragged myself over to

Ash's room, where we sat looking at each other, cursing every member of the assessment committee with considerable imagination. Misery does indeed enjoy company.

'I decided ages ago that if I didn't make it first time, I'm going to leave,' he said. 'If they don't want me, so be it, but I'm not just going to hang on here for ever, having to tug my forelock at the likes of Lucy and Elly. Buggered if I know what I'm going to do, though.'

I hated the thought of losing Ash from my day-to-day life, but knew how he felt. The way the power balance had shifted with Elly was especially distressing. Yet we were both institutionalised – scared of what life might be like outside our ivory tower.

So rather than explore our career options in any more detail, we found it far easier just to resume staring at one another, swearing softly.

But the law stops for no man, however utterly fed up with it he is, and so I at length dragged myself back to my office in an effort to polish off this bloody contract without including clauses such as 'The company guarantees that its solicitor, Graham Bentley, is an arse.' There'd be no danger of being sued over that one. Richard, however, was in situ with his head down on it already. I must have done something right in the last few months. I fell into my chair and received a look of pity from him – so my life had come to that, had it?

'Is there anything I can do?' he asked.

You could have a word with your old man because there's clearly been some kind of embarrassing mix-up over this whole partnership thing, I didn't say, and then the thought struck me that perhaps it was Richard who had done for me, the little weasel. I examined his shifty eyes closely, but I saw no guilt, and I was getting wearily used to recognising the signs.

'Actually, there is,' I said. 'I need you to speak to your father about something and I need you to back me up a hundred per cent. I'm relying on you, Richard.'

His eyes widened with the fear of responsibility.

353

Chapter Thirty-Eight

It was not a good day, punctuated by people popping their heads around the door to commiserate with us both, several of them more junior lawyers interested – in a 'there but for the grace of the assessment committee go I' kind of way – to see what the car crash of someone else's career looked like. It was not, I fancy, a pretty sight, but then neither was the display of my colleagues' social ineptitude.

Some were genuinely sorry, especially Sue, who had fancied the secretarial status of working for a partner and also knew how I'd put everything into it. 'I can't believe it,' she said for about the tenth time, wilfully ignoring the way I was doing anything but listen, 'especially when you think of some of the brainless misfits they do promote.' That didn't make me feel a great deal better, on the whole.

One smiled awkwardly. 'It's just as well. The hours would have been even worse,' she said, with a wave of her hand. 'Who needs the hassle of being a partner anyway?'

'Me,' I replied sullenly.

'A lot of people make the lifestyle decision not to become a partner nowadays,' another explained earnestly.

'Would you?' I asked.

'God, no,' he snorted as if I'd just asked him to forni-cate with a threshing machine.

There was one woman a year below me who took up residence in a chair in front of my desk, having appointed herself my social worker. To the entertainment of the entire department, she'd once manufactured a little sign for herself – 'I think therefore I care' – had it framed and put behind her desk. It has never lasted more than twelve hours without being defaced, most memorably 'I drink therefore I care' and 'I think therefore I quit'.

'There are plenty of smaller firms with less pressurised workloads, you know. I'm sure you can find yourself a partnership at one of those.' She was utterly thrilled to be helping.

I wasn't in the mood to be reformed and stared moodily at her.

'You're worried you can't do it, aren't you?' She leaned over the desk, but even a flash of cleavage didn't brighten the experience. 'The bastards have knocked your confi-dence so much that you're doubting yourself. I can see it in your eyes.' She shook with mild anger on my behalf, but had she really been able to read my eyes, she'd have been doing unpleasant things with my stapler right then. 'Come on, Charlie, tell me what you're feeling.'

Overwhelming though it was, I resisted the temptation to expound on my feelings at that moment. 'You know, Sasha, actually I'm really worried about Tom Gulliver. Telling people about this is a terrible strain. I overheard him saying that he wished he had someone he could talk to about it, someone who would understand. A woman, a lawyer, someone like that. He's really very sensitive, you know.'

Her eyes lit up with ecstatic expectation. Here was a once-in-a-career opportunity to show the head of depart-ment how much she cared and to suck up furiously for next year's partnership round. 'You are such a good person, Charlie. Even in your darkest moment, you're thinking of others.'

I leaned towards her. 'Sasha, I just want to see you get what you really deserve.'

I thought she was going to start crying. 'Oh, Charlie. That's the nicest thing anyone's ever said to me here.'

Sadly, I could believe it. She wasn't a bad person, just so irritating that you wanted to rip her tongue out, and however good a lawyer she was technically, there was more chance of my mum being promoted than her.

Sasha hurried off to comfort Tom as an e-mail popped up on my screen to announce this year's new partners and that the usual special party would be held in one of the boardrooms after work to celebrate this exciting time for Babbington Botts. It reminded me of the other weight I was carrying and I sighed heavily, sending an e-mail to Ash, who would no doubt be as well disposed towards all this as I was at that moment.

Excitement in the office mounted at the prospect of the evening's festivities and especially the partners putting their hands in their pockets to fund it. Albeit that this was normally a manoeuvre which baffled them (I, of course, would have brought wise generosity to their ranks), but I suspected that after the Christmas party this was the high-light of the social year for some staff. They could be at work but not actually work – a dizzying delight.

The clock eventually crawled around to the appointed time, and once I was sure that all the arrangements were in place, I headed off to the main boardroom on the top floor, uncomfortably aware that I could be on the verge of making a bad situation career-threatening. But then, what's another gallon or two of oil when your bridges are already burning?

The room was packed with at least two hundred and fifty people, and the babble of happy noise contrasted starkly with my dark mood. Clumps of chattering people stood aside as I walked past – all it needed was for someone to yell 'Dead man walking' for the scene to be complete – and reached Elly, who was laughing along with Tom Gulliver and Ian McPherson at some partner-level joke. Sasha was hovering nearby, summoning up the courage to empathise with Tom.

I regarded Elly sadly, but she mistook the expression and impulsively grabbed my hand in support – a social faux pas that would be forgiven just this once, I suspected – while Ian glanced at me shiftily, and Tom muttered a faintly embarrassed, 'Hello there, Charles.'

There was a silence that was more awkward for them, but I forced out some jollity to make them all feel at ease.

'I heard this new lawyer joke,' I said. 'A lawyer's in a car crash, and the other motorist comes over to see how he is. "My Rolls-Royce, my Rolls-Royce, just look at it," the lawyer says, but the other man shouts at him: "How can you be worrying about your car at a time like this? Can't you see your arm's been ripped off?" And the lawyer stares at his severed stump in horror and starts screaming: "My Rolex, my Rolex."'

They laughed dutifully, but lawyers don't really like lawyer jokes, however much they try to appear as if they do. All the time, I had been watching carefully to make sure every piece was there. Richard had done his job and the video equipment was close by, connected to one of those large roll-down screens. Almost all the key people had arrived. As Lucy joined us, Richard walked in with his father, holding a small package and searching for me. He caught my gaze and I nodded. Richard turned to his father and shooed him to the top of the room by the screen. Somebody tapped a glass for quiet and eventually hush descended so the words of our great leader could fall gently into our ears.

'Good evening, everyone,' he said. 'This is, as ever, an exciting day in the history of Babbington Botts. The day when we welcome our new crop of partners.' All over the room, glasses were tipped with varying degrees of enthusiasm and resentment at those who had made the grade. 'It is the custom for me not to say much about them – that would, after all, require me to remember their names – but you can take it as read that we think highly of them. Now, as a special surprise, I understand that some of the associates have made a video especially for the occasion. An excellent example of how times are changing in the legal profession, I'm sure you'll agree.' There was a stirring of excitement. 'Erm, now, Charles Fortune, where are you?'

Many eyes turned to me, none more surprised than Elly's. The people in front of us melted away to the sides so that my little group was now in front of the screen. I walked casually over to Richard, who gave me the package containing the video. I pushed it into the machine and fiddled with the switches as he lowered the lights. Finally, after all this time, he had done exactly what I had asked of him. I'd make a solicitor of him yet.

'The quality's a bit amateur,' I said loudly, 'but that's not because I was involved in it, I should add.' There was a small, nervous laugh – was I being self-deprecating or bitter? I'd always thought that the firm should either produce a guide to the etiquette of dealing with the deadbeats who fail to make partner, or get them out the door as quickly and quietly as possible so as not to upset any other staff.

I turned back to the crowd and saw, at a side door, that Ash had quietly come in with a Sparkle dressed from head to toe in a rainbow of spandex – I'd asked her to be inconspicuous, after all – and a nervous-looking trio of Bills dressed as smartly as their pensions would allow. Billy's best hairpiece shone like a worn nylon suit, and I wouldn't like to swear that Little Bill hadn't dusted down his demob clothes. Ash clenched his fist at me in support, while one partner stared at Sparkle like he had never seen anything as disturbing. Behind the Bills, I caught a flash of glossy brown hair and felt a surge of excitement.

The video spluttered to life on screen to show what the lawyers didn't know was the Bills' living room. The kitchen door had been almost closed, but left open enough for our newly purchased video camera to poke out discreetly from a darkened room with Sparkle at the controls. Ian was pacing around impatiently in the middle

358

of the screen; behind him stood a nondescript middle-aged bloke with short hair and a well-cut grey suit.

There was a murmur of confusion from the audience as Big Bill announced proudly, 'That's my front room, that is.' Several more heads swung his way and clocked Sparkle. A wave of shock swept the room. This wasn't a dress-down Friday, after all.

Sparkle was peering through the crowd. 'Mickey?' she cooed loudly, waving wildly. 'Mickey O'Farrell? Is that you?' Heavy-hitting insurance partner Michael O'Farrell waved back weakly.

Edward Greene turned to me and was about to ask what on earth was going on when the handsome star of the show walked into shot. 'Fortune?' Ian said to him. 'What the hell are you doing here?' I glanced at Ian and he was watching the screen with mounting horror. As instructed, Ash slipped behind him so that he couldn't make a rapid exit.

On screen, I was making a creditable effort at keeping cool. That tie really works with my eyes, I thought. 'I act for the people selling the house.'

'What do you mean, you act for the people selling the house? I keep getting letters from some poxy law centre.'

I admired how calm I appeared – you wouldn't have guessed that my jack-hammering heart had taken up residence in my bowels. If I had learned little else in the past eight years, it was how to handle myself under pressure. But it was time for a haircut, perhaps. 'That was me. I help out there once a month.'

'But ... but ... that's ridiculous.' Shaky though his grasp of ethics patently was, even Ian could see it was a bit tricky having me on both sides of a transaction.

I'd thought for ages about how best to approach this. Tease out the truth through inscrutable and elegant questioning, perhaps? Skilfully pull them in and snap the trap closed before they know what's happening, leaving them bewildered but grudgingly impressed? Or just strap the electrodes straight to the testicles? 'I know what you're up to,' I said flatly. 'I've worked it all out.' I hadn't realised my voice had a slightly nasal character to it. I must speak more from my chest.

The camera zoomed in slightly as his features curled into an innocent question mark. 'What on earth are you talking about, Charles?'

Even though I knew what was coming, my heart was beating fast now. This was it. 'Worthington Trumpet? Your little racket? I learned ever so much from that time I spent in your room the other week.' His enlarged face began to flush and I could sense Graham observing me from the other side of the room. 'I mean, keeping the key in the flower pot. How amateur is that?'

A litigation partner moved towards the screen and began to speak. 'Edward, I really don't think we should—' but before anyone could act, back at the show, a swarm of words burst angrily from Ian. 'What are you talking about, you shit?' But the fear I had sensed at the time radiated from the screen. 'I'll have your bollocks for earrings for this.' There were a mixture of titters and gasps from the rapt audience. I watched with grim pleasure as the senior partner's jaw continued its downward movement. Elly had a hand over her mouth in disbelief. 'I don't know what kind of game you're playing here, you little gobshite. But you don't want to mess with me.' His threats sounded so strange when delivered by that cut-glass accent.

The shot pulled back jerkily as I put my hands up defensively. But I spoke for the benefit of the camera. 'Maybe I've got it wrong. Maybe this isn't a money laundering operation. Maybe you haven't been circulating money through the firm's accounts for no good reason. Maybe you're not buying all this property with dirty money. Maybe you haven't had your thugs intimidating the defenceless old men in this house. Maybe this isn't the last bit of land you need before you can sell it on to a developer for a fat, dirty profit.'

On and off screen, Ian glared at me with ill-disguised hate.

'Oh shit,' Tom muttered.

Elly looked at me wildly. 'Turn it off,' she yelped, but nobody moved.

'You little fucker, you don't know what you're messing with.' Back on the screen, Ian was busy proving himself less of a City gent by the second as he pushed me roughly in the chest and back against the wall. He seemed ready for a fight, but I hadn't hit someone with anything more aggressive than a writ since I was sixteen, and Kevin Hadfield took his revenge on me for telling people I'd seen his mum naked (she claimed that she hadn't realised I was upstairs while he was getting drinks from the kitchen, but it's not like she covered herself up all that quickly).

I bounced back and squared up to Ian, looking ever so tough on screen, I thought admiringly. An all-action legal hero: if I can't negotiate them into the ground, I'll pound them instead. You certainly couldn't tell that inside I was all whiney and 'don't hit me, I fight like a girl'.

'Go on, Ian, you can take him,' someone shouted from the back of the room as the stand-off continued.

'Hit him, Charlie,' a woman countered. Nice to get the female vote.

'Wait,' said the other man and the shot lurched across to focus on him. 'Let's find out what your friend wants.' The voice was less cultured than Ian's; sounded if anything as if it was losing the battle to throw off cockney roots. This had been a major bit of luck. The boss was in town, a brief visit from his offshore haven, and had turned up to see the last piece of his property jigsaw fall into place. Perhaps he still had a thing for the East End.

Ian backed off slightly. 'He's a little piece of shit, Ernest. You don't want to bother yourself with him.'

'Ooh, harsh,' said someone behind me in the boardroom.

'But let's face it, not totally unfair,' said another.

'Yeah, guess so.'

I tried to concentrate on the action. 'Ian, Ian, Ian. Maybe he'd like a bit of the action eh? I'm always interested in new blood. Maybe the fact that he's here now is his way of saying he wants in?'

361

'Like we'd want him in,' Ian snorted. 'This one's even more useless than Gray.' I peeked at Elly, who had cocked her head like she couldn't quite believe what she had just heard. Her eyes were so wide, it seemed like her lids had given up and gone home. 'I can handle the legal side of things without having to put up with another chinless wonder.' The look Elly got from Ian at that moment was brutal. I turned away.

Instead, the dashing star of the show had known he had to sound interested. 'What are we talking about?'

Ernest waved at Ian, as if discussing such things was beneath him. Ian shook his head angrily but it was clear who was holding whose testicles in this relationship. 'Enough that you won't have to worry whether or not you make partner, that's for sure,' he said grumpily, and then his voice took on a cruel, mocking tone. 'I told them there was no way you were up to it, by the way.'

Tom returned my gaze with a raised eyebrow, which was a display of vivid emotion by his standards, and that wasn't just because he had Sasha at his elbow.

'Who needs to be a partner?' Ernest shrugged. 'I can give you so much that you can have whatever you want. Whatever your favourite pastimes. Women, cars ...' He examined Ian with a dismissive smile. 'Gambling.' He was bored, like we were just playing out a game he'd won countless times.

For the benefit of the slower partners, I had wanted to spell it out in letters ten feet high. 'Let me get this straight. You want me to join your money laundering gang?'

'I wish he'd stop using those words,' a property partner moaned from nearby.

'I wouldn't use the words "money laundering",' said Ernest, granting his wish. 'That's a very crude way of putting it. More of a redistribution of wealth. But yes, I think I could find a use for you. You can never have enough lawyers around, in my opinion.'

'We could do with a few more clients like that,' an assistant said loudly, seeking laughs and instead just getting a glance from Edward Greene that foreshadowed a Triple-R.

'I especially like having them from a firm as prestigious as Babbington Botts,' Ernest went on. 'Makes me feel very important.' He laughed gently to himself and I think I sensed every partner in the room go a little green. They won't be putting that commendation on the website.

'And if I say no?'

The idea seemed to amuse him further. 'Do you know something, Charles – can I call you Charlie? – I'm not entirely sure. Nobody's ever said no to me before.'

'This is all lies,' Ian shouted in the boardroom. 'Some kind of sick practical joke.' He made to move in my direction, but Ash got a tight hold of his arms. Ian turned, flashing anger, but Ash was immovable.

'I'll be the judge of that,' Edward Greene murmured, loud enough for Ian to hear, and though he struggled some more, he was eventually forced to subside, muttering obscenities that did not become a blue-chip City law firm, that's for sure.

On screen, it seemed as though I was thinking over his offer. 'I'd rather disembowel myself with a potato peeler than dirty myself with you people,' I said at length. Not a bad line, under the circumstances.

Ian's face reddened and he jerked forward like I had just given him an idea. Catching me by surprise, he was able to get a pinstriped forearm against my throat. To watch him as he toured the City's finest restaurants, you'd never have guessed that he had it in him. 'I'm sorry, Charles, I didn't quite catch that.'

He released the pressure slightly. 'I said, you can't stop me telling people.' Back in the boardroom, I rubbed my neck in recollection.

He had reeked of desperation and somehow the smell filtered from the film. 'Did you hear that, Ernest? I think he's threatening us. You've got bollocks, I'll give you that. And yes, you could go and tell people, but we wouldn't be very happy about that. And we are not people you want to displease.'

I lashed out at him, but I couldn't make him loosen his hold. On reflection, that said more about me than him.

The camera closed in on us. 'Let's not get melodramatic about this, Charlie,' Ernest said, although had I been able to get the words through my windpipe, I wanted to yell that it was a little late for that. 'This isn't some silly TV programme. The police aren't about to burst through the door and save you. You're deep in the shit, my friend. You can either go deeper, or take the only hand that's going to pull you out.'

Forgetting for a moment that I knew how this was going to end, I stood watching the screen and really hoping that the police would crash in just to see the expression on his face. Of course they didn't, but I had everything I needed, and thrashed around some more for effect before finally signalling my capitulation. 'I won't say a word,' I agreed, appearing defeated. And I had, in a way, kept to that. 'How do I know you will keep your side of the deal?'

Give the man an eye-patch and a cat to stroke and he'd have been in bad-guy heaven. 'As they say in the movies, you don't.'

'No,' Elly shrieked, jumping in front of the screen. 'I don't believe this. It's got to be a mistake.'

Attention turned to the first-hand drama. 'There's no mistake,' I said quietly.

'There must be. You must have dubbed it, or used actors, or . . . or . . . something.' It sounded feeble even to her. 'I refuse to believe it. Worthington Trumpet is my file. My client.'

Not the best time for that confession, I thought. 'They were just using you.'

The surrounds seemed to dissolve and all I could see was Elly. 'This is all your fault, isn't it?' she hissed. 'You just can't cope with the fact that I made partner and you didn't, can you?' Lucy moved towards her calmly but Elly's stare was so malevolent that Lucy shrivelled backwards.

I put my fingers to my temple in frustrated disbelief. 'I'm sorry? I made all this up because you became a

364

partner?' I moved closer in a vain effort to keep our voices down and try not to share what promised to be a moment of painful intimacy with the rest of the party.

This was the other Elly laid bare like I'd never seen her before. 'You've been like this for as long as I've known you,' she said, before faltering at the sight of countless saucer-shaped eyes around us. 'Jealous.'

The only green-eyed monster in the vicinity right then was her, but rather than make that point, I went for the more direct, if slightly less eloquent, 'You're off your bloody trolley if you think that.'

She got closer so we were virtually face to face. 'I'd hoped you'd be over it by now. I've finally given in to you. What more do you want?'

I forgot about Ian and Ernest and Edward Greene and Babbington Botts. 'What do you mean, "given in"?'

'Come on Charlie, you know exactly what I mean. You've wanted me since you were old enough to speak and now I've finally let you have me.'

I was fast losing my cool. 'You let me have you?' For a few seconds I just made incoherent noises, unable to counter this monstrous claim. Those around us strained to hear, but a glare from Elly saw them shuffle backwards in alarm.

'I thought you'd changed, grown up, become a real man. But it seems I was wrong. I thought you were just the kind of man I was looking for and then I find out that you're still the immature fourteen-year-old I always remembered.'

'Elly, I'm not the one acting for a fucking crook,' I said in a constrained shout. In my mind, I could hear my mother tutting so loudly they could hear it in Bedfordshire and telling me not to swear in front of the senior partner again.

I then took a deep breath as a strange kind of peace flowed over me. Elly genuinely had no idea what was happening. I had feared that she was so up to her neck in this that you could put a frill around it, but every cupboard, file and drawer of hers I'd looked in had convinced me she wasn't. And her reaction was one of innocent outrage. I thanked every god who may possibly have had a hand in making it so. I had achieved what I'd set out to. Sadly, the emotional price had quickly gone up with inflation from embarrassing to humiliating.

My voice was dispassionate, almost offhand. 'Elly, you don't understand what's going on here. These people are criminals. Just look at some of the things that have been signed off.' I pulled some Worthington Trumpet papers out of my inside pocket, filched from a file she'd brought home one night. 'What else could it be? You didn't even know they were buying property in the East End, did you?' A shadow of confusion chased across her face. 'This isn't your client. It's Ian's. They were just using you to put some distance between themselves and what's happening just in case things got difficult.'

There was a breathless silence. Elly peeked fearfully in Ian's direction, unable to look at him directly. 'Tell him it's not true.'

He ignored her. She rushed up to him and screamed, shockingly, in his face. 'Tell him it's not true.'

Ian's face was fixed. 'I'm not saying anything.'

'You might want to get yourself a lawyer,' I said. 'Do you know any good ones?'

I saw Lucy put her hand over her mouth in shock.

'You used me?' Elly's voice was suddenly fragile.

Ian choked out an exasperated laugh. 'Little girl, just go away. It's so easy to pull the wool over your eyes that I'm amazed you manage to find your way into work.'

Elly fought back tears as Ian suddenly tore himself away from Ash and ran towards the door. Where he thought he could go is anyone's guess, but there was a blur of colour as Sparkle's fist came from nowhere and landed solidly in the centre of Ian's face. There was a satisfying thud and he fell backwards, clutching his nose and swearing vividly. Ash and a couple of other assistants swiftly moved to sit on him.

Above, the film was coming to an end with unbloodied

Ian cornering me by the kitchen door. He was so close to the camera that I was terrified at the time that he would see it and everything would go to pot. 'Remember, if you breathe a word of this to anyone, you little fuck, it's over. Everything. Take my word for it.' And on that happy note, the screen went black.

Richard turned up the lights and there was an awesome silence. Elly was sobbing, Lucy had gone white, while I could see that Tom Gulliver was already calculating the damage and whether there was any way he could possibly limit it.

'There's one other thing,' I began to say, but Edward Greene waved me away. 'It can wait. I think we better call the police, don't you?' he said to nobody in particular. 'And can we clear the room?'

The party-goers slowly filed out, the partners presumably rushing home to put all their assets in the names of their wives just in case, while Sasha was crowding around Tom, saying she understood what he was going through. I heard Edward saying how pleased he was that this terrible crime had been exposed.

After the room emptied, I saw Edward Greene introduce himself to Sparkle and congratulate her on her upper-cut. 'I'd've put him down no problem,' Billy Whizz interrupted, and he threw an air punch with such force that his hair slid slightly askew.

Then he walked over to where I was standing with Richard, supervising Ian's detention. 'Did you know about this?' he asked his son.

Richard nodded happily in expectation of a big serving of fawning paternal approval; it would be nice to see a bit coming my way as well. 'Some of it. Charlie told me a few hours ago. He needed my help to set it up.'

Edward Greene, however, is not the fawning sort, and his smile dropped. 'I do not believe this. The combined intelligence of a senior associate with years of Babbington Botts training and my son came up with the idea – the oh so brilliant idea – of exposing this appalling fraud in front

367

of the entire firm. Did it take you long to dream up or had you both recently suffered head traumas?'

'Mr Greene—' I began.

'Discretion, Mr Fortune. That is what Babbington Botts is known for. That is what we look for in our lawyers. In our partners, especially.' He arched an eyebrow at me.

That didn't explain the now ex-partner who once turned up in court in a slinky evening dress he had borrowed from his wife as an innovative way of expressing his opposition to the tyranny of his job. It was, admittedly, a good way to part him from both the tyranny and the job.

Rather than recall this, I spoke over his interruptions and explained that public confrontation was necessary so I could be sure about Elly's role in the whole affair.

'And this was the only way you could do it? The most discreet way?' He was not convinced.

'It seemed so at the time,' I said, conviction faltering.

He turned to Elly, who was sitting on a chair, looking vacant. 'You should be pleased, Fortune, that there is someone in a lot more trouble than you. Once the police are done with you, Miss Gray, we'll need to have a long meeting. A very long meeting.'

Elly stared at me, utterly woeful. I couldn't help but love that face, despite everything. It had been so central to my life for so long.

She began to apologise, but he cut her off curtly. 'This is not the time.'

There was a long pause as Elly continued to hold my gaze. 'But sir, there is one other thing you should know. It's about Hannah Klein.' I stared at Elly with gratitude, and she gave me a brittle smile in return.

After she explained what had happened, the senior partner rubbed his forehead and looked suitable grave. 'Oh dear. This just gets worse and worse, doesn't it?'

'I'd been planning to get to what happened to Hannah,' I said, 'Which was the other reason this had to be in public. I wanted eveyone to know.'

At that moment, Tom showed in the police, as painful a

368

sight as I suspect Edward Greene had ever witnessed in the offices of his beloved law firm. Ian was led away, while an officer stayed behind to start taking details and was trying to get the Bills to speak in turn rather than over each other.

The senior partner turned to me once more, drawing a deep breath. 'We need to talk about this properly. I can see that you, well, shall we say, may have had your reasons for doing what you did.'

That was as good as I was going to get right then. 'I'm sorry about what this'll do to Babbingtons,' I said.

He sighed. 'So am I. It won't be pretty, but we'll cope. We always have. At least we – at least you caught him. It'll be bad for business, that's for sure. Hit profits. Maybe we won't be able to make up any new partners for a year or two.' But his face had taken on an ironic twist.

Then his mobile rang; he exchanged a few words with Tom Gulliver before shutting it off decisively. 'Right, I've got work to do. We will talk soon,' he promised, gesturing to both Richard and me, but the tone was not as grave as before.

He made to leave, but turned to Sparkle. 'Thank you ever so much for all your help.'

'Eddy – can I call you that? – it was a pleasure. And here's my number should you ever need me again.' The senior partner smiled in gentle confusion that such a thing could possibly come to pass, and placed the piece of paper carefully in a business card holder.

Tom motioned for Elly to leave with him, but instead she came over to me, dropping to her knees before me.

Her beautiful face implored me to forgive her. 'Charlie. I'm so sorry. I didn't mean any of it. I need you. I realise that now. I love you.'

I smiled without rancour and put a gentle hand to her face as I caught movement at the doorway. I looked up and there was Hannah, rubbing her wet eyes with the heels of her hands like a child. She dropped her arms to her side. 'Charlie,' she mouthed and at long last, I knew what I really, really wanted.

Eyes moist, I looked down at Elly. 'I love you too,' I said, 'but ...' And I got up and went over to hug Hannah with the intention of never letting go.

Chapter Thirty-Nine

'How does it feel to be a partner at last, Charles?'
Graham's smile hid his sadness that he could no longer
lead me by the nose.

'More than anything, it's just a huge relief. Nice to
know that in future I'll be working my nuts off for my own
enrichment, rather than for yours.'

Tom Gulliver laughed gently. 'And there are a lot of
nuts to be worked off, that's for sure.'

There was a collective wince at the months ahead.
Babbingtons had already lost some clients in the two
months of Worthington Trumpet fall-out, not least British
Pharmaceuticals.

But this was a celebration, and everyone welcomed the
chance to forget their worries, even if only for an hour or
so before they had to rush back to the office. I caught the
Bills stationed in front of the buffet, attacking it methodi-
cally.

'They're all very proud of you here,' Big Bill said in
between bites. 'We were just talking to one chap who was
saying how nobody thought you had it in you to do what
you did.'

Little Bill was eyeing a plate of sushi warily. 'Funny old

371

world, isn't it? We beat the bleedin' Japs in the war and they get their revenge by making us eat this.'

Billy Whizz was talking to a property partner, spitting little flakes of puff pastry in his direction. 'So, if Charlie's busy, will you do our conveyancing for us?'

The partner, who never dealt in anything smaller than £50 million office blocks, was hoping to escape but Billy had him cornered. 'Not sure it's really my thing.'

'We can afford you, don't worry about that. We're going to be quids in. There's this proper developer, you see, who's seen the potential of what the other geezers – you know, the bent ones – were trying to do. Charlie says we'll do really well out of it.'

'I can see you as an estate agent,' he said to me maliciously. That was high on the list of professional insults. And this from a man with the charisma of an accountant's calculator.

'Billy,' I said. 'Tell Malcolm here about that time when you were in Burma during the war.'

Billy's eyes lit up and he put a hand to Malcolm's arm to ensure that he wasn't going anywhere. For some time. I passed on happily.

Sparkle was holding court with a group of partners, not least Edward Greene himself. Richard was standing with them. She was brandishing a bunch of business cards she had made up specially on one of those machines you get in supermarkets. 'Make your evening Sparkle', they ran, before going on to proclaim that escorting lawyers and/or investigating corporate fraud was her speciality. 'Endorsed by Babbington Botts', it read across the bottom.

'I don't believe it,' Sparkle was shouting. 'Tell me again how much they charge you out at?'

Richard, who had now passed into the care of the litigation department – despite their attempts to get court orders to prevent it – blushed deeply. 'It's currently a hundred and forty pounds an hour.'

'That's twenty quid more than me. And which of us do you think provides better value for money, eh?' Sparkle's

372

hoots of laughter were enthusiastically echoed by her coterie.

'But most of my time's written off, anyway, because I'm learning.' Richard was trying, and failing, not to sound too whiney. Life had improved for him markedly at the firm since events in the boardroom and his reinterpretation of the story so that his role was considerably more central. 'Most of my work's effectively free.'

Sparkle looked as shocked at the admission as she had all that time ago in the law centre. 'Let me give you a word of advice about life,' she said. 'It's the golden rule. Never, ever do anything for free.' There was a wave of nods about her.

'We should hang that in every office,' I overheard one partner saying to another as I moved on, greeting the many guests, the strains of a string quartet in the background. There were a few well-wishers – I could see my mother taking a puzzled pensions partner through the dizzying variety of cakes she'd insisted on making – but most were either current or hopefully future sources of work. Breaking a multi-million pound fraud was good for business, we had learned.

I caught sight of Ash with his charm turned full beam on Maurice, the guy I had met at Sparkle's and who, it turned out, ran a large lawnmower company. My dad was on hand to provide technical back-up – and an ice-breaker in his lawnmower tie – as Ash worked hard to turn Maurice from one of Sparkle's clients into one of ours.

I was standing to one side, contentedly watching the scene when Elly ghosted up and put her arm through mine. 'It's a great feeling, isn't it? Knowing you've done it. Lived up to your own hopes. Lived up to everyone else's.'

'You still got there first.'

She shrugged. 'Natural order of things, I'm afraid. You've always been a step behind me.'

'Only because I like the view.'

Elly extracted her arm and wrapped it around my waist as we watched her father – wearing what he had told me

373

earlier was his 'pulling jacket' – say something to Lucy which elicited a sharp slap to the cheek from his wife. 'You deserve it, Charlie. More than I do, that's for sure.'

I turned to her. 'It looks like we'll always be together, doesn't it? Our lives are destined to be entwined, I reckon.'

Elly smiled. 'Suits me.'

We shared a moment where the past thirty-two years whizzed through our minds on a rapid showreel. It wasn't so bad, all in all. 'Me too.'

But then there was a gap in the crowd and I caught sight of a flash of shiny chestnut hair. Disengaging myself from Elly, I slalomed my way over there.

'Whatcha doing?'

Hannah and her parents were staring at a display board on the wall by the door. 'Reading this again. Feeling good. Feeling happy.' She looked up at me. 'Feeling well, fortunate.'

'So, your salary must be going up a bit now,' her mum interrupted, her voice laced with hope.

'Mum, stop it. Leave Charlie alone for five seconds, will you?'

Her dad pointed at the string quartet nearby. 'You know, I've always thought that marriage is like a violin. When the beautiful music's over, the strings are still attached.'

Even Mrs Klein laughed and I couldn't help but feel amazed by how my world had flipped over. I'd sent Ash to plead with Hannah on my behalf and, more to the point, get her to the boardroom. She had to see that I'd do anything to get her back, and Ash told me that it had taken his full reserves of magic just to get past Hannah's mother.

But I'd done enough for her to wipe the slate clean and give me a second chance. I wasn't about to bugger it up for a second time, and the last three months had truly been the most astounding of my life. For the first time in my life, whatever Sparkle had to say about the state, I felt wonderfully free – free of obligation, free of expectation, free of fear, free of the past.

'You two look great together,' Elly said from behind us,

and we turned. Was she jealous? A little part of me – the old me – hoped she was, but I was beyond that now. Kind of. It was the least she deserved, all in all.

'Feeling jealous?' Hannah asked with a smile.

Elly gave me a look as if to say what a sad little man I was – she knew what I was thinking. 'What? That you've got your hands on the man who virtually ruined my career? Jealously isn't the emotion I feel when I think of that.' But her face was almost placid. She'd had to come to terms with a lot of things about herself – and I'd spent a great deal of time helping her do so – and I liked this Elly so much more than the old one. But nothing like I loved this Hannah.

We all turned back to the board, which contained an enlarged copy of an article from the *Law Society Gazette*. I put my arms around Hannah as we read it together for the umpteenth time. 'Oi vey,' I said quietly.

'Good Fortune for City firm,' ran the headline.

Five former lawyers at City giant Babbington Botts this week launched their own practice amid continuing fall-out from the biggest fraud case to hit the Square Mile in years.

Charles Fortune, Eleanor Gray, Hannah Klein, Ashok Chaudhry and Lucy Sommersdale have left Babbington Botts, pledging that lawyers working at their new firm – called Fortune, Klein, Chaudhry & Sommersdale – will not be forced into the City culture of long hours.

Mr Fortune, who is said to have turned down partnership at Babbington Botts in favour of the new venture, told the Gazette: *'We hope to discover whether there is life beyond law. It may be that there isn't, in which case we'll put up everyone's billing targets by 50 per cent.'*

Ms Gray is the only one of the group who is not a partner in the new firm. Restrictions placed on her by the Law Society as a result of her role in the Worthington Trumpet scandal mean she is only allowed to work as an assistant solicitor under close supervision.

Former Babbington Botts partner Ian McPherson and his former client, Ernest Lewis, are currently awaiting trial for fraud. Mr McPherson also faces being struck off.

Edward Greene, Babbington Botts' senior partner, said: 'We are sad to see this group of fine lawyers leave the Babbington Botts family. With the training we have given them, I am in no doubt that they will be a great success. But the firm will go on just as strongly as before.'

In a double celebration, Mr Fortune and Ms Klein this week also announced their engagement.